T0051773

PROVIDENCE BLUE

David Pinault

Providence Blue

A Fantasy Quest

IGNATIUS PRESS SAN FRANCISCO

This is a work of fiction. Although the narrative makes reference to institutions and monuments actually existent in Rhode Island, the characters described as visitors, employees, and staff at these places are entirely fictitious and—with the exception of certain celebrated literary and historical personages from the past—bear no relation to any actual individuals affiliated with these institutions. Any apparent resemblance is entirely coincidental.

Cover design by Enrique J. Aguilar

ISBN 978-1-62164-489-7 (PB)
ISBN 978-1-64229-177-3 (eBook)
Library of Congress Control Number 2021933198
Printed in the United States of America ♾

For Jody, with love (she helped me up onto that Providence rooftop for a meeting with the Bug);

For Steve (together we endured those eleven-and-a-half-hour shifts at Guild Metal);

For Elle (she sent me Rhode Island oddities and news of Roger Williams);

And for Paul (he saw his life reflected in Bob Howard's Esau Cairn).

I

Cross Plains, Texas, June 11, 1936

Had anyone been paying attention, they might have sensed his spiral, might have glimpsed the signs of what he just might do.

He'd written to his publisher. "Dear Mister Farnsworth, no more stories foreseeable from me."

Then:

He'd made out his will.

Purchased a plot.

Borrowed a gun.

Placed the gun in his car.

Now as for Miss Novalyne Price. She would have noticed. Maybe. Educated, cultivated, sensitive. A teacher. But she was long gone, exhausted, her nerves exhausted, by him. "Do you have to shout," she'd say. She'd said that yet again the day before she finally gave up, before she left Cross Plains and gazed one last time at the house and the empty street and its dust.

"Do you have to shout. Do you have to rage."

"Well yes I do," he could have replied. "Yes I do." But aloud not a word. That last day with her he'd been in a mood to brood.

Glower, then rage. People could be forgiven for thinking that was all there was to him.

Just last week at the Magnolia Service Station he'd heard the man at the pump say as he was pulling away—his window was cranked down so he'd heard it all plain—"Doc Howard's boy Bob. Now there's a strange one."

Now there's a strange one. And that about summed up the judgment, he figured, in Cross Plains, and beyond.

Well let them think that then. Let them.

Suddenly he realized he'd been standing motionless, one hand on the screen door, for how long? He studied the predawn sky to the east. Ten minutes. Maybe fifteen.

If there had been observers, someone watching him—but there were no observers, nothing but wind-whipped dust and an empty street and, just barely visible, a crow on a telephone wire—if there'd been observers, they might have been thinking: *He's not sure he'll do it. He hasn't made up his mind to the fatal deed.*

No. Don't give them the chance to think that. He, a creature of doubt? He, Robert Ervin Howard, prince of brawny pulp fiction, creator of Bran Mak Morn, Kull the Conqueror, Solomon Kane the Swordsman, two-fisted Steve Costigan, Conan the Barbarian, Cormac the Slayer: a creature of doubt?

He would have laughed away the thought but he feared waking his dad within, and the cook.

Make up your mind to the fatal deed. He liked the ring of that, the drama.

Successful. Not everyone hereabouts knew it, but he was not just a writer, but a successful one.

Yes.

A famous storyteller.

Yes.

Known to every reader of *Weird Tales*. Not to mention *Oriental Stories. Gun-Smoke Mesa. Astounding Fantasy. Danger Trail.* Highly paid.

Yes.

So highly paid, and so successful, that when he finally got sick of folks saying, "Why doesn't Bob Howard go out and get himself a regular job, move out from home the way young men should, use his hands and work for a living instead of hunching over a typing machine all night and talking to himself so loud he troubles the neighbors": when he got sick of all that, just for the deuce of it he'd gone out one day in his old car and driven to the dealership in Cross Plains and bought himself a 1935 Chevy Standard Sedan, shiny new, gleaming black, running board, big silver grille, big bulging lamps.

Yes, and he'd paid cash, four hundred and sixty-five dollars—all earned from his writing, mind you, all thanks to Conan and Cormac and Kull the Conqueror—four sixty-five, laid out on the counter while pale salesmen and passersby gaped and stepped back. *Successful. Successful.*

Still motionless, still one hand on the screen door.

A caw overhead. First light in the sky. Enough so now he could see nice and clear: the crow on the wire. Studying him.

A herald of Odin, here to see him off?

Odin too had gotten tired of life. You could tell. You could spot the signs. Anyone who lets other gods and frost-giants hang him from a tree and tear out an eye just so he can squint with what's left into the future and catch time-to-time glimpses of things to come and get to call himself Wise. Odin must've been in some mood.

Or maybe just bored.

The crow cawed again, lifted its beak.

On another day Bob Howard would have stepped inside (ideas always came early mornings), typed a quick poem:

Lift him on his flaming pyre
To Valhalla through the fire ...

But if he did that now he'd wake up his dad and anyway he was through with poems.

Quietly he eased the screen shut. No stirring save from the crow. A long rasping croak.

Quick strides across the gravel. Just a few steps to his Chevy Standard, and now a hand on its driver's-side door.

And then a doubt. The shot would spoil the interior, and he loved this machine. He remembered the showroom placard: "Talk about value! You certainly get it, in overwhelming measure, when you buy one of these big, beautiful, finely built Chevrolets for 1935."

Value, overwhelming measure: yes, he'd certainly gotten it. Every time he needed a refuge, he had come out at night to sit alone in the car and keep the windows up and talk as loud as he liked, talk with Solomon and two-fisted Steve and them all.

A shame to spoil the interior.

But: on to Valhalla.

He opened the car door, slid behind the wheel, closed the door. Sealed in now, atop the pyre.

Dawn light stronger. The bird flapped a wing.

A Valkyrie, a chooser of the slain?

Glove compartment open. His neighbor's pistol. A three-eighty caliber Colt automatic.

Beautifully made. Shining metal, smooth to the touch. Smooth and blank. Blank, poems all done, stories all done.

Then, from within himself: voices.

One, meager and small. *Wait. This is wrong.*

Another (louder, stronger). *Do it. End it. You're a failure, a blank.*

War and clangor in his soul. *Shouldn't do this. Shouldn't.*

(Louder now, insistent.) *You're a failure. You know it. At least show you can go out with style.*

Bad to have a conflict storm when weighing life and death.

Worse to have the conflict with one's finger on a trigger.

Shouldn't do this. Shouldn't.

(Even louder.) *Failure. Failure. Show at least you can do this bit with style. Valhalla. Flaming pyre.*

Shouldn't. Shouldn't. (Weaker, diminuendo.)

Make an exit like no other: smoke and fire leaping high. Tower piled with skulls, stark and gaping at the sky.

(Barely whispered.) *This is wrong. Wr . . .*

The crow lifted its wings, rose up from the wire.

A last-minute plea?

Or a Valkyrie, come to escort me?

He lifted the gun to the side of his head.

(Barely a breath now, a gasp.) *Shouldn't. Shouldn't.*

The skull tower piled high. Tempting, tempting. Yes.

The skulls grinned. *Pull the trigger. Pull it.*

Time to join Cormac, Conan, and Kull? *Yes. In the halls of the slain.*

And now a voice so loud he could hear nothing else. *Pull the trigger.*

A final blurred glimpse: the crow flying right at the glass.

Then a spurt of flame from the three-eighty Colt.

2

Valhalla turned out to be mud.

Layer upon layer of it: viscous, thick, and dark.

Somehow he breathed within it all, he, a mud-worm, buried deep, slow deep breaths, deep within the dark.

No problem breathing, and why not: mud-worms love mud, and this was his world. Thick, dark. Mud-worms see nothing, feel only the breath of what might be other worms around them, feel breath bubbles form and float in the muck.

Lack of thought, all feelings stilled. Good. Good. No sound save a thrum, faint, that pulsed through the mud.

Peaceful, at least at first. No feelings, no rages, no brooding, no moods. Just the thrum, just the pulse, coming faint through the mud.

Blind mud-worm. Blind. No rages, no moods. Just the pulse in the mud. Breath bubbles formed afloat in the muck.

For how long like this, hard to say. But then something from above. A new sound, a hum.

And with that, a thought. Conan the Barbarian at the underworld court of the Blind and Coiled Vermicule-King. A new idea for a tale.

The humming grew louder, seemed to come from above.

Came the realization, drowsy and slow: *I need my typing machine.* Came the notion, a bit quicker now: *As a worm I'd find it hard to type in this mud.*

Humming from above: much louder.

The breath bubbles slowed. And then a feeling, sharp as a lance: panic. Followed by a writhing blind-vermicule thought: *What have I done to myself? What have I done?*

The humming from above: much louder now, just overhead, descending, coming closer.

At first he didn't notice. Valhalla mud-worms seldom do. Attention only for his one vermicular thought: *What have I done? What have I done?*

Not humming exactly, no. The whir of wings. Louder and closer.

Pressing in on him, a message: *What you did was wrong. Wrong. The self-killing: it was wrong.*

Another thought. *Sorry. I'm sorry.* He would have said it aloud, would have shouted it out, if he hadn't been a mud-worm with a mouth full of mud.

Louder and closer, the whir of wings.

What have I done? What have I—

And then he found himself lifted, out of the muck, out of the dark.

3

Back at his car. But not inside.

Standing, outdoors, in the early-morning light.

Not standing, exactly; he was too unsteady on his feet.

He found himself leaning against the bright silver grille, one hand resting on the hood.

And perched on that hood, head turned so as to eye him, that crow from the wire.

"*Hoo.*" Glad with relief, Robert Ervin Howard felt like talking to someone, and he didn't care if there was no one around but a crow. "You have no idea, little fella. For a moment there I ... I mean *hoo.* You have no idea. I thought I'd ... I mean I almost ... But things are okay now." He said it again. "Things are back to where they were. But you have no idea."

"Oh, yes I do." These words came from the crow. And that's when Howard realized things weren't quite as they had been.

The man stared at the bird. It held something in its beak. He would've said, wanted to ask, *Now what on earth do you have in your mouth*, but before he could figure out how to address a crow, it spoke again through its clenched beak.

"Put out your hand."

"Huh? What for?"

If a crow could voice exasperation, this one was doing it now. "Just put out your hand. What I've got won't hurt you."

Tentatively the man held his hand in front of the bird. Quick as a shot the creature spat the thing onto his palm.

Smolderingly hot to the touch. "*Ouch.* I thought you said it wouldn't hurt."

"I lied. Crows do that." A caw of delight. "Besides, you've no cause to complain, considering what I just rescued you from."

"Rescued?" Howard peered at the thing in his palm. And then he knew what it was: a spent cartridge from a three-eighty Colt. The tip was squashed, almost flattened.

An explanation from the creature perched on the hood. "It got dinged hitting the door frame after it finished going through, or at least after it starting going through, your, ah, how to put this delicately ..." Howard realized the crow was staring at the side of his head.

He couldn't help touching the spot: just above his right ear, where he'd pressed the barrel. Felt okay, no smear of blood on his fingers.

He studied the slug as it cooled in his hand. *Did I dream all that, the walk across the yard, getting in the Chevy, the Valhalla pyre, mud-worm in the muck? Maybe, yeah, just a dream. I'm still okay. Steady now, steady. Okay. Maybe still okay.*

A sudden chill breeze. He shivered. "*Hoo*. Starting to feel cold."

"Of course you feel cold. The dead always do."

"Dead?" The breeze whipped early-morning dust against his face.

"Turn around and look."

Within the car: a figure, a man, heavyset, the thick muscled shoulders of a fighter, a boxer. The figure's head slumped forward against the wheel.

"Say. That's me."

"Well, that used to be you. But not anymore." The crow tilted back its head and croaked a long piercing cry.

This scummy thing's laughing at me. No sooner came the thought than Howard shot out his fist. "You miserable ..."

The crow danced out of reach. "How about some gratitude? I got sent here to rescue you. Someone had to block that shot, or try to. And I had to catch that bullet with my beak. It hurt, too."

"Not much of a rescue," grunted Howard. "Look at him." He gestured to the body in the Chevy. "And look at me."

"Well, it was a sort-of rescue, a kind-of almost-rescue. Actually the best I could do. Don't ask for too much from a crow."

A tap-tap of claws on the hood. "I was forgetting. Introductions. Call me Kavva. Kavva the Corvid."

No response from Howard. *So this is death?* thought the man. *No change of realm, no blessedly annihilating sleep, just standing around in front of my old house feeling cold and being stared at by a crow?*

A cawed question. "So why'd you do it?"

"Do what?"

"You know. Pull the trigger."

There was so much he could have said in reply.

Successful, he'd liked to call himself. Yes. He'd always made a point of that success, rubbed the world's nose in it, shown everyone who'd ever called him strange or given him oblique jeering looks, shown them how wrong they'd been about him. He'd never been just some stay-at-home fool, over-fond of mom and dad, talking to himself, no real friends, talking to the air. He'd made money. He'd shown them all.

Talking to the air. Who was it that had said that about him?

One of the Earlson brothers. Used to work the pump at the Sunoco station in town. Tiny guy with big ears, something wrong with his leg. Howard sitting in the car for a fill-up, and this guy pumping juice for him, pumping juice while talking to grease monkeys from the garage, not seeming to know Howard could hear every word.

"I seen him, I tell you. Every time he comes in to get a fill-up, he sits by himself and talks to the air."

Tad Earlson. That was his name. Howard had silently named him Shrimp with a Limp. Must put him in a story someday. Make him a slave or a thrall. Make him cringe; make him crawl.

"Talks to the air. Hands going like this. I'm telling you. Like this. Fists, like he's in a fight. Talking, and I mean loud. Lookit. He's doing it now. That fella is strange."

Howard had said nothing to any of this, had wanted to swing open the door and get out of his car and pound the man one-two. That's all it would've taken with a shrimp like that. One-two and boy it would've felt good. One-two.

What Tad the Shrimp couldn't have known, what none of the Earlson boys knew, was that Howard had never been alone as he sat in solitude in his Chevy at the service station in town. Talking to the air? No sir.

The front seat had thronged with guests. From Valusia, from Cimmeria, from Hyperborea's outer reaches, travelers had made their way from afar. Grim iron-thewed men, swords sheathed at their sides, shields slung on their backs, who shouted for beakers of wine from full-bosomed vixen-eyed maids clad in the sheerest of silks.

Men who'd quaffed their brew and hailed him as Friend. Men who'd trusted him enough to tell him their names. Conan and Cormac and Bran Mak Morn. Whose chests rocked with mirth as they wrapped an arm around his shoulders and belched in his ear as they told him some joke. Who—best of all—confided their tales, boasted of the kingdoms they'd seen, the hazards they'd braved, the foul wizards they'd slain.

Howard had scarcely been able to keep up with it all. He'd mouthed their words aloud to remember, talking faster as his friends grew louder with their ale and their beer, pounding the wheel as they punched his shoulder for fun.

Until finally his head would be overfull and he'd crank down the glass and be hit with the smell of fuel fumes and dry Texas dust.

And then he'd growl at Tad Earlson the thrall, "No don't check the oil, just bring me my change," and then he'd race home to his typewriting machine. Get it down on paper, the latest he'd heard from his friends.

But how to explain all this to a crow?

And how to explain what had been worst of all: when suddenly these visits from friends had come to an end.

An end to the visits: which meant an end to his tales.

The question echoed. Maybe the crow had cawed it again. *Why'd you pull the trigger?*

He could have confessed that he'd fantasized that taking the Colt from the glove compartment was putting himself at the center of one more story.

He hadn't really tried to put a bullet through his head, he could've explained. He *was* the bullet, and the barrel of that Colt was a cannon that would launch him outward to a fertile new Earth, one that just might—who could tell?—offer more hope.

Like Esau Cairn in *Almuric.* (Two years now since he'd published that tale.) A fugitive, wrongly hounded by enemies, by cops, by the world. Desperate. Takes refuge in the mountains, in the lab of a scientist friend. The scientist tells him: "I've this device that'll shoot you out into space. Maybe you'll die. Maybe you'll find a fresh home." Esau Cairn shrugs: "I'll take the chance." Then *pow,* and off to new worlds.

Another *scritch-scritch* of claws on the hood. That crow and its question. *Why'd you pull the trigger?*

Aloud Howard said, "Dunno. Gone dry. Blank."

But he'd no sooner said "blank" than something came back. The memory of where he'd just been, or what he'd just dreamed. Valhalla-as-mud. Conan the Barbarian in the court of the Vermicule-King. The germ of a story.

But there'd been a problem while he was in the court of that king. What was it? Come on. Bring it back.

There. He'd been a mud-worm in Valhalla. Which hadn't mattered for an age and an age. He'd dozed to the buzz for who knew how long, until he suddenly felt a deep urge to write.

That's when he'd been hit by the thought: *Gosh how I'd like to be back at my typing machine.* But worms don't have hands, or at least not much more than vestigial stumps. Makes it hard to type. Hard to get down that tale.

Damn.

The crow tapped its beak on the hood.

He raised his gaze, stared through the windshield, again saw the body slumped at the wheel.

Longing welled up now. Regret, and keen sadness. Feelings he'd run from for who knows how long.

Remorse. *I truly am sorry.* He wasn't sure if he'd said this aloud.

He wanted to confess things, get it all out somehow, even if it was maybe too late now, even if no one seemed on hand to hear a confession aside from this crow on the car hood. "I was so confused. In one of my moods. But this time really bad. *Hoo.*"

The bird eyed him as he spoke. Can one get absolution from a crow? The man shrugged as if to shift his weight of sorrow. "I'm such a dummy. How'd this happen? Hard to think. Don't know if I can find the words to tell you." His voice dwindled.

Another raw wind-gust of dust. He shivered.

Damn.

He put his hand on the glass.

"Say." He stole another glance at the body behind the wheel, then looked at the crow. "Any chance I can have it back?"

"Absolutely not." Kavva jabbed its beak under a wing as if scratching an itch. "You chose to sunder spirit from clay. Choices have consequences. You have to live with yours. Or—pardon me—die with yours." A twitch of the muscles at the base of the beak: that might have been a smile. Hard to tell with a crow.

"Confound it." Howard pounded the hood so hard it made Kavva jump. "If I have to be dead, fine. But being lectured about consequences by some lousy bird while I'm standing around freezing and getting colder and colder. I mean, if that don't beat all. I shouldn't have to listen to this."

"I am not lousy, for your information." This with stiff dignity. (Howard realized he'd never been one to pay heed to the range of tones one could find in a crow.) "Not lousy at all. I groom myself daily and eat all my lice. It's not my fault you're now a Vespertine."

Now there was a word. If only he could get back to his typing machine, make a note.

Aloud he said, "Vespertine. Not sure if that's good or bad."

"A dusk-crawler. A dweller in the realm in between. Half light and half dark. And you know what happens to Vespertines?"

Howard sighed. "I suppose you'll tell me whether I want to hear it or not."

"Your life is gone." Kavva poked its beak under one folded wing, then the other. "Irretrievably. You can't have it back. Well at least not ..." Another beak-jab beneath a wing. *As if,* came the thought to Howard, *the creature was trying to find something it had tucked away and misplaced.*

A flutter of wings. "Where was I? Oh, yes. Irretrievably. But what you do have is an afterlife. That's all you have to work with. Work."

And now Kavva studied him with a gaze that impressed Howard as calculating, shrewd. "Work. Let's be precise. You're about to be put to work."

"Say. I'm not sure I like the sound of that." The man shivered again.

"You have no choice. Once you grow careless with your life and throw it away, someone else picks up your afterlife from the gutter and puts you to work. That's the rule. Someone who was watching you the whole time and studying you while you still had choices to make."

"Someone watching me?" Another shiver. Numbness advanced down his arms to his hands. It would be hard now to take story notes on all this even if he could somehow get back to his room and sit with his story thoughts crowding as companions around the typing machine. And how distant his family home seemed now, how remote, even if it was just a quick stride's distance away across the gravel!

Kavva had resumed poking its beak beneath one wing, then the other.

"Spill it, crow. Who's this someone who's been watching me?"

"Why, the same individual who's been putting me to use for ever so long." Another poke of its beak beneath a wing. "There." The beak now held something. "Was afraid I'd misplaced it. Then for sure I'd be in a spot."

"What's that?"

The thing in the beak was a small square of painted cardboard.

"Mister Howard, do you like to play cards?"

Truth was he'd indulged from time to time. Mostly to study the players' faces, enjoy the lingo—hear men bellow about their four of a kind or pair of ladies or inside straight—while he took furtive notes for his next Western shoot-'em-up tale. But no enjoyment now. The chill had crept from his icy palms to his fingertips.

"This is no poker hand, Mister Howard. No five-card stud. Just one card, from a tarot deck."

The man shivered again, thrust his hands under his armpits. "Not in the mood."

"Go ahead. Take a look. Give it a gaze." Kavva fluttered across the Chevy's hood, alighted right before Howard. Through a clenched beak came a low croak. "Just a look."

So Howard stooped to look. He didn't want to at first—afraid what he'd see—so he glanced away briefly to what had been his car. But that made him see the massive shoulders and the torn head slumped over the wheel—the body, once vital, once his—and so to steady his thoughts he did as he was told and studied the picture on the painted card.

A battlefield. The aftermath. Broken lances, slain horses, black sky. In the distance kites feed on the dead. Foreground: a corpse sprawled face down on the field near a river of blood. Numerous long-bladed daggers, knives monstrous in length, pierce the corpse, arms, legs, and back.

"Ten of Swords," announced Kavva. "Inauspicious. Destruction. Dead end. The scorching of hopes."

Howard shivered once more, wanted to turn away. Couldn't.

"Now watch this." Carefully Kavva placed the card on the Chevy's hood, just before the windshield, just in front of the steering wheel with its slumped body—but Howard didn't want to look at that anymore, averted his gaze just a second.

And when he looked again, Kavva was gone.

No. Not gone. There, beside the dagger-pierced corpse on the battlefield beside the river. Kavva cawed once, and the kites rose up crying into the black sky.

"Now see." The crow jabbed its beak into the dead warrior's shoulder and rolled him over so he lay face up.

A face Howard knew. The face of a one-time companion of Conan and Cormac and Solomon Kane. A face from whose lips once streamed a profusion of tales. The face of a writer, the prince of pulp fiction—once successful, now dead—named Robert E. Howard.

Kavva jabbed the Ten of Swords body again, and the corpse slid off the bank into the bloodstained river with a soft splash.

Soaking wet, and cold, even colder than he'd already been. Howard found himself floating face up in the swift stream. Corpse-kites wheeled overhead in the sky.

His body ached all over from ten dagger thrusts. A fast current bore him. Bobbing on the water's surface, flat on his back, studded with swords, eyes open wide, headed feetfirst downstream.

He tried to flail but couldn't. *Flap arms; swim; do something.* Zero response.

Zero, except a flap of wings, where Kavva the crow perched on his shoulder.

Perched uncomfortably close. The bird bent over his face, until the beak brushed his nose, and the crow's eye came to a bare inchbreadth above his own. Crow's eye. Cold black orb, smooth as polished stone.

The beak pecked his lips, and Howard wondered if this thing was about to snack on his face.

Crows did that to corpses, and he was a corpse.

Unless he could move, flap the thing off.

But the weight of ten tarot swords held him in place. All he could do was feel himself pulled, flat on his back, as an icy, bloodstained current tugged him downstream.

A flap of the wings. "Getting colder, are we?"

A vast struggle, and the man raised his head slightly. All he could manage. But Cormac wouldn't yield his corpse passively, nor would Solomon Kane. So neither would he.

"Go ..." A wave slapped his face, and he swallowed blood-water, sputtered and spat. "Go ... go to hell."

"Hell? Hell's what I'm trying to help rescue you from. But it will take some doing, my friend. And we *are* friends. You just don't know it yet." The crow shifted its perch on the man's shoulders. Howard felt the tread of talons on his cold skin.

"But before there's any question of rescue," continued Kavva, "there's no avoiding your being put to use. Sorry to say. But oh my."

The bird suddenly cocked its head to stare at something downstream. With a huge effort—getting colder now, and stiffer, and *damnation*, the weight of these ten back-piercing swords didn't help—Howard lifted his head. (In his place Kull of Atlantis would've made the effort, so he did too.)

Not reassuring. He was being borne swiftly feetfirst directly toward something that bobbed on the dark swell. Something that glimmered under the black battlefield sky.

A glass bottle, lying on its side.

A bottle of mammoth size. Bigger than a human, bigger than any ship. It lifted on the slap of water. Big. Its neck and open mouth lay exactly in his way: a huge tunnel of a maw about to suck in his oncoming feet.

Howard flailed, or tried to, tried to divert his course. He lifted his head again, glimpsed Kavva perched on his shoulder, claws scratching his cold flesh. Tried to say, "Don't want to be swallowed by that bottle." But water gagged his mouth and the Ten of Swords weight of his corpse held him down. All he could utter was a gurgle of dread.

Feet pointed straight at the giant glass bottle's wide mouth.

Howard gurgled and gasped, tried to say "Help."

Bottleneck closer now.

Sudden flap of wings. Again the claws scratched his cold flesh. A croak from Kavva: "Oh my. Time to go." The bird lifted itself up and away.

Onrushing current, corpse pointed feetfirst to the glass and its oncoming mouth, and all the man wanted—more than he'd ever wanted anything in thirty short years of life—all he wanted was to feel those claws, the scratch of a crow, the touch of some living thing, again on his flesh.

Kavva cawed something overhead in the sky. Sounded like "Yog-Sothoth"; no telling what that might mean.

A pause, and then the winged creature cried another utterance, something less cryptic. Hard to make out the words—maybe "still your friend"—and Robert Ervin Howard (prince of pulp fiction, Vespertine, Ten of Swords, deceased) would've asked the bird to say it again, would've loved to know for sure he'd heard one last time the word "friend."

But another wave slapped his face and rushed him up to the glass and into its mouth and right down its cold throat.

4

College Hill, Providence, Rhode Island, June 11, 1936

Howard Phillips Lovecraft was enjoying a pleasant summer evening, working on his latest tale for *Weird Fiction*, when one of his Elementals flew in through the window. The creature flapped its black feathers and croaked an announcement. The arrival, as ordered, of the latest delivery in the Pipeline.

Lovecraft felt no haste to lift his head or acknowledge the news. Here, in his apartment, he reigned supreme. Here, servitor-beings were constrained to await his pleasure. And his pleasure, at this moment, was to shape the paragraphs before him, here, at his writing desk, with its view of the city below. He put pen to paper:

> Now too late he realized: refuge in the cellar was no refuge at all. In the dark he could hear it, the Horror out of Innsmouth, descending the stairs. Its squamous skin scraped the stair-railings; its tread on each step, massive and slow, sounded the approach of the man's ever-nearing doom. So black was the darkness that he could see nothing of this; and yet he knew this blindness to be nothing less than a blessing; for human eyes were never meant to glimpse those things that breached the crevice between worlds ...

Another croak from the Elemental; another flap of its wings. Let it wait. H. P. Lovecraft reigned supreme here.

Where was he? *The crevice between worlds* ... A glance up from the page to rest his eyes. The view from his study window, always an inspiration. A sky flared with blood: western clouds, stained by the dying sun. Below him, at the foot of College Hill, the huddled shapes of downtown, domes, pinnacles, spires, shadowed by the onset of night. Amid them the bulk of the Industrial Trust Building, its rooftop beacon aglow all night: a sentinel eye to warn of invaders who might swarm out of the ever-encroaching Dark.

Well. Back to that cellar, and the crevice between worlds, and the Horror out of Innsmouth. He needed a line about how the Horror smelled; something about "fetid fungi-breath that induced a veritable ecstasy of fear." He frowned. "Fetid fungi"? Hadn't he used that before, in "The Crypt-Mouth Revelation" or perhaps "The Rats in the Walls"? He should keep better track of his words. Not that the editors of *Weird Fiction* ever seemed to mind. They bought it all.

Weird Fiction. Well. Let them classify his tales as fiction. He knew better. He knew to what truth he pointed, to the underlying pervasive Menace. He knew of the lurkers that swarmed just beyond the Barrier out in the cold black cosmic gulfs. He ...

And now Lovecraft realized his concentration was being scattered this lovely evening, and all thanks to that noxious Elemental. Another croak; another flap of its feathers.

Scattered, his concentration, so that uninvited memories of his latest neighborhood perambulation intruded on his writing efforts. He treasured his walks; but what he'd experienced had been distressing. Swarms of foreigners, recent arrivals, idling on his city streets. *His* Providence; *his*. Swarms of outsiders, swarms. The swart, the slant-eyed, the slope-browed, the pockmarked, the mongrelized, the wide-nostriled, the thick-lipped, the yellow-skinned, the dark-skinned, more and ever more. *Aliens, all of them, and all of them blind servants of my cosmic foe Cthulhu ...*

More cawing, more flapping of wings, beseeching his attention.

The distraction made the writer aware of other ambient sounds. From the sitting room behind him, the faintest *tink-tink*. Akin to a silversmith's hammer, delicate, patient, shaping a vessel for a client of taste.

Tink-tink again, from the sitting room. A bit louder now.

No, not a silversmith. Lovecraft knew very well the source of the sound, knew and enjoyed the sound because it signaled his mastery over everything that stirred in this apartment. Here was a more fitting metaphor: a dungeon-dweller clanking his chains, hoping for attention from his captor. *Tink-tink*. Lovecraft smiled. Let the captive wait.

But meanwhile: a cawed squawk, right at his elbow. The Elemental had flapped its way directly onto his desk. What infernal impudence.

Aloud he snapped, "Kavva, I've told you. Never intrude on my reveries when I've pen in hand."

Another cawed squawk. "Sire, you commanded me to let you know the moment I brought you what you wanted." Lovecraft was sure he detected impertinence in the black gaze of this crow.

"I've told you before. Don't call me Sire. It sounds medieval."

"As you wish, Magus."

Now he was sure the crow was smirking at him. "Simply call me Mister Lovecraft. Can you manage that much?"

"Yes, Mister Lovecraft." Another flap of the wings. "But what you wanted is in the Pipeline, and I think you'd best fetch it before someone else comes across it."

"Very well then." Night was coming on, his favorite hour for a stroll. And if more foreigners made an appearance? Well, he'd just pretend not to see them. "Let us exercise ourselves then with a walk down to Canal Street and see what the Providence River has brought us."

He stepped into the sitting room, lifted a coat from a massive stone-topped worktable in the center of the room. *Tink-tink.* Louder now, the sound. It came from something atop the table, a diminutive object no more than twelve inches in height: a stoppered glass jar of curious manufacture.

Tink-tink. Lovecraft stooped over the jar, addressed the contents. He indulged himself like this when he felt triumphant, when he felt things to be—even if only briefly—under control. "Ah, is that you gently tapping, tapping at my chamber door?" *After all,* Lovecraft told himself with a smirk, *my prisoner happens to be a poet—pathetically overrated, in my expert opinion. And what better way to torment a captive poet than to mock him with verses from his own poems?*

Louder now, and faster. *Tink-tink, tink-tink.*

"Ah, my friend, I seem to hear you tapping, tapping somewhat louder than before." Undoubtedly an indulgence, this mockery; but how pleasurable it was to taunt this particular prisoner with his own foolish rhymes.

A burst truly frantic. *Tink-tink, tink-tink-tink.*

Lovecraft's face split into a smile. Yes. In control, if only for a moment, against the crypt-mouth forces of the night. He snapped his fingers, and Kavva the Elemental settled onto his shoulder.

Tink-tink-tink came from within the stoppered glass.

"And now," said Lovecraft, smiling down at the glass, "this grim, ungainly, ghastly, gaunt, and ominous bird of yore has a word for you; and that is ..." Once more the writer snapped his fingers, and Kavva the crow obligingly croaked: "Nevermore."

As man and bird stepped to the door, Lovecraft called over his shoulder to the glass as its inhabitant tapped out a last despairing *tink-tink*: "Oh, and we'll come back tonight with a companion to keep you company, Mister Poe."

5

Howard residence, Cross Plains, Texas, June 1936, three days after the funeral

Novalyne Price hesitated at the front door, tried to make up her mind to knock. She had never been welcome here, not really, not as far as Bob's parents were concerned. How often had his mother refused to let her in, each time Novalyne stopped by after work? "He's trying to write. You wouldn't want to disturb him now, would you?" She had to remind herself that it was Bob's pa himself who had asked her to come by today.

Well no sense hesitating, girl. That's what Bob would have said. She drew a breath, squared her shoulders, and knocked at the door.

It was Ettie the cleaning lady who answered. "Miss Novalyne." She smiled as she let her in. Ettie had always been nice that way.

"Mister Howard sent me a note, wondered if maybe I could visit." She felt she had to explain herself. "The note mentioned his son's papers, correspondence, asked if I could sort through them and decide what to do with them."

"Yes'm." Ettie led her through the silent house to Bob's study, explained that Mister Howard was feeling poorly and sent his apologies and would she please forgive him if he didn't come out to welcome her the way he should.

"Of course." But Novalyne scarcely heard. The desk, the typing machine, the shelves sagging with heaped-up books. She remembered it all, remembered the afternoon she'd sat in that armchair in the corner while he typed up a story—or rather, talked through the story, sword thrusts and all, shouting out the good lines, pounding the air, declaiming threats, conspiracies, grand entrances. Novalyne Price taught elocution and knew a good speaker when she heard one; Robert E. Howard was one of the best.

"Five foot eleven and two hundred pounds of pure barbarian energy": that was how Bob described himself. His presence had certainly filled up this room.

And now. Now all she heard was a clock as it ticked in the house.

A polite cough from the cleaning lady. "I'll just straighten up these books."

"Of course. I'll get to work." Scatterings of paper all over the desk and on the floor. Notes for what might have been new stories, with jagged pen-strokes x-ing out each attempt. Balled-up sheets everywhere; angry crumplings. Notebooks, spines askew, their pages torn and dismembered. (What was it he had said one day? "If a story won't talk, just rip out its tongue.") A stack of letters, all from the same address, all postmarked from somewhere up north, jumbled and shoved in a corner.

And positioned all alone, atop the typing machine where she'd be sure to see it: an envelope with her name written on it, in a hand she knew well.

Within the envelope, a note:

> Sorry, girl. I've run out of steam. HPL is right. That fellow on the run, "flushed" from the ravine: that's me. Striped prison pants, blood on his leg: that's me. Nowhere left to go: that's me. That's me. Time to end this.

She puzzled over the note. "'Flushed' from the ravine": What ravine? "Striped prison pants"? What fellow on the run was he going on about? Strange talk.

But then he'd been talking strange and voicing dark thoughts all through winter and early spring. And everything he said like that, he said loud. Very loud.

Like those times she entertained him in the parlor at the rooming house in town for the young single ladies who taught at Cross Plains High: he'd bellow as if hailing her from across a wheat field. "The stories won't come. I've run out of steam."

Her roommates would take her aside and ask, "You going to be all right with him?" And the landlady: no end of admonitions from her. "That young man of yours will have to temper his tone."

Run out of steam. She knew now she should have paid more attention. But that last semester she'd been teaching elocution (three sections) plus English grammar and public speaking and ancient history. Plus, as she'd tried to tell him, she had three dozen students who needed help so they could graduate that June.

But did he understand? No. What he knew was Conan and Kull and all those other pals who packed his head full. And when his pals no longer came by, when the inspiration gave out and his typing machine grew still, then she should have been there, should have pulled herself away from her lesson preps at night, should have slipped away from the rooming house to see what was wrong.

Too late now of course.

She sighed, sat down at the desk, stirred the pile of letters from that address up north. She studied the postmark. Rhode Island. So this would be correspondence from that fellow fantasy-author Bob had mentioned. What was the man called? A funny name.

HPL. Like in Bob's farewell note.

Lovecraft. That was it.

H. P. Lovecraft.

A curious association. At first, Bob had been enthusiastic. "An older gentleman, genuine New England type, distinguished British ancestry and all that." That was how Bob had described him at first. A friend, Bob said, a real writer with a real reputation, someone who understood, who knew what the creator of Conan was trying to do as he built the worlds of Cimmeria and Stygia and lost Atlantis.

But then things had gone wrong. The two men started quarreling in the letters they exchanged, arguments over she didn't know what. Toward the end Lovecraft starting looking down his nose at Texan writers, Bob said, at pretty much anyone who wasn't from New England. And Lovecraft had come up with a belittling title for Bob Howard, something Bob didn't like, something really insulting. What was it? Bob had told her once at her rooming house when he was in a truly foul mood.

She glanced through the pile of letters. Each piece had been mailed recently, within three to four weeks preceding the suicide. The one with the most recent postmark must have arrived the day before Bob died. Each envelope had been opened, the contents hastily reinserted after Bob had read them.

None of her business, of course, what this Lovecraft had written to her Bob. She shouldn't pry. Bob was buried and gone.

HPL is right. What could Bob have meant by that? Had Lovecraft played a role in what happened? Might there be a clue in all this correspondence?

But it wasn't her place to open a dead man's mail. Wasn't really right.

Yet her hand strayed to the pile. She stopped herself, hesitated. Indecision.

Then a memory of Bob Howard's voice, clear as if he sat across from her now. "Girl, you just go right ahead."

She snatched up an envelope from the top of the pile. The postmark showed it to be the most recent arrival.

At first, a disappointment. No letter inside at all. Just a news clipping, neatly snipped from the *Providence Journal*, dated June 1, 1936. It featured a boldface page-one headline:

> Louisiana Convict Killer Dies as Posse Closes In: Wilfred Lindsley, Baton Rouge "Bad Boy" Responsible for Five Killings, "Flushed" in Ravine, Turns Revolver on Self When Rifle Jams.

Why on earth would Lovecraft have mailed such a news item to Bob? She read on:

> Wilfred Lindsley, 23-year-old Baton Rouge "bad boy" responsible for five killings, added a sixth to his score today and it was himself. Lindsley, object of the greatest manhunt in Louisiana in recent years, killed himself as a posse closed in on him and bullets from their guns spattered around him.

Hastily she skimmed the piece:

> ... youthful escapee from the State penitentiary ... object of a manhunt with bloodhounds and armed men following him ... found wearing the clothes in which he had fled—striped pants with blood on the knee, and a blue shirt ... ate blackberries and drank water from little creeks ... walked in the middle of the creek to fool the bloodhounds ... As the possemen advanced, laying down a barrage,

the convict shot himself through the chest with a revolver and toppled forward.

Certain phrases in the article had been carefully underlined in blue ink: "killed himself"; "the convict shot himself through the chest with a revolver." And someone had penned a comment in the margin (it matched the handwriting on the envelope, so it must have been Lovecraft): "What that boy did was the only honorable way out for a failure. But what about Two-Gun Bob? He *points* the pistol, but he never dares shoot."

Two-Gun Bob. That was it. That was the name Lovecraft used against her man.

Quickly she opened all the other pieces of mail. More news clippings, all themed alike:

Nephew of Prominent Politician Shoots Self on Argentine Ranch ... Bankrupt Businessman Slain by Own Hand ... "It's No Use, Can't Go On": Heartbreaking Last Words ... Found After Trail of Blood Leads to Sorry Doom ... Found Hanging in Closet ... Found Drowned ... Found Dead ... Dead ...

She stopped scanning the headlines, studied instead the primly penned comments:

A failure: you're blocked and you know it. A failure: nothing left in you. A failure: Two-Gun Bob, you've been "flushed" from your ravine, so now it's over. A failure: pull the trigger. It's over, Two-Gun Bob: pull the trigger. PULL THE TRIGGER.

Two-Gun Bob. A name to belittle the action-pulp stories that had meant everything to Robert E. Howard. A name intended to madden, and sting, and goad her man to death.

To death.

Mister Lovecraft, sir, you are a truly *damnable* piece of work.

"Miss Novalyne?"

She'd forgotten the cleaning lady was still in the room, didn't realize she'd been talking aloud.

"Sorry, Ettie. Just mumbling to myself."

"Yes'm. I do understand." Ettie stepped to the desk and laid a hand on her shoulder.

Abruptly Novalyne Price stood, gathered up the clippings with their blue-penned comments, held them firmly in one hand as she turned to the cleaning lady.

"Ettie, your uncle Ned has an automobile, doesn't he?"

"Yes'm. It runs good."

"Fine. Fine. Do you think he might take me to Abilene tomorrow?"

"Abilene? Sure, Miss Novalyne. You want to see the picture show? They're showing that new one with Carole Lombard. *The Princess Comes Across*. You'll like it. Do you good."

"No." Novalyne Price smiled. "No picture show. Abilene is where I can catch the bus for Fort Worth."

"What you gonna do in Fort Worth?" The cleaning lady wrung her hands, stepped forward as if to hug her or hold her in place.

"Fort Worth bus station is where I transfer to catch the Greyhound. Long distance, up north."

"Up north. What for, Miss Novalyne?"

"To have words with a gentleman. A gentleman in . . ."—she lifted the envelopes, consulted the return address again—"in the town of Providence, Rhode Island."

6

Canal Street, Providence, Rhode Island, June 1936

What woke him was the stench.

Sewage. Damp garbage. Plus urine-streaked sludge.

He opened his eyes. Darkness. A sense of movement, being bobbed back and forth.

Water sloshed his face. He sputtered, lashed out with his hands. To either side, curved walls of glass.

Then he remembered. Dagger-pierced he'd been, by the tarot's Ten of Swords. But the knives were gone now; he could move.

Abruptly he sat up and at once banged his head in the dark. Above him—cautiously he felt about with his fingers—was another smooth surface of glass.

Slowly the memory returned: the long Sadness; the gunshot to end it all; that crazy crow. (Its name had slipped away, like most things in a dream.) And what happened next: the tumble into a river by a battlefield. And then: the imprisonment somehow in a giant vessel or carafe of some kind that swallowed him whole and bore him downstream.

To where? A waterway of limitless night? Had he died yet again, to awaken in a yet darker afterlife?

No. Ahead of him. Comfort: a pinpoint of light. Distant, but something to gaze on. Slowly the light neared, grew brighter.

And the darkness yielded enough so he could see: he was in a tunnel, being borne in his receptacle prison along some underworld stream.

His nose twitched. Diesel oil. Far above him somewhere, beyond the tunnel: an air-horn blast, the shrill of a whistle. Screech of metal on metal, boxcars being shunted onto sidings. He knew that sound.

He couldn't be dead, not really. Not unless they had train yards and freight trains in hell.

Another smell: mixed with the sewage and sludge, a breath of brine. Ocean air. He was being shipped to the sea.

And then the tunnel ended, and he was out in the light.

He peered through the glass of his vessel. A river embankment and houses built into the side of a steeply sloped hill. Office buildings and warehouses. Cars and buses. Sunset, and crowds of people along the embankment, hurrying home at the end of a working day. They rushed on, head down. A pair of young men paused long enough to light cigarettes and look out over the water and enjoy the westering sun.

"Hey." He tapped the glass. *How can they not see me?* He tried to shout. "Hey, fellows." *I mean, how often does a city river offer the spectacle of a mammoth receptacle, transparent to the view, presenting all five foot eleven and two hundred pounds of the King of Pulp Fiction?*

They were staring straight at him. How could they not see? He couldn't be more than ten yards from shore. He had to be the biggest thing on the water. "Hey." He pounded again at the glass.

They flicked away their smokes, laughed at some joke, slipped back into the crowd.

"Hey." But the current carried him off.

Only to confront him with another problem. Lying athwart the way was a fallen tree, its giant limbs adrift on the water. Impaled on one branch was a big rectangular white sheet, the size of a sail on a three-masted schooner.

The tree caught his vessel in the crook of a limb. Becalmed, he gazed at the sheet that enshrouded much of the tree. Up close like this, he saw there was black lettering that filled the face of the sheet.

He stood and pressed his face against the glass of his vessel to gaze on this lettering—typeface that screamed at him skyscraper-tall. "Providence Journal," it read, and "Price Two Cents."

"Now wait a minute," he protested to the cosmos at large. That was no schooner sail. That was a newspaper. In which case: what had snagged the paper wasn't a tree, but more like a twig. He rubbed his eyes, shook his head. Tree, or twig?

All sense of scale in the world fell away.

Disheartened, he slumped in a heap.

That was when he noticed the thing affixed to the top of his prison vessel. It seemed a label of some sort. He gazed up at it, too exhausted at first to care.

The label was torn. From one corner it trailed a peeling tendril in the current.

Words. Words on the label, facing outward to the world. From within the vessel he strained to read them backward.

"A-D-O" ran part of one word.

"M-A-E-R" ran the reverse lettering for part of another.

He struggled back to his feet for a better view. A wave sloshed through the vessel's mouth to soak him once more and knock him awry. Stubbornly he braced his hands against the glass roof and peered more closely. His neck arched, his nose all but touched the glass beneath the bottom of the label.

Laboriously he spelled out the lettering. One more word in reverse. "E-I-X-O-M."

Oh. Oh.

"Moxie Cream Soda."

And beneath that, the size: "10 oz."

A discarded soda bottle: so this had been his chariot out of Valhalla.

Wait.

How could a fellow five foot eleven, two hundred pounds, fit inside a ten-ounce bottle?

No time to puzzle this out. For at that moment, pale talons, each longer than the length of the captive's whole body, swooped down and plucked vessel and prisoner clear of the current.

Not talons. Fingers. Monstrously long, pale writhing hydras. Warrior Conan had fought such things in the caves of Lemuria.

Pale hydra fingers. An arm sheathed in black. Teeth and a mouth that all but swallowed him in a smile.

And a countenance: cadaverous. Yes, that was the word. But the prisoner knew, as the bottle was lifted level with the mouth, that "cadaverous" was overused, a spent image. Yet here it was apt: the pale visage of a cadaver, a corpse that still breathed. He had seen this being but once, and that in a photograph. But he knew who it was. Someone he'd once admired and honored but had since come to loathe. Someone he'd had in mind in his pulp-fiction writing when he created the foulest of his own fever-dream villains: Skull-Face.

And now here was Skull-Face come to life in the flesh.

And it seemed Skull-Face had a companion. A crow that flapped uneasily on his shoulder. A crow Howard knew. Hadn't it claimed to be his friend? But now it turned aside its head as if to deny it had ever mouthed such words.

The Skull spoke. "Welcome to Providence, Mister Robert E. Howard. What a historic moment. Howard Phillips Lovecraft meets Two-Gun Bob. You don't mind if I use your pet name? Since, after all, you're about to join my menagerie of pets."

He held the bottle high so the two men were eye to giant eye.

"Wait." Howard's protest was cut short: Lovecraft shook the bottle so water sloshed the prisoner full in the mouth.

Howard sputtered, tried to shout.

"Go ahead, little man." Lovecraft inserted the bottle into a capacious coat pocket. "No one in this crowd of passersby can see you; no one can hear. All they'll notice is a gentleman who's just plucked a bit of trash from the river. A bit of trash containing a yet smaller bit of trash."

Lovecraft smiled as he turned to stride back up College Hill. "You see, Two-Gun Bob, for your afterlife you've been miniaturized."

From within the coat pocket Howard could hear the footsteps of workmen hurrying on their way home. He bellowed for help.

"Miniature size, miniature lungs," said the Magus with a smirk. "Too small to be audible. It's a bit hard to be heard when you're not even two inches tall."

The bird paced about on its master's shoulder.

"Come, Kavva. Say something to welcome our new guest."

Squawked the crow slave: "Nevermore."

"No, no. Save that for our *other* guest." Lovecraft lengthened his stride for the climb. "I'm eager to introduce the two to each other. I'm sure they'll get along just splendidly. But if they don't, no matter." He shrugged as he walked. "They'll each be expendable servitors for my vital project."

The prisoner sloshed about in his Moxie Cream bottle. The Magus giggled. The crow squawked. And night folded its wings upon College Hill.

7

Mouth of the bay called Narragansett, frontier of the Plymouth Colony, April 1636

Cold earth. Raw dawn. Wet leaves by his head, from last night's rain.

He unwrapped himself from his cloak and sat up.

Even as he murmured a prayer of thanksgiving for this gift of a new day, he listened.

Drip of water from the trees. Gurgling from the river; *slap-slap* of waves over stone.

Nothing amiss. Yet some sound had stirred him from his bed.

Bed. He smiled at the word. His couch for the night had been no more than a wallow scooped from damp ground. He recalled the lines he had penned on the day previous—for even in this his exile, he kept a journal, applying his quill to the end-papers of the Gospel he secreted always on his person: "I have been sorely tested, for fourteen weeks, in a bitter winter season, not knowing what bread or bed do mean."

Bitter winter. He recalled what he had seen, on the third day of his travels. Snow falling, his feet wet, a night of moonlit frost that left his fingers numb. He had splashed his way across a stream, only to stop and marvel at the creatures he encountered: a family of beavers. Later, even as he shivered, he added another note to his Gospel:

> Observation. A Beast of wonder; for cutting and drawing of great pieces of trees with his teeth, with which I have often seen fair streams and rivers damm'd and stoppt up by them: upon these streams thus damm'd up, he builds his house with stories, wherein he sits dry in his chambers, or goes into the water at his pleasure.

Sits dry in his chambers. How fervently had he shaped a pleasant fantasy: to repose in hospitality among these beasts, warm and sheltered against the wet, to listen to their chatterings and try to divine their tongue.

Divine their tongue. Yes, that was what he needed: a key into the language of America (this vast new continent), a means of speaking to all the Lord's creatures he encountered in his journeys, whether animal or man.

"A key into the language of America": someday I will pen a book with this very title.

Well. No haven had there been for him that night. But he had staggered on through the long winter's dark, consoling himself with the words of Matthew: "The foxes have holes, and the birds of the air have nests; but the Son of Man hath nowhere to lay his head."

Yet now, in this April dawning, winter was waning, thank the Creator, and just as the Israelites in the desert had been granted manna whereby to survive, so too had he been given a rude but sufficient victual in this vast wildland. Dried chestnuts, brought him yester-eve by mild-hearted Pocassets (subjects of the sachem of the Wampanoags).

The Pocassets had brought not only food but a warning.

"Are you the fugitive sought by Boston, the man named Roger Williams?"

He had nodded that he was.

"Then hear this tiding." Even here, they informed him, distant as he was from Boston, after months of travail on foot through forest, he was not beyond the Crown's reach. For in this encampment, perched as he was on the Bay's east shore, he was still within the lands claimed by Plymouth Colony. And Plymouth answered to Massachusetts, and Boston had issued a decree to arrest this heretic and freethinker wherever he might be found within the confines of the colony.

Yet Plymouth's governor had sent these Indians to him with a warning most cordial: if the fugitive were simply to remove himself to the west shore of the Seekonk, to the tribal lands beyond the arm of the English, why then, Williams would be at liberty to establish for himself a home wherever God most gracious might be pleased to place him.

Yet he must hasten, the Pocassets had warned before they withdrew. For Boston deemed him an outlaw so disturbing to the colony's peace that the Puritans would surely arraign him unless he found refuge among the feared and powerful Narragansetts.

That had been last night's message. And now—Williams rose stiffly and shook his cloak free of dirt—he had best make ready to go.

There. A noise of some kind, the very same that had first awakened him. Pursuers coming through the forest, intent on his arrest?

No. Simply the wind in the oaks, setting their leaves to rattle and chatter. And yet a strong wind, and unseasonable.

Louder now, the rustling of the oaks. Tree limbs swayed and danced.

He shivered, reminded himself of his own simple motto: *Solitary, but never alone, with the Lord as my companion.*

He shivered again in the wind. Truly, time to go.

But first a reading with which to strengthen himself. He opened his Gospel and read aloud from John: "They said therefore unto him, What sign showest thou then, that we may see, and believe thee? What dost thou work? Our fathers did eat manna in the desert; as it is written: He gave them bread from heaven to eat."

Yes, he knew this passage well: the people doubting the Son of God, asking him for a sign, for sustenance, just as the Israelites had been given bread from heaven in their Exodus wanderings.

Which reminded him: in his hunger last night he had eaten almost all the food brought him by the Pocassets. Should he take time now to forage through the woodland here for nuts or berries or wholesome herbs? Or should he make use of the dugout given him by the kind Pocassets and flee across the wide river at once?

For guidance he read further in John:

> Then Jesus said unto them, Verily, verily, the bread of God is he which cometh down from heaven, and giveth life unto the world.
>
> Then said they unto him, Lord, evermore give us this bread.
>
> And Jesus said unto them, I am the bread of life; he that cometh to me shall never hunger.

Here then was his answer. Williams smiled. He would not tarry in this wilderness, hunting anxiously for manna to hoard against future want, when at any moment the Crown's agents might appear with their manacles and shackle him to a future dubious. No, he would set forth now, and trust for his bread to God's own Providence.

But even as he pocketed his Gospel and took a step to the shore, came a manifestation wondrous.

The wind blew afresh, howled now so as to lift him nigh off his feet. The oak nearest him flexed its limbs as if in struggle. Its dead winter leaves rattled and flew skyward.

And in the sky: out of the north, a great cloud, rapidly nearing, a fire enfolding itself within. It paused, a brightness about it, and in its midst a pulsation as of amber.

The cloud lowered itself till it all but touched the oak. The brightness grew greater, flared itself in a downward jagged stroke. Too much for human eye; too much for oaken wood. The man stooped and turned his face; the tree burst into flame.

What wonder was this?

His heart hammered as he steadied his gaze. The tree now was no more than a smoking black stump.

Yet what drew his view was that which approached. For a moment he saw, and saw clearly. A retinue of lights, diminutive globes that bobbed and touched one another, as if to converse each unto its neighbor.

Demonic, or godly? Devil's play, or divine?

Even as he wondered, the retinue drew near, then hesitated. The man felt for his Gospel, swallowed hard.

Hesitation, then the retinue withdrew, a pace, another, until it hovered over the charred ash of the stump.

Is it possible ever truly to learn the tongue of another race, another class of beings? Sincerely had Roger Williams labored, while a guest in the lodges of the Sakonnets and Wampanoags and even the war-hungry Pequots, to learn the language of that part of America called New England. Now here before him was a yet greater challenge.

For he believed he sensed a language at play within the retinue. No words emerged, no tongue could he hear. Yet he sensed as it were a sigh as the globes touched and bobbed above the stump they had ruined. *Regret*, came the thought. *That is what they feel.*

Of a sudden the globes straightened and lengthened as if to stretch forth an arm. A dazzlement, so that once more the man had to turn away his face. And when he looked again, he beheld a tree renewed, its blasted stump now a strong trunk, its limbs sprouting with green leaves that spoke of verdant spring.

A healing. And then the globes withdrew from the tree and approached the man and dipped and curtsied as if in salutation.

Ever courtly himself (although his heart still hammered), he bowed in return.

He sought for something to say in greeting, tried uttering the first word of the language of America that he had learned in these wildlands: "Netop."

He smiled, said it again. "Netop."

He raised his hand in welcome, said the word now in his own English tongue. "Friend."

The globes brightened and pulsed and then slowly faded. An end to the vision.

Yet still there somehow, of that he was sure. A radiance, palpable if not visible. An aura. A presence.

Whatever these beings, they were not of the Dark. Were they, like him, also seeking their way?

He gestured to the canoe. "I must perforce journey westward across this body of water and entrust myself to providential care. You are most welcome to join me in this wandering."

And with that he pushed the dugout into the water and stepped lightly aboard. *Solitary, but not alone.*

8

Rhode Island, Providence River landing, Dyer Street, downtown, present day

Joseph Bonaventure stood uncertainly amid the crowd of some hundred volunteers. He glanced about. No one he knew. No surprise. He'd been away too many years.

Seven-thirty A.M. People sipped coffee, turned their backs to the breeze coming off the river. Too early in the day to talk. Quiet group, except for a pair of women behind him. Speculating about which boat they'd be assigned to. One of them said she hoped they'd get the *Icarus* again. She said she liked the skipper on that boat.

Individuals with clipboards stepped forward and called names. Serving on the *Apollo*. Serving on the *Phoebus*. Serving on the *Eos*. Volunteers followed their minders to each vessel's gathering point.

Finally there were only some ten or twelve people left unassigned. A pleasant-faced woman wearing a pilot's cap addressed them. Said her name was Linda, captain of the *Icarus*. "You folks are with me."

A loud *yay* from one of the two women behind him. "We got what we wished for."

Joseph Bonaventure normally kept to himself as much as possible. Keeping to himself maximized his privacy, which in turn maximized his time to think his quiet, organized thoughts. So now he fought any impulse to look over his shoulder to see who was making this celebratory *yay*. Probably not the kind of person he wanted to talk to.

Then he reminded himself why his therapist had pestered him into volunteering for this festival. "Mix with people. Do you good. Take you out of yourself."

"Maybe I don't want to be taken out of myself."

"Oh yes you do. You just don't realize it yet."

And with that, Doctor Cartwright had gone online and signed him up for Riverglow on the spot. (Not that Bonaventure had any idea what kind of work this volunteering might entail.)

And what would Doctor Cartwright say now? "Go ahead. Chat with these two women."

So he turned and moved his mouth in what he hoped was a smile. For months—what felt like forever—he hadn't had much practice.

The yay-brayer smiled back. She had a nice smile. A small woman, sturdy, up there in years, to judge from her wrinkled, weathered skin. Tight jeans. White T-shirt with a faded Foxwood Casino logo and a picture of a grinning demon holding a dollar bill in one hand and an ace of spades in the other while above its head a caption read "Ya gotta pay to play." Rolled up in one sleeve of the shirt was a pack of cigarettes.

"I'm Janey. This here's Barb." Barb stood large and tall beneath a head of high frizzed hair. The hair was dyed metallic purple—almost a color match for the capacious muumuu she wore. Barb was chewing gum, loud and fast, but she paused enough to say "Hey."

"Hey. I'm Joseph Bonaventure."

"We'll call you Joey," decided Janey.

"I prefer Joseph."

Janey announced she liked Joey better.

Barb told Janey to shut up so they could hear what the skipper had to say.

Captain Linda was making a welcome speech. How for over twenty-five years the Riverglow festival had been bringing together visitors from all over Rhode Island and New England and beyond. How Riverglow gathered musicians and dancers and artists and food vendors and enticed big crowds to what used to be a derelict downtown. How the heart of the action, what made Riverglow Riverglow, was what the volunteers assembled here now did on summertime Saturday nights: going out on these boats lined up here at the dock to ignite the midriver braziers and feed them wood and keep them alight to cheer the riverbank crowds through to midnight and beyond.

Janey had apparently heard all this before. "So, Joey. What do you do?"

What do I do? He hated that question. Especially after everything that had happened to him these past umpteen years. *Well I could tell you folks what I used to do. How I used to feel pretty high and mighty before I came crashing down hard and screwed up my life but good.*

Aloud he said he was a teacher. "But not teaching at the moment. Kind of between jobs right now."

"A teacher? Cool. What do you teach?"

"Used to teach. Long time ago. Like I said, I'm kind of between jobs at the moment. But I used to teach American literature."

"Huh." A pause. "I read *Romeo and Juliet* in high school. Part of it, anyway. Saw the rest on video."

"Don't be so stupid-ass." A reproof from Barbara between chews of gum. "That's not American. That's Shakespeare."

"So what. It's still literature. I'm just trying to make conversation here."

Captain Linda was offering introductions now, pointing out individuals, reading out names. Hard to hear. Janey and Barb behind him were right at his ear good-naturedly quarreling about something.

The captain announced his name. "And this is Professor Joseph Bonaventure." "Professor": he hadn't called himself by that label for ages, certainly not since he'd come back to Rhode Island, not since he'd been booted from his last academic post, not since the scandal. How did Riverglow know about this? Somebody must have researched him online.

"Professor, huh?" Janey looked impressed. "Is that cool, or what? Not just a high school teacher, but a professor."

He started to say he was actually only a grad student and had never been more than a temporary adjunct lecturer, that "Professor" was no more than a courtesy title in the classroom, not a rank he'd really ever deserved in any way. But he mumbled his explanation, talking more to himself than to the world at large. (He did that a lot these days.)

Barb interrupted. "Talk louder. Can't hear you."

He said he wasn't really a professor. "Just a student." He turned back to the captain, trying to signal this was a topic he'd rather not pursue.

But Barb wasn't willing to let him off so easily. "Student? Lookit him. Lookit." She nudged her companion. "I see a lotta gray hair on that head of his. This guy's getting up there in years." She appraised him full-voiced as if he weren't standing right there, able to hear every word like a stab to the heart.

"He's too old to be a student." Barb shifted the gum in her mouth, chewed as she spoke.

Janey suggested maybe he was still writing his dissertation. Said she'd heard these things take time. "Is that it, Joey? Still doing your dissertation?" The fact that he kept his back to them both didn't seem to stop the chatter. "How long you been working on it?"

Without turning his head: "Too long."

"Yeah? How many years?"

He said quite a few.

Janey persisted. "Ten years? Twelve?"

"Longer. Way longer." He hated being reminded of this, the sputtering wreck of his so-called academic career, one failure among many.

"Get outta here." Barb stopped chewing long enough to squeeze a world of scorn into those three words. "Twelve years and counting, scribbling away and nothing to show for it?"

Another stab to the heart. Bonaventure resolutely kept his back to them both as he replied. "Let's just say there's been a hiatus."

"A what?"

Janey translated. "I think he means he took time off for a while."

"How come he didn't just say so?"

Bonaventure fought the impulse to flee, reminded himself once more he was there on a therapeutic assignment, made himself turn briefly to Janey and Barb and grit out a reply. "That's right. I took time off for a while. A long while. Now I've come back to Providence. Planning to ease back into my studies." He turned away again to let them know "Let's drop this subject."

Barbara wasn't quite done. "Gotta feel a little sorry for him though." She nudged Janey. "I mean lookit him. Pitiful scraggly. Unhealthy, like he's not eating right. Raggedy-ass bony. Yup: getting up there in years." She said she could see it in his face.

Janey punched her in the arm. "You're a fine one to talk. You and me, it ain't like we're a pair of spring chickens."

"You got that right, girlfriend." A barked laugh from Barb.

Getting up there in years. Yeah, and I feel the weight of them all. Bonaventure pretended he'd heard none of this, tried to make himself focus on the Riverglow preparations in front of him.

Captain Linda was still going through the introductions. She pointed to a thickly built man in his sixties. Big, capable, calloused carpenter's hands. Baggy cargo shorts, baseball cap, sweatshirt with a logo: "Francis Xavier/Federal Hill." Father Something, Linda called him. Amid the volunteers' babble, Bonaventure didn't catch his name. The man nodded agreeably and smiled in acknowledgment.

"Father?" scoffed Barb. "That guy don't look like no priest. I mean, he ain't even in uniform."

Janey countered that priests didn't exactly have a uniform.

"Sure they do. You know, robes. Dressed in black."

"Maybe he's off duty."

"Priests are never off duty."

"Who made you an authority? You just done a survey?"

"I'm serious. They're never off duty. They're priests, and nothing but priests. Period. Like, all the time. Twenty-four/seven. Period. Joey, am I right, or what?"

Bonaventure flinched. "Um." *Great. Now I'm being propelled into somebody else's squabble.*

Janey half-turned and gave him a conspirator's wink as if to say "It's okay just make my friend happy."

Bonaventure cleared his throat and murmured yes that sounded right to him.

"See?" Barb elbowed her pal. "The professor agrees with me. I'm always right. My take is"—and this in a voice loud enough for everyone to hear—"that guy must be going incognito or whatever because of all them sex abuse scandals."

"Hey can you blame him?" Janey tugged at Barb's muumuu and muttered a fierce "Would you please shut the hell up?"

Father Something must have heard the exchange but simply bestowed on them an unperturbed smile.

Bonaventure liked the priest's placid creased face, asked himself the question he often silently posed nowadays in meeting someone new: Could this person be trusted with secrets? A lifelong Catholic, Joseph Bonaventure had kept the habit of respect for clergy, the news-media revelations of clerical abuse notwithstanding. Sooner or later, Bonaventure knew, he'd need to take a risk, share with someone the burden of his past, of everything that had happened in the catastrophic years that trailed behind him.

With a jolt he realized he'd lost focus on the present—something he did all too often these days. The captain was almost done with introductions. But she'd just said something to snap Bonaventure back to attention. What was it? What had he heard?

The word "Athenaeum." That was it. The name of the very library he was hoping to visit here in Providence. The place connected with the project Bonaventure had dreamed up in hopes of making some kind of comeback into academia after all these years of disgrace.

But who was it the captain had been introducing? Linda had just nodded to a young woman standing next to Father Something, a petite blonde, hair cropped no-nonsense short, one ear studded with silver knobs of intricate make. The knobs were arranged in an arc along the outer lobe. Was this silver-lobed volunteer an Athenaeum employee? Would he come off like a fool (he often felt like a fool) if he, a complete stranger, just waltzed up and said hi?

In any case Earlobe stood frowning as if uncertain whether the whole morning's venture had been a good idea (a doubt Bonaventure shared—but then he imagined Doctor Cartwright reprimanding him with a stern admonition to "Get out and socialize").

He was almost—or at least tentatively—at the point of daring all and risking ruin and walking over to Ms. Earlobe and saying, "Hi I'm Joseph Bonaventure and I'd love to ask you about the Athenaeum if that in fact is where you work because the Athenaeum boasts a treasure that might pry me out from under a dark rock and repair my academic reputation and bring me back into the warm light of scholarly approval if you'd just be kind enough to help me" (and oh how proud his therapist would be to see him now!)—he was yes just grimacing in grim determination and taking that big first step toward her when Captain Linda slapped her clipboard and said, "Okay everybody that's it for intros and now let's get to work."

Bonaventure blinked, stood frozen. The group moved away.

"Wassa matter with him?" Muumuu'd Barb made a face.

Janey came back for him. "Come on, Joey." She tugged the sleeve of his coat. "Wake-up time. I've had mornings like this too."

9

Alexander Finster already knew he was going to hate this assignment. And it didn't help that the woman in the pilot's cap kept smiling and calling them all volunteers.

Well, the rest of them might all be here voluntarily. But he sure as hell wasn't.

In court the judge had given him three choices.

Choice A. Two months in the Adult Correctional Institution in Warwick. Alex had just turned eighteen, so no more juvie hall for him, which meant two months hard time at the ACI. Not a good choice. Especially, the judge reminded him, given the fact that his fellow inmates might not warm to him once they found out what he'd done to land himself in prison.

Or, said His Honor, Alex could select choice B. Highway trash pickup in the breakdown lanes of I-95. Fill big plastic bags while trucks sped by and belched filth in his face.

Alex had asked how long would that be.

Ten weeks, said the judge.

That hadn't sounded so good either.

Or choice C. Four hundred hours community service with Riverglow on the Providence River.

Alex Finster knew zilch about Riverglow but figured the river had to be safer than the ACI and cleaner than I-95.

"Riverglow," he'd said.

Except now here he was, in downtown Providence on a lifeless Saturday morning in June, temperature hot and getting hotter, and he was surrounded by dipshits and dorks. No one looked anything like him. He stood out. Muscled torso, sleeve and neck tattoos, shaved head.

For the first twenty minutes he'd paid attention, listened up (which was what his probation officer had told him to do). The woman in the hat had read off names, pointed out faces. A librarian, a professor, a priest. Boring, all of them. Dipshits and dorks.

Especially the one she'd identified as a professor. Skinny, nervous, twitchy type. Oxford shirt with buttoned-down collar, chinos, tweed suitcoat. Didn't the jerk know this was no kind of outfit for hauling wood on the water? All he needed was a bowtie at his throat and a piece of chalk in his hand and he'd be all set for boring people to death in some classroom. No question: a dork.

He scowled at the volunteers and made up his mind. All of them boring as shit. Not a creative spark in the whole lot of them. Whereas he: he was an artist.

And if the world just happened to consider his particular art form a crime?

Tough shit.

One consolation: No one here seemed to know who he was. Which meant less hassle, less need to talk.

His consolation didn't last long.

"Hey." Some oversized bitch in a purple dress was nudging her friend, pointing at him. "I think I seen his picture somewhere. Maybe CNN, or WPRI. No, I got it. The *Providence Journal*. Yeah." Nice and loud, so every frigging person in the crowd could hear.

"Tagger. Hey Tagger. Yeah you." She pointed straight at him.

He muttered his name wasn't Tagger.

"It is now. Cuz it fits what you did."

The wood planking of the dock creaked under her weight as she strode toward him. Now she stood just inches away. "Get this, everybody. Punk kid moves here from out of state, makes it his nighttime hobby to spray-paint graffiti all over the place. The front windows of the Dunkin' Donuts on Gano Street. The overpass right by the State House. The Amtrak tunnel downtown. You name it. He tagged it."

She looked about to make sure she had everyone's attention.

"And every time, you know what slogan he sprays? Always the same thing. Tell 'em, Tagger. Tell 'em what you sprayed."

Alexander Finster glared but said nothing. *No way do I play along.*

She challenged him with her gaze, turned back to the crowd. "Okay then I'll tell 'em. He sprays the same thing every time. Three big fat letters. 'RMH.' When he gets arrested later on he says it's cuz he hates it so much having to live in Rhode Island, and he's so proud of being from Colorado, he's gotta spray 'RMH' every place he can."

Dimwit dork in the suitcoat scratched his head. "RMH?"

"Rocky Mountain High," she explained, "cuz he's from Colorado, right? Like he's on some John Denver singalong."

She paused, and for one grateful second Alex Finster thought she was done. But no. She was just amping up.

Spray-painting a Dunkin' Donuts, she continued, wasn't enough to make him headlines as a standout bad-ass tagger. His type always craved publicity. "So he had to do something worse. He had to go and spray the one monument everyone in Rhode Island loves. The most beautiful thing in the city of Providence." She was breathing hard now, and Alex wasn't sure if she was about to burst into tears or punch him in the mouth.

"You know, somebody told me even the *New York Times* called it iconic. Can you imagine?" Now she really was in tears, but she didn't slow down a bit. "Can you imagine, people calling something we got here in Rhode Island iconic? And this creep here had to go spray it. The one thing everyone agrees makes this state of ours special."

Alex retreated a step, his back to the river, before the focused scowls of the crowd. Everyone seemed to know precisely what beloved monument it was he had tagged. Everyone, at least, except for that dimwit professor in the tweed jacket, who scratched his head again and asked, "What thing was it that got sprayed?"

"And so right now," she concluded, "we're stuck with this puke for how long? Tell us, Tagger. How long?"

Again he said nothing.

"Four hundred hours." She supplied the answer. "Which means for four hundred hours right here in our Riverglow crew, we got ourselves the most hated guy in Providence."

"In Rhode Island," said someone.

"In the world," said someone else.

Alex Finster backed away another step. More frowns all around, from everyone, except for the guy they said was a priest, who had a look on his face like he felt sorry for him—*as if that's gonna do me any good*—and the dipshit professor in the coat, who scratched his head some more and seemed more confused than ever.

"That's enough, folks." The captain waved her clipboard. "We're here to work."

She formed the volunteers into two squads. One was assigned to several picnic tables near the landing. Piled atop the tables were stacks of old newspapers alongside plastic bags and a dozen cans of Duraflame charcoal lighter fluid. The captain said this squad would be in charge of making what she called fuse bags, whatever they were.

Alex Finster found himself assigned to the other squad. Mounds of firewood five feet high lay stacked along the landing.

The instructions were straightforward. Carry the logs to the skiffs dockside. Fill each boat to the gunwale. But leave free space on the port side. That's where the crew would stand later, when each boat was out on the water, as crewmembers grabbed wood and stacked the midriver braziers.

Nice and simple. Loudmouth was over at the picnic tables making fuse bags, still moaning about something, but here by the dock he couldn't hear and didn't care. No one in his squad seemed inclined to talk to him, which suited him just fine.

Armfuls of wood from the pile to the dock. Step down into the boat while dodging the arms and legs of others in the way. Dump logs on the starboard side. Climb back up from the boat to the dock. Repeat.

Mechanical. Nice and simple. It let him go into what he called robot-mode. No need to talk. No need to fuss. Just move and dodge the arms and legs of others in the way.

Iconic. Most beautiful and best-loved monument in Providence. Funny. He'd barely glanced at the thing that night, just sized it up as a big piece of metal, a good surface for his statement art in a high-profile place.

When he'd scrambled up onto the roof that night and tagged the thing, he'd mostly thought about how impressed his rival taggers back in Denver would be. *Selfies of tag-artist Alex Finster and his tag-line "RMH" sprayed along the skyline of this little shithole state.*

Yeah that was life: tagging and tats. He saw bodies and wondered how they'd look inked. As for the rest of existence: he sought out exteriors and shells, things he could tag. The connection between his obsessions: spray paint was a way to tattoo the world, a way to snarl forth his general hatred of things.

Tattooed or sprayed. And as for everything else: they were just ciphers and blanks.

And there was a whole frigging lot of ciphers and blanks in a shithole state like this. Yup. A place filled with dumb-bastard dipshits and dorks.

He grabbed another pile of wood, wiped the sweat from his face. Only midmorning, and already humid and hot. Going to be another slow summer day. He lifted his wrist, studied his watch. Ten o'clock. Three hours down. Just three hundred ninety-seven to go. Hey. At this rate he'd die of boredom long before he'd done all his time. Man how he hated this place.

Dumb-bastard dipshits? He directed a grim inward laugh at himself. Hadn't he himself been just a little bit dumb, hanging around up there on that roof to admire his work and take yet one more selfie, so pleased with himself he didn't hear the police till they'd swarmed up that ladder?

Smart all right, tagging a big icon with his own "RMH." But maybe not so smart what came after: resisting arrest, and spraying a cop in the face.

He'd gotten away: blitzed right off that roof, down a fire escape, and zap he was gone. Clean getaway.

Except for that one mistake. Posting selfies on Instagram and his Facebook account. Self-portrait with that big metal icon and "RMH." *Rocky Mountain High, dude. Way cool.*

Surprising how fast the police had found him. His lawyer called him stupid for photographing himself alongside his work for everyone to ID.

But hey. If you're going to make art you want to get a little credit, right?

What time was it now? He told himself fiercely not to keep checking his watch. But his resistance died fast.

Just before eleven. Three hundred ninety-six hours to go. Yeah maybe he was just a little bit dumb.

He sighed, returned from the dock, stooped for yet another armful of wood.

And then came the movement.

A stir of shadows among the piled logs. Then: a silent blur, a flash of white tail, and a rabbit dashed into the sunlight. Across the landing, under a chain-link fence, and a burst of speed into the dark green of bushes out beyond the fence.

Well yeah, came the thought. *Wish that were me, Mister Rabbit. Wish I could join you. Just run away and be free.*

And then something even stranger. For the first time all morning he truly paid attention to someone else in his boat-loading crew. That dipshit professor dork in his tweed jacket, holding an armful of wood. The guy was staring beyond the fence at the bushes where the rabbit had vanished. And the expression on the dork's face was plain as anything to read. Envy, and longing; a desire to follow the creature into the dark green and disappear.

The same set of feelings, in fact, that Alex Finster had just felt.

Which made Alex take a closer look at the dork.

The guy had rolled back the sleeves on his tweed jacket to do this work with the firewood. *Lose the coat, dude. Not a smart thing to wear.*

But what caught Alex's attention now was the man's exposed forearms. The dork had been inked. Each arm was tattooed.

Nothing elaborate. Alex Finster, tattooist and tagger, prided himself on his own sleeve-tats. What this dude had was simpler, just some lettering. Alex cocked his head to read it.

The dork suddenly realized he was being studied and rushed off with his wood to the boats. Not as fast as the rabbit, but almost.

Nonetheless: this dork was of interest. For one brief instant—no, make that maybe for all of two minutes—Alex Finster eased off of being resentful and bored.

10

By eleven A.M. Fay MacConnell was starting to think volunteering for Riverglow had been a truly sappy idea.

It had sounded acceptable enough last week. That's when her Athenaeum supervisor had circulated a memo urging staff to consider weekend community service "to build good will with the city." Her boss especially recommended Riverglow.

Her first thought had been *Okay, maybe, if that's what's expected. Get outdoors; be out on the water; sniff the fresh river breeze. The change might do me good.*

Not that she always handled change well. Nor was she an outdoor recreation type. Far from it. Her natural setting: well-stocked wooden shelves, old Britannicas lined up in welcome, leather bindings worn smooth by the affectionate hands of bibliophiles before her, floor-to-ceiling stacks that enclosed one in a kind of printed-matter privet hedge. And at the heart of this indoor garden: thick oak tables with ample surfaces, where one could open wide some folio volume of travels or faded atlas of rare maps and dream oneself into places far away. Books were good friends.

Better friends than humans; much better friends than men. That last guy she'd been dating (someone she'd met right after moving to Providence): whew. The romance conformed to her usual pattern—entanglement, a month's infatuation (maybe we'll even get married!), then rapid disappointment. The end of the business: late-night solo stare-in-the-mirror moments of *How'd I manage to do this to myself again?*

Luckily for her, Fay MacConnell's current best boy was a literary type who for the past century and a half and more had been very safely dead. Dates with him involved a lamp and desk in a reading room and a volume of his poems, while nearby reference clerks stacked books on shelves and kept things in their place.

Yes. Libraries. Old libraries, the older and calmer the better. So when the Athenaeum (the building dated to 1838, though the institution was even older) posted an opening, she'd given up her job at the Regenstein and moved from Chicago to Providence just like that. The Regenstein was okay if you liked Brutalist concrete but she'd been there sixteen years (straight out of her master's degree in library science) and enough was enough.

Three months in, and she loved her new Athenaeum perch, loved coming in every day. Then last week her boss, Tristram Schaefer, had stopped by her desk and said some staff person should take a turn this weekend doing community service with Riverglow. "Show the flag, and all that. Get our name out in the city. Fifi, you're the fresh young face in town. Why don't you do a round?"

The fresh young face in town. Plenty to object to in that sentence if she'd been in the mood to pick a fight. Problem was she'd just turned forty: she didn't feel fresh and she no longer felt young. In fact one night about a week before leaving her Regenstein job she'd discovered something that made her feel plenty old. Standing at the stove stirring a macaroni-and-cheese mix, watching a David Janssen *Fugitive* episode from the sixties (she loved TV shows about folks on the wrong side of the law who are always fleeing, fleeing, fleeing), she'd scratched her head and tugged loose errant strands of hair that proved to be prematurely, unreasonably, and distressingly gray.

Old-age onset? She'd voiced a firm "no way."

Off to CVS that very evening, the personal grooming aisle. She'd scanned the goods. L'Oréal. Garnier Nutrisse. Clairol Nice'n Easy. She liked the sound of that: *easy, easy.* Transform herself from blah brunette to blonde: it couldn't be that hard. After all, she was about to start a new job in a new city; why not new hair to go with her new life? (She had a lot of old life to leave behind and run from.)

Trouble was (this would be her rueful insight-in-hindsight) she lacked the patience to do a dye job right. (Even though she loved to say "I'm a do-it-yourselfer.") She'd barely glanced at the warning label on the bleach box: "Results vary. You may not achieve quite the color you see on the label."

Subsequent outcome, four weeks later: a blonde mane, yes, but with dirt-streak stripes and brunette roots showing amid those golden hues. Not to mention that—depending on the light—her hair glowed brassy: splotches of rust-flake red and metallic green and what she called sickly banana-yellow.

She sighed. *Splotchy hair to go with a splotchy life.*

If she'd been the type to trumpet her troubles (she liked to think she wasn't, though she knew she had her moments), Fay could have said to her boss: "My hair's losing its color and the only way I stay faux-blonde is courtesy of dyes from Vidal Sassoon and Friends" ("with anti-aging formula," it had said on the box: she'd been a sucker for that). "So please don't patronize me with words like 'fresh' and 'young.'" She'd bitten back the words, but nothing could keep her from thinking the thoughts.

And another thing (she could have added to her shout-out list): this business of people calling her Fifi. Tristram had coined the name for her during her first week on the job and he enjoyed it so much she didn't have the heart to say she preferred, instead of Fifi, just original-flavor Fay. But the new name had caught on at work and now all her colleagues followed Tristram's lead and called her Fifi too (or sometimes Feef, which was worse).

"And besides, Feef"—Tristram knew how to cinch an argument—"you'll see a lot of Providence history from the river's waterline. Whole new perspective. Refreshing. I promise."

And so now here she was, a Riverglow volunteer; but thus far this morning she wasn't finding the perspective any too refreshing. Anticipating the heat, she'd dressed in a sleeveless T-shirt and shorts and flip-flops. But her outfit provided no protection against the wood she'd had to lug all morning. Within an hour her biceps, elbows, forearms, wrists, and fingers felt abraded and sore. By noon she was aching all over and sticky and sweaty.

And then came the accident.

Captain Linda—a good person, Fay had decided, low-key and reasonable—had called out, "Okay, *Icarus* is full. Let's head out and go stock the braziers for tonight's gig."

Each *Icarus* volunteer—the priest, the professor in the tweed jacket, the graffiti guy they called Tagger—seemed to have the same thought: jump aboard fast, get out on the water, hope for a midriver breeze. Fay MacConnell hurried after them—a quick *flap-flap-flap* in her sandals from the dock to the boat.

Behind her someone cried, "Hey guys let me tag along for the ride." The volunteer Janey, in each hand a plastic fuse bag stuffed full.

Just as Janey caught up, Fay slipped in her sandals at the dock's edge. A wild wave of arms as Fay banged into Janey. Janey dropped her bags and tried to catch Fay.

A try that only propelled Fay right over the dock.

Chin-first pratfall straight into the skiff—or would have been. For at that moment Joseph Bonaventure had been standing in the boat, gazing out at the river. The noise made him turn.

What Fay saw as she fell was a face contracted in self-absorption, then eyes that went wide with alarm. The man twisted in place, made an awkward lurch forward.

He too tried to catch Fay but all he caught was her ear.

Which made her land hard on a bag, while Janey landed on Fay.

The plastic burst with a pop. That's how Fay MacConnell discovered up close what a fuse bag contains: balled-up newspapers soaked in Duraflame fluid.

The professor pulled her to her feet, asked if she was okay.

"Fine. I'm fine." She shook free of his hand. "You practically tore my ear off."

A mumbled "sorry" from the man.

"Damn it." Her fingers probed the curve of her earlobe. "One of my studs is missing."

Another "sorry." Forlorn but unhelpful: uselessly he stood there, scratching his useless head. "What's it look like?"

"Little silver knob. Engraved with tiny spirals, sort of a curlicue design. Like the others I'm wearing." She flicked him an irritable glance.

He stooped, began poking among the logs in the pile.

"Forget it. It's too small. You'll never find it. Not with all this wood everywhere."

He was on all fours now, studying the deck.

The guy looked foolish. "I said forget it." Her voice packed more harshness than she'd intended. It was just that—and this was something she most definitely didn't want to share with a boatload of strangers on a day that was turning out to be stressful and breathless and hot—this was her lucky set of earrings, bought by her mother to wish her success when she left Chicago for the new job in Rhode Island.

Stressful and hot. Fay sat down suddenly on the portside gunwale.

Janey sat beside her. "You sure you're okay?"

"Fine. I'll be fine." She sniffed at her shirt. "Whew. Barbecue lighter fluid. At least I'll be fine as long as nobody strikes a match."

The guy in the tweed coat stayed on all fours, turned over more wood. He stammered something from the deck. Something about just trying to help; something useless. His head bumped her legs.

"Hey, lay off, will you? You'll never find it."

More mumbled apologies.

"You look a little pale." Janey patted her arm, asked again how she was doing.

"Well, maybe not so fine. Exhausted. Smelly. Highly flammable. Now I know how Icarus felt when he flew too close to the sun. What a name for a boat."

Up came Barbara in her purple muumuu. She announced she was done fixing fuse bags so she figured she would join them on the river. Her nose wrinkled at Janey and Fay.

"Whew. Ain't you two a mess. Some kinda accident scene here?"

Janey told her to go stick a sock in her mouth.

The guy in the tweed jacket was still on all foolish fours, inches from her knee, oblivious to infringements of personal space. Fay wanted to snap, "Excuse me but I'm tired why don't you back off can't you see you've done enough harm for one day?"

But then she noticed two things.

The first was that even as she was thinking how foolish he looked, she saw that someone else as well was watching him search. The teen they called Tagger. The young man stood apart, made no motion to help, on his lips a big smirk—a smirk that seemed to include all in his view. The boat was too small for that much ill will.

The second thing: from where she sat she had a good high-focus view—closer than she wanted—of this clumsy Professor Bonaventure. Hair thinning, badly combed, going gray (a condition with which she could sympathize). Skin on his face pitted and blotched. The light picked out a long raw red patch along his jawline, where the flesh stood puffy and raised, like a bad graft. He seemed older than she'd first thought. Old, and also tired. Maybe pushing the half-century mark, maybe a few years past fifty. *But hey,* came the thought at her, *there are days like today when I don't feel so youthful myself.*

"Really," she said to him, but this time she wasn't so harsh in how she said it, "forget it."

He turned his head to reply but instead bumped her knee. Which made her mad all over again: she fought off an urge to reply with a kick or a curse. More muttered apologies as he scrabbled away, head still close to the deck.

"Hey." Janey seemed to be seeking words to hearten Fay. "At least the day ain't likely to get any worse."

"Don't be so optimistic." The librarian rubbed her ear where the stud was missing.

Moodily she stared at the river. Not exactly the vista she'd hoped for. Right beside the boat, atop the water and taking up a space that must have measured some twenty feet by thirty, was a surprisingly dense trash gyre: a big fetid slow-stirring pile. Shredded plastic bags, wispy as ghosts, lay snagged on floating tree branches, along with plastic bottles, plastic lids, and plastic take-out wrappers. A diminutive bird of some kind was walking atop this mess, inspecting, pecking, stepping from garbage bit to garbage bit. The bird peered at a Marlboro wrapper. Fay hadn't had a cigarette for three-and-a-half days. She'd been trying to quit. Now the thought hit: *Geez I'd love a smoke.*

I could be back at my desk, cool and dry instead of out in this heat. Plus I've lost part of my earring set, the ones that are supposed to be bringing me luck.

Beside her Janey was staring at the bird and the Marlboro wrapper. She unrolled the cigarette pack from her T-shirt sleeve. Unfiltered Camels.

"You know I'd love one of these." Janey sniffed at the pack.

"So would I." Fay gave them a longing look.

"Except they smell like Duraflame fluid. Got a bit damp. Afraid if we lit one, we'd go up like a torch."

At that they both laughed, and Fay felt not quite so bad.

Captain Linda said something to the priest about needing a minute to check the ignition and fuel lines before getting started. "In the meantime, Father, since you're the senior volunteer, why don't you give our crew your orientation talk?"

"Be glad to, Skipper." The priest smiled at the others in the boat and introduced himself as Jim Cypriano. "Lifelong resident of Li'l Rhody, native of Federal Hill, not very far from here"—he waved an arm vaguely behind him—"and a longtime fan of Riverglow."

To Fay's relief the guy in the tweed jacket interrupted his earring search to sit up and listen.

Father Cypriano spoke in a low, pleasant voice Fay found easy to listen to. "But more important than me"—he patted the gunwale beside him—"is the *Icarus*. It's a flat-bottomed open cargo skiff, twenty-four feet in length. Like the other Riverglow vessels, it's painted black, so as to be inconspicuous on the water at night. For the twenty thousand visitors who'll show up here tonight, the focus will be on the fires that'll make the river glow."

He paused for emphasis. "Which reminds me. Every volunteer on the skiffs will be required to dress in black tonight. We want to be invisible servants, stagehands backstage, so to speak."

"'Scuse me for asking, Father"—the interruption came from Jancy—"but speaking of dress, my friend Barb was wondering how come you're dressed like a civilian. Is that the right word? 'Civilian'? Anyway, how come you're out of uniform? I mean, are you really a priest, or what?"

Fay felt embarrassed for the man. "Hey." She tapped Janey's arm. "Don't give him a hard time."

"You're right." Janey grinned at her, then at the priest. "Bless me, Father, for I have sinned. But I'm gonna plead an extenuating circumstance. My Camels are soggy and smell like lighter fluid and I'm dying for a smoke."

"Three Our Fathers and three Hail Marys," he answered with a smile, "and for extra penance go easy on the smokes. But as to your question"—here he grew serious—"yes, I'm a priest. One hundred per cent, civilian clothes notwithstanding. And I'll tell you a story about that."

He said a week ago he'd been in New York to concelebrate a Mass. He'd taken the subway to get to Saint Pat's. "I'm standing there. Crowded train. Delays and unspecified stops. Sweltering hot. The usual. And there I am, wearing my full priestly getup. Dog collar, black clericals, black cassock. And I get spat on. Twice. And people start unloading on me, shouting in my face. Sexual abuse by Bishop X. Cover-up by Cardinal So-and-So. Payoffs. Denials. No end to the scandals. And how dare I appear in public as a priest?"

Another smile, this one not so cheerful or bright. "An old buddy of mine from Woonsocket puts it to me like this: 'Jimmy, if you're part of the team, you wear the jersey, you wear the logo. At least once in a while. No matter how many hits you take.' And he's right. After all, you could say I'm married to the Church."

Cypriano's shoulders sagged. He added in a murmur, as if talking to himself more than to his listeners, "But now and then I like to just wear my civvies and take a break. Like when I volunteer for Riverglow."

Then he brightened and directed the crew's attention to the view before them on the east shore of the river. "This view always puts me in a good frame of mind. All this history on display. College Hill. Brown University. The Rhode Island School of Design. The Athenaeum." He nodded at Fay MacConnell. "The First Baptist Church. You can see its spire on the lower reaches of the hill, over there to the left. Established by Roger Williams, the man who founded this whole colony and the city of Providence in 1636."

He invited them to imagine Roger Williams' first Rhode Island voyage, all those centuries ago. "A fugitive, you know, from the Massachusetts Bay Colony. Persecuted as a religious freethinker by fellow Puritans. He comes rowing on his own in a canoe, looking for some place to settle, not knowing how the native folk will treat him. And he passes a spot called Slate Rock, not far from Fox Point"—he gestured to the right—"and he sees a group of Native Americans at the rock, standing by the shore. So he waves hello with his paddle, not sure what to expect. And they stare at him and finally one of them lifts a hand and says in a mix of English and Narragansett, 'What cheer, Netop?'—'How's it going, Friend?' And that's when Roger Williams knew he'd found himself a home. Yes. Some beautiful vistas, out here on the river."

"Beautiful? This river?" Tagger had been hunched all this time in a corner of the skiff, and Fay had forgotten about him. Now he pointed to the trash atop the water lying in a massed pile beside the boat. It was the same mess Fay had noticed when she boarded. Dispiriting to see; it had dimmed her mood. The same bird she'd seen before was still making its tentative way over the pile.

"Look how ugly all that is." Tagger thrust a hand at the water. "Beautiful vista? I call this a crappy little bird stuck in a crappy little plastic world."

"But don't you see, my friend?" Father Cypriano peered over the side and pointed below. "True, for the moment that *is* in fact this bird's whole little world: an archipelago of plastic, bits of waste placed end to end. But that plastic holds him up. And look how thoughtfully he steps, and how carefully he makes his way from one piece of waste to the next. And at each step his world holds him up. See how each bottle, each bit of Styrofoam, yields a bit beneath him but keeps him afloat."

From the prow Captain Linda spoke. "Engine check done. Cast off mooring lines fore and aft."

"Fore and aft aye." The priest cast off the lines and made them fast on the *Icarus*. The bird cocked its head at the humans, then resumed its march atop the trash.

"You know," continued Father Cypriano, "when you travel lightly, like when you weigh only a few ounces"—he chuckled at this—"you can make your home for a bit even on a plastic coffee lid. Now look at how he's stepped up onto that empty Coca-Cola bottle. Again, it yields a bit but keeps him afloat. The pleasure he must feel as each step is confirmed."

He waved at the captain to let her know the mooring lines were secured. "And that pleasure, I feel sure, is a form of gratitude."

"Gratitude." Tagger poured a lifetime's scorn into the word.

"Yes, my friend. Gratitude. That bird feels grateful for the world he's been given. And I'm convinced that this feeling—gratitude for the givenness of this world of ours, this world into which we've all been sent, birds and humans alike—this gratitude is part of what helps hold our cosmos together."

"This crappy cosmos?" The young man barked a bitter laugh. "It's just a throwaway world."

"You're right. It *is* throwaway: nothing down here lasts. He can't stay perched on that Coke bottle forever. But it's still precious to him because for the moment it's his home, and he's making the best use of it he can. And look what he's just found down there." Still balanced atop its bottle, the bird was pecking at a pair of wet candy bar wrappers.

"Reese's Peanut Butter Cup," exclaimed Janey, "and a PayDay bar. Not bad."

"Not bad," agreed the priest. "He makes the best of his world, trashy as it looks to us, draws life from it. You don't have to be a biologist to see the pleasure he takes in the chocolate he's found.

Soggy and stale? Doesn't matter. He takes pleasure in it. And as I said a moment ago: that pleasure he feels is a form of gratitude—his own form of thanks for the givenness of this world into which he's been sent. Now I'm not saying that's what our friend out-and-out *thinks*. Probably all precognitive. But that pleasure in his eyes, and that gratitude, they're a kind of hymn of praise."

"Dude, it's just a crappy pile of trash." Tagger turned away in disgust. But the rest of the crew gazed in thoughtful silence at the priest.

The engine burbled as the *Icarus* moved out from the dock. Waves lapped the archipelago. Plastic rose and fell in the wake. The bird flapped its wings but kept its perch.

"Just look," the priest marveled as he cast a last look astern, "how that bottle bobs and yields beneath him but pushes him back up and still keeps him afloat. Wonderful."

11

Silence. That was what Jim Cypriano liked best. Silence and solitude.

Not that he didn't enjoy human contact. If needed he could be very good company. But opportunities to be quiet, and meditate, and pray: these were what he instinctively craved. Nonetheless he had long ago learned to balance this desire with the job of engaging with those souls that were so frequently placed in his path.

As was the case today, on the Providence River, here on the deck of the *Icarus*. Captain Linda had asked him to give his orientation talk to this boatload of Riverglow volunteers. So Father James Cypriano, S.J., brought his heart back to Earth and summoned a smile for the crew.

While Linda piloted the skiff north along the river from the Dyer Street dock, he reminded the volunteers that decades earlier much of this waterway had been buried beneath concrete. "This open expanse you see was once old train tracks, shunting yards, parking lots, and boarded-up warehouses." Now the Providence River had been freed and dredged and widened, its embankments made welcoming with Victorian street lamps, cobblestone paths, and waterside cafés.

The *Icarus* motored under the downtown bridges that span the Providence River. Crawford Street Bridge. College Street Bridge. "And if you were to disembark here," he said as an aside, "and climb up the embankment and go straight up the hill, you'd pass the address where a famous horror-story writer lived back in the 1930s or so."

"H. P. Lovecraft." Joseph Bonaventure supplied the name.

"That's it." The priest looked impressed.

"And that College Street address," added Fay MacConnell, "is just around the corner from Benefit Street, which is where the Athenaeum is. One of the very oldest private libraries in America."

"Say." Jim Cypriano smiled at them. "You two know Providence."

The librarian and the professor essayed a glance at each other, then looked quickly away. *Sizing each other up*, thought the priest. *They're not sure yet they like what they see.* He wished that Bonaventure had been able to find her earring.

As the skiff passed into the dark beneath Washington Street, Jim Cypriano stood and stretched a hand upward to touch the damp archway that curved overhead. "A comfortable fit now. Plenty of space. But at high tide tonight remember to crouch as we go through this tunnel or the bridge will give you a crack on the head."

Back out into the daylight. Linda eased the throttle and the boat slowed. A big *V* of land jutted before them, parting the river. Confluence Park, it was called, also known as Citizens Plaza, where two streams converged to form the Providence River. The starboard-side stream was the Moshassuck ("where the moose come to water," as the native Narragansetts named it). "If we were to take this branch and go upriver just two hundred yards," explained their guide, "we'd find the spot where Roger Williams stepped from his canoe and made his new home. Providence, he called it, because he felt sure God had guided him and provisioned for him that very place."

The very sense of trust, he wanted to add, *one needs for navigating life*, but the priest warned himself not to get preachy. Instead he simply announced that the Riverglow route always followed the Woonasquatucket branch. (Another Narragansett name, he explained, one that means "where the tide ends.")

He nodded to the skipper, who steered the boat to the northwest. Along the way they passed dozens of braziers, jutting above the water one after another in a long midstream line. Other boats would be responsible tonight for keeping this part of the river alight, explained Father Cypriano. "Our post is farther upstream."

Beneath three more bridges they passed: Steeple Street, Exchange Street, and Waterplace. "And now," he said, "here we are. Our assigned post for today and tonight. They call it the Basin."

Here engineers had widened the river to form a vast circular pool. Along its watery perimeter was a circle of braziers. "Twenty of them," he said. "We'll be in charge of lighting and stoking them throughout the evening." Stairs led from one side of the basin up to a platform and a large stage of polished planks.

"At the moment it's pretty much empty," their guide observed. "But tonight up on that stage is where the donors and all the other performers will congregate." Politicians, corporate sponsors, big donors would have their choice seating nearby. "Right here is where the crowds will be thickest."

Not only ringside, around the Basin. "But also out here on the water. Gondolas, kayaks, different types of pleasure boats. They'll be swarming all around us, watching what we do. Twenty thousand guests, giving us the eye. We'll be at the heart of it all, right here in the Basin, where the *Icarus* has been assigned. Everyone will be giving us their attention. That's why we'll want to look sharp and make sure we do it right."

Up to that moment the crew's attentiveness had been slack. *Tired from hauling wood and doing chores at the dock*, he noted sympathetically. Barbara had been complaining about the sun and asking how come the boat didn't have an umbrella to give them shade. Janey had been telling Fay she was getting hungry. Unsmiling Tagger had been playing a game on his phone. And Bonaventure had been peering at the deck as if he still hoped to find the young lady's earring amid the wood.

But now Jim Cypriano had them. All of them—even that don't-give-a-frack kid—suddenly wore the same expression: *Oh. Twenty thousand guests, all looking at us. This is high pressure. This could get bad.*

He clapped his hands. "And that's why I'll ask you to give the captain your full attention. She'll show you how to load our braziers for tonight. And she'll go over what you need to know to make this evening a success for all concerned."

Linda guided the *Icarus* in a tight, slow counterclockwise loop around the braziers, keeping the objects on the boat's port side. Now the volunteers had their first close-up view. Each brazier rose some three-and-a-half feet above the water: a wide metal basket atop a thick metal stem. Four spheroid buoys were chained to each stem. All but invisible in the dark water below was a subsurface anchor chain that kept each brazier in place.

As they neared the first brazier Linda tapped the throttle down just enough so that the *Icarus* eased alongside the empty basket. Its protective buoys bobbed in the wash from the boat.

Linda nodded to Father Jim. Part of the pleasure of working with her, he felt, was that they'd been paired so often they needed few words.

He stooped and unwound a length of cable attached by one end to a cleat on the portside gunwale. He payed out the line and in one languid toss lassoed the brazier's stem just beneath the basket. A sharp pull on the cable to ensure it was taut, and then he made the line fast to another cleat on the gunwale.

"You make that look easy," marveled Janey.

"You should have seen me the first time I tried," he grinned. "Practice helps." Now that the *Icarus* was snugged alongside the brazier, he said, loading would be less hit-or-miss. "Too easy for logs to fall in the water if the boat and the brazier start floating away from each other."

Then the captain showed them how to build the woodpile. Under her direction they made what she called an "inner-core package": thin strips of kindling bundled around a fuse bag and a long braided-cotton wick. They bound the package together with knotted twine and placed it in the center of the empty brazier basket.

Next all around the core package they stacked upright lengths of wood in concentric rings until the basket was full.

"There," she said. "From the shore, no one will be able to tell that we've cheated by balling up newspapers soaked with lighter fluid inside a plastic bag. But this way once we light the wick tonight the whole thing is more or less guaranteed to catch fire even if we get one of those summer storms that can come up fast this time of year."

Then on to brazier number 2. Then number 3. And the next. And the next, counterclockwise around the Basin's rim. Linda formed them into a relay team for the work. Barbara and Bonaventure plucked logs from the pile and passed them to Tagger, who passed them in turn to Janey and Fay, who had the job of stacking and shaping the basket array. The priest noted with admiration how the skipper had placed Tagger in the middle of the relay. Each time he tried to check his phone he found his hands filled with another length of wood.

Overall they worked well together. No one dropped a log on anyone's foot (the most common mishap on a crowded woodboat).

Only one glitch, a slight one. At brazier 18, Barb pivoted with a piece of chopped pine, and a protruding knob snagged the sleeve of Bonaventure's tweed coat. (The priest had thought it odd that the fellow kept it on even in this heat.) The sleeve had pulled back to reveal inked lettering on the man's forearm. "GIR ..." Father Jim spied the first three letters of what seemed to be a long inscription but before he could read more Bonaventure hastily pulled the sleeve back in place. The priest pretended he'd seen nothing at all, simply making an encouraging comment to the effect that they were almost finished.

"And number 20." Linda told them they'd done a good job. "We're all stacked for tonight."

For a few minutes they rested, the boat motionless on the water, the buoys of brazier 20 tapping the side of the skiff.

The tapping made him think of Angelus bells. Which was silly, thought the priest, except that this quiet now, out here on the water, with the work done and everyone too tired to talk, put him in mind of Vesper prayers in the cathedral downtown. A good time of day.

But hot. Past midday now, and in the open skiff they had no shelter. Just thick humid heat from a hot baked-metal sky.

Yet he didn't mind. The dull, sweaty air put him in mind of old times, good productive times, his years as a Jesuit missionary in Indonesia. He closed his eyes a moment and remembered. The work had not been easy. Christian mission efforts were outlawed. His capacity for silence and patient restraint had served him well then. Simple witness worked better than sermons in words.

Number 20's buoy spheres tapped against the skiff in a pulse that in this heat made him think of Javanese gamelan gongs. He breathed deep, slow breaths.

"Hey." An exclamation from Janey. "What do you make of that?"

He opened his eyes. She was pointing to the western shore and the office-building skyline of Providence's downtown. Everyone on the boat stared where she pointed.

A flash of light. It winked, disappeared, on some surface along the skyline.

"There. 'Dja see it?" Janey's voice rose with excitement.

"Not sure what that was." Linda stood beside her. "Probably just the sun reflecting off a window."

"There it is again. See? Now it's blinking nice and steady. That ain't no sunlight."

"I wonder where that's coming from." The captain took binoculars from a locker by the wheel.

"Have a look, Father." Linda handed him the glasses. "Seems to be coming from near the top of the Superman Building."

"Superman Building?" said Fay.

The priest smiled. "That's our local nickname for the Industrial Trust Building. Biggest structure downtown, a business-office complex from 1928. Twenty-eight stories high. Easy to spot. It has that big tower with a black cupola of some kind on top." He asked if anyone remembered the old George Reeves Superman TV show from the 1950s. Fay shook her head no.

" 'Able to leap tall buildings in a single bound'? Anyway, the building Superman leaps over in the old TV show looks a little like our Industrial Trust Building. So bingo, everybody around here started saying that shot must have been filmed right here in Providence. People here in Rhode Island liked the feeling that maybe we were getting some national attention."

He handed the binoculars back to Linda. "Seems to have stopped. Whatever it was, for a second it was going all out like a heliograph. Strange. That building's been out of business for years, boarded up shut. The whole place is empty."

"Except for the pigeons," interposed Janey. "I saw online there are busted windows up in the tower and pigeons fly in."

Barbara said the pigeons had nothing to do with flashing lights and so no need to say anything about them.

"Who knows?" wondered Janey. "Maybe the pigeons really *are* involved. They're the only ones up in the tower."

"Yeah, right." A snort of scorn from Barb.

"Look, it's a theory. I saw on YouTube once you can train pigeons to do just about anything. You know, peck for food and tap out Morse code while they're at it."

"Girlfriend, you're getting overheated like you always do." Barb threw up her hands to dramatize her exasperation. "You telling us the pigeons up there are operating a heliograph?"

"How should I know? I'm just speculating. No harm in that, is there, Father?"

Cautiously he agreed there shouldn't be any harm.

"See?" She gave her friend a shove.

"It's a signal." This from Alex Finster the Tagger. For the past hour he'd said not a word as he handled logs on the boat. Now he gazed up from his phone, eyes on the Superman tower. For once he looked serious rather than sardonic.

"A signal?" The priest turned to him.

Tagger saw everyone stare and returned his gaze to the phone. "Nothing."

Linda started the engine, nosed the *Icarus* downstream back to Dyer Street. "Well, the pigeons seem to be done with their helio for the day. We'll just have to call this one of the many mysteries of Providence."

As they neared the landing she checked her clipboard. "I just remembered. One more item for tonight. I'm going to need two volunteers for extra duty." She explained that low tide on the river would come at eleven P.M. The depth would drop to just under three feet. "Too shallow for the *Icarus* or any of the other skiffs. But Riverglow lasts until one in the morning, so we'll need two people in a canoe to take wood from the dock to the braziers and keep the fires going for the last part of the night. The canoes have a nice shallow draft, perfect for low tide. Anyone interested?"

Father Cypriano said by way of encouragement, "Think of yourselves as following in the footsteps—or paddle strokes—of Roger Williams."

"I could try," blurted Bonaventure. "I'm big on American history."

Barbara challenged him: "Are you also big on canoeing?"

"I admit I'm a novice." The expression on his face showed he was starting to doubt the wisdom of his offer. "Or actually zero experience."

"Zero experience is fine," Linda assured him. "All you need is a good sense of balance. You'll be the feeder in the prow. Now I just need a good canoeist in the stern."

Tagger surprised them all by raising his hand. "I'm a good canoeist."

"You are?" Barb measured the teen with a skeptical eye.

"I just said I was, didn't I?"

"I'm sure you'll do fine." Linda stepped between them. "Alex in the stern. Joey in the prow."

"It's Joseph. Not Joey." But no one seemed to hear.

"Well, just tell those two to be careful." The expression on Barb's face proclaimed "This here is serious stuff." "Those things tip over easy. And who wants to go for a swim downtown in the Providence River? All that guck and garbage down there. Ugh. I mean who knows what you could catch falling in the water. Tetanus. Typhoid. I mean seriously."

Linda raised a finger to her lips. "No need to scare the new volunteers."

"Forget typhoid," exclaimed Janey. "I say tell 'em to watch out for ol' Spike-Head."

A sharp rejoinder from the captain. "Now don't start in on that again."

"I'm not starting nothing. Just trying to warn them for their own good."

Tagger stared glumly at his phone. Bonaventure looked uncomfortable or scared. The priest watched him and wondered if the professor was doubting the wisdom of his offer to serve in the canoe.

"Spike-Head?" asked Fay.

"Yeah." Excitement in Janey's voice. She wiped her dirty hands on her Foxwood Casino shirt. "There's something in the river. You see it sometimes at night. Comes up alongside the boats." She unrolled her T-shirt sleeve and gazed longingly at her Camels, then settled back into her tale as the skiff neared the dock.

"I never seen it clearly. Water's too muddy. Shows up only at night. But sometimes you can make out the outline. Must be six feet long, maybe longer."

"Really?" Fay looked from Linda to the priest as if hoping for help in sorting this out.

"Really. I seen it."

"You never seen nothing." Barb folded her arms in a quarrelsome stance. "If it's six feet long how come no one but you ever seen it?"

"Cuz it's always at night. Hard to see. Hard to be sure of anything at night. Anyway I'm not the only one. Two weeks ago Stubby Rattanak over on the *Persephone* saw something."

"Yeah? And what was it you think he seen?" Barb was getting louder. "Sasquatch? A yeti? Maybe the Abominable Snowman?"

Janey grinned at Fay. "She says that every time I report a sighting."

Barb snorted again, enjoying her heaping of scorn. "A sighting. Right. Sounds so official, like a UFO report for the government. You know what, lady? You should go back to your pigeons in the tower and tell 'em to send some more Morse code or whatever with their heliograph. They can give us their opinion on your sightings."

Janey told her good-naturedly to shut up.

Then she finished her tale. "Spike-Head, I call it, cuz it's got sharp spiny things sticking up from the back of its head. That's the way it seemed, anyway. Hard to tell for sure." She shrugged. "Whew, I could use a smoke."

The boat bumped to a stop at the dock. Linda reminded everyone to be back at eight for the show.

The priest helped Fay clamber up from the skiff to the landing. They walked together a moment along the embankment.

"Father, do you think there's really something swimming in that river?"

"Janey has a good imagination. That's one of the many things I like about her. In any case, I've seen too much to rule anything out."

He turned. Everyone from the *Icarus* had scattered in search of shade and rest before the evening Riverglow show. Everyone except the professor in the tweed coat, who squatted on the landing, peering first at the boat, then at the dock.

"I guess he's still trying to find your earring stud. I admire his persistence."

"I told him to forget it." Her pale face flushed red. "Boy. I hope he doesn't show up tonight, so I don't get my other ear torn off. Enough of him for one day."

She sniffed at her shirt. "I have to go change out of these things and get rid of that barbecue fluid smell. Plus I have to work the afternoon shift at the library before tonight's show. I'd better get moving. Thanks, Father."

He stood and watched as she took the footpath over the Crawford Street Bridge and hurried away up the steep climb to College Hill.

The priest paused by the water's edge. Glassy. A smoked-mirror surface. No movement in the afternoon heat. No monsters in the deep.

A glance up at the Superman Building. No more helio winks from Janey's pigeons. A signal, as the teen Tagger had claimed?

Over at the landing the figure in the tweed jacket still squatted and crab-walked about the dock. Jim Cypriano considered joining him just to provide the poor guy a morale boost in his quest.

Then he remembered: he was on the roster to say the five o'clock Mass at the cathedral and if he hurried he might have time first for a moment of solitary prayer in the side chapel.

Quiet, and a bit of blessed silence. Yes. That would be good.

12

As soon as she walked through the door, Fay MacConnell knew she badly needed the quietest possible afternoon at the Athenaeum. Problem was, she was scheduled for four hours at the circulation desk. The thought of dealing with the public right now was simply too much. She'd had her dose of human contact for the day.

She wanted to tell her supervisor "Please I'm all used up can you give me something else," but as soon as Tristram Schaefer saw her he started right in. "Feef: Didn't I tell you it would be fantastic? A restful morning out on the water. Invigorating, right? Just the ticket. I'll bet you're ready for anything now." He opened his arms as if to receive a bouquet of thank-yous.

"No, I'm not ready for anything now," she shot back. "And especially not the guests and tourists and all their yappity-yap questions." She was about to add, "Especially after a morning of falling down splat and getting doused with Duraflame fluid and losing something super-special from my mom and all because of you and your stupid Riverglow suggestion."

But then she saw Nancy Clayton standing behind Tristram waving her a warning and silently mouthing a frantic "Shut up shut up."

So Fay bit back the trash-mouth and simply said she felt a bit tired.

"Of course she's tired. Look at her." Nancy had been doing her best to watch out for Fay from day one. The mothering type. (More precisely white-haired grandmotherly: she'd come out of retirement—"It was boring"—to claim back her old job.) Sometimes annoying, Nancy could be. But at the moment Fay didn't mind. "See, she's all sunburned. She's been spending the day hauling timber. Or tree stumps or redwoods or something."

Fay said it hadn't been that bad, more like little lengths of pine.

"Same difference. The kid's tired." Nancy offered to work circulation, said someone needed to check membership renewals and that was nice soothing work so how about letting Feef simply do that?

Tristram shrugged and said fine.

So now Fay was comfortably settled in her favorite work perch. Upstairs, mezzanine level, at an old writing desk overlooking the atrium of the Ath (the nickname used by staff and visitors in the know). The best indoor view in the world, as Nancy liked to say.

And Nancy was right. Down below, mahogany flooring beneath worn oriental rugs: arabesques in woven umber and auburn and gold. Shelves twenty feet tall stuffed full with books. Guarding each shelf, positioned on high pedestals, were busts of intimate friends: Demosthenes. Shakespeare. Homer. Dante. Sir Walter Scott. On and on down the aisles. No end of pals here.

Below near the main door stood another good friend: an eight-foot Athena, her marble head bowed in pensive mode. And overhead a skylight shed a soft late-afternoon glow.

Under this same skylight, under this same soft glow, many a bygone thinker had paced and thought and pulled books from the Athenaeum's shelves. The Transcendentalist Margaret Fuller, colleague of Emerson and Carlyle and Elizabeth Barrett Browning. The poet Sarah Helen Whitman, once courted by Edgar Allan Poe, who'd taken the train from Baltimore just to ask her to be his bride. Disaster, of course, as with all things touching Poe. Still. The two had had their trysts in a book-strewn alcove just beside Athena and her pensive smile.

Poe. Fay MacConnell's childhood craze and lifelong passion, the reason she'd sought this job. The chance to handle the books he'd touched. The chance to roam where he'd once roamed, once loved, quarreled, and made a general mess of things.

Poe. "He's Fay's fave," Nancy Clayton always told guests, and it was Nancy who'd made her the guide for the special twice-weekly tours at two. Poe at the Athenaeum. Poe and Whitman. Poe as Horror-Goth. Fay MacConnell did them all. It was way more people-contact than she wanted, but at least it was for the sake of someone she loved.

Now she scrolled idly on her laptop through membership renewal files and remembered a favorite verse from Baudelaire (a poet who had idolized Poe almost as much as she did, which made him okay by her). The Frenchman imagines an escape to some dreamy ideal realm: "There, all is indulgence, calm and sheer serene bliss." Unthreatening membership files, no-brainer work, Athenaeum mezzanine perch, afternoon hush. *Sheer serene bliss*. Yes, this was it.

For fifteen minutes at least. At which point Fay emerged from her bliss enough to note the voices downstairs.

Nancy Clayton's post at the circulation desk was near the rear door. From where Fay sat she couldn't see who was engaging her colleague in talk. Both voices were low.

Then Nancy's tread on the mezzanine stairs. She stood beside Fay's desk. "This really is a fine place to work."

Fay repeated a thank-you for being sprung from circulation for the afternoon.

"Come on, we're Ath-mates. Gotta look out for each other. Plus you're new here, and you remind me of me when I was your age. All thorn-brambled and thistle-tipped."

"Thistle-tipped?"

"Uh-huh. Nettlesome. Brittle. Prone to moody sass. Liable to get suspended or just plain booted out. Which in fact happened to me many, many moons ago. Twice. I had to beg and plead my way back in. I just want to spare you that pain."

Fay said she wasn't sure whether she'd just been given a compliment or a complaint. "But thanks."

"You're welcome, sweetie." Nancy went on to say she had a visitor downstairs who wanted to get into Special Collections and study the Egyptian Cabinet.

The cabinet. Fay had never given it much attention, knowing only that this piece of furniture had been built in the nineteenth century to hold a twenty-five-volume French archaeological treatise called the *Description de l'Égypte*.

"Could you handle it for me, Nance? You know I'm beat."

Nancy said she'd offered to take the guest straightaway to see the cabinet. "But he says he specifically wants assistance from you."

"He asked for me by name? Who is this guy?"

"Didn't say. Just asked for Fay MacConnell. And that, my friend, would be you."

Fay stood up from the desk and leaned over the mezzanine rail but couldn't see who was down there. The visitor must have been standing at the very rear of the atrium.

She asked what he looked like.

"Getting up there in years. But still younger than I am." The older woman smiled. "Cute, in his own way. Or potentially." She tapped a finger against her nose. "Let's see. Tall. Nice face. But some kind of mark near his chin like he'd hurt himself there. Also jittery, twitchy. A bit unkempt. I've seen better grooming. Polite, but nervous."

Fay asked was he wearing a beat-up coat.

"As a matter of fact, yes."

A long sigh from Fay. So much for sheer, serene bliss.

"I take it you know who this gentleman is?"

"Yeah I know who he is. And I thought I'd get a break from him after this morning." Another sigh. "Well, let's go downstairs and serve the public, such as it is."

Nancy protested he didn't seem all that bad.

Fay just shook her head. "You might not say that if he'd torn off your ear. Which he did to me."

"He did?"

"Well, almost."

"Now I'm intrigued. Let's take a closer look at this wild man of yours." She followed Fay down the stairs.

"He may be wild," grumbled Fay over her shoulder, "but he's definitely not mine."

They found him standing twitchily, shifting from one foot to another, before a portrait bust. But not one of the marble greats that have been in the Athenaeum since 1838. This was a new addition, in bronze; smaller than the others, installed at eye level. A man of the early twentieth century, in suit and tie. A bronze unsmiling and blank.

"Oh. Hey. Hi." Joseph Bonaventure turned and offered his hand, then dropped the attempt when he saw Fay fail to respond. She stood and said nothing. He gave the two women a feeble wave of the hand.

"This statue, this writer. This is someone I study." He swallowed, tried again. "H. P. Lovecraft." He pointed. "I know him. I mean, I know his work."

"So do I. He was a creep. We shouldn't have anything here to honor him."

Placatingly Nancy reminded Fay that after all H. P. Lovecraft was a Providence native who'd frequented the Athenaeum throughout much of the 1930s.

"So what. The guy was a racist. He hated Italians. Hated Blacks. Hated foreigners and just about anybody who wasn't a hundred per cent New England Yankee like he was."

Bonaventure agitated his shoulders, shifted from foot to foot. "True. But a great writer."

"Hah. He wasn't so great. All he did was imitate Poe and never give him credit. He hated Poe."

Bonaventure pleaded in Lovecraft's defense. "He didn't hate Poe. He admired him. He started reading Poe when he was eight years old."

"Maybe." She glared at the bronze as if she'd a mind to knock the thing down. Nancy took a protective step toward it. Fay afforded herself the luxury of a bit more of a rant. "But I still say he hated Poe and envied him. Just like Lovecraft envied every writer who wrote better than he did."

"Okay. Okay." He raised his hands in surrender.

Nancy asked Bonaventure to excuse them a moment, then grasped Fay by the arm and guided her firmly down a secluded book-lined aisle. "Hon, don't forget what Tristram said at your first training session. Keep your temper with the public. And that gentleman out there is a member of the public."

"Yeah," hissed Fay, "but look what that member of the public did to me this morning." She pointed to her earlobe. "He messed up the stud set my mom gave me."

"Okay, so he messed up your stud set. But he's still part of the public. So go ask how may you help him. And for crying out loud how about trying to smile."

She propelled Fay back out to where the man still nervously stood. Then she nudged the junior librarian forward with a growled "okay, kiddo."

Fay cleared her throat. "Sir, how may I help you today?" A light airy voice, a wisp of a light airy smile.

Nancy beamed. "There." She nodded at the circulation desk. "I'll leave you two to it."

With the older woman gone the smile vanished too. In a low voice: "I still say he hated Poe."

"Fine. Fine. He hated Poe." He extracted a bright red bandanna from his pocket, wiped his face. "Whew. Warm in here."

"No air conditioning in the atrium. Just ceiling fans. The way I like it." She placed her hands on her hips. "It's getting late. We close at five. My colleague says you're interested in the Egyptian Cabinet."

"Yes." He wiped his face again. "I stopped by, wanted to study it. Or at least begin studying it. But turns out it's under lock and key." He said that surprised him. "I was here a long time ago, and I remember it was in the reading room downstairs, where anybody could just walk up and have a good close look."

She said that had been then and now it was kept locked up and protected in Special Collections.

"Protected? How come?"

She said lately there'd been too many creeps coming by. "A whole bunch of crazies. Poking and prying at it. Talking about making it offerings."

"Offerings? What kind?"

"How should I know? Something about 'intersubjective pharaonic rituals,' whatever that means. Three individuals came by one time saying they'd pay cash to be alone with it at night after hours. Course we nixed that." Thereafter, she added, came the board's decision to place the cabinet in Special Collections. "Double locks. Motion sensors. The works."

Which meant, she said, that now there was a protocol. "You want to see the cabinet, you go to our website, fill out the form online, request an appointment, state your interest."

The atrium grandfather clock struck the half hour. "Four-thirty. We close in thirty minutes. No time today to see anything anyway."

"Wait. Could I just show you something?" From an inside pocket he brought forth a sheaf of folded papers.

"There's not really time."

"Please." He held out the papers. "The best way I can explain my interest in the cabinet is to show you what I've found."

"Why the cabinet? I thought you said you study H. P. Lovecraft."

"I do. He's connected to the cabinet. Well, not exactly connected. I mean ... Maybe the best way to explain is to have you just read what I've found. It won't take long. I promise."

She rolled her eyes. Another kook. She was just about to say "Time to leave" when she recalled Nancy's reproof: "Don't forget what Tristram said—keep your temper with the public—and how about trying to smile."

So she set her mind to it and made her best effort at an upward twitch of the lips.

She pointed to a table by Athena. "Let's have a seat and see how much we can see"—she peered at the clock—"in the space of twenty-eight minutes."

"Okay." He unfolded the papers, smoothed them with his hands. *Still grit under his nails*—she noticed this kind of detail—*from the morning's boat-work*. For that matter his hair stood out at odd angles as if he hadn't combed it in a week. Or maybe ever.

"Okay." He rubbed the raw red patch of skin that ran in a line from his jaw to his chin. "First, an explanation. These papers are photocopies of what I found recently in the archives at Miskatonic University."

"The H. P. Lovecraft Cthulhu Collection. Deposited there shortly after he died in 1937."

"That's right." He looked impressed.

"I'm a librarian," she said simply. "I'm supposed to know these things."

"Right. Of course. Absolutely." He brought out the bandanna again, wiped his face. "Whew. Really warm in here. Anyway." He scratched his head. "This morning the captain of that Riverglow boat described me as a professor when she was making her introductions, but that's not quite accurate. I'm still a grad student, just an adjunct lecturer. Many pay grades below professorial rank. I teach courses piecemeal whenever I'm given the chance and as you can imagine I barely get by. But been a while since I taught anything. I'm still writing my dissertation. Or trying to, when I can find the strength and time. Still a long ways to go before I get my Ph.D."

He scratched some more at his head. "Anyway. If you know Lovecraft at all, you know he's in vogue right now. Resurgence in popular interest. Dark visions. 'Life as an engulfing fathomless abyss,' he says in one of his letters."

Fay observed drily that dark visions were all the rage these days. "Which makes sense," she added, "with the kind of world we're living in now. All screwed up. But that's good for you, right? If he's so popular and you're a Lovecraft scholar, everyone'll want to read whatever you write."

"Except there's a lot of competition. Researchers going up to Miskatonic all the time, reading through the Cthulhu Archive, possessive of whatever they find, peering over each other's shoulders, each worrying they're going to get scooped by someone else. And some of these people are well funded. I mean they get grants that let them book a room and stay up there for weeks. Months. Me, I can't do more than one day, maybe two, at a time. Then I've got to fret about earning a bit of money again to keep my life together."

He balled up his bandanna, wiped his neck. "It's just—I've been needing a breakthrough bad. I'm trying to restart things. After what h—" He paused, gulped. "I mean, jumpstart ... It's just, my career's in a bit of a slump right now."

Hastily he glanced at her, looked away.

"Let me start over. Last week I took the bus up to Miskatonic. At first I thought it was going to be a bad day. There must've been a dozen scholars up there in the Cthulhu Archive, hogging all the Lovecraft files, each file packed in its own storage box. Stories. Essays. Correspondence. Testimonia. Each researcher at a separate desk, looking murder at everyone else. I almost gave up, figured I'd just catch the bus back to Providence."

Fay suggested he come to his point before it was time to close.

"Right. Sorry." He said only one file had been available on the shelf: Cognate Writers. "I'd never bothered with it before. Didn't seem all that relevant. But now here I was, waiting for the other guys to finish, so I said what the hell."

The file contained material on fellow fantasy authors of the period. "Clark Ashton Smith. Arthur Machen. M.R. James. Writers who might have influenced Lovecraft, or maybe he influenced them. I figured ho-hum. But then I found this."

He jabbed at the photocopies, smoothed out the pages again. His voice grew in confidence; his eyes shone; his twitching ceased.

"Must have been misfiled. A holograph manuscript. Anonymous, but it's unquestionably his style. His handwriting. I know his pen. Never seen anything quite like this. Definitely unpublished. This could be the break I need."

"So what's it say then?"

"Read it. Just read."

"It's getting late. Almost a quarter to five."

"Just read it. Please."

So she read. And he did too, gazing over her shoulder. So unselfconscious did he become that he removed his tweed jacket, rolled up his shirtsleeves.

Together they read:

Howard Phillips is the name by which I am known, though I have borne other names in other times. Proud offspring of this fair and noble citadel of Providence, always have I loved the antique and refined, and little care I for the present age, where coarseness reigns and mongrel breeds swarm the mongrel streets.

"'Mongrel breeds'?" She rolled her eyes. "Talk about racial obsessiveness."

"Granted. Absolutely. But keep going."

And so from a tender age I rarely ventured outdoors. Fortunate enough to have received a sufficient inheritance, freed from the dull labor that hobbles the minds of common men, I spent my early years enclosed in my retreat on College Hill. With curtains pulled tight to admit no ray of sun, I spent my days in reading, in the study of forbidden lore and the arcana of ancient lands. A lamp by my armchair, while throughout the house reigned a long and comforting gloom.

Till twilight, when I would emerge from counterfeit domestic dusk into the true sable of evening's legions, descending the hill for an evening's refreshment along Canal Street and the Providence River. Clad in a black cape even on the warmest of nights, I felt myself sealed fast against the swarms that swirled about me. And up and down the river's length the city's antic play of electric light and shadow furnished me those infinities of mental excitement that oft gave rise to my next uncanny tale.

"He's stealing from Poe here." She grimaced her irritation. "Imitating the beginning of 'Murders in the Rue Morgue.' A pretty weak imitation, by the way."

"I know. Shameless. And funny you should mention that particular author. Because look what Lovecraft writes next."

Much has been made of one Edgar Allan Poe, and his frequent trips, nigh on a century ago, to our storied city of Providence. One might have thought, given his interest in tales of the imagination, that he would have availed himself of the rich lore of College Hill and its cobblestone streets. So much was here, right under his nose.

But no. Overlooked by pompous Poe, reputedly master of ratiocination, father of the detective story, sharpest of all for detecting the presence of the grotesque, overlooked, I say, was the presence of a Curiosity—a Curiosity that, had he had the wit to see it (and he most assuredly did *not*), would have hatched in his febrile mind a pullulating mass of horrific tales—and all of them horrifically *true*.

This Curiosity is housed in an establishment it was his wont to frequent, an establishment where I too am pleased to spend my time. I speak here of the private library that has stood since the early nineteenth century at the corner of College and Benefit Street, its granite steps and Doric columns and pedimented roof entwined with ivy making it an authentic embodiment of Greek wisdom. I speak of the Athenaeum.

"Huh." Impressed despite herself, Fay hitched her chair closer.

"Keep reading." He tapped the page. "It gets better."

Much-vaunted Poe failed to note this Curiosity, on display though it was even in his day, because he allowed himself to be befuddled on every visit by a ravishing widow, one Sarah Helen Whitman. His repeated dalliances and failed attempts at playing *le galant* with this poetess (and with numerous other members of the frail sex, may I add) led him to miss many a clue that would have let him detect the depths of a veritably fathomless abyss.

The Curiosity: I speak here of something on view on the ground floor of this library, something built to contain tomes linked to Bonaparte's fabled expedition to the East, something commonly called the Egyptian Cabinet.

The cabinet. Daily the innocent staff pass unwarily to and fro; daily well-intentioned but ignorant members of the bibliophiliac herd brush carelessly by this Thing. All unknowing they loiter and lean their elbows on this Horror that they house.

The Egyptian Cabinet. Unknown to the bibliophiliac mob, to the Athenaeum staff, yes even to much-vaunted pompous Poe, is a simple truth: This cabinet is a Portal.

"Five minutes to five," Nancy Clayton called out from the circulation desk. Visitors hurried by on their way to the exit.

Fay called out in return. "Be right with you." She turned to Bonaventure. "She wants to lock up."

"Just read a little more. Please."

A Portal. Yes, this Egyptian Cabinet, so innocently—and recklessly—housed within the Athenaeum, is, I am persuaded, a passageway leading to yawning depths before which the mere mind of man staggers.

For, painted on one end of this "innocent" cabinet—ostensibly a mere coffer of antiquarian books—is an image of a pharaonic barque, the same barque that bore Egypt's mummified kings to a mighty subterranean stream. For this is the truth I have gleaned: Here in this cabinet, barriers of time and space collapse. New England blurs into the Orient. Here, via this barque, the Providence River flows into the underworld Nile.

By what psychometric means I have discerned this truth I dare not say for now. For first I must test this thesis I have psychometrically divined.

Dangers, you say? Of a certainty. But also perhaps rare fortune, for those willing to brave that Portal, to open the cabinet. And as an offspring of this citadel is it not in my blood to hazard such a venture? Am I not of a lineage to attempt such a thing? Was it not from the very wharves I have so often seen, from Packet Street and Merchant Street and Fox Point, that many a Providence Indiaman set sail for the very limits of the East?

Yes. A venture. But like any good scientist (for scholars of arcana are also scientists of a kind) I will first conduct a laboratory experiment to test my hypothesis. I will dispatch Elementals (and I am in the process of acquiring several such servitors), just as Noah sent forth birds to see if land awaited him on the far side of the Flood. These Elementals will be sent through the Portal of this cabinet on a quest I have devised (a quest of greater cosmic import than any man of our era can imagine). If all goes well these Elementals will return with treasures that will serve a purpose I dare not disclose till all is safely in place. Treasures that will cause me to become—But soft, it would be unwise to trust such secrets to paper at this time.

And if something befalls the Elementals once they are dispatched through the Portal, if they unfortunately fail to return?

Well, I will find yet more Elementals to subdue to my service. I will find more.

"Is that it? Is that all?" Fay MacConnell pushed back her chair.

"Yes. It breaks off here. It's an unfinished draft."

"You know, what's creepy is that he writes as if he believed all that. Portals from Providence to some subterranean Nile, and all of it starting downstairs. *Brr.*" She shuddered. "Well, if he's convincing, I guess he learned that from Poe."

"Yeah, with Lovecraft when he gets really weird I have to remind myself sometimes it's all just a story. That's the thing with him; you're never quite sure how seriously he himself took all the fantasies he spun."

He stood and plucked the tweed coat from the back of his chair. "Anonymous and uncatalogued, but no question this is a text by Lovecraft. The style, first of all. You can find the same motifs in 'The Shunned House' and 'The Case of Charles Dexter Ward.' And of course calling the narrator Howard Phillips. Those were Lovecraft's given names. He used them for the protagonists in his initial drafts until he could come up with a good solid name that would stick."

He flung his coat over one shoulder, his shirtsleeves rolled up, his forearms exposed. Excitedly he stooped over Fay. She saw his eyes flash. "Hey. I know it's late and everything but do you think there's any way we could go downstairs and get a really quick peek at that cabinet?"

The clock sounded five.

"Sorry. Gotta go." She stood and stepped back.

"I mean, this would be just the thing for my dissertation. An unpublished Lovecraft fragment: that's good. But to discover an artifact, I mean, an Egyptian-style book-cabinet that's been hiding in plain view at a famous library like this for years and years, and no one's ever realized it inspired a Lovecraft story: I mean, for a literary critic that's like finding the tomb of King Tut!"

Lights began flicking off in the Athenaeum's atrium. Nancy Clayton called out from the back. "Are you two still there? Time to go home."

"We're just leaving." Fay turned to the graduate student. "Look. I'm sorry. Time's up for today. Next week maybe."

"I mean, if I could just confirm there's a pharaonic barque painted on one end, like it says in the story. Maybe even ..."

"Sorry. We gotta go. I've got only a couple of hours to take a break before I have to do this Riverglow thing again at eight."

"Oh yeah? Me too. Maybe we can be on the same boat again."

Oh joy and maybe you can tear another earring off my head. She just managed to keep herself from saying this aloud. *Remember not to lose your temper with the public.*

Nancy turned out the last of the lights. "Come on, you two." She ushered them out the front entrance, locked the doors behind them.

The three stood in the portico a moment. "So did you both have a lot to talk about?" She beamed them an encouraging smile, the kind of smile that—to Fay's cynical and all-too-experienced eye—meant that Nancy was hoping to play Cupid for this cute little scholarly pair.

Which made Fay annoyed. "In fact what our guest showed us," she rasped, "was a text that makes fun of my man Poe and also steals a bunch of lines from the 'Rue Morgue.'"

"Oh. Okay." Nancy descended the granite steps with a cheery wave of the hand. "Have fun, you two."

Which left Fay and the grad student alone in the Athenaeum's portico.

Or almost. Some tourists milled about taking snaps.

Bonaventure stared vacantly at them a moment, started to say something, changed his mind. From the coat over his shoulder he extracted his red bandanna. "Whew. Hot. Even hotter out here than inside." He wiped his neck.

"Hey." He turned to her. "I just want to say sorry about your earring thing."

"I told you already. Forget about it." *Not that I've forgotten about it one bit,* she thought. Plus she was still sore about that Lovecraft piece he was carrying that made sport of her Poe.

"Well I just wanted to say I can tell it meant a lot to you. So I'm going to keep looking."

"What are you going to do? Hoover it up from the bottom of the Providence River?"

That was unkind. As soon as the words were out of her mouth she wished she could take them back. But too late. He looked foolish and shamed.

But damn why'd he have to practically tear off my ear and make me lose part of the set that was supposed to bring me luck?

He scratched his head, mumbled something indistinct.

And as he scratched she saw his upstretched arm with the shirt-sleeve rolled back.

Which gave her a quick glimpse of what was inked on his arm: the words "Girlie you look like—"

Which was as much as she could see before he realized what she'd seen, at which he rolled down his sleeves and feverishly threw on his coat.

In a none-too-friendly voice from her: "What the hell's that?"

Another mumble. "Oh nothing."

"Looks like a tattoo. With a logo that's pretty blatantly sexist."

"It's from a long time ago." He backed away.

She said that wasn't much of an excuse.

He said it really wasn't much of a tattoo.

"It's enough to put you in bad with anyone that happens to see it. Like me for example."

He backed off another step. "Well that's why I generally never take this jacket off." He stopped, then opened his mouth as if to find better words in the air that might serve for apology or escape or just help him disappear. "You see, I . . ."

"Excuse us please." A pair of tourists, holding out their phones, asking could he possibly take a photo of them. Beside the entrance. Include the ivy. And please also a picture of them beside one of these old Greek columns.

"Oh. Okay. Sure." He stepped away from Fay, took the phones, one after another, took the snaps, gave the tourists back their phones, heard them say thanks and retreat down the steps.

He looked around. He wanted to resume his apology, say sorry about the earring, about the "girlie" tattoo, about Lovecraft and Poe.

But he stood alone in the portico. The Athenaeum was locked and his librarian had slipped away.

13

Four hours down. Three hundred and ninety-six to go. *Shit.*

Alexander Finster's mood was not good.

He strode south along Canal Street, head lowered, fists clenched, on his way to his nighttime Riverglow shift. The crowds slowed him down. He was going to be late. He couldn't care less.

Tourists from out of state. Families from Pawtucket and Bristol, Seekonk and Cranston. Gawking at the lights, the T-shirt stalls, the souvenir stands, the star lanterns hung from trees. Exclaiming at the musicians and mimes. Laughing as they stood in the twilight and ate clam cakes and quahogs, popcorn and hot dogs. A bald vendor, some senior-citizen type, called out to him, "Young man how about buying an official Riverglow kitchen magnet to support our local festival?" He wanted to scream in the guy's face "I did four hours of slave labor for Riverglow this morning, I've got another four hours tonight, and I'd just as soon stuff that kitchen thing down your throat." Instead he said nothing and kept moving.

Let's see. After this shift tonight, he'd have 392 hours left to serve. This community service sentence was going to last forever. *Shit.*

But Riverglow wasn't his main gripe tonight. What was burning him bad was how his afternoon had gone.

His mom had insisted on personally driving him to his three o'clock appointment with Mister Delmonico at the state employment office. Alex had muttered he could get there himself but his mom pointed out he'd skipped his last two appointments and this time she was going to make sure Alex kept his date and in the process avoided violating the terms of his parole.

"Awfully nice of your mother to bring you here herself." Alex wasn't sure whether Mister Delmonico was trying to taunt him with a comment like that. The counselor knew he hated his mom.

Alex wanted to fire back with "Yeah and it was likewise awfully nice of my mother to split up with my dad and sell our house and drag me from Colorado just so she could have a new life as an academic dean of whatever at Brown University out here in this shithole state." But he wasn't about to let this employment counselor or anybody else know how close he was to losing his cool. Instead he said nothing and popped a stick of Juicy Fruit in his mouth.

Mister Delmonico typed something on his laptop, showed Alex the screen. "You'll be glad to know I've found you a job."

Alex said he already had a job. "Four hundred hours with Riverglow."

Mister Delmonico explained yet again that Riverglow wasn't a job. "It's unpaid service. Restitution for vandalism, as mandated by the court. But the court also stipulates you demonstrate responsibility by securing fulltime employment. Which I've just found for you."

Alex longed to say he didn't want a job here, he just wanted his old life out west. But he already knew what the counselor would say, the same warning he'd issued before: "Get a job or go to jail."

"You're going to love it. I found you a gig that'll make good use of your skills. Your particular skills." Mister Delmonico said this with a slyness Alex didn't like. The counselor sported a tidy three-piece suit with a tidy, well-knotted tie that matched the suit hue for hue. Which triggered in Alex the kind of thought that had gotten him into trouble before: *What I wouldn't give for a can of Liquitex or Scribo and just give him a quick squirt and mess up his day.*

Mister Delmonico stared at him hard as if reading his mind. *Which the bastard is probably capable of doing.* Hastily Alex looked away, eyed the decoration on the wall. The flag of Rhode Island. An anchor with thirteen stars, and below them the one-word state motto: *Hope.*

Yeah. Right. Hope. Shit.

Mister Delmonico handed him the address. "You start work Monday. A place called Guild Metal."

"Guild Metal? What kind of job is this going to be?"

"You show up and you'll see. Factory job. High class. You'll love it."

"You'll love it." Alex eyed the flag again on his way out the door. *Hope.* In this shithole state? Be more honest to change it to "Hopeless."

And now here he was, on his way to Riverglow slave labor, with the prospect of dull factory work clouding his Monday, in the midst of mindless mobs having their loud, mindless fun.

And just to make his gloom complete, at that moment some mindless little girl waving a big wand of cotton candy ran smack into him. The kid's mom peeled her off, smiled a "so sorry," and left him with a shirtfront of sticky candy floss. *Shit.*

Ever since the divorce, ever since being dragged to this place, he'd been feeling blocked off, locked up. Whether they made him do hard time at the ACI or let him wander the streets made no difference. He was screwed. He was trapped.

And the more trapped he felt, the more extravagant his fantasies of tagging.

Like right now. Right across the river, in the heart of downtown, reared up the bulk of that high-rise Superman Building. Man, how cool it would be to do a throw-up piece on that surface, a big blast of jungle green from a can of Krylon, bubble letters—"RMH"—three stories tall. *Rocky Mountain High.* That would tell the shitheads here where he was from, where he'd rather be. Cool.

Of course it was tagging that other site with his signature "RMH" that had gotten him into so much shit to begin with. *Damn.*

The Superman Building. He'd seen that light this afternoon glint off the top, some funny Morse-code thing. Had given him a strange feeling, a lift for a second, like a message speaking only to him. Not that he'd known what it meant.

But now, mobs of strangers, in a place he didn't belong, with night coming on fast.

He came to a dead stop. "Man. I hate all this." He said it out loud.

And that's when three individuals stepped before him, blocked his way. At first he paid them no attention. His mind scanned and dismissed them: *Ciphers. Blanks. Like everyone else in the crowd.* Until one of them spoke.

"Do you want out of all this?"

He blinked, studied them. All young, like him, a chick and two guys. All dressed exactly the same, shoulder-length hair, gray chinos, gray polo shirts. Some kind of gender-neutral unisex shit. Strange.

In the collar of each shirt, a little lapel pin: "GGCG." Whatever that meant.

It was the chick who spoke. "Do you want out of all this?"

How did they know his thoughts? This was weird shit. "Who the hell are you?"

Instead of answering, the chick nodded at the Superman Building. "I think you received our flash. We were sending you a signal."

"What are you talking about?"

No reply. They just stared. He felt his heart beating hard. All the sounds of the mob died away.

"If you want out," she said, "we'll get you out. We'll signal you again. We'll let you know."

"Of course," said one of the guys, "if we help you, we'll expect you to help us. That's how it works."

"But who the hell *are* you?" He felt his breath coming hard.

No answer. Another hard gaze. Then they stepped away, off into the swarm.

Gone.

He swallowed, called after them. "You're damn right I want out."

But they were gone, just like that.

Shit.

14

"Joey, whaddya think you're doing? This is nuts. C'mon. Stop wasting your time." Janey Evans addressed this critique to the hunched form of Joseph Bonaventure. He squatted on the Dyer Street landing, head bent down, fingers palpating the wood planks of the dock, straining his eyes in the gathering dusk.

What Joseph Bonaventure was doing was telling himself a story—a story of how he was going to make things okay. He often did this after making a big mess. In this particular story he was going to find the missing earring-piece and present it to Fay MacConnell just as she came walking up for the night shift. Then maybe she'd forgive him and smile. That would be nice to see. She didn't smile much.

Except it was getting dark and dozens of Riverglow volunteers milled about on the dock and kept bumping and tripping over him.

"You'll never find it. Give it up." Janey grabbed him by an arm and hauled him to his feet. "Here. Sign in." She handed him a clipboard. He jotted his name under *Icarus* and scanned the list for others who had already arrived.

"You looking for your little friend?" Janey was watching him.

"I'm not sure she'd call me her friend."

"She got here half an hour before you did and switched her registration to another boat."

He looked about. All seven vessels for the night's Riverglow were now lined up at the dock, prow to stern, gunwale to gunwale. There was his *Icarus*. Already aboard were Barb, Father Jim, and Linda the skipper. Nearby were the other skiffs, each crowded with its crew, the *Aphrodite* and *Apollo*, the *Eos* and *Phoebus* and *Prometheus*. Yet no sign of Fay.

But there, yes, on the *Persephone*, a petite figure, cropped blond hair, clad—like the other night-shift volunteers—in a black T-shirt and black jeans. He tried a timid wave of the hand. No response. Maybe she couldn't see him.

He stepped down onto the deck of the *Icarus* and sought out the captain. "Linda, do you mind if I switch over to a different boat? I'd like to share duties with someone I know."

"I can't spare you. That kid Tagger hasn't shown up, and now we're shorthanded. Sorry."

He gazed helplessly as the *Persephone* pulled away from the dock, followed by the *Prometheus* and *Aphrodite*. Too shy to call out her name—afraid she'd snub him in front of thousands—he raised his arm in a tentative salute. But she was too far away now to see. Each skiff headed upstream, weighted with wood, black hulled and low to the water, a red pilot light on its prow, another on its stern.

A friendly hand on his shoulder. "Here, help me cast off." Jim Cypriano smiled and nodded at the mooring lines.

"Oh. Sure, Father. Thanks."

The *Icarus* formed the tail end of the convoy. As it followed the other vessels Linda stood behind the wheel and instructed her crew. "Not many people on the shore along this part of the river," she explained, "but a little while after we leave behind the College Street Bridge there'll be a gazillion folks packed on the embankments, with their eyes all on us. So once we come out from under that bridge, we'll be part of the performance, and I'll want you to look professional, you know, formal, like you're part of the show. Because you are."

She had them stand one behind another along the portside gunwale: "Let's do it by height, tallest at the back. Janey, you in front. Then Barb, Father Jim, and Joey, you at the rear." The captain told them to keep their eyes front and center for the first few minutes until they reached the Basin and had to start their work as fire tenders. "No swivel-neck gawking in all directions. We're in a procession, and this is our ceremonial entrance. Lots of out-of-state visitors, so let's make Rhode Island look good."

It was just as the *Icarus* passed under the College Street Bridge that the music began. From hidden shoreside speakers resounded a recording of a quasi-Tibetan chorus. The boomed gutturals of a chanted mantra. A deep thud of drums and the prolonged bray of mountain horns. The sounds echoed and rolled around the dark curve of the arch.

They emerged from under the bridge into a vast sunset sky. Piled-up clouds in the west, burnt orange, pink, violet blue, against a horizon line of the Superman Building and the other high-rises of downtown. Ahead of them on the water, the black hulls and pilot lights of their companion skiffs. And on either side, crowds in their thousands, perched on the bridges, seated on the shore, and on the stone steps of the embankments.

The chanting soared high, and the onlookers went silent and lifted their heads, as if their hearts had been snatched heavenward—or at least Bonaventure knew that was what had happened to him.

"Yeah, this is the payoff," enthused Janey in a low voice. "This is what makes it worth doing."

It was only because Bonaventure was standing so close to Father Cypriano that he saw him wordlessly make the sign of the Cross. The priest turned to him with a smile. "The best view in Providence."

"All right, people." This from the captain. "We're going into action in a minute or so. Let's look sharp."

Under the Washington Street Bridge, past Confluence Park, then a starboard turn into the ring of the Basin. Here the crowds were massed thickest. Their attention was on the large performance stage on the Basin's east shore. Here a throng of officiants waited as a double file of women bearing four-foot-tall torches descended from College Hill to the stage.

One behind another, the skiffs came to a halt in the water just before the stage. Linda eased the *Icarus* into position so that its prow just touched the stern of the *Phoebus*.

Marching in perfect accord, torches held effortlessly high, the double file made its way to the stage. "Dancers from the Rhode Island School of Design," commented the captain.

Elegantly the dancers handed the torches to a knot of individuals who seemed considerably less confident as they received their fiery burdens.

"Those people getting the torches," explained Linda, "are businessfolk from the Trogliflex convention. That's the corporate sponsor providing the funding for tonight's event." She said the guests would briefly board the boats and have the privilege of lighting the braziers to inaugurate the evening's Riverglow.

The torchbearers clambered awkwardly into the waiting skiffs, two to each vessel. "Here come ours," observed Barb. "They don't look too sure of themselves."

Advancing toward the *Icarus* was a pair of portly suit-coated men. They stopped, peered about uncertainly.

Father Jim helped the guests onto the boat. "Just be careful to keep your torches upright."

"Plenty warm this evening." The stouter of the two loosened his tie. "I'm Vance Mattingly. Senior exec, human resources at Trogliflex." He introduced his colleague. "This here's Bert Stoddard from accounting."

Bert from accounting looked like he earnestly wished himself ashore. "Hafta confess I've never spent much time on the water."

"Me neither," agreed Vance. "Unless you count the shallow end of the pool at the Y." He tried for a businesslike air. "Well. I understand we're supposed to do the honors and light up some barbecues for you or something."

"Something like that," agreed Linda mildly. She explained that the *Icarus* was assigned to ignite braziers 18 through 20. The skiff swung in a wide arc around the metal baskets and dodged the mill of other boats.

"Whoa," exclaimed Bert. He gasped something about not quite having his sea legs.

"Don't you worry, sir." Janey offered him reassurance. "You're as safe as in your bathtub back home. We'll have you back on the dock in no time."

As they neared number 18, Vance leaned over the gunwale. "I got it." Barb pointed to where the fuse protruded above the basket's piled wood. "Just hold the torch there for a second. Nice job." The fuse ignited with a sharp snap.

Number 19 went up just as smoothly. The flame traveled fast from the fuse to the concealed bag of lighter-fluid-soaked papers. "Pretty good," marveled Vance. "Not as hard as I thought."

"Maybe I could try the last one," ventured his Trogliflex colleague. The *Icarus* slowed alongside 20 and Bert leaned far over the portside gunwale.

Too far. A sudden yelp, and a plunge forward.

Only to be saved by Janey and Barb. Barb grabbed the torch, and Janey the accountant.

"Easy does it," Janey laughed. "No swimming in the Providence River. You don't wanna meet ol' Spike-Head."

The Trogliflex man could manage no more than a confused "huh?"

"Yeah. It might just jump up and bite you in the butt."

Now the man looked scared.

"She's just messin' with ya." Barb lit number 20 and gave Linda a thumbs up to head back to shore.

Back at the performance-stage landing, Bonaventure helped the guests scramble onto the dock. Bert Stoddard straightened his suit and breathed a long sigh of relief. "Not sure I'm cut out for these sea voyages."

"Just be glad you don't have to go out later tonight in a canoe," called Janey after them, "like our Joey here." She grinned at Bonaventure. "Things could get hairy at low tide."

But for the next two hours Bonaventure was too busy to worry overmuch about what might happen come low tide. As the fires burned low, the *Icarus* swung round the circle of braziers within the Basin, slowing just long enough at each basket for the stokers to pile on more logs.

Clearly Barb, Janey, and Father Jim were veterans who worked smoothly as a team. In the narrow space between the portside gunwale and the starboard woodpile they turned nimbly back and forth, sidestepping each other as they grabbed logs and stoked the flames. With Fay and Tagger both absent, Bonaventure was the only rookie on board, and at first he mostly tried to stay out of the others' way. On the darkened boat the five-foot pile of wood was no more than an indistinct mass. Each time he bent and stooped to find a log and pull it free he had to be alert to avoid a clip to mouth or head from a piece of wood pulled free by someone else.

In his haste at first he fed the fire by tossing the wood atop the brazier. Showers of sparks blazed up as cinders flew and scorched his wrists and hands and burned holes in his shirt. "Bad move," said Janey. "Don't throw 'em. Not safe. Just do it like this." As the *Icarus* glided by the next brazier she gently stacked two logs on the outer edge of the basket. "Tell you what. You work with me. You grab pieces from the pile, then pass 'em to me."

Which improved things. It allowed for an effort that had its own flow. For Bonaventure it felt good just to work and try not to think—not about his past, nor about the scandal that had ruined his life and cost him his job and marked up his face, nor about the attempts to restart his academic career, attempts that so far really weren't going so well. And as for Fay MacConnell—he jeered at himself: *Hey aren't you the ladies' man.* At which point he collided with Barb, who told him to watch where he put his stupid feet, which reminded him: *Man, turn off the thoughts. Give it a rest.* He recalled his therapist's injunction: "This Riverglow service, think of it as a relaxing mental-health vacation." To which he had replied: "I'm not exactly the vacation-relaxation type." His therapist had said what she always said: "Just try. You can do it. Just try."

And every time flames jumped from a brazier he had to tell himself not to flinch. Fire scared him, spooked him, ever since ... *But then that's why I'm out here now, trying to get over it. Best not to think. Turn off the thoughts. One step at a time.*

"Whew. Hot night." Janey fanned her face with her hands.

From the wheel Linda called out. "Just checked Weather-dot-com. Eighty-five degrees out here on the water."

"And a lot hotter," added Barb, "every time we go near those flames."

In this heat everyone on the skiff wore a T-shirt. Everyone except Joseph Bonaventure, who wore a black, long-sleeved shirt to cover his inked arms and would have worn his tweed jacket too to cover them even more if the coat had been the mandated black instead of its ratty worn brown.

He should've had the tattoos removed. *Why not just excise them? By now they're old and splotchy and a bit blurred—like me, like my soul. And they keep causing me grief, like they did today, when she saw just one part, the part that reads "Girlie you look like . . ." Wow the look on her face. Just as well she didn't see the rest. I don't want to have to explain it all, explain any of it.*

Yeah maybe just get them removed, gouge 'em, cut 'em, blot 'em all out. And then Joseph Bonaventure arrived at the same thought he usually did: *But hell these tats are part of me, part of my past and who I am, and I'm not sure I want to just let all that go. Can't anyway, can't run far enough, no matter how much I gouge and cut away.* Worriedly he rubbed the puffed ridge of flesh that ran from his jaw to his chin.

"Ten o'clock." Linda announced it was close to low tide and time to head for shore.

At the western end of the Basin was another dock, this one reserved for Riverglow boats.

Two volunteers were sliding a canoe into the water. Janey grinned at Bonaventure. "All right, Admiral. There's your battleship." Then she pointed to someone sitting slouched on the landing, head bent over smartphone. "Hey, and there's Tagger."

Bonaventure climbed from the boat to the dock and said he was sure glad to see him. "I thought I was going to have to do this canoe thing all by myself." By way of greeting, Alexander Finster tilted his head and shrugged.

The captain stood over Alex. She reminded him he was over two hours late.

Slowly the graffiti artist got to his feet. He mumbled something about how yeah well he was here now.

"You sure you're up for this?" Linda studied his face. "We need someone reliable in the stern to paddle and steer while Joey feeds wood to the braziers. We need someone good."

He mumbled well relax because he was the best.

Linda shook her head and turned to Bonaventure. He took a deep breath and said he was sure it would all work out fine.

Not that he was feeling at all fine himself. *In fact plenty scared, and getting more scared by the minute.* He fought hard to keep the fear from escaping into speech.

Not just because he was a novice at canoes, and likely to make a fool of himself in front of the Riverglow crowds. That was the least of it. His therapist had insisted he do this because of Bonaventure's "anxieties" about fire. Understandable, said Doctor Cartwright, in light of what she diplomatically and ever so therapeutically termed "the Incident." *Well Doctor how about calling it what it really was? How about calling it a calamity, a disaster, a frigging trauma, for me and for everyone in my world, the moment that divided everything into Before and After, an ax that sliced my soul in two, a giant twelve-ton steel-tipped boot grinding into my neck for the rest of my life?*

"I see you're still upset." Soothingly Doctor Cartwright had urged him to put the Incident into perspective. A bit fearful of flames even at this distance in time? Understandable. But Riverglow would afford him an exposure to fire that would be manageable and supervised. "And in a setting," the therapist beamed, "that will help you practice socializing and reintegration."

Stupid, stupid, stupid. How did I ever let her talk me into all this?

"Joey?"

Bonaventure looked up. Father Cypriano had tapped his arm. Confusedly the ex-lecturer glanced about, tried to orient himself.

The canoe was positioned alongside the skiff. Alex Finster had already taken a seat in the stern. Jim Cypriano and Barb were loading wood from the *Icarus* into the canoe. The priest was saying something to him, something about his needing a gaff.

"I need a what?" He snapped his focus back into the present.

"This." Father Jim handed him a big metal hook fixed to a three-foot wooden pole. "Use this to grab hold of each brazier by its stem as you come up on it. That'll keep the canoe and the brazier locked onto each other so you don't drift away while you're trying to feed the fire. It can get tricky. And watch your hands. Also your eyes. You'll be close to the flames, and the wind's picking up on the river. We don't want a gust to go burning your face."

Bonaventure nodded, swallowed hard as he stepped down into the canoe. Fear dried his mouth. *Burning your face.* He already knew something about that. *The Incident.*

"Here." The priest handed him a pair of welder's gloves. "These may help." Padded thick, the gloves covered Bonaventure's arms up to the elbows. "And these, for the eyes." A pair of safety glasses.

A comfort. "Thanks, Father."

"You'll do fine." Jim Cypriano laughed. "The two of you just need to remember: no sudden moves, and you'll have no trouble staying afloat."

Alex Finster lifted a paddle to push the canoe away from the dock, and Bonaventure was thinking *All I need is a distraction to take my mind off the fear,* when in fact a distraction presented itself. Hurrying along the dock came a young woman. Gray chinos, gray polo shirt, shoulder-length hair. Behind her came two young men dressed the same way.

She crouched at the edge of the dock, her eyes fixed on Tagger. Graffiti-boy seemed to know who she was. Surprise, then pleasure: it looked as if Alex Finster might even smile.

She stooped, whispered something, handed Tagger a note.

Which gave Bonaventure a second to note her lapel pin. "GGCG." Cryptic; made no sense.

But something else, intriguing: a second pin, set just above the first. It read "HPL was right."

Some people say the world is full of coincidences but Joseph Bonaventure knew that wasn't true. For him there was only one HPL and it had to be his man.

She stood and turned, clearly ready to leave. Bonaventure wasn't normally the type to talk to strangers but he had to find out about this pin. "Hey. Right about what?"

For reply, a tight little superior smile.

Try again. "What was Lovecraft right about?"

She turned away with a toss of her hair. "You may find out. You may all find out, if our plan doesn't work." With a glance she gathered up the other two polo-shirted youths, and the three strode off into the dark.

Tagger was grinning as he read the note and tapped something into his phone. The kid seemed so pleased Bonaventure decided to chance a question.

"Girlfriend? Love note?"

"Better'n that." Alex Finster punched a fist in the air. "Dawg, this is my ticket outta here."

And that was all. A big push with the paddle against the dock, and Tagger launched them out toward the Basin's circle of braziers.

At first it all went better than Bonaventure had expected. Alex Finster in fact knew what to do. Expertly he maneuvered the canoe so they came neatly alongside brazier number 1. With the gaff Bonaventure hooked the stem pole just beneath the basket. He gripped the gaff hard with one hand to keep brazier and canoe fixed in place side by side. With his free hand he reached behind his seat, grabbed a length of wood, and hoisted it up and atop the basket. Then another log, and a third, until he'd piled up the requisite replenishment quantity of six.

At which the wind on the river gusted and the fire flared and fear likewise jumped up in his throat. But he repeated the mantra he used whenever doubts and worries about a misspent life bedeviled him as he tried to write his dissertation: *Focus on the work.*

And so on to brazier number 2, and number 3. Hook the stem with the gaff, grip the gaff hard to hold canoe and brazier in place, grab a half-dozen logs to keep feeding the fire.

Number 8, and number 9. Flames blew at his fingers as he lifted another piece on the pile. But the welder's gloves cushioned him, made him feel safe. *This isn't so bad.*

Number 14. Number 15. Not a word in the stern from Alex Finster, but so what. Skillfully the teen guided them from brazier to brazier. As the wood load grew depleted around Bonaventure's feet, the kid used his oar to push logs from the rear to within his partner's reach.

Number 18. Number 19. More gusts of flame, but now it wasn't so bad. *Just like with the dissertation: Focus on the work.*

Number 20. Topped up and done. The fires blazed nicely from all the braziers in the ring. *Hope the crowd on shore appreciates our efforts.*

Work completed, for the moment. It would be some thirty minutes before the baskets needed restoking. Just past midnight. Came the realization: *Man am I bushed.*

Alex paddled them in a slow circle around the braziers. With suddenly nothing to do, Bonaventure dipped an experimental oar and began to paddle too.

Hey this is actually fun. He paced himself to Finster's strokes and began to enjoy himself. *Doctor Cartwright would be proud. I'm doing something therapeutic.* He imagined Roger Williams, the year 1636, paddling just like this, coming up solo along the Providence River. *What a yo-yo of emotions Williams must've gone through: a hunted man, alone and on the run, not knowing if his voyage would end in capture, ruin, or worse. And then rising up from shore a sudden welcome from the Narragansetts: a reassuring "What cheer, Netop." Always nice to find someone willing to call you Friend.*

And just at that moment, as he was feeling so good that he thought he'd try to chat with Alex Finster, ask him if he knew about Roger Williams or maybe ask him about his girlfriend or whoever that gal was and maybe also ask him about that cryptic lapel button that said "HPL was right"—just at that moment from the Superman Building flashed a sudden flare of light.

Bonaventure started to say "Hey what on earth is that."

But he never got the words out of his mouth. For at that moment Tagger's smartphone pinged.

And before Bonaventure could do a thing the canoe suddenly flipped.

A mouth full of water. Cold shock to the skin. Flailing and panic. *I'm not a good swimmer.*

Wait. Low tide. Water only a few feet deep. No risk of drowning. He stood and was safe, water no more than waist-high.

Even if he felt a fool in front of umpteen thousand people. From the shore some idiots hooted and clapped. Other witnesses, more sympathetic, shouted, "Hope you're all right!"

He stood cold and dripping, looked about for Tagger. But the kid without a backward glance was wading toward the embankment.

Bonaventure called after him, asking "What happened" and "Hey are you okay." No answer.

Hell. It was almost like the kid deliberately ... He started to follow Alex to shore but then remembered the canoe. It lay bobbing nearby. He turned toward it and then realized he'd lost the gaff the priest had given him.

He stooped and studied the water but the dark murk revealed nothing.

He didn't much like the idea of sticking his face in the Providence River again—he remembered Barb's warnings about typhus and typhoid—but there seemed no alternative. So he squatted and submerged his head and opened his eyes.

There. The gaff. He grabbed it.

But something else. Swimming toward him, from maybe fifteen yards away. Something long and big and fast.

Mostly a blur. Spine-crested head. Thick flailing tail. Limbs with sharp claws. Claws six inches in length.

Plus eyes that burned red, and a big gaping mouth.

He tried to scrabble away, tripped on the gaff, plopped hard onto river mud.

And now the thing was on him. Eyes that burned red, and a big gaping mouth.

A mouth that held something. A large metallic sphere. Giant, translucent, like a glowing pearl, but impossibly big, like an ornamental globe on a suburban backyard lawn. *Crazy.*

Bonaventure scooted backward in the mud but couldn't move fast enough. The mouth came right up to him and spat out the sphere so it landed at his feet.

Then the swimmer-thing veered and swung around him and vanished in the murk.

But the sphere was still there. Bonaventure got to his feet and stooped to touch it and at once it shrank in size. Shrank until it was no more than a small silver knob in the palm of his hand.

A silver something Joseph Bonaventure had been looking for. A stud that belonged to the earring set of a librarian he happened to know.

15

"Wait. Run that by me again." Disbelief flared from Fay MacConnell's eyes. "You're saying some ... What was it?"

"Some kind of ... of creature." Joseph Bonaventure rubbed hard at the scar on his jaw. She'd noticed before he had a habit of doing that. He seemed to do it when he got agitated.

"Fine. Some kind of creature. And you want me to believe it came swimming up to you in the Providence River and handed you my lost earring stud."

Just her luck: an irritating supplement to an irritating Monday morning. She'd slept badly, bad dreams that woke her at three (this happened often), then she'd lain awake for hours till almost dawn, then dozed off, only to wake with a jolt: 8:45, and horribly late for work. A glare at her alarm clock: it hadn't gone off. *Why'd you have to betray me?* She flung it across the room (just missing her cat). Only later did she realize she'd forgotten to set the alarm.

No time for breakfast, no time for coffee, no time for the precious smoke she'd rationed and promised herself as her sole cigarette of the day. She'd arrived at the Ath out of breath, her mind on the Camel she craved, and there was Nancy Clayton. A big maternal smile. "Your gentleman friend is back."

"Who?" Fay was too sleep deprived to have any clue whom Nancy meant.

Nancy's smile widened. She'd obviously gotten plenty of trouble-free sleep. "You know. Your Egyptian Cabinet fellow."

"Oh no." She'd said this out loud, which was rude. For there he was, standing right behind her near the circulation desk.

"Hey. Hi." He was wearing old jeans and that ratty tweed jacket, the same as before. *Doesn't he have any other clothes?* He offered a feeble wave of the hand, shifting from one foot to the other, like he wasn't sure he had any right to take up space on the Earth. *Hell knows*

I can sympathize with that feeling, but right now I just want to be alone with a smoke.

She'd tried to be polite (after all, Nancy was standing right there), said she was glad to see him but had no time to socialize because after all she was supposed to work and had overslept and shown up late and was now trying to make up for lost time.

And then he had reached in his coat pocket and pulled out her earring-piece. And now he was stammering some far-fetched explanation about falling out of a canoe and something swimming up to him and handing him her stud.

He was still talking at her. With an effort of will—*damn, I can't believe how bad I need a smoke*—she steadied her attention and listened.

"Well, not exactly handed it to me," he was saying. "More like, spat it out at my feet. And you should have seen the thing's eyes. Glowing red."

Did he seriously expect her to believe such a tale? "Mister, it's too early in the morning for this razzmatazz dumb-ass shit."

"Fifi. Feef." Sharp reproof from the circulation desk. "That's not nice. He's just found you your earring. Say thank you."

She wanted to snap "Don't call me Fifi and don't call me Feef my name is Fay MacConnell is that too much to ask." Instead she muttered "thank you" and snatched the stud from his outstretched palm.

"There." Nancy stepped between them, took them each by an arm, and guided them across the atrium like a chaperone at a junior-high prom. "Why don't the two of you have a seat here." She deposited them at the table beside pensive Athena—the same table where they'd sat the other day. "I'm sure you both have a lot to discuss." The older woman leaned close to Fay so only she could hear. "Remember what Tristram said. You're supposed to keep your temper with the public." Another smile, and Nancy walked back to her desk.

Fay turned on Bonaventure at once. "Why can't you just say you found it on the dock, like a normal guy would? Why make up a dumb-ass story? Why do you have to dramatize?"

He said he wasn't dramatizing and he wasn't making up a story. "It's true." Stubborn insistence in his eyes, but only for a moment. "Unless maybe I'm going nuts. Jeez." He rubbed his chin, ran a hand through his hair.

She almost said, "Well that makes two of us wondering if maybe you're going nuts," but she bit the words back. The problem with this guy, she told herself, was that too much emotion, too much angst or something, was too close to the surface, always about to break out. She winced to see so much of her own unsureness in him. She'd been treated too poorly for too much of her life to have spare strength for cases like him. He made her feel like her own defenses could crumble at the slightest shove. *Especially now when I could really, really use a smoke.*

"Oh. I almost forgot." He was saying something else. "Just before the canoe flipped there was a flash from the Superman Building, up top near the tower. And then that kid Alex, the one they call Tagger, you know? Right after the flash his phone pinged. And then plop, over we go. As if that ping had been a signal."

She suggested maybe it had been nothing more than a text message on the kid's phone. "Just a coincidence."

He said the world was too small for coincidences. "Okay sure it was a text message. But that text message was a signal. And something else." He glanced up at Athena, as if unsure whether they should be allowing the statue to overhear them. "Just before we leave the dock, some gal comes up to Tagger and gives him a note. She's wearing a button that says 'GGCG.' Beats me what that stands for."

"Beats me too."

"Plus a button with a logo that says 'HPL was right.'"

"HPL as in H. P. Lovecraft?"

"Gotta be. I told you: the world is too small for coincidences."

"And what's Lovecraft supposed to have been right about?"

"My question exactly. The girl gives me a know-it-all look, says something cryptic, and just walks away. And of course I can't pry a word out of Tagger."

She fought down the impulse to exclaim "You're sure you're not making up all this stuff?"—one look at him was enough to confirm he'd probably twitch himself into self-tortured knots if she showed any further doubts—so instead she just asked, "Where do we go from here?"

"Well." He sat up straight, tried to square his shoulders. "I googled 'GGCG' and found nothing useful. The next time I see Janey I'll ask her about that thing she says she saw in the Providence River, what she calls Spike-Head. But meantime I've got my dissertation research. That Lovecraft manuscript I showed you the other day, the one I found up at Miskatonic: I really, really want to examine that Egyptian Cabinet you have downstairs in your Special Collections unit, see if it matches at all the description Lovecraft gives in his unpublished text. This is the kind of thing that could make my dissertation big. I mean big."

His air of uncertainty briefly vanished, and his eyes flared and glowed. Like the murderer's eyes in Poe's "Tell-Tale Heart." (The thought came to her: *Ugh, unfortunate comparison.*) Or maybe like the eyes of that thing that Bonaventure claimed had come swimming up to him in the Providence River. She was having trouble deciding whether he was lying or deluded or mentally unwell. Or maybe all three. Which led to the thought: *Would it be safe for me to be alone with this guy?*

"... is why this request means so much." He'd been saying something more.

"I'm sorry. I must still be sleepy. Could you say that again?"

He said he'd be really, really grateful if she could take him downstairs right away and show him that cabinet.

"Now?" At this early hour there was no one else downstairs, which meant she'd be alone with him in the vault. ("Vault" was her private name for the Ath's backroom dedicated to Special Collections; in her mind the name offered the space a nice Gothic tone, something she was sure her pal Poe would've liked. Which would be an amusing thought at any other time, except here it was early Monday morning and she hadn't had her coffee and she was facing the prospect of touring the Egyptian Cabinet at close quarters with a freak who saw eyes that glowed red in the river and she wasn't sure this was safe and boy oh boy she badly wanted a smoke.)

"Yes. Now. Please." Again his eyes glowed.

She hesitated, said nothing. The glow died. He slumped defeated in his seat.

She sighed and scolded herself. *Look girlfriend he did find the earring for you—even if he'd been the one to tear it from your head. If he gets weird you can handle this. Worst-case scenario you just start yelling for Nance.*

She stood and nodded for him to follow. "Come on then. I'll get the keys and we'll see how well our Egyptian Cabinet matches up with this Lovecraft of yours."

While Fay hunted behind the circulation counter for the Special Collection keys, Nancy Clayton exclaimed over Bonaventure's interest in the cabinet. "So nice that someone shows an appreciation for that piece," she gushed, and then for his benefit she enumerated data points about all the things that made the Egyptian Cabinet unique.

How it had been custom built in 1840 by local furniture makers to house the twenty-five mammoth elephant-folio volumes of the *Description de l'Égypte*. How the *Description* had been the product of the combined efforts of some hundred and fifty *savants*—the adventurous scholars and scientists who had volunteered to accompany Napoleon and the French army in their expedition to Egypt in 1798.

How the Athenaeum's copy of the *Description* had once belonged to a French nobleman named Jules Armand de Polignac. "Very high up in Parisian society, mother a confidante of Marie Antoinette, living quarters at Versailles, very royal lifestyle, very posh. But then came the Revolution and the guillotine"—it was clear Nancy had given the Special Collections tour so many times, she had the details down by heart—"and Polignac's family had to flee to London or else they'd have gotten the chop."

Polignac returned to France in Napoleon's time but remained a lifelong royalist and supporter of the *ancien régime*—which in the turbulent years of early nineteenth-century France earned him ongoing trouble and banishment and the confiscation of all his worldly goods. "Including his books, which got put up for auction. The Ath was lucky enough to snaffle his copy of the *Description*, for five hundred dollars—an impressive amount to pay for a set of books in the Providence of 1840." With so much money invested in the purchase, the Athenaeum's board of directors decided they needed a special receptacle worthy of housing these volumes—hence the commission to create the Egyptian Cabinet.

She paused for breath. "Come to think of it, young man, you're the first person to ask about the cabinet since we made the decision to lock it up. Shame we had to do that. All because of those kooks and eccentrics pestering us to allow them to do some sort of séance with it. Which we certainly weren't going to allow."

"Séance?"

"Yes. One of the strangest sets of guests I've met in thirty-five years at the Ath. In fact ..."

"Got 'em." Fay waved the keys.

The senior librarian called after them as they descended the stairs. "Fifi, remind our visitor to ask me sometime about that whole business of the séance."

Fay said she'd be absolutely sure to. Once safely in the silence at the foot of the stairs, she rolled her eyes and murmured, "I love that woman, but whew. Yakkity-yak. Too early in the morning." Quickly she unlocked the entrance to Special Collections and turned on the lights. "Here we go. Your Egyptian Cabinet. Have to admit I haven't paid much attention to this piece since I started working here."

Standing three feet tall and some nine feet in length, the coffer was constructed in the shape of an Egyptian temple, complete with sculpted lotus columns and, all over its wooden surface, painted figures of gods and worshipers and winged cobras guarding the disk of the sun.

Other things crowded the confined space of the room. Shelves of rare books. Old maps of Providence and Narragansett Bay. A large magnifying glass set on a metal stand. And a coral-encrusted amphora beside the stuffed figure of a raven. "A prop," explained Fay, "for when we have events in honor of my man." Her hand caressed the stuffed raven's head. "We call this little guy Nevermore."

But Bonaventure's attention was elsewhere. He swallowed and spoke in a low, urgent voice. "In that piece I found at Miskatonic, Lovecraft described the cabinet as a 'portal.' Does this thing have doors of any kind?"

"Sure. Here, around the corner, at the left end." They crouched before the narrow transverse end of the coffer. Confronting them was a pair of closed doors. Bonaventure licked his lips, ran his hands over the sealed pinewood surface. "Do you have a key for this?"

"Right here. It's the original. Nancy said to open this gently; it's a pretty fragile antique." Carefully she fitted the key in the lock and eased the doors open.

Before them was a series of seven narrow knobbed drawers, one atop another. Impatiently the graduate student pulled open the topmost. "Empty."

"Hey. Take it easy. You damage the wood, you damage my job. Let me do this."

"Sorry." She could see him make a visible effort to restrain himself. He drew a deep breath.

With vigilant care she opened the second drawer. A burst of irritation beside her. "Another empty."

And so too with all seven. "Nothing in any of them," he said. "I don't get it."

"Not surprising," she replied. "I checked the Ath's master catalogue and it says the twenty-five volumes of the *Description* were transferred to a climate-controlled storage unit years ago to keep the brittle paper from disintegrating. So this cabinet doesn't contain a thing. A nice-looking container, I know, but a disappointment once you get to the inside. Kind of like life in general."

He slumped to the floor and eyed her. "Are you always this much of a pessimist?"

"Sorry. That's caffeine deprivation talking. To say nothing of my need for nicotine. And maybe even something to eat." Breakfast was taking shape in her mind, and at the top of the menu: a deeply inhaled drag on an unfiltered Camel.

He was saying something: "... thought there'd be more. Can't be just empty." He shook his head. "Remember what Lovecraft wrote in that fragment? 'Here in this cabinet, barriers of time and space collapse. New England blurs into the Orient. Here, via this barque, the Providence River flows into the underworld Nile.' "

"Sounds like you've memorized the whole piece."

"Not quite. Almost." He laughed at himself. "Crazy, I know. I guess I was just hoping for ... expecting ... I don't know what."

"Let me guess. Hoping to collapse the barriers of time and space, right here inside this piece of antique wood." She snorted. "Did you think you could just stick your hand in there and get warped through to some other dimension? Get real."

A murmured reply, akin to an incantation. " 'Anywhere, out of the world.' "

"Hey. That's a line from Baudelaire."

"That's right. He's a French poet."

"I know he's a French poet, damn it. He was one of Poe's fanboys. I like him."

"I like him too." Confusion and embarrassment on his face, as if he feared he might have said too much. In silence he stared at the cabinet.

She started to say more about Baudelaire but saw Joseph Bonaventure was focused on something else. From where he crouched he lifted his head, tilted his chin, *like a bird-dog*, she thought, *sniffing the air.*

He snapped his fingers. "Wait." From his tweed coat he pulled the photocopies of Lovecraft's Miskatonic text. "I'm so stupid. I almost forgot. Listen to this: 'Painted on one end of this "innocent" cabinet—ostensibly a mere coffer of antiquarian books—is an image of a pharaonic barque.'" He sprang to his feet, almost fell onto the frail wood of the coffer.

She sprang up too. "Hey. Don't wreck the joint. I want to keep this job."

But he'd already hurried to the other end of the cabinet. "Now this is more like it. Facing west. Seems appropriate. The realm of the sunset; the Egyptian land of the dead."

There it was: the painted figure of a pharaonic barque. Seated in the vessel was a mummiform pharaoh wearing the crown of upper Egypt and holding a flail and jackal-headed scepter. The prow and stern of the ship were shaped in the form of papyrus fronds. Perched atop the prow was a bird. "Probably a Horus-falcon," mused the grad student, "meant to guide the king through the underworld Nile."

He tapped the wooden surface beside the painted barque. "And this is what our friend Lovecraft must have meant to draw attention to." To the right of the image was another pair of closed doors. His hands clenched and unclenched; he almost danced in agitation. "Come on, come on. Let's open it up."

She was really wishing now she'd had a coffee and smoke before coming to work. "Hey, calm down." She crouched before the door with her keys. "No need to breathe down my neck like that."

The lock seemed much stiffer and did not yield so easily as the doors on the other end. "I don't think any of the Ath staff has touched this in who knows how long."

Bonaventure said nothing but she could feel him twitching right beside her.

"There." The doors swung wide.

Seven drawers, the same setup as the other end of the coffer. She began from the top.

Nothing.

She opened the second drawer.

Nothing.

Drawer number three. Likewise nothing.

Mister Twitch (by now that had become her private label for this guy) hissed a nervous burst of distress.

"Stay calm," she urged. "Let's take it slow."

She opened the fourth drawer.

And this one held something.

"Let me see." He swooped low beside her, bumped his head into hers.

"Ouch." She shouldered him aside. "Do you mind? Give me space."

"Sorry." But Mister Twitch clearly itched. His fingers danced and shivered on the painted coffer-doors.

She lifted clear the contents of drawer number four: large oblong lengths of tissue and, cushioned underneath, a pair of elephant-folio sheets of paper. Tinted engravings, illustrations. One depicted a kestrel in flight. The other showed an owl perched on a branch.

"These look like they're from a copy of the *Description de l'Égypte*," exclaimed Fay. "Someone must have excised them a long time ago from the book with the idea of framing them and selling them piecemeal for buyers to display in their homes. This is a real discovery. These drawers feel like they haven't been opened for a hundred years. I'll bet the Ath has no record of this whatsoever." For the first time all morning Camel cigarettes weren't uppermost in her mind.

"Mmm." That was the only response she received. Mister Twitch was stooped over the open drawer, his nose a bare inch above the wood.

"There's something else in here." He felt about in the drawer and delicately extracted an object the mere length of a spent fingernail clipping.

"Dead insect." She glanced over his shoulder before returning her attention to the engravings. "We get them every now and then. Infestations. Looks like that one's been here a long time. All these drawers need a dusting."

He lifted it close to his face. "Dead insect. Yes. But something strange about it."

Fay opened drawer number five. "More engravings, labeled in French like the others. A vulture. And this one's a peregrine falcon. Nice."

The grad student seemed not to have heard a word. From its shelf he grabbed the magnifier and peered at his minuscule find through the lens.

"Don't tell me you count bug collecting among your hobbies." No word of reply from her visitor.

Well if Mister Twitch was so distractable she'd just go on with her own discoveries. She opened drawer number six. "Another pair of engravings. More birds. Cool." Which led to an idea: *Why not generate some publicity, contact the* Providence Journal, *get them to write up a newsflash—"Junior staff member at Providence's oldest library unearths treasure in Athenaeum vault." Publicity like that would make the Ath look good and maybe make Tristram and Nancy overlook my little failings like getting grumpy with the public and showing up a tad late.*

She started to voice her good idea but the grad student was still studying his foolish tiny dead thing under the glass.

"Look," he declared, bent over the magnifier. "Look at how all the legs and feelers are intact. All of them arched, too. Curled in a snapshot of striving. As if this little guy had been struck down—heart attack, maybe—trying to do something important. Can bugs have heart attacks?"

Bugs and heart attacks. The thought resurfaced: *Is it really safe to be alone down here with Mister Twitch?*

He was saying something about a dream he'd had the night before. "So in the dream some midget creature is trying to communicate with me. Microscopic. So small I can barely see it. Maggot, larva, termite, slave ant. Not sure what. Opening its mouth. Trying to say something. I dreamt this Saturday night, right after falling into the Providence River and seeing Spike-Head or whatever that thing was that came swimming at me. And I had the exact same dream last night. Trying to communicate. And now I see this."

Lying, deluded, or mentally unwell? What difference does it make? Fay wanted to finish up, get away, gallop upstairs, go outside and grab a smoke. She took a step back. "Listen. We've got just one drawer left. Number seven. Let's open it and then take a break."

"Look. *Look.*" Urgency now in his voice. "This is no ordinary bug, or beetle, or whatever it is."

"How can you be so sure?" Overcoming her own nervousness at his proximity, she stepped closer to the magnifier.

"The head. Something funny about it. Almost as if . . ." He stopped himself, glanced at her, then away.

"Almost as if what?"

"Almost as if someone had altered . . ." His voice trailed off. He pawed about in the drawer, pushing aside the Egyptian folios.

"Hey. Easy with those. I could lose my job if those pages get torn, right when we've made a discovery down here."

"Yeah well I think we've got another discovery in this drawer. Something a lot stranger than stray pages from the *Description of Egypt*."

"There." He reached elbow-deep into the very back of the drawer, then extracted a small object and held it to the magnifier.

"Let me see that." She took it from his hand: a miniature glass vessel, two inches long, with a wide mouth and flaring neck.

"What was this doing in there?" she asked. "It didn't belong in the drawer."

"I wonder." He held up the bug husk and the flask. "I have a theory. And if I'm right then somewhere in here we should also find . . . Half a sec." He stooped again over the cabinet. "Yup. Here we go."

He plucked from the drawer a tiny cork stopper, dried but intact. "See? It fits this bottleneck perfectly."

This was all going too fast. "I don't get it."

"You see, I think this bottle was a prison."

"Wait." *Is this guy truly nuts?* "A prison? For whom?"

"Or for what." Solemnly he held the bug husk in the palm of his hand, as if it were a warrior borne on a shield. "I'm thinking this little guy died—maybe heroically—gasping out its life trying to break free and scrabble clear of the drawer."

"Heroically. That bug. Uh-huh." Fay stared at him, started to say more, started to say "You're kidding right you can't be serious." Then she saw his eyes—which glowed, just like that underwater thing he claimed he'd seen.

She shook her head. "How about we stay on task. We've got just one more drawer to check. Number seven. Then we can call it quits and I can go out and find myself some breakfast."

"Just look. Please." Again he placed the bug husk beneath the magnifier. "There. The head. Right there. Look."

"Okay. I'm looking."

"The eyes. Don't they strike you as atypical? And the whole face, or what passes for a face on an insect: Doesn't it look mutated or something, almost quasi-human?"

"Are you an entomologist?"

"No, but I told you I've been having this dream ..."

"Which does *not* make you a specialist qualified to pass judgment on what rates as typical or atypical for dried-up insects you find in a drawer."

He looked hurt, disappointed. Then he flinched, as if he'd just been bitten or stung. "Whoa."

"What's wrong?"

"It just flipped in my hand, or jerked about. Or at least I think it did."

"The only one getting jerked around right now is me." She snatched the magnifier and thrust it firmly back on the shelf. "Put away your little friend, okay? I want to look at number seven and then get out of here."

She knew she sounded harsh but this clown was really too much. *Dead bugs flipping about in his hand. Right.*

Thoughtfully he placed the bug in the flask and then stoppered the flask with the cork.

She fixed him with a stern gaze. "So will that thing keep for now?"

"Yeah. It'll keep." His voice took on a hopeful tone. "Hey. Do you mind if I hold on to this?"

"The dead bug?"

"Uh-huh. And this glass thingy. Just so I can give him a resting place."

She was about to tell him no, the institution's regulations were very strict on this point: anything discovered within or among the library's artifacts—and that would have to include the flask and stopper and even any dried-up insects—automatically became property of the Athenaeum. But then she noticed the look of longing on his face.

"Okay," she relented. "I know I shouldn't be doing this. But if it'll make you happy and get you out of my hair faster you can keep the glass thingy and your husk along with it. On one condition."

"What's that?"

"That you promise to stay quiet and act normal long enough for me to open this last drawer here and see what's inside."

"Okay. I promise." Sheepishly he pocketed the flask.

Drawer number seven: she was expecting additional folio sheets of birds. What it disclosed was altogether different. At first all that came to view was unsurprising: a dozen thicknesses of protective tissue. Side by side the librarian and the student stooped and riffled the sheets.

"Nothing," she said. "No. Wait."

Near the very bottom of this last and lowest drawer, nested among the layers of tissue, lay something else: old sheets of paper, creased and folded, minutely inscribed with closely packed lines of script. The ink was faded brown with time but the writing was still legible.

Fay read aloud the inscription atop the first page. "Journal of Novalyne Price. Prov., RI, July 1936."

"What's this doing here?" she wondered. "And who's Novalyne Price?"

"Robert E. Howard's love interest," explained Bonaventure. "Or maybe that's too definitive a word. More like his on-again off-again sweetheart."

"Howard as in Conan the Barbarian pulp fiction?"

"You got it. But this isn't what I was expecting at all." He rubbed the puffed flesh near his chin. "Based on my Miskatonic fragment, I was secretly hoping Lovecraft had maybe stashed another unpublished manuscript here. Not sure exactly why or how he would have done that, but then he was someone who did a lot of strange stuff. But Novalyne Price."

He tapped his chin. "Not sure of the connection. All I can say is, I know Howard and Lovecraft corresponded, exchanged a lot of letters, though the correspondence broke down when they developed some difference of opinion over something and got irked with each other. Irked over what, exactly, isn't clear. Not all of their letters survive. At least they're not all in the Miskatonic archive."

He began pacing before the coffer. *Going into Mister Twitch mode again*, noted Fay. *Getting agitated.*

"So where does Miss Novalyne Price fit in?" He stooped and boomed the question at the cabinet's open doors as if he expected a reply from some oracle within. "I've read all of Lovecraft's correspondence I can find and there's no record he ever mentioned her or spoke to her. And this Providence dateline. That's weird as well. Price was never in Rhode Island, and neither was Howard. And this date of July 1936. That's a month after Howard died. Shot himself, at the age of thirty."

"Pretty grim." She made a face. "Guess he'd used himself up."

"Yeah. Or something. But why would his lady friend have come from Texas all the way to Providence, just a month after his death, and leave a journal behind in a library that was the longtime haunt of H. P. Lovecraft?"

From his coat pocket he extracted the flask that held the bug husk. He caressed the glass, turned it about in his hand. "Unless ... I wonder." His lips quivered and his eyes glowed—an expression that made the librarian think: *Uh-oh here comes his warning light.*

He stooped so suddenly to the open cabinet doors that Fay thought for a second he'd try to thrust his whole head straight through the drawers and do his best to make those barriers of space and time collapse.

Instead Mister Twitch subsided and a relatively rational look returned to his face. "Well. I guess the easiest way to get some answers"—he reached for the papers where they lay in the drawer—"is simply to read Price's journal right now."

"Unh-uh." This was what she'd feared. She snatched up the journal sheaf. "I'll tell you what we're going to do." She stood and nudged him away from the coffer drawers. "I need a break and I gotta have a smoke. I'm going out and I'm taking you with me. Can't have you wandering loose down here getting into who knows what."

"But I just want to sit and read that ..." His arms flailed about.

"Absolutely not. I'd never get you out of here."

"Then how about we take the manuscript with us for breakfast? I'm sure we can sneak it past the front desk."

My worst nightmare, come to life. "I'd just as soon not lose my job, thank you very much."

Downcast and stricken: he looked so woebegone she knew she had to offer him something.

"Tell you what I'll do." She pulled out a phone. "Half a sec." Turning the sheets quickly, she photographed each page of the journal, then placed the manuscript back in drawer number seven and relocked the Egyptian Cabinet. "Technically I'm not supposed to take pics of unpublished library files without permission, but we'll just keep this between us. And now we can read what your Novalyne Price has to say while we go out and have something to eat."

"But couldn't we just sit quietly and ..." He gave the flask a beseeching look as if hoping for verbal support from the bug husk within.

She pushed him out past the Special Collections doors, locked them in place, then bullied him up the stairs.

As she propelled him through the atrium: "You like pepperoni pizza for breakfast?"

He gulped, looked confused. "For breakfast?"

"What am I saying. Of course you do. You're from Providence."

She waved a "'Bye I'm on break" to Nancy and thrust Joseph Bonaventure out the rear library door and onto College Street.

"I know just the place," she announced. "Angelo's. On Thayer Street, near Waterman. By Brown Bookstore."

"But pepperoni pizza for breakfast?"

"Washed down with a can of Mountain Dew. You'll love it. I promise."

And with that she nudged Mister Twitch up the streets of College Hill.

16

"The usual?"

Fay MacConnell nodded.

The woman behind the counter chewed gum and surveyed Joseph Bonaventure. "And for your sweetheart?"

"My colleague." Fay liked to keep things precise. "Not my sweetheart, for your information. This is business." She turned to Bonaventure. "Flavia does this every time I bring a guy in here. She figures 'Ah this is it, this is romance, this is true love.' She loves to bust my ass." She turned back to the server. "Just my colleague, okay?"

"Fine. Fine. Just your colleague." Flavia flashed Bonaventure a broad mascaraed wink. "What'll you have, hon?"

Fay spoke before he could clear his throat. "He'll have the same as me."

The grad student shrugged a helpless shrug.

"Okay then, four slices, pepperoni and cheese." Flavia slid them in the warmer. "And to drink. Mountain Dew, as usual?"

"Yeah. No. I'm in a Coca-Cola kind of mood. Make it Coke."

"And your colleague?"

Bonaventure asked what they had in diet.

"Diet? A stringy beanpole like you? Don't tell me you gotta watch your figure." Flavia shifted gum from one side of her mouth to the other and eyed him up and down. "What you want with diet? Make it classic Coke."

He raised his hands in surrender. "Okay. I'll have a classic Coke."

"Atta boy. Keep your girlfr—sorry—keep your *colleague* company on her mad path to hell."

"See?" Fay tapped his coat sleeve. "She loves to bust my ass."

"No I don't." Flavia folded her arms and leaned across the counter. "All I do is point out you have bad taste in boyfriends. Or you have had until now." Chin in hand she studied Bonaventure. "Course it could be your taste is changing."

"He's a colleague. That's all."

"Course he is, honeychild. Course he is." Flavia shifted her attention to the warmer. "For here or to go?"

"To go. The only way I'll get to eat in peace without someone dissecting my personal life."

"Pizza. Cokes. Napkins. Straws. There you are."

A row of tall glass shakers lined the counter. The librarian took two, one of parmesan, the other red pepper flakes.

"Do you mind? I'll bring them back."

"You said that the last time."

"This time I will. I guarantee."

As they turned to leave, Flavia called after Bonaventure. "You make sure she brings them back. She's forgetful."

He said he'd do his best.

"And hon a word of advice." Another mascaraed wink. "This girl snaps a lot. You just snap right back."

Back out on Thayer Street, Fay announced Brown campus as the place they would sit. "We'll call it a picnic."

They walked down Thayer, turned right at Waterman, crossed onto the campus. Fay said since it was already so hot they needed to find a nice shady spot.

"This'll do." She had them sit beneath an elm. Before them, an expanse of green lawn, thick leafy trees, and old brick lecture halls and dormitories. Summer-session students crisscrossed the quad.

She handed him his first pizza slice. He said he'd rather see the phone and learn what Novalyne Price's journal had to say.

"No way." She patted the shirt pocket where she kept her phone. "Keeping things in order is how I keep myself together. That means rules and regulations. And the first of them is: don't spoil a good meal with texting or emails or electronic this-and-that. Just eat. We'll get to your Novalyne Price. She'll wait for us."

He nibbled tentatively at his pepperoni-and-cheese and watched as she took from a bag the two glass shakers from Angelo's and methodically shook the contents over her food for a full twenty seconds.

"Whew," he observed. "That's one snowstorm of flakes."

"Grated parmesan. The great key to happiness in your day-to-day. The pizza slice is no more than a delivery device." She ate through both her pieces in quick tearing bites.

He was still nibbling at his first. She pointed at the other. "I'm hungrier than I thought. Do you mind if I take just a bit?"

"Take the whole thing. It's too early in the morning for me to confront pizza."

"I'll just have half." She popped open a Coke, drank a long gulp, reached for her Camels.

"You know those things will kill you."

"What, has life been that good to you, you wanna live forever?" Lovingly she lit her cigarette—*my only one of the day, make it last, make it good.*

"Live forever?" He said he felt as if he'd already lived a very long time.

"Okay then." She breathed a deep plume of smoke. "In that case maybe you have some idea how I feel."

At that he studied her with what looked like real interest. For a moment she thought he was about to ask how exactly did she feel about life—in fact she had a brief sensation: *Hey this guy seems genuinely intrigued with what I say and how I feel*—but he evidently reconsidered and went back to chewing his pizza.

Another lungful of smoke and a long pull on her Coke. Then: "Flavia says I snap a lot. I guess I do. Sorry."

"Don't be. It just means you have moxie."

"Yeah?" She paused with the cigarette at her lips. "You're the first guy that's ever said that to me. I mean the first guy aside from my dad. He used to say that. He called me his Moxie Girl. You know, he named me in honor of someone he said had real moxie, the star of *King Kong.*"

"He named you after a movie gorilla?"

"No, you idiot." She laughed. "After the gorilla's costar, Fay Wray."

"I thought in that movie she just screams a lot."

"Then you should go watch it again." She said the best part of the film was the first fifteen minutes. "In the movie she plays this girl surviving on the streets of New York in the early 1930s—Great Depression, everyone jobless, everyone desperate—and she's stealing apples, getting through life any way she can. Then a big-name cameraman comes along and says 'Take a chance, come with me on my freighter ship to a faraway island and I'll make you a movie star.' And on the spot she says yes and gets on that ship and decides to take a chance.

My dad said that took moxie and so he named me after her. He said that's what a girl has to have to get by."

The grad student surprised her then by proposing a toast. "Well here's to getting through life."

They clinked cans of Coke. She nodded agreement. "To getting through life." She tilted back her head, breathed another plume of smoke, suddenly realized she felt relaxed. *This Mister Twitch,* came the thought, *maybe he isn't so bad. Okay he tore off my earring and then made up that whole drama about an underwater creepy-crawler finding it for him. But still. He did find the thing, and he seems to take an interest. An interest in me, and what I have to say. Which when I think about the guys I've known is pretty good. Pretty good.*

Another long pull on her cigarette. "Maybe this is just the pizza talking, or a sugar-rush blitz, or my Camel nicotine high. But I'm going to ask you something. How'd you ever get into H.P. Lovecraft? That's a hell of a gloomy dissertation topic. With Lovecraft you've got paranoid sensibility to the max. Cthulhu cults, human sacrifice, horrors in basements, horrors from alien outer space. I mean dark doesn't begin to describe him. You're gazing deep into one twisted gizzard."

"Says the gal who's a pal of Poe."

She grunted. "Okay, you got me there. I'm a fine one to talk."

He said his grad school choice of dissertation topic all had to do with bad choices he'd made in his reading when he'd been a kid. "This will sound strange"—he shot a glance as if to assess how she might react to what he would confess—"but even when I was little I liked anything that hinted at transcendence, at realities larger than the flat indifferent surface of things, realities just waiting for us to notice what lies beneath the humdrum routine of our lives. Realities bigger than what some people seem satisfied with. Yeah." He wiped his mouth, set his pizza aside. "I wanted transcendence, but hey I was twelve and I wanted it delivered with a lot of pow, a big pulp-fiction punch—the result of reading too many comic books like *Tales to Astonish.* Then I found Lovecraft and his stories. Titles on the order of 'The Haunter of the Dark' and 'The Rats in the Walls.' Talk about hidden realities most folks don't notice. *Brr.*"

He sipped from his Coke. "Fast-forward to grad school on the West Coast. Stanford's American lit program. I needed a dissertation topic no one else had tackled. Hawthorne, Dickinson, Longfellow; they'd all been done to death. Other students in my classes asked me where I'm from, and their response was 'Providence where's that? Rhode Island where exactly is that?' All they'd ever heard of was Newport. So I wanted to put Providence on the map. But not a lot of Rhode Island authors to choose from, not for someone with my peculiar tastes. And then I remembered 'The Rats in the Walls' from when I was twelve. So for my dissertation I tell my advisor I'll go with Lovecraft."

He laughed. "Except that now, going back to Lovecraft as what passes for an adult, I begin to realize just how repellent his worldview was. The vision he offers is pretty grim: we humans are the victims of cosmic forces that are sadistic and, to put it mildly, don't exactly wish us well."

"But you're sticking with it?"

"Yeah, I figure, put my time in, finish the dissertation, then I'll be free of him, free of all his rats in the walls. Actually I was supposed to be done by now, supposed to have finished ages ago. But then stuff came up. Things got in the way." He tapped his chin agitatedly, ran his hand through his hair, not realizing, Fay suddenly noticed, that his fingers were greased with tomato sauce from the pizza. She offered him a napkin but he was too far sunk within his own thoughts to notice. *Uh-oh*, she realized, *here comes Mister Twitch*. "Things got in the way," he said again. "Stuff happened." He scratched at his coat sleeve, which reminded her of the inked arms beneath. And which also reminded her of the tattooed inscription, at least the little bit she'd glimpsed: "Girlie you look like ..."

"Anyway." He studied his hands, saw they were streaked with tomato grease. He grimaced. "I seem to have made a mess." Absently he accepted a napkin from her and tried wiping at his sleeve, at his face. "Don't mind me."

He crumpled the napkin. "But I've been wondering. How did you wind up devoted to Poe?"

Why Poe? She knew he'd ask. She welcomed the question; dreaded it, too. For it brought up her lifelong challenge: How much should she say, should she risk? Keep inquisitors out, or let them in? Build towers, or a bridge? She'd often privately pondered the enigma herself: *Why Poe?*

To get at reasons, she could have started way back—the fights, ongoing, between her mom and dad, how as a child she'd wanted nothing better than to find a way to make them happy and keep them together, how once they'd split up—when she was all of six—she blamed herself and fretted over how she might entice and cajole them and reassemble the broken bits of what had been a family. She tried, but nothing worked. Dad went off, she stayed with Mom, and that was that.

So that when she started first grade she'd had nothing to say to people who couldn't see what she needed most. She lived at home with Mom, longed for Dad. This went on for years. So school meant nothing, it had nothing to say to her, offered no help, so she said nothing back.

Classmates noticed her silence, called her strange, called her weird, found ways to make sure she'd know she'd never fit into their world or any world. And more than once her teachers too would go along with the dynamic, yielding her up as a sacrificial goat (staked out for blood) for class-communal taunts, so that instructors and pupils alike could define themselves together as not-weird, not-strange, not-Fay.

Moxie: that's what her father had said she needed for getting through life. So she clenched her teeth, remembered her dad, did what she could, all with the goal of just getting through life.

Even now, all these years later, I still know by heart, could recite off the top of my head if I wanted for Mister Twitch here, a poem I wrote in sixth grade:

> School days—nothing but noisy cliques and noisy groups:
> Group pressure, group preening, group crowds.
> Silent kids stand out.
> What's forbidden, what's allowed,
> Gets determined by the crowd.

And how had she survived elementary school and junior high? By hiding in the library—skipping gym, study hall, cafeteria lunch, torture sessions all. And in the library she found a soulmate, a friend: one Edgar Allan Poe.

Fay emerged from her reverie to notice Joseph Bonaventure beside her on the green campus lawn. Quietly he sat awaiting her reply.

Why Poe? No way of course I can share all these memories, or even almost any of them. Who'd want to hear it?

Aloud she murmured, "A lot of stuff happened when I was a kid. Problems at school. Bullying."

"And Poe I bet was a way to strike back. At least in your mind." Unmistakable sympathy in Twitch's voice. "'The Cask of Amontillado.' 'Hop-Frog.' No one beats Poe for tales of payback and revenge."

This man startled her: he understood.

Fay smiled, chuckled ruefully. "That's right. Revenge." A long sigh. Boy all those years she'd reveled in Poe's elaborately staged vendettas. The much-insulted Montresor getting the obnoxious Fortunato drunk and luring him into the catacombs, then trapping him in chains and brick by brick walling him up alive. Or Hop-Frog the humiliated jester-dwarf, tying up the abusive king and the king's complacent courtiers, then tarring them all with pitch and grabbing a torch and setting them alight. To read stories like that: man had that felt good.

Till one day—in seventh grade, was it? No, eighth—some pack of goons from the crowd-that-was-loud stood around her table where she sat in her library lair and heckled her long and hard. She reared up from her Poe and turned on them a Gothic eye that buried them all alive. "The look," she called it, and it must have disturbed them. One girl said, "She creeps me out," and they all backed away.

For one second, in the now-empty room, dark joy, and then the realization: *Poe's cruelty mirrors the cruelty I've been shown. I keep this up I'll just turn into them.* And after that things shifted a bit in her mind. She still ran fantasies of "The Cask of Amontillado," but now instead of inflicting torments she found herself within the role of the walled-up and unfortunate Fortunato. And in this new version of her imaginings she wriggled loose from the chains and unbricked the wall and sloshed through waist-high sewer-waters and dank catacombs forever. Utter silence and darkness; but nonetheless the freedom to move. Yes if nothing else: the freedom to move, to disappear, to hide. Not the happiest life, but a way to survive. All she needed was moxie; and her dad had always told her she had plenty of that.

Aloud she said simply, "Revenge. Yeah. I kinda burned out on that. These days I'm more into his poems. Less anger; more sadness. They give you some sense of Poe as a passed-over genius. A wounded spirit."

"I like 'The Conqueror Worm.' "

"You do?" She'd been just about to name that as a fave. Most people had never heard of "The Conqueror Worm." Hell, these days most people had never heard of *Poe.*

A long thoughtful drag on her Camel. She considered Joseph Bonaventure afresh, felt a sudden surge of kindness. "Um, I didn't do a good job of saying thanks for finding me my earring stud. Sorry."

"Wasn't really me that found it." He was wiping his head with a paper napkin from Angelo's. Maybe he felt sweaty or was just trying to get the rest of the pizza sauce out of his hair. "The credit goes to that underwater swimmer-thing. It spat your piece out right at my feet. I'm just sorry about the Providence River muck on your earring. Plus Spike-Head had his mouth all over it. Bit of a yuck factor." He smiled. "Or guck factor. Hope that won't keep you from ever wearing it again."

There he goes again. Mister Twitch and his Spike-Head obsession.

She cut off the mental complaint: *Hey, make an effort with this guy.*

She gulped more Coca-Cola and said, "Don't worry. Your Spike-Head won't stop me. I'll wear the piece again. Probably tonight."

"Good. I'm glad. Hey, do I still have pizza on me? I'm thinking of using a little of this soda to wash the stuff off." He wetted a napkin from his Coke can and ran it over his head, which succeeded only in making his hair stand up in stiff tufts. "Successful?"

"Not entirely. Speaking of spike-heads." She laughed but then stopped when she saw he looked stricken. "Coke's not the best substitute for a good wipe-and-dry."

Another lungful of smoke. "Okay. I'm nicely topped up. Pizza. Tobacco. Ingestions of chemicals and sugar." She took out her phone. "Time to examine this manuscript of Miss Novalyne Price."

At once he gave up fussing with his makeshift wipe-and-dry. "Fantastic. Let's have a look."

17

Journal of Novalyne Price

Prov., RI, July 1936

I have finally arrived. Of course now I must ask: To what end?

The Greyhound took me all the way from Fort Worth to New York. More tiring than I had foreseen. A man in the seat behind me coughed all through the night. A mother in the row across kept shushing her noisy boys, which did little to make them sit still. Long hours on the bus. But at the station in Philadelphia where I stepped down to buy a paper, a colored woman at the concession stand slipped me a packet of mint drops, saying she thought I might need something sweet to buck me up for my journey. An act of kindness, for which I thanked her.

By the time I reached Manhattan I was so stiff from my seat that I indulged in an extravagance: I bought a train ticket so I might go by rail for the last leg of the trip.

And thus into Providence, an early summer morning. I'd kept all the letters and envelopes and showed the station clerk the address I wanted: 66 College Street. He pointed east and said Thataway. So suitcase in hand, I set off at once, telling myself, "Do it now, you'll only grow more tired."

On foot through downtown, the bag dragging at my wrist, crossing a small bridge over what I learned was the Providence River, then a steep climb uphill. Until at last I stood before it—a big fine old wood house, two stories, black shutters, tall chimneys. Everything prosperous, fresh, and well kept. Back in Cross Plains, sun and wind would peel paint and warp wood before you could spit.

I raised my hand to knock, and then I hesitated. Not because of the early hour (I saw by my watch it was only six-thirty) or any fear of disturbance—Mister Howard Phillips Lovecraft had not only disturbed but destroyed the life of the man I now knew I loved.

No, I realized of a sudden I hadn't thought this matter through.

Oh, I knew all right what I wanted to say: "You, Mister Lovecraft, you kept calling Robert Howard a failure. You mocked him with the title Two-Gun Bob. Again and again you wrote him and urged 'Pull the trigger.' Well, sir. Now he has. That's what I'm here to tell you. Now he has. And I have one simple question for you: Are you satisfied with what you've done?"

And then what?

Stand on his doorstep, make a great scene, wave the letters, collar him like a common hooligan?

Mister Lovecraft might simply point out there's no law against writing letters—even if those letters served the purpose of hounding a fellow to death.

And then this estimable New England author might summon the law to remove a troublesome Texan vagabond woman from his front step.

No this wouldn't do. There were other questions too for which I wanted answers.

On the Greyhound—when I wasn't dozing in my seat—I had read through all Lovecraft's many letters to my Bob. (And I hope, now that Bob's gone, he won't mind this use of the tender possessive "my.")

In December of last year H. P. Lovecraft wrote:

> I have a special project underway. It will necessitate methods unorthodox for a secret contest supreme, methods shocking perhaps to unlearned minds but justified when I consider that a whole world is to be defended and kept secure.

And in January of this year he penned the following:

> So you wish to know more? The squeamish will cry Profane and immoral. But what do any of them understand of the high aims for which I strive? Ages hence I will be hailed as Reanimator, Resuscitator. My researches in the Necronomicon have shown the way. Serendipitous that a copy is at hand in this very locality, at the Athenaeum (though little do they know the risks inherent in even owning a copy!).

And this, from a letter posted in March:

> My Indo-Malay sources suggest what a magus (their word is *dukun*) might do with those who are three-quarters dead, with those who are dead-but-not-quite. Ah my dear Two-Gun Bob, you like the majority will not understand—but perhaps you can be induced to serve.

All of this intermingled with ever-increasing slights at my Bob and his stories.

"The dead-but-not-quite. The three-quarters dead." I don't know what Mister Lovecraft had in mind, but I mean to find out. For the sake of Bob's memory, and for my own peace of mind. And simple doorstep denunciations won't provide answers. This requires finesse, not a frontal attack.

I stepped back from the house and eyed the silent windows. I will be back, I promised, and so I walked to Benefit Street.

I will need work to support myself if I'm to stay here some time, and I know just the place to seek employment.

July 7

Thus far I've fared better than I dared hope. I presented myself at the Athenaeum (on Benefit Street, a scant minute's walk from the Lovecraft house) and announced myself and my desire for a job.

(Will confess here I felt afraid. A stranger, and, despite my education and all my elocution classes, I knew every word I spoke proclaimed a central Texas accent, a very far cry from this New England town. But I could all but hear Bob say, "You just go and do this, girl. Do what Conan or Kull the Crusher or Bran Mak Morn would do." I wanted to reply "Well Bob I'm not sure I see your barbarian friends lining up for jobs of quite this kind," and the thought was enough to make me smile. Which gave me the little boost I needed.)

Spoke with a Mrs. Dexter and told her what I've done at Cross Plains High, maintaining the school's book collection while teaching fulltime. I told her I'm well organized and know the Dewey decimal system and feel qualified to be a librarian.

Mistake! This woman sniffs and looks down her nose and says, "Qualified for rural Texas, no doubt. But this is Providence. We have high standards."

I came back sharp (sharper maybe than I should have, which I'm afraid I often do) with "Yes Ma'am but I have high standards too and you'll find I work hard."

She said nothing and let the silence spool out. I was just turning for the door when she allowed as to how of course there was no question of employment as a librarian but it so happened they had need of someone to help with filing and if that was acceptable I could start right away.

I said that was very acceptable. And I could all but hear Bob beside me say "Yes that's my girl."

On my way out one of the younger librarians stepped up and introduced herself. Margaret Johnson is her name, and she said just call her Maggs. She asked if I'd found a place yet to stay and when I said no I'm new in town she told me I should try Mrs. Torrance's, a boardinghouse for single women at 144 Benefit. Just up the street from the Athenaeum, Maggs said, and she also said that's where she stays too. "So we'll have plenty of chance to chat if you like"—which was kind of her to say.

In a strange city I feel I've just made a friend.

July 8

First day of work at the Athenaeum, and Mrs. Dexter has kept me, to use her own phrase, "painstakingly employed." Refiling books, filling membership invoices, restocking shelves. If I had time to remark them, there would be many things to describe for the other teachers out in Cross Plains. The way the afternoon sun shines a soft glow on the portrait busts at mezzanine level; a light so different from what we have back home. The feel of oriental carpets underfoot, and the sense you're not alone in seeking wisdom with a tall statue of Athena beside you in the hall. The hush in the downstairs reading room, where the painted coffer they call the Egyptian Cabinet makes you feel you're settling down to read at the threshold of a tomb. If I had time ... but I don't. Mrs. Dexter keeps me too busy.

Embarrassed to admit by day's end I felt a bit dizzy. In the restroom I steadied myself with both hands on the washstand sink. Maggs Johnson came in and stood beside me at the mirror and proclaimed herself bushed. "Also hot," she added, as she leaned in close to the mirror to refresh her lipstick. She smacked and rubbed her lips to ensure those lipsticked lips puckered just so. I couldn't resist asking if there was some young gent she was looking to please.

She said she was looking to please herself with a walk downtown and she'd take me along too and show me the sights such as they were. I pleaded fatigue but she said our boardinghouse rooms were simply too hot until that western sun went down and so I was coming too. "Don't bother arguing," she said, so I didn't.

Downtown we went and walked along streets with unfamiliar names, Weybosset, Dorrance, Empire. She showed me buildings she liked, the Turk's Head, the Arcade, the Majestic Theatre. I asked if we could sit for a bit so we stopped at Haven Brothers, her favorite dinette. (A wagon, really, that gets hauled downtown every afternoon.) Maggs had a root beer and burger. I sipped a ginger ale and ordered grilled cheese. Too hot to feel much like eating. I fed half my sandwich to the horse that pulls the dining car.

Then a slow return sunset walk up College Hill. "One more place to show you," said Maggs, and I said please no I was too tired for more. But she insisted I'd like this, and she was right.

Prospect Terrace Park juts forward on a promontory high above downtown. An evening breeze blew and cooled us. We watched the sky darken and lights appear in office buildings. From a tower in the tallest a red beacon flared; Maggs explained that was a landmark called the Industrial Trust.

We weren't alone in enjoying the view. Couples on benches cuddled close and talked low. (I remembered Bob and tried not to feel blue.) A solitary man, tall and very thin, stood at the park parapet's very rim, studying the sky as if watching for signs. Dressed entirely in black—black fedora, black suit, and matching black slacks; while there circled just above him, in the fast-dwindling light, a solitary black crow. The man turned and strode along the parapet, and the crow winged behind him in pursuit. He stopped and gazed out again, and the bird circled once more above him in the gloom.

I mouthed some silly joke to the effect of "Oh look an undertaker and his pet" but my companion shushed me with a muttered "Not so loud." That, she explained, happened to be an Athenaeum patron. "One of our more unpleasant ones," she said. Never smiles, seldom talks; doesn't trouble himself with "thank you" or "please."

The oddest tastes in reading. "And when he signs out books," said Maggs, "he gives himself fanciful names. Paracelsus the Alchemist. Zosimus of Panopolis. Abdul Hazred the Damned. Of course as soon as he fills the card in I just jot down his real name so everyone knows who's who."

Feeling sleepy I half listened and watched the evening lights of downtown. To make conversation I asked what was his real name.

"Actually a bit of a celebrity in these parts, at least as authors go. His name is H. P. Lovecraft."

No sooner did she say this than the man strode purposefully from the park, followed by the flapping crow.

I pointed at his retreating back and said just for fun let's follow him.

Maggs objected with something to the effect of "I thought you said you were tired."

I told her "Not anymore."

Good-naturedly she trailed me as we followed in his steps. Downhill he went, to the embankment along the Providence River. He walked along the shore, then paused. Awkwardly he stooped and studied the water as if on the watch for something. Above him the crow silently circled.

Then the crow cawed. The man's hand struck the water. We stepped closer to see. His hand seemed to close on something. In the growing dark we couldn't tell for sure.

He stood, one hand wet and clenched. With his other he extracted from his coat a handkerchief and wrapped it about whatever it was that had been snatched from the river. He pocketed the linen and strode fast up College Street. The bird cawed again and followed. We kept mum and followed too.

At number 66 the man hurried up the steps and unlocked the front door. He disappeared within. The unlit door stood a bit ajar.

Temptation; impulse. I felt the urge to go through that dark door and interrupt the man with whatever he had in his pocket and shout "Aren't you ashamed of what you did to Robert E. Howard and what's this you wrote about the three-quarters dead and the dead-but-not-quite and what's it all got to do with my Bob?"

When you tend to be headlong it's good to have a friend to head you off at the pass. Maggs grabbed fast at my arm. "Don't. He's a bad one."

There was still one more sight to behold. That singular crow flopped down to the pavement before number 66. With a flap of wings it hopped atop the first step, then the second and third. It paused before the door, cawed once, and stepped inside the unlit house.

And then the door snapped shut.

July 9

Weather even warmer today; humid, too. "I am simply not going to stay cooped up tonight in Mrs. Torrance's cage." Maggs announced this to the Athenaeum at large.

I told her our boardinghouse wasn't really all that bad.

She came back with something to the effect of "You can say that because you've been there only a few nights but once you've put in four months the way I have you'll know what I mean."

She said we need to be out and about tonight. I asked what she had in mind. She said she'd study the paper and come up with something.

What I really wanted to do at work today was pore over the circulation register, find out just what books make up the reading matter of our Paracelsus or Abdul Hazred or whatever other Mardi Gras name this Mister Lovecraft chooses for himself.

But Mrs. Dexter kept me chockablock with chores. Six trips upstairs to the mezzanine, to fetch books for customers at the desk. Five, maybe more (I lost count), downstairs, to bring antiquarian titles from Special Collections.

And it was on the last of these trips, near the close of the day, that I met our Zosimus of Panopolis. Our alchemist Paracelsus.

"Met" is perhaps too strong a word. But I got a good glimpse.

Arms folded, chin in hand, he stood before the Egyptian Cabinet, peering at the closed doors at the coffer's west end. He laid his hand flat on a figure painted to the left of the doors. I couldn't see much. The painting seemed to show a king with a crown seated in a boat. As Lovecraft touched the wood he bowed his head and moved his lips as if in prayer.

As I descended the last of the steps he looked up. What I saw was mostly his face. Long, angular, pale. Mouth sealed and pinched shut. Hair carefully brushed and combed back. Eyes blank and withdrawn, a gaze that flicked over me, assessed me an instant like a butcher weighing up beef, then passed on in search of something worthwhile. Wordlessly he brushed by me and straight up the stairs.

I paused by the coffer, bent over the doors he'd been perusing. They were shut fast and secure. Except that—and here I bent closer—there seemed to be faint scratches around the keyhole, as if someone had made an attempt with a penknife at forcing the lock. I'd never studied the cabinet before, so I couldn't be sure. What was this man up to?

I found my assigned texts and climbed back up the stairs and was still pondering this when Maggs Johnson approached with a flourish of the *Providence Journal*. "Let's go to the pictures. Double feature at the RKO Albee."

I said how about we just go to our rooms and rest quietly this evening. She said that was no way to celebrate the end of the day especially when the night promised to be so muggy and stale. "The Albee's like a cave. Nice and big and cool. I need an evening out and so do you. It's the best entertainment we can get for fifteen cents. And don't but me no buts. Save your breath and come along."

What else to do? I saved my breath and came along.

And in fact the evening was fine—except for what happened halfway through.

The first feature on the bill proved to be something Bob would have liked. *I Am a Fugitive from a Chain Gang*. We sat in the dark and watched, and there, up on the screen, were all the ideas Bob hammered home in his pulp-action tales. Desperate men in desperate straits. Civilization stripped away, so a man is forced to attack problems with nothing but sword or stone or fist. Brutal punishments, brutal escapes.

Plus the notion of being on the run. The line in the picture that hit me most was when the hero up on the screen says to his girl: "I can't do nothing but keep moving. That's all that's left for me."

A lone man fleeing, bloodhounds howling, guards panting in pursuit. "Keep moving. That's all that's left for me." An idea that always gripped Bob hard, especially toward the end ...

Toward the end of his life. Hard for me to say that, to say yes he's gone, even though it's been weeks now. Because no matter his rages and frustrations, he always seemed so energy-filled and alive, so full of ideas for the next tale he just couldn't wait to tell.

"Dead-but-not-quite. Three-quarters dead." Those were the words I remembered most from Lovecraft's letters to Bob. Whatever those words meant to Lovecraft, they also said something to me. Because that's how I felt: Yes maybe dead-but-not-quite.

I wiped my eyes in the dark. Maggs looked over at me and squeezed my hand, said "Yeah this picture's sad but just wait till you see the vaudeville number they've got lined up for intermission."

And if one wanted distraction the intermission show certainly provided that in full. From behind the curtain a chorus line of floozies dashed forward onto the stage. Called themselves The Dancing Georgia Peaches. Wearing not much more than wispy little sashes, like outfits on magazine-cover heroines from the pulps Bob used to write. They locked arms and pranced and kicked high and sang. The audience clapped and laughed. The whole business was so silly I clapped and laughed too. "See?" said Maggs. "This is just what we needed."

Which was fine, until halfway through the number someone came and sat in the dark right beside us. I paid no attention at first. People always coming in late to these shows.

But a minute later I felt I was being stared at so I turned my head to look.

There in the seat beside me: Paracelsus the Alchemist. Zosimus of Panopolis. Abdul Hazred the Damned.

Otherwise known as Howard Phillips Lovecraft.

But in fact he wasn't looking at me. He had his eyes fixed straight ahead, frowning hard at the Georgia Peaches as if he wished them in hell.

But something else was staring at me, or seemed at least to be.

Lovecraft was wearing a stickpin or ornament of some kind on his lapel. It was figured in the shape of an insect, carved in a green enamel so bright it glowed even in the dark of the theater. And there were two points in particular that glowed: the insect's bulging eyes, which bulged a fiery red. For a second—and even as I write this I know how odd it sounds—I felt the eyes staring, yes staring straight at me, and with a look I'd have to call beseeching.

Can a stickpin insect have beseeching eyes? Not in any world I know.

I was just trying to figure out how to divert Maggs' attention from the dancing Peaches and get her to take a peep at the stickpin without alerting Lovecraft when the problem resolved itself all at once.

The man abruptly stood up, barely a minute after he'd sat down, and without ever acknowledging us hurried away from the row and up the aisle. Maggs never saw a thing.

Enough strangeness for one night. More than enough.

But the night wasn't quite through.

For when we got back to Mrs. Torrance's, we stopped in the foyer and checked the announcement board as we always did. The usual. Lost-and-found items. Did anyone want to share a bus ride to Boston for the weekend game. Opportunities for employment.

One opportunity in particular. A listing that must have been posted only today, because I'd looked at the board yesterday and it hadn't been there.

The listing ran: "Wanted—Cleaning girl/domestic help. Part-time/light work. Apply 66 College Street, 2nd floor."

66 College Street. Home to a doorstep-hopping crow and a gentleman who wrote about individuals that were dead-but-not-quite. A gentleman who might have answers to questions I scarcely knew how to ask.

A gentleman named Howard Phillips Lovecraft.

I snatched the announcement from the board.

Maggs yawned and asked what I'd found.

"Just an opportunity to make an extra dollar or two." And just maybe, I said to myself, a chance to snoop around a murderer's den.

July 10

Walked to work this morning with Maggs. Bright sunlight through the trees on Benefit Street. Crickets already singing. Another warm day.

Maggs was still full of last night's picture show. Turns out she'd already seen it twice. "And yet I keep coming back for more," she said. "And you want to know why I get such a terrific kick out of *Chain Gang*?" (She didn't wait for me to say "Yes please tell me.") "After a show like that you can't help but feel no matter how awful the troubles you got, suddenly they don't seem so bad. Gives a girl perspective."

I had my mind on the employment listing I'd seen last night in the foyer but I did my best to pay attention.

"Take my boyfriend. Cute guy, sweet. But he has this habit. He asks me out, then forgets or something. He's stood me up two, three times, which I tell him is two or three times too many. He's got to treat a girl with dignity."

I'd heard these travails before but nodded encouragement.

"So I was gonna give him the gate but now I think I'll keep him around a while. I mean at least he's not a fugitive from a chain gang. I don't have to worry about him showing up for a date in shackles." She giggled at her own imaginings, then switched to a new topic. "Say, you got a boy?"

Without thinking I said yes then corrected myself to no. Then I said I wasn't a hundred percent sure.

"Well gosh Novalyne which is it? I mean you do or you don't."

A phrase from her companionable chatter resonated in my mind. "I was gonna give him the gate." Yes, and I had been about ready to give Bob Howard the gate too, had told him without mincing words I was worn out with his temper and vexations and moods. And a week after that, he climbed behind the wheel of his fine car and shot himself in the head.

"You got a boy?" Maggs' question lingered. How could I, with Bob dead and buried? I'd attended the funeral. And yet, the longer I'm here in the town of Providence, the surer I feel the thread between us is unbroken, is still there in some form. And that somehow that unbroken thread runs through an upstairs apartment at 66 College Street.

I stopped and turned to Maggs on the cobblestone path. "Can you do me a kindness?"

She said sure just name it. (Maggs is truly a friend.)

I said I knew we have plans to go downtown again tonight but I want her to wait for me an hour while I do something first. "I'm applying for a second job. Part time. I need the money, to send home to my ma on her farm in Brownwood, Texas." All of which was true enough.

She said why sure but what kind of job?

I told her domestic help for a Mister H. P. Lovecraft.

She all but threw a fit. "You can't do that. That man is poison."

I said I knew but I had my reasons. "I'll meet you back at Mrs. Torrance's at seven tonight. It'll be fine. I promise."

She said she sure hoped so. "But if I get worried I'll come fetch you myself from that nasty man."

At six I finished at the Athenaeum and walked around the corner from Benefit to College Street. I'd scarcely knocked before the door yielded and there in the doorway stood the man himself. How had he raced down from the second floor so fast? It was as if he'd known I was coming, and precisely when, as well. Without a word he preceded me up the stairs.

Only one room did I see on this visit, a large study with a big west-facing window offering generous views of downtown. My host sat himself by a desk near the window but didn't invite me to take a seat. He said not a word.

I glanced about. In the room's center was a long table topped in stone. Almost half the table's surface was taken up by an oblong object some two feet high that was covered by a rough burlap shroud. Beside the shrouded object was clustered an assortment of small glass vessels, flasks, retorts, alembics. The remaining table surface was taken up by scattered piles of books. In fact books lay everywhere in this study, on shelves, atop sofas and divans, spilling from stacks across the floor.

So quiet was this study, so wordless my silent host, that from another room I clearly heard the ticking of a clock.

And something else as well: a faint repetitive sound, a noise so indistinct I couldn't trace its source. Tink-tink. Tink-tink.

I gazed about, anxiety-stricken—irrationally, I told myself—by that sound. Where was it coming from?

Howard Phillips Lovecraft sat by the window, one languid arm on the desk, and fixed me with a cold, ungiving smile. I pretended not to see him stare. On the walls, framed portraits, daguerreotypes, family ancestors perhaps. And in the corner, an object I hadn't noticed: a tall coatrack. Mounted thereon was a relic of the taxidermist's art: a stuffed crow, its beak agape, its figure stooped. Its glass eye gleamed black.

I thought at once of the bird that had followed this man to the river and then up the hill to this house. Stuffed, or perhaps not? Preserved, or alive? It held so impossibly still. I stepped in for a closer look.

And then in my face a flap of wings and a great big raucous caw.

I leapt back and almost fell while my heart jumped fit to burst.

A dry chuckle from the desk. "You must forgive Kavva. He has a streak of mischief. Impish, for one so old. So very old."

The crow flapped its wings again and settled itself back onto its coatrack perch.

There: that sound again. Tink-tink. Tink-tink. Could it be coming from the bird called Kavva? But now it was as motionless as any inert toy.

My prospective employer asked if I'd come about the position. I nodded. My heart was still pounding hard from that bird's little joke.

Again: tink-tink. Tink-tink. Not quite so faint now. Louder. Mister Howard Phillips Lovecraft was saying something about how I was the very first to apply. "Commendable. This suggests an ethic I approve. A willingness to be useful."

Tink-tink. Tink-tink. Louder now. Definitely coming from within this room.

"I said you must have a name. If you would be so kind as to introduce yourself."

So distracted had I become that I almost hadn't heard his request.

I said my name was Harriet. "Harriet Hopkins." Something warned me not to entrust my name to this man and his joking crow. I said my friends call me Hattie.

"Very well. Hattie."

There. Tink-tink. Tink-tink. Even louder now, and urgent. Coming from the worktable in the center of the room.

"Hopkins. A fine distinguished New England name, worthy of our Puritan pedigree." He frowned as he stared. "But you have rather dark-complected skin, don't you, and such luxuriant black hair." Even though he sat across the room it was as if he were running his hands across my face. "Perhaps there is some Portuguese in you, or Italian."

I don't advertise my blood but I'm not ashamed of it either. I told him how my ma said the story goes by way of my grandma we might well be part Indian. I saw him stiffen. "Maybe Comanche," I added. "Best to tell you now in case that might pose a problem."

He frowned and started to say something but then seemed to change his mind. "Let me hasten to assure you it will be no problem. You will serve quite well. You will do ideally. Consider yourself hired."

But I only half heard because there it was again: tink-tink. Tink-tink. From the worktable, from the oblong thing within its burlap shroud. More urgent, ever louder. Tink-tink.

The crow cocked its head to eye me.

"Perhaps before you leave," offered H. P. Lovecraft, "you'd like to see my vivarium?"

He rose and in a few quick strides stood by the worktable. With a flourish he removed the shroud.

Before me reposed a glass tank, some two feet by four, and a bit more than two feet in height. At first glance it seemed to contain no more than forest debris—crumbly black earth, branches, leaves, and twigs, to a depth of six inches. To the side lay a small pool of water.

But in an instant I saw the source of the sound. Atop the dirt lay a small metal object. I stooped to see. "Yes, come closer," urged H. P. Lovecraft.

A metal object. Circular in shape. I bent nearer. A silver coin. An American dime, lying flat on the earth.

And then one end of the coin began to rise. Slowly, a fraction of an inch at a time, as if pushed from beneath. Uncanny; I barely suppressed a gasp.

I stooped closer. Beneath the coin, becoming visible now as the dime rose, was a pair of minuscule creatures. Bugs of some kind. Caterpillars, maybe, in color vivid lime-green, coiling and arching, pushing the silver coin upright.

I blinked in surprise at the sight. Lovecraft's voice came from right beside me. "Laborers. Toilers." He watched me as I watched them. "Yes. Workers struggling to who knows what end."

The bugs arched themselves to full height, gripped the dime in their multiple appendages. For a moment the coin wobbled, so that I saw first the winged Mercury on one side, and on the other the insignia of olive branch and rods and ax. From where I crouched the words "Liberty" and "In God We Trust" were clear to read. Even the date, 1935, and a mint mark, S for San Francisco.

Then the creatures or caterpillars or whatever they were steadied the coin between them in their wriggling arms and rammed it hard against the glass of the enclosure.

Tink-tink. And again: tink-tink.

I bent so close now my nose pressed the glass. One of the bugs fixed its gaze on my face. Red eyes that glowed. Beseeching red eyes.

"The insect world is underestimated, I think"—I'd forgotten: that horrid man Lovecraft was standing right beside me—"in its strivings, in its torments, in its dreams. Do you ever wonder, Miss, ah, Hattie, of what do insects dream?"

I said nothing. My attention was all on the bug.

Tink-tink. Again the bugs tapped with the dime. Another coiled effort of massed caterpillar arms. Tink-tink.

And still that one bug looked up at me. Red eyes. Beseeching red eyes.

Sending a tap-tap message. Pleading for help.

Tink-tink.

And then disaster. The silver coin wobbled; the bugs scrabbled, straining mightily to keep the thing upright. Flailing feelers, waving antennae, a last flare of red eyes, and then the dime toppled, Mercury head up, ax and rods down. Both bugs were trapped beneath as the coin hit the earth.

Green fluid squirted and spattered the glass.

I feel foolish writing this, but I confess I may have screamed.

A sudden pounding at the door downstairs.

Placidly my host refitted the burlap shroud atop the vivarium. "Ah well. Such is aspiration. In the insect world as in the human, not always crowned with success." He gave a little smile.

I dashed to the window, darted a glance down, and to my relief, saw Maggs Johnson waving worriedly up at me from the street.

I must have said goodbye—I can't recall—just knew I had to flee. The crow cawed and the man said something as I rushed from the room and descended the stairs and burst out from that house.

Before Maggs could say a word I squeezed her hard in a grateful hug.

"I think I could go for a ginger ale," I said, and propelled us both downhill.

July 11

Early Saturday morning, and most of the tenants at Mrs. Torrance's afford themselves the pleasure of sleeping late.

But not I. A hot sleepless night. I lay thinking of Bob, of those bugs. Red beseeching eyes. What did they want?

No use lying in bed. I put on a housecoat, wandered the hall, sat in the foyer with nothing to do.

I gazed about, restless. A wallpaper design of tropical parrots. Cheery plumage, red, blue, and green. Green like those bugs. Like the one that—and again I admit this is nonsense—stared straight at me. What did it want with those big bulbous eyes? A creature on the cusp of speech. I teach elocution, and back in Cross Plains many's the voiceless student I've coached. "Everyone has the words," I tell them. "Search your heart, breathe in deep, let the speech come out with your breath. Ask yourself: What is it you most want to say?"

The foyer felt cold. I eyed the wallpaper again. The parrots were mute. Or maybe a message: "Just go back to bed."

Which I did. Again I lay wide awake. Something returned to my mind that Lovecraft had said in that horrible room, something I'd only half heard at first: "Those creatures are pawns in a game. A serious game, that I play for great stakes. Chess, at cosmic scale. Knights, rooks, and pawns: I can afford to sacrifice them all. They'll simply be replaced by yet more that I'll find."

Enough. I got up, washed my face and dressed, slipped out the door.

Absolute quiet on Benefit Street. No destination; I just wanted to think. Found myself descending the hill, walking the riverbank where that dreadful man had paused with his crow. A breeze blew and rippled the water in waves.

Bob Howard always said he liked the waves in my hair. Hair Indian black he said.

He brought up that point every so often. I fired back "So what if I do have Indian blood?"

"Girl I think you look swell. It's just that"—I remember so clearly his saying this—"people got to stick with their kind. Not go mixing. But here I am mixing with you."

I came back at him. "People I can stand to talk to, those are the ones that make up my kind."

Bob said he'd have to puzzle over that.

"Well keep puzzling Mister Robert E. Howard. But even though you're so twisted up, I see something in you. Even with those many moods and melancholies of yours."

I recall Bob's admiring look. "Say, you're all right. You're a gal that's got sand. You've got the grit to see a thing through."

So clear was his voice it was as if he stood beside me now by the Providence River.

Hard to accept he was gone.

"Three-quarters dead. Dead-but-not-quite." What had Lovecraft meant by those words?

Back up to Benefit, and Mrs. Dexter had just unlocked the Athenaeum's entrance. "Well, Miss Price, you're certainly up and about with the dawn." I told her I'd been unable to sleep and asked if I might sit downstairs for an hour before the start of the morning shift.

Mrs. Dexter is generally stern and I was expecting her to say no you just make yourself useful. But she nodded understandingly and said I had plenty of time before nine o'clock. "There's a couch down there. It's comfortable. You go right ahead."

I took the stairs slowly. Felt worn away, tired.

My plan was head to the couch, put my feet up an hour, try not to think.

But at the foot of the stairs the first thing I saw was the Egyptian Cabinet. And there, by the wood surface I'd seen that awful man fondle, the door at the west end of the coffer stood ajar.

This was odd.

I stepped to the cabinet. One of the drawers within had been opened, even if by only an inch.

I pulled it out all the way.

Within I found something. A bit of circular metal.

A coin. Nothing more than a dime.

I picked it up. The head of Mercury. Stamped with the date of issue, 1935. And S for the place of minting, San Francisco.

The same as the dime in the vivarium. Coincidence?

I turned the coin about. The familiar image: olive branch and ax. Except the ax on this coin was thick with green slime.

Green blood.

The blood of my Bob.

Yes. It had to be. The blood of my Bob.

Call me crazed. But if readers ever see these words I defy them to go through what I have and think any different.

I staggered to the couch, sat heavily with my head in my hands. Three-quarters dead? Yesterday, somehow, I had seen him die—again—but this time before my very eyes. Crushed flat by a dime, with no company but another bug.

So much for my fine plans, such as they were. The Greyhound and train up from Texas, the scheme to be a domestic and spy on H.P. Lovecraft, to interrogate him and learn why he'd written those letters to hound Bob to pull the trigger. And now this business with the bugs. And all for naught. I'd learned nothing. Get Howard Phillips Lovecraft to yield information? He was too hard, too opaque, too in control. Might as well try to pry talk from his crow.

Came the thought: I've failed; and I threw myself face down on the couch.

He's dead. This was my one thought. Not just three-quarters. But well and truly gone. Dead. I can never go back to that wretched room on College Street. I may as well give notice at the Athenaeum, pack up, and go home. Back to Cross Plains and try to put together the broken parts of my heart. Of my life.

I must have slept. For at once I dreamed, and in the dream I was visited by my own dear Bob. Except Bob came to me as a bug. Wounded, gouged in its thorax, from which a green fluid bled. But still very much alive. That was what counted. Still very much alive.

The bug stared up at me with bulging bright eyes. Eyes that beseeched me. And a mouth that was voiceless. But wanted to speak.

In the dream I told the bug to take its time: "I'm an elocution coach and I can help." I told it everyone has the words.

The eyes beseeched. The mouth moved without a sound.

I said "Take your time. I'm a teacher. I've coached all kinds of pupils. Search your heart, breathe in deep, let the speech come out with your breath. What do you most want to say?"

In the dream I leaned in close and the bug opened wide its mouth.

Nothing. But then a sound, faint at first. Nothing more than this: tink-tink. Tink-tink.

"Enunciate more clearly," I said. "What do you most want to say?"

The bug oozed green slime, opened its mouth wider.

And this time I could hear the words.

"Please stay. Don't go."

"Please stay. Don't go."

The bug oozed more slime, and the voice grew fainter. Tink-tink. Tink-tink.

I woke from the couch with a start.

And now I knew just what to do.

Upstairs in a flash, where I sought out my supervisor, asked her to confirm that Saturdays at the Athenaeum we work only a half day.

"That's right, Miss Price. You can use the afternoon to rest and relax."

I said, "Actually, Mrs. Dexter, for this afternoon I have alternative plans. I've taken part-time employment as a domestic just around the corner. At 66 College Street."

"Oh yes." Mrs. Dexter smiled. "With that interesting eccentric gentleman. Mister Lovecraft."

"That's right," I agreed. Inwardly I said "And you just watch out, Mister Howard Phillips Lovecraft. And you too Mister Kavva the crow. Because this gal has got sand. Plus the grit to see a thing through."

18

"Whew." Fay MacConnell put away her phone. "That stuff is pretty far out there."

"I wonder." Joseph Bonaventure was patting at his head again with an Angelo's napkin.

"Wonder what?"

"Just wondering if there could be a connection between that bug we found in the cabinet drawer and those bugs Novalyne Price says she saw in Lovecraft's apartment."

"Wait. You talk as if you take all this seriously, all this stuff she wrote."

"Sure I do. Don't you?"

"Maybe. Not really. Don't know." She pulled out her pack of Camels. *No more than one a day, girlfriend, and you've already had yours.* Regretfully she put away the pack. "I mean maybe your Novalyne Price was trying to imitate her sweetheart Robert E. Howard, King of the Pulps. Maybe she wanted to go him one better with a yarn of her own. In diary form. An homage, or whatever you call it."

"No, no. That can't be." Half the time the things this Mister Twitch said he tended to mumble. But now he grew strident. "What Novalyne Price wrote was out-and-out serious. No fantasy, no make-believe. I can feel it. I'm one hundred percent sure."

The tone grated on her. How many times had she had to listen to guys in her life, boyfriends of various kinds, hold forth and say they knew it all and were one hundred percent sure. Not that this twitchy grad student with the pizza sauce in his hair could ever qualify for the status of boyfriend. Not in a thousand years.

He was still carrying on. "I mean, I'm as sure of what she wrote as I am about what I saw in the Providence River last weekend. That underwater swimmer-thing with red eyes. Pretty sure, anyway." His voice faltered. "I mean, I saw it just for a second. Nothing much more than a glimpse with all that mud stirred up."

Then he regained confidence. "But hey it spat out your earring-piece at my feet, and now you've got it back, and that's pretty good by way of rock-solid proof."

"Please don't start in again on your little swimmer-thing."

"It wasn't little. It was a good six feet long."

"Listen." She was losing patience. "If you actually saw a red-eyed six-foot something swimming in the Providence River Saturday night, and if what Novalyne Price wrote is even halfway true, then I'm not sure what constitutes the real world anymore."

"Join the club. I have those doubts every day."

They would have argued more but an interruption intruded.

"Hey babes long time no see."

Standing before them was someone Fay MacConnell knew all too well. A big individual, bulky and broad; he scratched at his paunch and slurped a Monster Energy drink as he waved a hello. Boardshorts in Day-Glo orange; an open aloha shirt over a Jurassic Park T-shirt. A tattoo on his neck of Jimi Hendrix in concert. Pale wavy ginger hair dangling down past his shoulders; a jutting bushy beard plaited in ginger dreadlocks.

He bent over her where she sat, offered a sloppy knowing grin. "Well aintcha gonna say hi and introduce me to your friend?"

"This is Jeff Boudreau." *I can't believe this is happening.* "My ex-fiancé."

"Ex-shit. You were never my fiancée. We had some laughs is all."

She nodded to Bonaventure. "You can already get some idea why we split up."

Before the grad student could say anything Boudreau cut in. "You forget, babes. These days I prefer to go by Treff. Treff as in Jeff the T-Rex. T-Rex as in Tyrannosaur. Got my own band now. Treff and the Raptors. A cool name, huh? Treff as in Tyrannosaur, cuz I'm an apex predator. Spin you on your head-ator. Smack you so you're dead-ator."

"Okay, Treff. We get the idea. You're a cool hip-hop artist now. Or wannabe rap star. Or whatever." Her throat went dry, and she suddenly, desperately, needed a smoke.

"Wannabe?" His indignation boomed so loud passersby on the quad turned to get a look. "I'm the top of the food chain, babes. Tip of the spear. Large and in charge."

Large and in charge. How that carried her back. Her dad used to describe himself that way too when she was a little girl. "I'm large and in charge and I'm going to take my princess for a ride." He'd been a big guy with a big merry voice. She loved the attention then and had missed being fussed over ever since he abruptly disappeared from her life.

Living proof, this Treff Boudreau, of her tendency to choose poorly when it came to men. *Of course I have a long history of this. I get picked up by guys who say they're large and in charge but they're just full of crap.* She suddenly remembered a college creative writing class where the instructor had asked everyone to jot down their thoughts about true romance. She'd written "In my roadrunner sprint down the highway of life my love-lusts have been nothing but fender benders, sideswipes, and breakdown-lane busts." Trying to say something positive, the instructor had praised her for her "automotive creativity." Looking glumly at Treff, she mentally posted an addendum to her old essay: *How about this, Professor? My latest tower-of-power was worse than a hundred-car pileup at Friday rush hour.*

She'd slipped so far into the past she missed some of what Treff was saying. "Dude. I know you. Joey B, right?" He blinked, belched, stared agape at Joseph Bonaventure. The grad student curled as if he hoped to crawl away through the grass.

"Babes, you know who you're dating?"

Fay tried to point out they weren't in fact dating. Treff was so excited he didn't give her a chance.

"Dude, I seen you perform five, maybe six times, when your band was still based in Rhode Island. At the Providence Mouthpiece before it closed down. I was just a kid then, years and years ago. But you. You were the Senior Statesman of Rock. Friggin' indisputable. Uncrowned kinga New England." Fay was astonished: the expression on Treff's face was one of openmouthed, reverent awe. "Course that was before you went on the road. California. L.A." Through all this Bonaventure said nothing.

"But what's with the tweed coat? You could almost be a respectable citizen. And your hair, man. It's gone short. You used to wear it longer'n I do." He laughed. "You shoulda seen him, babes. Hair down to his ass. Righteous."

He slurped more Monster drink and flashed at Bonaventure a conspiratorial we're-in-on-this-together grin. "Dude. You still got those tats inked up and down your arms? I'll bet you do. 'Girlie you look like the Queen of Diamonds.'" He turned back to Fay. "Babes, that's from his all-time best hit. Definitely numero uno." He threw back his head and bellowed out across the campus lawn:

> Girlie you look like the Queen of Diamonds
> Burning your cigarettes right down to the bone.

Treff offered Fay an explanatory aside. "My favorite lines from my favorite song of his. But babes you shoulda seen him and his group in concert. Man how he packed 'em in. Crowd would go nuts. High school cuties in miniskirts throwing themselves at the stage. That so totally rocked."

Bonaventure murmured, "It was something I did on the side. To pay the bills in grad school. At least until ..."

Treff interrupted. "But dude you did okay. You got outta this lousy city. Outta this lousy state. You got out and seen the world."

"Yeah. I saw the world." Bonaventure patted his head with a napkin.

"Don't know why you'd ever come back to a place like this. Cuz dude you'd made it. You so totally rocked. You did okay." Treff belched again, more softly this time, as his face took on something approximating thoughtful recollection. "Okay, at least till all that shit happened. I read about that."

In response Joseph Bonaventure flinched as if he'd been stung. Apparently Treff hadn't noticed. He nattered on. "But dude the way those girls were all over you. Just swarming the stage. Awesome."

Fay abruptly stood up. "I'm sure you two boys have lots to discuss. Me, I should've been back at work half an hour ago." She strode off without goodbyes.

"Babes, did I say something?" Treff flapped his arms wide to ask the world, "Hey what's the problem with her?"

Bonaventure trailed in her wake but she fiercely waved him off. "No." He persisted for half a block. She spun and faced him. "No." *Damn*, came the thought. *I really need another smoke.*

"But couldn't we collaborate on that manuscript, talk about Novalyne Pr—"

"No." She wheeled and walked faster.

As she descended College Street she glanced once over her shoulder. He stood in the street, looking crushed, looking squished, like a bug under a Mercury dime.

As she stormed down the hill to Benefit she realized that bad as it was, seeing Treff Boudreau hadn't been the worst of her morning. Being reminded of the hundred-car pileup of her life was of course ugly. But she realized she also felt disappointed.

Despite her disagreements with Joseph Bonaventure, and his obsession with that underwater thing he claimed he'd seen, and his general pizza-tufted messiness, she'd actually been enjoying his company. They'd actually been able to talk. At least until Treff Boudreau came along and peeled away a layer of Mister Twitch's past that made the two men begin to look much too much alike. "Girlie you look like the Queen of Diamonds": What kind of guy inks his arms with words like that?

Such thoughts preoccupied her throughout the afternoon. It wasn't her best day at work. Luckily Nancy seemed to sense her distractedness and gave her the easiest chores to do.

It was with relief that Fay MacConnell punched out at six and walked home amid the surging end-of-day crowd. She felt a sense of welcome and escape every time she entered her building, the Westminster Arcade in the heart of downtown. She liked the Arcade's age, its two centuries of history, its Greek Revival columns, the fact that her man Poe had often passed by this place—she could feel it, she was sure of it—on his way to woo Sarah Helen Whitman at the Athenaeum.

"Dupin, I'm home." Dupin was her cat, a fierce tom she'd gotten from the rescue who hated all humans except Fay alone. They shared a bare-bones one-room apartment, 225 square feet, on the floor overlooking the shops in the Arcade's atrium.

Pets weren't allowed but she'd listed Dupin as a service feline. Which wasn't much of a stretch, considering how hard it often was for Fay just to make it through her day. And the thought of her cat rubbing up against her in welcome, just like he was doing now, gave her something every day to look forward to, definitely helped her mental health.

She toasted two slices of Wonder Bread, diced a cucumber, popped open a can of tuna. She pulled blueberry yoghurt from her mini-fridge and on impulse decided she'd also have Cheerios. (Sometimes she'd eat them for breakfast and then have another helping for supper but that was the advantage of life alone with a cat: there was no one to say she couldn't have cereal twice in a day.)

They curled up on the couch that doubled as a bed and watched TV and shared the tuna. "Guess what, Dupes? Remember that earring stud I lost last weekend? Well, some crazy man found it for me. The same guy who'd torn it off." On impulse she drew the stud from her pocket, fitted it to her ear. "There. Good to have it back."

The stud itched a bit in her ear, something it had never done before. So glad was she to have it back she scarcely noticed.

Worn out from the day's work and from all her strange encounters, she reached for a notebook and pen she always kept by her couch. Vacantly she jotted, then cast aside unread what she'd written.

The cat sat in her lap. While the TV buzzed she plucked a paperback from the book pile that lay mounded at the foot of the bed. *Complete Poems of Poe.* She leafed through the pages, came to "The Conqueror Worm":

> Lo! 'tis a gala night
> Within the lonesome latter years!
> An angel throng, bewinged, bedight
> In veils, and drowned in tears,
> Sit in a theatre, to see
> A play of hopes and fears,
> While the orchestra breathes fitfully
> The music of the spheres . . .

She read the familiar lines and remembered: Twitch said he too liked "The Conqueror Worm." She wondered which stanzas he especially favored. *I should have asked.*

Again the sensation. The stud itched a bit in her ear. Unthinking, unknowing, she reached once more for her journal. Additional scrawling. Words unspooled from the tip of the pen.

Pen and notebook slipped from bed to floor.

"Whew. I'm just too tired to read." She put aside the poetry volume and patted the cat's head. They surfed TV channels until they found an old Brad Pitt movie. *Seven Years in Tibet.* "Dupes, why can't all guys be as sweet as luscious Brad? I just get the weird ones."

A third time the itch. Absently she scratched her ear, touched the ear-stud. At once, unbidden, pen and paper found their way once more into her hands. The cat rubbed its head against her knee to signal it wanted more attention. No success. The woman kept writing. Eyes closed, breathing erratic, she scrawled words across the page, slowly at first, then faster. From the foot of the couch the cat watched the pen move to and fro.

The pen stopped.

The woman blinked and flinched and opened her eyes.

Fay MacConnell came back to herself.

"Sorry, Dupes. Must've nodded off."

Slack in her hand lay the notebook. "Hey. What're these notes?" She studied the fresh scrawling:

> The weight of sword and scabbard
> A hot Sahara sun.
>
> Warnings from a statue.
> Tears trickle down a carved stone face.
>
> Fangs drip blood.
> They drip.
> Winged cobras seek a victim,
> Seek to feed.

"Whew. Crazy stuff. Don't remember writing any of this. Musta done it half-asleep." She felt a sudden shiver. "Talk about disordered thinking. Guess that's what comes of mixing 'The Conqueror Worm' with Cheerios and tuna."

She reached over to her roommate. "C'mere Dupes and give your mom a hug. I could use some reassurance." The cat obliged by curling onto her lap.

"That's better. Yeah." She yawned and put her head back. The TV muttered a companionable murmur. She fell asleep still wearing the earring.

Dupin the cat, as the only other soul in the room, was also the only individual to witness what happened once Fay had fallen asleep.

The stud in her ear began to glow red. The stud that had been mouthed by the Providence River swimmer known as Spike-Head.

19

Father James Cypriano, S.J., was writing at his desk in the rectory of Saint Francis Xavier Church—a last jotting of thoughts before tea and bed—when there came an unexpected knock at the door.

Unexpected, but not that unusual. As one of the few priests on duty at FX (as parishioners affectionately called it), he was accustomed to requests for help at all hours.

"I know it's late. But you said I should feel free to drop by anytime." Standing in the doorway was Gladys Trevor, pastor of the First Baptist Church downtown. "So tonight I'm idling about and at loose ends and thought I'd take you up on your offer and invite myself in."

"Glad you did." The priest waved her into the rectory parlor. Pastor Trevor was no-nonsense and ferociously well organized in her management of time, not one to drop by aimlessly at ten P.M. So he doubted she'd simply been idling about. Chances were she had something important—and urgent—on her mind; and he calculated it wouldn't take long to come out.

He said he'd been just about to put on the kettle when she knocked. "Earl Grey? Oolong?"

She asked if he had any chamomile.

"Chamomile it is."

Pastor Trevor glanced at his desk. "Let me guess. Writing a sermon."

"Yup. About half-done."

"That reminds me. I've still got mine to write for Sunday." She looked about the room. "Say. I want to rest my feet. And this here is one tiny chair for my considerable bulk. How about asking me if I'd like to sit on that comfy couch over there?"

"Help yourself. I'll squeeze my own considerable heft into the chair."

With the tea poured and a tray of cookies laid out—"Pepperidge Farm is all I have at short notice," he apologized—Father Cypriano sat quietly and waited.

"Think I'll try this mint-and-chocolate number," she decided as she took an offering from the tray. "There." She settled into the sofa and saluted him with her tea mug. "Cheers." Nibbling her cookie, she made small talk and asked about parish activities at FX. Then she put down her cup and ran a hand through her hair. She wore it in long intricately braided cornrows gathered over one shoulder.

"And if I know my Father Jim, he's probably asking himself why the pastor of First Baptist is showing up at his door at ten o'clock at night."

"Not at all. I'm just glad for the pleasure of your company."

"Which shows what a sweet man you are. Well. I believe you're already aware of my research into the ministry and life of Roger Williams." Gladys Trevor's interest made sense, given her own ministry. The First Baptist congregation over which she presided had originally been established back in 1638 by none other than Williams himself. Cypriano had worked alongside Trevor on many projects—civil rights, interfaith dialogue, the Providence Homeless Coalition—and he knew these were all endeavors of which the seventeenth-century preacher would have approved. For Williams had fled to Rhode Island from the Puritan intolerance of the Massachusetts Bay Colony. What he'd sought: "soul liberty," a haven for those "distressed of conscience," individuals like Williams who were being persecuted for their beliefs, whether as Quakers, Catholics, or freethinkers.

"One second." Cypriano darted into the rectory kitchenette and reappeared with more food on a tray—cheese, grapes, a package of crackers.

"Triscuits," she enthused. "I love those."

"I should lay them out on a plate. Dress things up a bit for you."

"Just let me eat them straight out of the box," she countered, "and then I'll feel right at home."

"Wheatberry Clusters." He read from the package. "New flavor. Supposedly healthy." He grimaced.

"Of course the healthy thing," she shot back, "would be to admit we're both well into our sixties and this late at night we shouldn't be eating anything at all. And instead here we are." She took a bite of her Triscuit.

"Amen, Reverend. Now where were we?"

"Roger Williams."

"Right. Your research. You've found some unpublished text? Something interesting?"

"Yes. Something, and somebody. A trio of somebodies. And strange cases, all three."

"You've got me intrigued."

"Okay, let me show you the text first. Then I'll tell you about this trio I had to deal with." She asked if he was familiar with a book published by Williams called *A Key into the Language of America.*

"I've heard of it."

"Something he wrote in 1643. Researchers specializing in Williams are familiar with it. He'd studied the local dialects spoken by Native Americans and wanted to share with other colonists what he'd learned. He wanted to convert the local tribes to Christianity but he also respected their customs and was frankly fascinated by their culture. And he wanted other colonists to see the locals as he did, as fellow children of God. You can get a sense of how widely his interests ranged from the subtitle of his book. Here. Take a look."

From a handbag she withdrew a small volume and laid it beside the cookie tray on the sofa. Opening the book to page one, she read aloud its title in a rich sonorous voice:

> A Key into the Language of America, or An Help to the Language of the Natives in that part of America called New England. Together with brief Observations of the Customs, Manners and Worships &c. of the aforesaid Natives, in Peace and War, in Life and Death. To which are added Spiritual Observations, General and Particular by the Author, of chief and special use (upon all occasions) to all the English Inhabiting those parts; yet pleasant and profitable to the view of all men.

She lifted her head from the text and smiled. "Now *that's* what I call a book title. Rambling, freewheeling, leisurely in style—part of why I love reading this man and everything he wrote. But that's not why I'm here tonight eating your cookies and Triscuits."

She reminded Cypriano that for years she'd been working on a biography of Williams and checking the usual sources—"the Athenaeum, the Providence Public Library, the Rhode Island Historical Society"—to see if she could find any texts that had been overlooked by other scholars. "Nothing much. But then it occurred to me to check the Westminster Arcade."

"You mean that renovated building on Weybosset Street? The one that has a gallery with shops on the ground floor and micro-apartments for rent on the upper two stories?"

"The very one. Back in the 1820s or so, the Athenaeum got its start in downtown Providence, storing its books and renting a reading room in the Arcade. When the new Athenaeum building was opened on College Hill in 1838, the books were transferred from the Arcade. Researchers have always assumed that nothing of interest remained downtown."

"But they assumed wrong."

"You got it. Of course for many years in the twentieth century the Arcade had been shuttered and out of business—no shops, no customers, just an empty shell. But once the Arcade reopened, not so very long ago, I contacted the new owners and asked them to let me visit the old reading room on the ground floor. The manager told me there were no books in there, nothing of interest at all, just a few pieces of beat-up furniture that were going to be hauled away as trash. 'Not worth your time,' he said. I said could I just take a peek. He said all right but I'd best hurry because a truck was coming the very next morning to clear everything out."

The priest paused in mid-cookie-bite and sat up in his chair. "But you got there in time?"

"I most certainly did. Five o'clock, almost closing time for the Arcade, with the manager pointing at his watch saying I'd have to hurry. And in that reading room, amid all the cobwebs and dust"—*No question,* thought Cypriano, *this woman is gifted at holding an audience's attention*—"inside a broken-legged desk—one of those roll-top cylinder numbers, you know what I mean?—in a concealed closet-compartment, I found"—and here she reached once more into her handbag—"this little thing."

With a flourish she displayed two sheets of paper. "Of course these are just photocopies," she explained. "I've donated the originals to the Athenaeum, and the supervisor there, what's his name, Tristram Schaefer, that's it, he's promised not to give anyone else access till I've published them. Just two pages, but my Lord, they have something to say."

She said the pages in question seemed to be an unpublished fragment of Williams' *Key into the Language of America*. "In his own hand, mind you, part of his chapter on Native American religious beliefs. But it contains information—information relating to his own personal spiritual experiences—that for some reason or other never found its way into the published edition."

"New data on Roger Williams' personal spiritual life? For Rhode Islanders in our line of work, you can't get much more intriguing than that."

"Well. I wouldn't come knocking at your door at ten o'clock at night unless I had something good."

The priest gestured eagerly at the text she held in her hand. "So what does it say?"

"You know that famous 'What cheer, Netop' moment in Williams' life?"

"Sure. He's been condemned as a heretic by the Puritans in Boston and spends weeks as a fugitive in the forest before camping out on the east shore of the Seekonk. After which he paddles across the river till he comes to the spot called Slate Rock. There he sees a group of Narragansett Indians standing around and he wonders how they're going to treat him. Then they give him the 'What cheer' greeting that lets him know they're hospitable and he's going to be okay. From there he paddles around Fox Point and up the Providence River." He could have added that he himself thought of Roger Williams in his canoe every time the Riverglow crew was out on the very same river, joining Jim Cypriano in stoking the braziers to light up the night. *Separated from Williams by less than four centuries*, came the thought, *a mere exhalation of Spirit in God's sense of time, a motif I hope to work into my new sermon somehow*—but he refrained from voicing the thought so as to allow Reverend Trevor to have her say.

"You got that right," she replied. "But now just give a listen to what Williams has to offer in this unpublished version I found. He's inserted what seems to be a personal reminiscence into his discussion of Native American beliefs. Do you mind if I read this aloud?"

"Not at all. I love your voice. You know on some Sundays I stop by the First Baptist just to hear you preach."

"I've said it already. You're a sweet man. Well. Here goes." And then she read aloud the text:

> He that questions whether God made the World, the Indians will teach him. I must acknowledge I have received in my converse with them many Confirmations of those two great points, viz: 1. That God is. 2. That He is a rewarder of all them that diligently seek Him.
>
> But thereupon comes Misery into the Indian Faith. First, they branch their God-head into many gods. Secondly, they attribute it to Creatures. First, many gods: they have given me the Names of thirty-seven, all which in their solemn Worships they invocate: as Kautantowwit the great South-West God, to whose House all souls go, and from whom come their Corn, Beans, &c., as they say.
>
> Even as the Papists have their He and She Saint Protectors, as Saint George, Saint Patrick, Saint Denis, Virgin Mary &c., so too do the Natives have Squauanit, the Women's Deity. Muckquachuckquand, the Children's Deity &c.

At this Father Cypriano interrupted with a chuckle. "So he sees us Catholics as having something in common with Native American religion. I like that. I like that a lot."

She smiled in reply and then affected a tone of rebuke. "Just you let me keep reading." She sipped chamomile and resumed:

> Secondly, so worship they too the Creatures in whom they conceive doth rest some Deity, as Paumpagussit, the Sea; Yotaanit, the Fire-God. Supposing that Deities be in these, &c.
>
> When I have argued with them about their Fire-God: say they, Can it be but this fire must be a God, or Divine power, that out of a stone will arise in a Spark? And when a poor naked Indian is ready to starve with cold in the House, and especially in the Woods, often saves his life, doth dress all our Food for us? And if it be angry will burn the House about us, yea if a spark fall into the dry wood, burns up the Country?
>
> And in truth I privately applaud their acuity of Vision:
> *Presentem narrat quaelibet herba Deum*—
> "Every little Grass doth tell,
> The sons of Men, there God doth dwell."

And here, in recording their converse about Yotaanit the Fire Deity, I am minded of an incident that befell me when first I fled the Massachusetts colony in a bitter January, knowing neither bed nor bread for fourteen weeks.

For I awoke one dawn by the shore of the river called Seekonk to behold a Sight wondrous: Sublimities of radiance, descending from the Heavens. Most like unto six-winged Angels, wherefore I named them Seraphim, as doth tell us the Prophet, Is. vi.2. In alighting they did brush lightly an Oak, which at once was consumed all in Flame, and I grew afraid. But as if in Sorrow and Penitence for what they had done all unknowing, they turned to the Tree and lo!, I saw it renewed, its stump that was withered now a strong Trunk, its Limbs sprouting with green Leaves that yielded a promise of verdant Spring.

Then turned they to me and did dip and bow with Curtsies most gracious and formal, so that by their kindness of Presence I knew them to be Envoys of our own Father of Mercies and His Son our Lord Jesus Christ. And thus reassured I did return their Salute and bade them fair Welcome and spoke to them saying I must perforce journey westward across this River and entrust myself to Providential Care.

And so saying I did embark in my Craft and set forth onto the Water. And as I did so the radiance of these Seraphim diminished so that they dwindled from my View. And yet knew I well that though solitary in my journey I would not be alone.

And thus came I to the western Shore till I spied on a great Rock a gathering of Natives who gave no sign as I neared. In greeting I lifted my oar and wondered mightily if they would present me a Countenance of Peace or of War.

Then one of their number broke silence and raised high his hand and with a Demeanour most cordial spoke forth and said What Cheer Netop. And how greatly encouraged was I (giving thanks to the Lord God in my heart) to hear that word Netop (for every Exile in a strange land doth long to hear the word Friend) commingled with the familiar What Cheer.

And even as we hailed each the other, another of their Number (whom I surmised by his garb to be a Priest) began to agitate his limbs and point, not at me but as it were beyond my right Shoulder. And as he did so he broke into a laborious bodily service, unto Sweatings, and spent himself in strange Antick Gestures, and Actions even unto fainting. And again and again he cried out in a loud Voice, saying "Manitou-wock Manitou-wock." Which in their tongue is to say They are gods that attend him, they are gods that attend him.

"And that's it." Reverend Trevor replaced the sheets in her bag. "That's all we have. But this business about Williams encountering those beings he calls Seraphs, and how a Narragansett priest identified them as Manitou or 'gods': none of that is in any of the published sources."

"Congratulations. This will be a nice addition to your biography." Jim Cypriano nodded at the tray of cookies. "Just wish I had something more than Pepperidge Farm to offer by way of recognition."

She leaned forward and grabbed the box of crackers. "Another Triscuit or two will be recognition enough." She ate in silence a moment. "But interesting as it all is, this unpublished text isn't the main reason I dropped by tonight."

"So that group of individuals you referred to as the trio is what you mostly wanted to tell me about?"

"Father, you read my mind. The trio, and how they reacted—or more precisely, how one of them reacted—when they walked in on me and I let them read this text."

"Wait. You let a group of strangers get a look at this manuscript discovery before you've published it?"

"I know, I know. Kinda dumb, right?" She crunched another cracker. "Well. Let me tell you how it happened. It all started when the three of them dropped by unannounced at my office at First Baptist."

Three of them, she repeated, a woman and two men, all very young, all dressed exactly the same. "Polo shirts and chinos. Gray and bland and blah. Same hair styles, too, straight shoulder-length. And they all wore little lapel pins too with tiny lettering but I didn't have my bifocals on so it was hard to read. The three of them struck me as a little strange, but hey no business of mine."

They'd asked if they could have a tour of the church. "Or rather, she asked. The two young men did just about no talking at all. She said her name was Alicia Wheatley and she was a spiritual quester. She'd heard about what an important and wonderful historic church I had here and she said she'd be so grateful if I could take a minute to show them around."

First Baptist had its own cadre of volunteer guides and normally the pastor didn't give tours but it had been near the end of the day and the last of the guides had just left for home. "So I said sure I'll give you folks a quick look-round and just step this way."

At first Gladys had found young Alicia quite charming. "She laid it on, you know? We walked around the church and she kept hitting that religious-quest theme. Said she'd been spiritually adrift for years, seeking God, often in the wrong places, but hoping to find a mentor, some wise older person. Said she'd heard about Roger Williams, how he'd been a seeker too, and now here she was, the very congregation he'd founded, and gosh I was so nice to show them about." Gladys shook her head. "She played me, you know? Pure flattery. But hey my profession is spiritual guidance, and I was so pleased she took such an interest." Even though, the pastor added, it was a little curious how the two young men kept silent throughout the whole tour.

"Anyway, I showed them the usual sights. Outdoors, the Georgian architecture and the 185-foot-tall steeple, still in place since 1775. Indoors, the main auditorium, with the box pews and a big pulpit in place of an altar. The Palladian windows and the fluted columns, with each column the solid trunk of an oak. I showed them how some of the columns had cracked over the centuries from alternating extreme spells of heat and cold. Impressive and interesting stuff, if I say so myself. But after about twenty minutes I started to get the feeling my guests weren't really listening. This Alicia kept glancing every which way as I talked, just saying *Uh-huh uh-huh* and staring off in one direction and then another, as if she were looking for something inside my church and was disappointed she couldn't find it. And the two young men just watched her and looked where she looked and paid no attention to me. It started to feel strange, if you know what I mean."

"Plenty strange," agreed the Jesuit.

"The worst of it was when I was telling them the history of First Baptist. I told them how in the old days the Blacks and the Native Americans and the colored freedmen all had to sit segregated in an upstairs gallery, cramped in what they called 'pigeon holes' way up high and far away from the comfortable pew-seats downstairs where all the white folks sat. And I said what I usually say on these tours, how as an African American I like to remember this history because if the good Lord had assigned me to live in the eighteenth century instead of the twenty-first, I'd have been cooped up in that pigeon's hole too instead of being allowed to fly high and rule the squawking roost—and don't you smile at me Father Jim just because of that extended metaphor I use—from my very own pulpit."

She frowned at the memory. "Usually when I talk about all that I get some kind of response. Questions, requests for more information. But nothing from those three. Zip. Finally this young lady stops dead and stares at me and says, 'But no statues in this place, no icons, no crucifix, no cross.' Just like that. Like she's disappointed. So I tell her, 'Darling, this is a Protestant congregation. For crucifixes and statues, you'd best look into a Catholic establishment. Like Saint Francis Xavier, over in the neighborhood called Federal Hill.' And this Alicia turns to the young men and says, 'Saint Francis Xavier. Federal Hill. Make a note.' And the two young men hurry to pull out their phones and start typing away. Silent. Like zombies. Then they go back to gazing at her like they're waiting for her next command."

At which point, continued Gladys, Alicia asked a question the pastor had never encountered before. Didn't First Baptist have anything in the way of apotropaia?

"Apotropaia?" interrupted the Jesuit, leaning forward in his chair in a sharp show of interest. "As in things to ward off evil?"

"Which is precisely what I asked this young lady," agreed Reverend Trevor. "And she looks me right in the eye and says 'That's just what I mean. Consecrated things. Holy-water things. Things that pack power. Things that pack punch.' Well. I told her straight off First Baptist isn't into holy water or consecrating objects and I say to myself *Well now. This is more my buddy Jim Cypriano's turf.* And I told her that, which maybe I shouldn't have, because now I suspect she's going to be headed your way."

The priest smiled and quietly said he'd served twenty-plus years as a missionary overseas and had had his share of strange visitors and would do what he could to take this new batch in stride.

"Which is another thing I like about you. You do take things in stride. You're a calming presence, you and your Triscuits. In fact I'll take another before I go." She consulted her watch. "My word. It's getting late."

She lifted her bag and stood up to leave but then turned to her host. "Oh yes. Almost forgot. After all that off-putting talk about apotropaic objects and 'things that pack power' let me tell you I was ready to kiss that trio goodbye. But right after that, this Alicia Wheatley seemed to sense she'd overstepped bounds and tried to charm me again with a tale of her errant youth. How the kind of life she'd led as a child and young teen had made her sometimes confused, how she'd frequently become spiritually lost, how grateful she was that I'd given them this tour, and how she could tell I'd be a wonderful mentor and could we just sit in my office and talk for a bit. Well. I was plenty tired and I should've just shooed them all out. But as I said: she knew how to play me. So foolish me I said yes."

The Jesuit patted her arm. "I would have been foolish and said the same thing."

"I'll say it again. You're a very sweet man." She squeezed the priest in a quick hug. "And that's when the strangest thing of the night happened. We sat in my office and she sees those two pages I found in the Westminster Arcade and right away she says something like 'My my what's that?' And I mentioned 'Oh just an unpublished text by Roger Williams I found' and I start to put it back in my desk, thinking *Gladys you should never be so dumb as to leave such things lying about.* But then this Alicia's all over me saying 'Oh how wonderful, Roger Williams' and 'Oh how exciting, an unpublished text' and she'd love to hear about my discovery and it would make her so happy if I'd just read it aloud real quick and Oh could I just please please please. You get the idea."

"Yeah." Jim Cypriano sighed sympathetically. "So you read it out loud to the trio."

"I did. And you know what happened? Remember how in the text Roger Williams describes paddling across the river in his canoe and he gets to Providence and the Indian shaman can sense the presence of the Seraphs?"

"Yes. A lovely passage. Haunting, and very moving."

"Just how I felt. Anyway, I finish reading the manuscript for them and this Alicia jumps up and says so loud she nearly yells: 'So that disgusting Roger Williams must have been the one who did it.'"

"Well. That shook me up. No more melt-in-your-mouth nice-nice from Little Miss Charming. I say to her, 'Must have been the one who did what?' And this girl looks at me wild-eyed and says, 'Brought the infestation into Rhode Island. The infestation of those things he calls Seraphim.'"

The Jesuit blinked. "What?"

"My reaction precisely. I said to her 'Young lady, the manuscript makes clear Roger Williams interacted with these Seraphs, whatever they were, and he was convinced they were completely benevolent.' And my guest practically spits at me and says 'Then Roger Williams was a fool.' Just like that. 'Roger Williams was a fool.' "

The Baptist pastor stooped and plucked another Pepperidge Farm cookie from the tray. "For the road." She shook her head at the memory. "Yeah. And the young lady turns to her two young men and barks 'Make a note. Roger Williams. Seraphim. Infestations. Data points of service to the Magus.' Then she growls a poor excuse for a thank-you and goodbye and storms out the door, with her two zombies tapping at their smartphones and trotting in her wake."

"Of service to the Magus?" The Jesuit helped Gladys Trevor put on her coat.

"I have no idea whom, or what, they were talking about. Anyway." She buttoned her coat. "As I said, I've a hunch this little trio is going to be headed your way."

He asked if he could give her a lift home.

"I brought my car." She hugged him again and stepped out into the night.

20

James Cypriano, S.J. was up early next morning. He followed his usual routine: prayer and a meditation from Ignatius Loyola's *Spiritual Exercises*, then a half hour kneeling in devotion, rosary beads in hand, before a wall-mounted crucifix. Scotch-taped to the wall beneath it was an old holy card—something an uncle had sent him from Rome—showing Christ on the Cross. No strife or anguish in this picture of Jesus. The artist had chosen instead to show a Christ fully at peace—beautiful long wavy hair, beautiful lowered eyes in a beautiful youthful face. The card bore an inscription:

> If you want to know
> How much Jesus loves you,
> Consider how wide
> He stretched open His arms
> Upon the Cross.

Gladys Trevor had teased him about the card the first time she saw it. "So sentimental. So Italian."

Jim Cypriano reminded her his family was from Italy and his parish of Francis Xavier was in Federal Hill. "The heart of Italian Providence." In reply Gladys had laughed and said in that case she'd have to give him and his holy card a pass.

He recalled her words and smiled as he knelt now before the cross. Sentimental? She was right. But he loved that old picture.

After prayer he sat at his desk and resumed his task from the night before—translating a text he planned to incorporate into a sermon. He'd been working on it for days. Dictionary at his elbow, he wrote out his translation, an adaptation of a play by the French poet Claudel.

The play opens with a violent sequence sure to catch an audience's attention (and Jim Cypriano jotted notes so he could summarize the action for his own congregation). The sixteenth century, and a sailing ship sets forth from Spain to the New World. Its passengers: Jesuit missionaries (*kindred spirits*, thought Cypriano, smiling), eager to win souls for the Church.

But mid-Atlantic Ocean, pirates attack. Cannonfire sinks the ship, shreds the sails, wrecks the rigging and masts. The pirates kill the crew, kill the priests.

All save one. A single Jesuit, his head streaming blood, but still alive. (Jim Cypriano had a vivid imagination, and he stored up these details so he could share them in his sermon.)

In savage sport the pirates take the surviving priest—his cassock torn, his torso cut with criss-cross saber-cuts—and bind him with ropes, lashing his legs and chest and neck to what's left of the stricken ship's mainmast. Then the pirates stretch out his bloodstained arms and tie them fast to a transverse spar jutting at right angles from the mast. After which they set the wreckage adrift—mast, spar, and captive priest—to bob atop the cold Atlantic depths. The pirate ship vanishes from view in the west, and the survivor is alone spitting salt spume.

So much for the opening scene. The part to which Jim Cypriano gave particular care was the prayer addressed to God by the bound and wounded priest as he regains his senses and lifts his head an inch from the slapping waves and the rough wood of the mast:

> Lord, I thank You for having thus attached me so closely to You! True, in the past I've sometimes found Your commands onerous to follow; and my selfish will has sometimes been restless and perplexed when confronted with Your rule.
>
> But today I could not possibly be bound to You any more closely than I am now, in every part of my being, in every one of my limbs. And there is no part of me now which could in any way be separated from You by even the slightest bit.
>
> For in truth I am made fast to a cross—a condition You, too, as Lamb of God have eternally known.
>
> My cross has its own special terror—for it floats free on the sea. But if ever I fear being lost, I have only to wait for the resurgence of that unfailing power beneath me that seizes me and lifts me high and heavenward in a heartening rise from the depths.

I am tightly fixed to the innermost core of God's holy will, having renounced my desires for the sake of His own.

I have given myself to God and now entrust myself to these cords that bind me fast to Him.

Jim Cypriano put down his pen a moment and thought over what he'd just written. *Bound fast to a cross that floats free on the sea: Wow, that's an existential circumstance that can speak to many a soul today. Now, how to link this imagery to the meditations that well up in me when I'm out on the Providence River with the Riverglow crew?* Crouched at his desk, grateful for the flow of ideas, he scratched notes for his sermon.

Only to be interrupted by a knock at the rectory door.

Reverend Trevor had been right in her prediction. There stood the trio.

The young woman wasted no time. "Father Cypriano? I'm Alicia Wheatley." Without waiting for an invitation, she strode into his study, trailed by her pair of silent young men.

But none of them wore the gray polo shirt and gray chino pants ensemble described by the Baptist pastor. This morning all three were clad in frayed short-short cutoff jeans and brightly colored peasant smocks. But where the young men's shirts were baggy and shapeless, hers was low-cut and tailored to show off her trim figure. Buttoned to their smocks were pins that read "GGCG" and "HPL was right."

He puzzled over these while Alicia Wheatley crossed the room to his desk and its flanking bookshelves. She studied the top shelf of books to the right of the desk, ran a lingering hand over the spines of the texts. "Ah." A long appreciative breath. "I see you're a scholar. Titles in Latin. Greek. German. French. You must have a deep knowledge of history and culture. Impressive." She turned around and fluttered her eyelids and flashed him a big-eyed oh-gosh-you-are-so-wonderful darling-girl smile.

What had Gladys called her? Little Miss Charming. He could see why.

Then a quick curt command to her young men: "Make a note. James Cypriano. Scholar. History and culture."

"Do your friends have names?" Annoying, to see how she ordered them about.

"I call them Jack and Junior. Doesn't matter. They'll answer to anything. And no, to anticipate your next thought, they don't mind being told what to do. They're used to it. Besides, leadership requires mental discipline. They lack the knack. And people who lack the knack, well, they find themselves put to use. But natural leaders like me, and like *you*, Father Cypriano"—more fluttering of eyelids, more little-girl charm—"we instinctively follow the motto voiced by the Magus: 'Use everything that comes your way and crosses your path, and then dispose of it as you like.' "

"The Magus?"

"Our mentor," she said with quiet pride. "Howard Phillips Lovecraft."

Jack and Junior bobbed their heads as if in reverence at utterance of the name.

This was startling enough. What she said next startled him more. "You know, the Magus used to keep you under surveillance."

"Oh?" Surprising, considering that Lovecraft had died a long time ago. Jim Cypriano was well into his sixties but not quite ancient enough to have caught the attention of H. P. Lovecraft.

"I mean your church. Saint Francis Xavier. You can see its tower and steeple all the way from College Hill. It's an old building, and our Magus used to contemplate it from a distance. He kept a telescope or something in his College Street apartment. He enjoyed using the glass at sunset to study the western skyscape of Federal Hill."

He asked how she knew this.

"It's all encoded in his stories. Especially 'The Haunter of the Dark.' "

"And that button you're wearing: 'GGCG.' " Jim Cypriano could see she wanted him to ask. "What does that stand for?"

"Gnostic Guardians of the Cosmic Gate."

"Sounds ambitious." He arched a skeptical eyebrow. "Where's this cosmic gate located?"

"We've determined it's right here in Providence." She announced this with the rock-solid confidence of someone tapping at a map and pointing out a Dunkin' Donuts or Krispy Kreme or other local landmark.

"Wait. Right here in Providence?"

"Yes. It's called Yog-Sothoth."

"Yog-Sothoth. Okay." He cleared his throat, glanced at her, then the twins (couldn't help thinking of them that way, they acted so much alike) Junior-Jack. All three GGCG-ers gazed back at him blankly. "If you don't mind my asking: How do you know all this?"

"The Magus told us."

"But your Magus died, let me see now, well over eighty years ago."

"1937."

"So how could he have told you?"

"It's all in a manner of speaking." She bestowed on him the patient-but-pitying look of a kindergarten teacher minding a toddler. "If you read works by the Magus such as 'The Dunwich Horror' you'll see he spells it all out."

"Okay. And that other button. 'HPL was right.' Right about what?"

"Do you mind if I sit down?" Before he could speak she flopped onto his sofa and kicked off her shoes. She leaned forward and traced an idle hand down her thigh. She had shapely tanned legs and she knew it—and clearly she wanted him to know it too. Junior-Jack flanked the couch and stared straight ahead.

"Right about what." A long exhalation of breath. "You're not an initiate or a Guardian—though who knows maybe someday we can fix that—but this much I don't think the Magus would mind if I say." Her head tilted back and she half closed her eyes as if recalling scripted lines for a recitation.

"Right about the nature of our world. This Earth is a random product of chance. There's no Creator that loves us. There's nothing out there but hate. Cold hostile spaces and cold hostile gods. I say gods but not really because that implies maybe some need for worship. They're demons. Djinns. Old Ones. They predate us by eons. The Magus discovered some of their names. Azazoth. Cthulhu. And they definitely don't wish us well."

All this in a persuasive voice that left no room for doubt. Junior-Jack bobbed their heads in a silent amen. Jim Cypriano knew a skilled preacher when he heard one and this young lady was tops.

He shook off the spell. "But how can you be so sure of all this?"

She spoke on undeterred. "This world is an outpost. Alone in the cosmic wastes. It's a fortress. And we Gnostics, we the ones who know, we're the Guardians. Because Cthulhu and Azazoth and all the Old Ones, they seek to enter and swallow and press in on our weak points. Because, my friend, there are in fact weak points and we're living in one."

"Here in Providence?"

"Precisely so."

"Where exactly in Providence?"

She said it was on this the Magus had been laboring at the time of his death. "There are hints that he found it—the cosmic entry point, the gate called Yog-Sothoth—shortly before he died suddenly of cancer in 1937. But knowledge of its location died with him." She paused, very evidently savoring the attention paid her by the priest and her two devotees.

"The Guardians have been seeking Yog-Sothoth's location ever since. And we Gnostic disciples of the twenty-first century are narrowing down the search even now. We can't buttress the weak point and shore it up against invasion until we locate it with precision. But we're close to knowing. Very close." She gave a tight-lipped, inward-gazing, superior smile.

"Which brings me to you. To you, Father Cypriano." Now her smile turned outward and radiant. She crossed and uncrossed her tanned, shapely legs. "We, all of us, are facing an invasion, as I said, and we can't ward off the Cthulhu hordes all by ourselves. The GGCG is in need of apotropaia to plug up and buttress Yog-Sothoth."

"The cosmic gate," he said skeptically, "that's supposed to be somewhere in Providence?"

"Just so."

"And what do you want from me?"

"Apotropaia," she said firmly. "Things that ward off evil. The evil we're confronting in this Cthulhu-horde invasion. Consecrated things, that's what we need. Things that pack power. Things that pack punch. Crucifixes, holy water. Whatever your institution uses to ward off demons or whatever you choose to call them. And mind you, the GGCG is eclectic. For decades we've been collecting and gathering—in secret, of course—objects of power from all over the world. Amulets, talismans, ghost daggers, juju-wands. From Africa, Egypt, Mesopotamia, Java, Tibet. You name it. Whatever might work."

She raised an arm as if hailing a whole conclave of initiates. "Of course the Magus amassed such a collection too in the 1930s. He sent out emissaries to locate apotropaia and did his best to plug Yog-Sothoth. But it's in the nature of such objects that over time their virtue wears off, especially if they're in heavy use as sealants to block up a gate. So more artifacts must continually be added with the passage of years."

Her voice rose as she spoke. "Hate against hate. That's what our Magus taught us. Apotropaic artifacts to buttress the gate. Coercion and force. Terror and the threat of harm. That's the only language the agents of invasion understand. The hot force of hate against cold, hostile gods. *Try to enter and we'll crush you.* That's the message we need to post at our gate. That might be enough to push Cthulhu back."

"Wait." Jim Cypriano sat down at his desk chair. "I don't know about the amulets and so forth you've collected, but in our faith tradition at least that's not how such objects work. Just take a look for a second."

He directed the trio's gaze to the wall. "The crucifix isn't the sign of a god who crushes and hates. It's the mark of a god who operates out of love, who feels so much solidarity with the creatures he loves that he empties himself of any privilege of power. Empties himself to the point that he makes himself vulnerable—vulnerable to suffering, and even death on a cross."

The priest jumped to his feet. Affectionately he touched the visage of Christ. "Study that face, and you know what it tells you? Coercion and force aren't the fundamental principles undergirding the cosmos."

"I see. You're playing hard to get. You don't want to give away something for nothing. Well, fair enough." She delivered all this in a kittenish tone, crossing her legs and leaning far forward to offer him a good peek down the front of her shirt. "Tell you what. You let us borrow some of your church's things, and in exchange you and I can have a private conference. One on one. Without these boys or anyone else standing around. A tutorial. I could instruct you. One on one."

But he only half heard. He wanted to say to her *The question isn't whether I experience temptation from you, or from anyone else. The question is one of focus. Kierkegaard was right: "Purity of heart is to will one thing."*

Serving God leaves little room for distraction. And what you're offering is quite simply distraction.

Which led him to think of the verses he'd just translated from Claudel. How could he convey to this young woman the depth of love and sense of trust conveyed by the poet? Cypriano wanted to share with her this portrait of a Jesuit lashed to a mast, adrift on the sea, but able to endure all he suffered because he loved a God who also has suffered, a God whose cries of thirst from the Cross allow all sufferers to know that at least they don't suffer alone.

The Gnostic Guardian apparently mistook his silence. "Or if you prefer, and if your tastes run that way"—at which words her expression shifted from kittenish to sly—"I could arrange payment—consider it a rental—in the form of one of my acolytes. Junior here, or Jack, whichever you like. He can be your altar boy, or server, or whatever your institution calls them, for a week or two. And if you're *very* cooperative, you can take them both. For as long as you like. Your private own. I can always get more."

He gazed at the crucifix on the wall a long moment. Then he turned to the Gnostic on the sofa. "You know, what you just said demonstrates a pretty low opinion not just of me but of Catholic priests and the Church in general. And to tell the truth I don't mind that so much. God knows we as an ecclesiastical hierarchy have failed our congregations, again and again, in our mission and in our responsibilities. We've indulged ourselves and dishonored our role as shepherds."

He paused. When he spoke again he did so more sharply. (He realized he was angry—furious, in fact—and normally in such states he'd try to count to ten first before saying anything but now—bang—he just let himself go.) "What I do mind is your willingness to use other human beings—these two young men here—as disposable tools. As with every created being, they're uniquely precious, not things you use and throw away."

She disregarded what he'd said, feigned a look of concern. "It must get lonely, you living here all by yourself."

"Actually, I'm not living alone." As he spoke his gaze lifted up to the crucifix.

"Oh?" Once more she purred in her kittenish tone. "You've got a little special someone tucked away here in the rectory?"

"Not so little. But special, yes."

"Well in that case. Perhaps you'd like a cash donation—for your church"—a conspiratorial wink—"but also for that special person of yours?"

"No thank you. Cash is never uppermost in that Person's mind."

"I suggest you wise up." *So much for Little Miss Charming,* he thought. *Get ready for a blast of bile.* "Before you throw away what I'm offering, I suggest you take a good hard look in the mirror. You're old and overweight and going bald fast."

Ouch. A bile blast, for sure. Double-barreled, and right on the mark.

She wasn't done yet. "Plus your face is all wrinkled up and every time you smile people can see your teeth look like shit." Her expression was that of a prosecuting attorney offering a desperado a last-minute plea bargain. "You should grab what you can while you can. What kind of deal are you holding out for?"

"Actually," he said (by now he'd begun to feel calmer), "I've already been offered a great deal." He smiled up at the crucifix.

As he spoke he felt a compassionate stab in his heart and wondered: *And what cross has this young woman been bound to? What burdens was she made to carry, perhaps too early in life, that embittered her so much and brought her to this habit of bitter contempt?*

She wasn't quite through with him yet. "Well, if you're too ignorant to help, we'll find others who will. We'll find other juju-wands, other apotropaia. We'll locate Yog-Sothoth and block up the gate and stop the Cthulhu invasion. And we'll remember the ignorant ones—like you, you blubbery old fool—who stood in our way."

With a toss of her hair she summoned the twins. Obediently they formed up behind her.

She fixed James Cypriano, S.J. with one last withering look before she burst out the door. "You and your cross."

Gently he closed the rectory door behind her. "Whew." Aftershocks of anger—pity, and sorrow, too—trembled through his frame. Briefly he pressed his forehead to the wall, breathed a prayer for patience and for help in dealing with his temper.

More closely than ever he felt freshly akin to Claudel's Jesuit, lashed to the mast on a cold, stormy sea. *Bound tightly to you, dear Christ. Just keep me afloat.*

21

Five-thirty-five. As usual, Atith Rattanak drove into the lot twenty-five minutes early to supervise first shift at Guild Metal. And as usual, after he parked he sat in his car a moment, enjoying the cool air of dawn and happily humming along to something playing on AM radio. He couldn't make out the words, but it didn't matter, because just sitting like this at the start of a new summer day made him feel good. It never took much. His threshold for feel-good was blissfully low.

This car for example. A '63 Impala he'd bought decades ago from a scrapyard in North Providence, some four years after arriving as a refugee in the States. "Needs just a bit of work," the dealer had optimistically declared, and Atith's uncle—who had been the young man's sponsor when he landed in Providence—snarled with scorn that what this old piece of junk needed was new tires, new brakes, a new windshield, and a new motor that might actually have a prayer of starting when you turned the key in the ignition. "Junk," his uncle repeated in English to the dealer, and then he turned to Atith and gave him a string of reasons in Khmer to say no to the deal.

But Atith had smilingly paid his uncle no mind. "This car looks like a good egg," he told the dealer. "I'll take it."

Atith Rattanak had learned much of his English at age ten at the Puerto Princesa transitional resettlement camp on the island of Palawan. A hut marked "Library" held a stack of yellowing, salt-dampened *Reader's Digests*, and Atith had spent contented hours puzzling over columns like "It Pays to Increase Your Word Power." In some such column he'd discovered the expression "to be a good egg." A lover of vivid language, he'd considered that phrase his prize find of the day—that, and an advertisement he saw in the same issue for a sky-blue four-door 1963 Chevrolet Impala. He'd rushed out of the hut past the nearby palm trees and showed the ad to the first aid worker he saw and cried, "This is a good egg." Which had made her laugh, and Atith along with her. "A fine flexible egg," he'd improvised, just loving this new language and new life and the prospect someday of a sky-blue Impala.

And now here he was, many years later, seated in his reconditioned fine flexible egg, about to start a fresh morning shift at Guild Metal Products. The car radio played low while he sipped coffee and ate two buttered croissants—an eating preference dating back to childhood. The bread made him think of Siem Reap, and the French tourists who came to see Angkor and sit in cafés and drink coffee and eat croissants just as he was doing now, after which they'd hire bicycle rickshaws to go gaze at the shrines and the cryptically smiling stone Buddhas at the temple entranceways. All that of course was before the Khmer Rouge and the end of his whole family's old life and the beginning of what he bracketed in his mind as The Great Sadness.

Whenever he reached this point in his early-morning thoughts Atith Rattanak knew it was time to punch the clock and get to work. There was a reason he drove himself hard and put in fifty-eight hours a week. No good giving yourself too much time to think.

And being first-shift supervisor at Guild Metal gave him plenty of problems to occupy his mind. To judge from the way Jorge Ramirez was flapping agitated arms at him from the office doorway, it looked like the morning's newest challenges had already arrived.

Jorge had the perfectionism one hoped for in an assistant foreman. He wore his customary frown, forehead furrowed in concentration—"And what can you expect," he'd say when asked why he always looked worried, "I've got to keep track of a hundred and eighty-seven workers, and that's just the morning shift, never mind the second or third."

Ramirez gulped Red Bull—by six A.M. he'd have downed two 8.4-ounce cans, which he said set him up so he could get through his day—and waved Atith into the office. "Stubby, we have a situation."

Inexperienced neophyte FNGs (Frigging New Guys) at Guild Metal tended to assume people called Atith Rattanak "Stubby" because his height was so diminutive. True he was short but when any FNG asked Ramirez in private why Atith was nicknamed the way he was, Ramirez simply said, "Just look at the man's mitts," and sure enough three fingers on his right hand and two on his left were truncated and really nothing but stubs. "Which doesn't slow him up a bit," Ramirez would tell the new guy, "or keep him from being the best boss you could want."

From day one at Guild Metal, Atith had gotten along with everyone he met. Maybe because of his innocuous size—"At five foot nothing you're no threat to no one" had been the assessment of Crazy-Chester Metcalf, the loudest loudmouth on the loading dock. Or maybe because Stubby Atith perpetually seemed to find the cheerfullest side of things no matter the circumstance.

A mentality which Atith Rattanak would need to call on right now. His assistant foreman handed him a personnel file from Human Resources. "Our latest hire," said Ramirez, "and our latest problem child. Due to start work this morning. Some boys on the shift just heard he's coming and are already saying no way they're gonna have him around. This is one FNG they already hate."

Atith asked if they knew the man personally.

The foreman said just by reputation. "Must be the most unpopular guy in Rhode Island. Ever since that exposé article about him in the *Providence Journal* came out and identified him as the perpetrator."

"Perpetrator? What was it he did?"

"I'll tell you what he did." A voice from the other doorway in the office—the door that led out to the factory floor. Two men stood there. Troublemaking Chester Metcalf and his drinking pal Dree Duarte.

"I'll tell you," Chester Metcalf said again. "He painted graffiti all over Providence's Big Blue Bug. What was it he sprayed on it?"

"'RMH,'" supplied Dree.

"Yeah. 'RMH.' Rocky Mountain High. Cuz that shithead's from Denver. Thinks cuz he's from Colorado he's way cooler than us folks in Li'l Rhody. Sprayed 'RMH' all over our Bug. Shit."

Only 6:05 A.M. and already Crazy-Chester sounded irked enough to punch dents in the wall. (Atith had seen him do precisely that on one occasion.) "You can't lay this on us, man." Chester glared straight at the supervisor. "You can't put him on our shift."

"Stubby's from Cambodia, dude." This contribution from Dree. "Not likely he's gonna appreciate the finer points of our Bug."

Actually Atith knew quite a bit about the Bug. Like most Rhode Islanders he'd actually only ever seen it from a distance in passing while driving by on 95. A three-dimensional advertising gimmick—fifty-eight feet of winged metal termite—the Big Blue Bug perched high atop the roof of New England Pest Control and overlooked the highway and the industrial zone and freight-loading wharves of Narragansett Bay. For years the Pest Control proprietors had made a ritual of dressing up the Bug and fitting it with costumes to match the changing seasons.

Which was what the loading-dock boys were trying to explain to their Cambodian-immigrant boss. "Fourth of July it gets a scraggly Uncle Sam beard and a twenty-foot-tall stovepipe Stars-and-Stripes hat," enthused Dree. "Halloween they give it a black witch's cape and a big-ass trick-or-treat pumpkin. Come Christmas it's dressed up in a Santa Claus outfit and a fat red nose like Rudolph." He paused as if grasping for a sufficiently philosophical way to sum up. "For homeboys like us the Bug is the thing that says Providence. It's like the Washington Monument."

Crazy-Chester corrected him. "More like the Alamo."

"Nah. Niagara Falls."

"Bigger. Grand Canyon."

"Dude. Whatever." Dree turned back to Atith. "Crazy and me, we're just saying. Please keep that Tagger off of our dock. For his own good."

Atith said he'd do his best to keep their thoughtful wishes in mind. The two turned back to the factory floor.

Tagger. Now he knew why this story sounded familiar. Atith studied the name on the personnel form. Alexander Finster. Of course. He had some idea who this Finster was, and all thanks to Janey Evans.

Atith Rattanak loved many things about Providence but one of the things he loved best was Riverglow. He served on the *Persephone* but after ten years volunteering he knew all the regulars on all the boats. Janey was just as sociable as Atith and the two had become friends. Last Saturday night after the boats had been berthed and swept clean she'd walked along the river with him and chatted about this and that. Including the topic of a new crew member on the *Icarus*. A sullen and uncooperative teen she called Tagger. "Could scarcely get a lick of work out of him the whole night."

So this was Guild Metal's new hire. Oh well.

The curious thing, came the thought, was that by coincidence this Alex Finster would be the second FNG in the course of a few days to have some connection with Janey Evans.

For just last week she'd phoned Atith and asked if he could do her a favor. "I mean a really big favor. For my nephew. He needs a job. Needs one bad."

Atith had asked what was his name.

Augustus Valerian Tessario, she'd said. "Pretty grand, huh? But we just call him Gusto. Or plain Gus. Or even Gussy, but that's my pet name for him."

A good kid, she'd insisted. Been in some trouble from time to time. "But hey ain't that true for us all."

Atith had equably agreed and asked what kind of trouble.

"Substance abuse. Addiction. Like with so many people today. Then detox. Rehab. But he swears he's past all that now." She'd said what the kid needed was a second chance and a clean sheet, something to hold him steady and keep him grounded, and she saw from Help Wanted that Guild Metal was hiring and "hey Stubby how about it could you put in a word and land him a job?"

So Atith had said sure and put in a word. Which had gotten the kid a job and—just as Atith had privately anticipated—had created a whole lot of extra angst for himself.

Speaking of Janey's nephew—Atith Rattanak stepped from the office out onto the factory floor—there before him now was the young man in question, Augustus Valerian Tessario, punching in at the time clock, under his arm the skateboard he always rode to work.

Jorge Ramirez tapped at his wristwatch. "Eighteen minutes late for his shift. This kid is hopeless."

Atith mildly observed this was an improvement from the day before. "Yesterday he punched in almost an hour behind the clock."

"That's supposed to make me feel better?" Ramirez stepped forward to give Tessario a scolding. The kid stepped back and flinched.

Atith disliked seeing anyone have to start their day like that. And this was Janey's nephew after all.

"Gusto." He raised a hand in greeting. "Good to see you."

A shrimpy stoop-shouldered kid, this Augustus Tessario. A narrow gentle face, with wispy curls of a goatee sprouting from an unshaven stubbly chin. He clung to the skateboard under his arm like it was—(Atith paused to consider: he liked to make his language vivid even when thinking to himself; after all as the *Reader's Digest* said, "It pays to increase your word power")—yes as if that skateboard were some wooden teddy bear.

But in that case, thought Atith. *kind of an unfriendly teddy.* The skateboard bore a skull-and-red-thunderball logo. The skull breathed flames and grinned wide in a big derisive smirk.

And at the moment the skull looked more alive and more electric than did Janey's nephew. Uncertainly his gaze flickered about the vast spaces of the factory floor. This after all was only the kid's sixth day at work and everything was still new.

His eyes were what the supervisor had learned to watch. Sometimes—seldom—they glittered, decisive, hard-edged, bright. More often they lacked focus, suggesting a spirit hungry, abstracted, wrapped in longing, adrift.

As seemed to be the case this morning.

"What's happening, my man?" Atith boomed out his best six A.M. greeting and steered Augustus Tessario away from the assistant foreman, who was still lecturing the youngster on tardy arrivals.

Atith told Ramirez to look sharp for Alex Finster. The foreman growled that Finster was already almost a half hour late for his first day of work. "These FNGs."

Atith said he'd set up Gusto with some tasks for the morning. Gently he guided the young man among the machines and the barely contained chaos of the Guild Metal floor.

From the first day finding chores for Gus Tessario hadn't been easy. Atith knew better than to put him in Shipping and Receiving. The kid was too tentative, too delicate to be entrusted to Crazy-Chester's crew on the loading dock. They'd likely gouge him with a forklift or drop a crate on his foot. Spray-painting in the Industrial Metal Goods section? No. That demanded precision and nonstop attention—not good for sleepy-eyed dreamers like Gus. And for the same reason the kid wouldn't do as a caster. Pouring molten metal required steady hands, and every day so far he'd come to work with the jitters. Getting spattered with hot liquid steel was no joke.

So Atith had consulted with Jorge, and the assistant foreman had agreed they'd start Gus as a floor boy.

Gus had blinked confusedly when they first told him his job title. "Floor boy?"

"Factotum," Jorge had explained. "Gofer. You'll be our all-purpose errand-runner."

Errand-drifter, it had turned out. Augustus Valerian Tessario could successfully fetch what he was told. You just had to allot him plenty of time.

"You do realize he's not worth even minimum wage?" This had been Jorge's assessment after the first day.

"Give him time." Atith knew the kid was slow. But Janey Evans had begged and Gus was her nephew and Atith could see the boy was actually a good egg and Atith and Janey were boat-mates after all from the Riverglow crew. "Keep Gusto busy," Janey had pleaded. "Give him plenty to do. It's probably the only way to keep him tethered to planet Earth. Otherwise he's liable to just float away from us." So the kid had lasted into week two and now here they were at the start of a fresh day.

Atith explained what needed to be done. (He had to step close and bellow to be heard over the whoosh and roar of ventilators and overhead air ducts.) He pointed out the two-wheeled hand trolley by the freight elevator. "The sprayers are running low on paint. Harvest gold. Avocado green. Autumn glory. Also acetone. Go down to the basement and bring up some fifty-five-gallon drums." He reminded the kid not to do what he'd done last week, leaving a barrel of cleaning fluid near an open soldering flame. "You don't want to make us all go boom." Gus nodded in frightened assent. Atith knew he understood. Jorge Ramirez had blasted the boy with a ten-minute safety-reminder after last week's close call.

There. That should keep the youngster occupied a while. Atith turned and jogged back along the factory floor to the front office. He wanted to be there before Alexander Finster arrived so as to head off any possible problems.

Too late. There stood his newcomer now, slouched by the back door. Looking exactly how Atith had expected: a defiant, scowling punk crawling with tattoos and bad attitude.

Speaking of attitude: confronting Finster now as the supervisor approached was Crazy-Chester Metcalf, shaking a fist and calling the other man something that sounded like "shithead Tagger."

Chester turned to Atith with a voice of indignation. "There's a reason we call these fresh hires FNGs. Too many new guys are just too much frigging trouble to be worth the bother. Shithead Tagger here's a case in point."

"Mister Metcalf." The supervisor suggested pleasantly that if he had nothing to do in Shipping and Receiving, work might be found for him this morning down in the basement. "Like shifting two hundred barrels of paint thinner from one end of the lower level to the other."

Crazy-Chester backed off fast. "Just keep away from my dock." A last shake of his fist at Tagger. "You hear?"

Atith apologized, introduced himself. Alex Finster folded his arms and said nothing.

"I understand from your file you decided to choose Guild Metal because you like to paint."

"I didn't get to choose shit. State Employment stuck me here."

"Oh." This was going to be harder than Atith had anticipated. But after imprisonment by the Khmer Rouge the worst that life could throw at him just made him laugh. He simply smiled back at the teenager's sass. "Come with me." He had just the task for someone with graffiti-artist skills.

Atith led the FNG to the Industrial Metal Goods wing, then to one wall where a dozen workers labored at a row of tall booths that each stood open in front. The chemical smell was everywhere in this factory—Atith had long since become adjusted so now he scarcely noticed—but here the sting of burnt alloys and solvents and fumes was particularly bad. "You'll need this." They put on face masks and coverall bibs and two pairs each of gloves. "Inner pair cotton," said Atith, "to absorb sweat. Outer pair insulated rubber. For protection. Now come."

They stepped closer and watched as a worker went to a nearby rack and lifted out a tray containing assorted stamped-aluminum parts. "This is Thomas," indicated Atith, and the worker nodded at them. Thomas brought the tray to the booth and placed it atop a large flat disk some four feet in diameter. With one hand the man lifted free from a holster mounted on the side of the booth an apparatus consisting of a nozzle, trigger, paint jar, and hose. With his other hand the man spun the disk containing the tray. As the disk spun, Thomas stepped in close to the booth and pointed the nozzle at the stamped-metal parts and squeezed the trigger. A fine dispersion of paint covered the parts, and a fan at the back of the booth sucked the cloud of spray that emerged.

"You have to lean into the booth a bit to get just close enough," said Atith, "but don't get too close." He explained that the vibrations sometimes shook the shield loose and left the rear fan exposed. "And that could chop your hand into chop suey chop-chop." He held up his own hand that happened to be missing three fingers. "People here call me Stubby. You don't want them calling you Stubby too."

That got Tagger's attention to the point he actually said something. "You mean you lost your fingers here on this cruddy job?"

"Oh no. Not here. When I was ten. Back home. Far away. Nothing for you to be scared of." He patted the young man's arm. "Just be mindful."

The paintwork complete, Thomas lifted the tray clear and walked down the hall to a large adjacent room. The pair followed and watched. In the room stood a pair of ovens some eight feet in height. Atith explained this was the room where the painted products were baked. "He's going to open the door. We might want to stand back." Heat blasted them, furnace-hot, as Thomas quickly slid in the tray and closed the door shut.

"Very nice. Now I leave you to Thomas. He'll show you what to do." Atith wished him success in his new career as an industrial spray painter.

"Career. Yeah. Shit." Tagger was still muttering as Atith left him to learn his trade.

Not that the supervisor was done with him for the day. By no means. At eleven-thirty Atith gathered up both Alexander Finster and Augustus Tessario and took them outside to the gravel lot where the food trucks stood parked and waiting.

There was a lunch room indoors but that was where the likes of Crazy-Chester and Dree sat and mouthed off. "So I sit in the fresh air away from the fumes and the mouths. And you two will sit with me too."

Atith Rattanak's idea of fresh-air dining was to perch inside his Chevy Impala with all the doors open, with the car parked facing the food trucks—"in case I need to get refills, and just to watch the daily show." He had Gus beside him in the front seat. Alex Finster sat in the back.

The show Atith had in mind commenced right away. Amid the constant in-and-out of delivery trucks and cargo vans wheeling through the lot, and workers sweating in the sun as they lined up to buy food, there was a third wave of traffic: pigeons that gurgled and finches that cheeped, bobbing and pecking at crumbs on the gravel. A bird three inches tall tore hopefully at a cigarette butt, only to see useless tobacco blow away in the breeze. A sparrow got too close to a human and his boot and had to scoot to avoid a swift kick.

"The life they live is hard," observed Atith, "but they waste no time in complaint. Big lesson there, you bet."

In the rear Alex Finster ate in silence, his nose to his phone. Same with Augustus Tessario in the front seat.

Janey Evans wouldn't like this antisocial smartphone obsessing, would probably think this unhealthy. She'd given Atith instructions. *Keep him tethered to planet Earth. Otherwise he's liable to just float away.*

So what would Janey do? Talk to them. Draw them out of themselves.

Atith swallowed a bite of sandwich. *But what should I talk about with them?* In the rearview mirror he saw Tagger had finished eating and was simply staring into space. Not in a friendly way either.

Beside Stubby in the front seat, dreamy-eyed, vacant Augustus wasn't unfriendly but was still immersed in some search on his phone. Wasn't polite of course to peep at other people's searches but Janey might like to know for her nephew's own good and with that excuse in mind Atith leaned in for a view. The kid had just tapped in the word "redrum."

"Redrum"? Gusto didn't strike him as the type to get big into drink.

The boy suddenly turned his head and shut off his phone and asked where was the restroom.

Atith watched from the car as the youngster crunched gravel underfoot and politely stepped aside to make way for the lunch line and finches and pigeons.

Once Gus had entered the main building, Atith turned in his seat and knew at once that Tagger too had been watching from the back as the skateboarder tapped queries into his phone.

"Redrum." Atith said the word aloud. He knew Alex Finster wasn't much for conversation but Atith was worried about Janey's nephew and needed someone to confer with and it was either Tagger or the pigeons *so here goes.*

"Redrum," he said again. "Some kind of alcohol? I woulda thought he was into drugs."

"You were right the first time, Dawg."

The supervisor said "redrum" was a funny name for drugs.

"Try googling "Apache." Or "China white." Or "China girl." All the same thing."

"China girl? Sounds like an international dating app."

Tagger took a deep breath and flicked him a knife-edged gaze that all but screamed "Why do I have to exist in a world full of dorks?" "It's called 'China girl' because the stuff you're talking about comes straight from China. Imported from Shanghai, places like that. Anyway," he added grudgingly, "redrum's a code word. You have to read the word in reverse."

"Redrum" in reverse. "Murder?" *This doesn't make sense.*

"It's meant to describe the effect the junk has. Kind of an advertising boast. If you're a customer you want a high that steps up to the edge of putting your lights out for good. I mean like terminal. I mean like how close can you come to dying without actually stepping through the Door. Though of course," Tagger added, "sometimes you go too far and you actually do."

"And then," whispered Atith, mostly to himself, "it really is murder." How was he going to explain all this to Janey? He turned once more to Tagger. "So I guess Gus is maybe into heroin."

"Worse than heroin. Fifty, a hundred times stronger. Fentanyl."

"Fentanyl? But that's awful."

"Dude. Your boy is messing with some serious shit."

And now here was Augustus Tessario, coming out of the restroom and back across the lot. Atith saw him pause a moment among the traffic-flutter of birds. A minute later the kid was settled once more in the Impala's front seat.

"Guess what." Beatific innocent smile. "One of those pigeons. I got it to take a bite of my sandwich. It looked so happy doing that." Another smile. "A really big bite."

22

That night Atith Rattanak texted his friend Janey Evans. Texted his worries about her nephew. How Gusto might be back into drugs. Might be into junk that would put out his lights. Into redrum. Into China white. China girl. Fentanyl. What to do?

At once his phone pinged. She'd texted right back:

"U got to say sth to him."

Great. This landed the mess smack back onto his lap. He tapped a reply:

"Spends 100% of his free time researching stuff online. Probably drugs. Doesn't talk. What do I say?"

Another fast ping:

"Get his head outta that phone. U got to say sth. Thanx!"

She wasn't being much help. Gus Tessario was her nephew, not his. Why couldn't *she* map out a plan? Of course Atith would never voice this vexation aloud.

His head had begun to ache. Nothing that bad. Probably just the day's leftover Guild Metal fumes. Still the throb made it hard to think. He was so tired (it was past ten P.M.) that all he could text was a plaintive:

"Tell me what to say. What do I say?"

To which in reply came the third and last ping of the night:

"You'll think of sth. You're a fine flexible egg. I trust u.♥♥"

Tired as he was, he had to smile. Ever since the first time she'd heard him use the phrase, she'd been egging him on now and again with fine-flexibility jokes. *Sweet of her to say she trusts me; and she hearts me enough to let me talk to her nephew. But she gives me no clue how to do it.*

Enough for one night. He closed up his phone, fell like a lump into bed. Too exhausted to think. Ten hours of Guild Metal. Gus Tessario. Alex the Tagger. Enough.

The dream came again that night. Except that as always the dream matched closely the events that had actually swallowed him up at age ten. Matched so closely that the dream qualified almost as an

"Atith-this-is-your-life" documentary film-clip or maybe simply a reincarnational obsessive-repetitive loop.

It started as always in his father's study in their old house in Siem Reap. His father, home from work. An interpreter and guide for the French archaeologists at the École Française d'Extrême Orient. Evening quiet. Lamplight, and shelves lined with books. His father putting on his reading spectacles and selecting a book from the shelf. Khmer mythology.

His father, an educated man, loved to read aloud to Atith. Stories linked to the carvings on the walls of Angkor. Tonight it was Vasuki and the churning of the cosmic ocean and the creation of *amrita*. Vasuki is a *nagaraja*, a monstrous water serpent, what in Chinese is called *longwang* or dragon king. (By now Atith knew the details by heart but loved his father's voice so much he wouldn't let him leave anything out.)

Gods and demons all hunger for *amrita*, the elixir of deathlessness, of immortality. To obtain it they must churn the ocean to whip the salt water into *amrita*-foam. To do that they need a churning-rod and a rope to twirl the rod back and forth. At this point his father always looks up from his book and peers over his reading glasses at his son and asks: "And do you remember what the gods and demons use as a churning-rod and churning-rope?"

Of course Atith knows. His father has read him the tale a dozen times or more. "For the churning-rod they use Mount Mandara, a crag snapped from the cosmic mountain Meru. And for the churning-rope they catch hold of the *nagaraja* Vasuki."

His father smiles and says "That's right my son" and goes on to read to him how the gods and demons entwined the captured Vasuki around the mountain. The gods pull hard on Vasuki's tail and the demons pull hard on his head. Back and forth they tug the snake so that Mount Mandara begins to twirl, fast and ever faster, so fast that just as the deities desire, the ocean foams up into *amrita*.

At this point his father pauses for a wise aside on the nature of snakes. "If you tug them back and forth and spin them too much you'll make them not only peevish but queasy." And this is what happens to Nagaraja Vasuki. He begins to vomit streams of poison and foul-smelling flames, just as you might expect when you wear out the patience of a king cobra.

"So he's puking out his guts," cries a delighted ten-year-old Atith.

"Yes," agrees his father. He indulges his son. "Vasuki's puking out his guts."

And here comes the heroic moment, in the myth and in the dream.

Gods and demons are all alarmed. They've made the *amrita* they long for, but now the immortality elixir is going to be spoilt by gooey gobs of snake vomit. (Atith squeals again in delight.) Yet the god Shiva steps forth and without a moment's hesitation volunteers to drink up the bile so everyone else can enjoy their elixir unspoiled. So bitter to taste is the vomit bile it turns Shiva's throat blue. Which is why Shiva is the god with the divine title of Blue-Throat.

His father always concludes by laying aside his spectacles and saying to him, "It takes a generous heart to drink up the poison so no one but yourself will be harmed."

And the dream always shifts to what happened next, in April 1975:

The conquest of Cambodia by the Khmer Rouge, with the backing of Mao Tse-Tung and Communist China. The forced evacuation of Phnom Penh, the emptying of the towns. The remaking of society. Year Zero.

The arrests and the killings. He has to stand and watch as they bind his father's hands and place a cord around his father's neck. The Khmer Rouge turn to Atith and say "Your father wears glasses. He's an intellectual. He's an enemy of the agrarian classes."

Then they ask ten-year-old Atith: "Why does your father wear glasses? Why does he read books?"

In the dream as in 1975 Atith thinks if only he can give a good answer maybe they won't kill his father.

The Khmer Rouge ask him again: "Why does your father wear glasses? Why does he read books?"

In the dream as in 1975 he never knows what to say.

Tonight in the dream the prompting comes in the form of Janey's text:

"U got to say sth. You'll think of sth. Thanx!♥♥"

Atith Rattanak awoke with a jolt. The bedside clock let him know it was 3:45.

He shook his head, swung his legs out of bed. On nights when the dream came there was no returning to sleep. Might as well start his day.

He dressed and put on a jacket. He had a spare hour before having to leave for work. He knew just what he wanted to do.

He slipped from his apartment and closed the door behind him as quietly as he could. No one else in the building was likely to be awake at four.

His apartment was on the second floor of the Westminster Arcade. Janey Evans had recommended the building to him—tiny rooms, she said, but big enough for people living solo, and a great location downtown. Plus another Riverglow volunteer was already living in the Arcade and had given it a thumbs up. A young woman, a petite blonde, by the name of Fay MacConnell. He had met her last Saturday night on the *Persephone*.

Silently he walked along the corridor to the stairs. The second apartment from the end of the hall was Fay MacConnell's. He smiled as he passed; apparently he'd been wrong about everyone being asleep. From under her door came a low murmur and a pulsing red light. A bit unusual: Was Fay an all-night video-gamer? She didn't seem the type. But he had his own thoughts pulsing at him and Fay MacConnell slipped from his mind.

Down the stairs and out the front of the Arcade, with its shuttered shops and tall gray neo-Greek columns.

Then along Weybosset Street, past the Turk's Head Building and the old Hospital Trust, and out to Memorial Boulevard and the Providence River.

This was something he loved about Providence, about living downtown. Everything in walking distance, the river in easy reach of his door. Small city, manageable world. Manageable: he liked that word, after everything he'd been through.

He decided to run a bit and jogged south along the river. Glad he'd brought his jacket. A stiff breeze blew in from the water. Weather-dot-com said it might rain. Moist gunmetal clouds piled up dark in the sky to the east.

Gunmetal clouds piled up like this in Siem Reap too in Cambodia in April and May of 1975. And as he ran his memory took over from where the night's dream had snapped shut.

When the Khmer Rouge ask "Why does your father wear glasses? Why does he read books?" the only thing Atith Rattanak can think of to say is "Please don't hurt him."

An answer not good enough. They lead his father off—the last time Atith ever sees him—with a cord round his neck.

As for Atith. They take him to a shed and pen him all day with a hundred other children identified as enemies of the agrarian class. Without thinking he asks for water, which singles him out for notice.

For fun the guards lead him out in the hot afternoon sun to a stained concrete slab and splay his fingers out and unfold a big knife and—

But Atith had long since trained his thoughts to jump ahead to the things that happened later that same night in '75. Much better things. (And besides, nowadays if new acquaintances at Guild Metal or Riverglow happened to ask about all this in any way, Atith was in the habit of saying "Hey I've still got two left on one hand, three on the other, and that's plenty enough to let me eat pizza." Which made people laugh, and was all Atith wanted.)

April '75 and the Khmer Rouge lock the children in the shed for the night. No guards are posted; they're confident the prisoners are too terrified to attempt an escape. But monks from the temple come and break open the lock and lead the children out into the dark and on foot through the forest. Atith can't move—he's curled in a ball, just him and the pain—but a monk lifts him gently and carries him the whole way. Three miles of forest jungle scrub, until they reach Angkor.

Of course the guards come searching. But Angkor is vast. Labyrinths of chambers and chapels and long halls carved with demons that ward off intruders. The Khmer Rouge get bored and give up and move on to plunder Phnom Penh.

Atith is laid on a grass mat in a shrine within innermost Angkor Wat. The first day and the second all he knows is the pain. Monks have bathed what's left of his hands and wrapped them with white bandages that quickly well up red. He lies on his mat beside a broken Bodhisattva that's missing an arm. The statue is clothed in robes, brilliant saffron and yellow on lichen-gray stone. Gnarled tree-roots twine about the fragmented wall and tower up through the open roof. Every morning the monks come and change the robes on the Bodhisattva and drape it with fresh garlands and change the wrappings on Atith's hands for clean white cloths that are quickly stained red.

Until after some days—or is it weeks, or a month?—they say it's no longer safe for the fugitive children to stay. One night the monks take them out to the lake. Boats await. Atith is placed in a sampan—he has a last glimpse of Angkor, a giant smiling face of the Buddha atop a stone tower—and then he's laid under the cover of an atap-palm awning. Children are packed in alongside him, until the boat is crammed full.

From the lake southward to the Tonlé Sap River the water is mild. But where the Tonlé Sap joins the Mekong the current becomes rough and the sampan is tossed back and forth. Vasuki the *nagaraja* gets tugged this way and that to churn up the elixir. And just like Vasuki a very sick ten-year-old Atith pukes up his guts. And every time Vasuki-Atith vomits, the pain throbs in the stubs of his much-mangled hands.

Throbs for days down the Mekong and then out into the South China Sea. Where the sampan is sighted by a U.S. Navy frigate and the children are taken aboard and delivered to the Philippines, to a transitional resettlement center on the island of Palawan. Nicknamed Vietville because of all the refugees from Saigon, but there are Cambodians there too.

Months of recovery, of slow healing, until the bandages come off for good. And part of that healing: the hut marked "Library" and those piles of salt-dampened *Reader's Digests* and the bright prospects of the English language and a sky-blue Chevy Impala.

Atith slowed in his running. To his left was the Dyer Street landing and the berths for the Riverglow skiffs. He walked out onto the dock. First light in the east among the dark clouds. Rain coming for sure. A pair of seagulls cried overhead. He studied the water.

Of course he hadn't been able to come straight from the Palawan camp to the States. He'd spent a long three-and-a-half years in Manila until his uncle arrived in Rhode Island and arranged sponsorship for him. Manila, and work in a cramped rattan-and-wicker shop, where the proprietor at first had said he'd be useless—he lacked sufficient fingers to be employable like the other children in weaving bamboo-fiber mats. "Just watch," a youthful Atith said and quickly proved the man wrong.

He lingered a moment longer on the Dyer Street dock. Early-morning wind slapped waves against the berthed skiffs. He picked out the *Persephone*. His boat. His favorite.

Strange to think: on time's currents the Mekong flows straight into the Providence River. And borne on that flow: a fragile palm-thatch vessel, not much more than a raft, carrying a sick little kid with maimed and mangled hands. Three fingers on one hand, two on the other—enough to weave mats with, or eat pizza. On mornings like this when Atith woke up from bad dreams it was good to remember his grittily determined ten-year-old self.

Part of me of course will always be on that sampan, vomiting up bile like any other long-suffering snake with the job of churning up elixir. But hey. Nagaraja Vasuki survived. And so have I. So have I.

Which reminded him. Two weekends ago, or was it three, he'd been out on the river with the *Persephone* crew. Almost midnight. They had expended their wood and lit the last of the braziers. The skiff came about to return to the dock. He was alone in the prow, stooping low to retrieve and coil a line.

That's when he saw it.

Something in the water. Swimming hard with a lithe wriggling motion. Some two meters in length. Briefly alongside the boat, and then gone.

"Did you see that?" he'd cried out. But no one else had. *Stubby, you're tired. Could have been a shadow on the surface. You know, cast by flames from the braziers.*

Shadow on the surface. At the time he'd agreed maybe so.

Later he'd told Janey Evans. Who promptly said, "Spike-Head. Mystery beast. You're not the first to see him. Riverglow has its very own monster."

He'd said, "More likely just a shadow on the surface."

But now a different thought came, after the shadow cast by the dream: *How far can a* nagaraja *dragon king swim? Could Vasuki have followed me all the way from Angkor? Distances are always slighter than they seem. And after all you were just telling yourself: the Mekong flows straight into the Providence River.*

In that case I'd best look sharp for snake vomit.

The thought made him smile. A thought to share with Janey. And maybe even with her nephew.

Which in turn made him think of Guild Metal. He looked at his watch. Time to jog back and head off to work.

23

At ten the rain came hard in a burst.

Which was good for Guild Metal. Storm gusts blew through cracked windows and old intake vents and briefly thinned the paint spray and acetone fumes.

Still stormy at eleven-thirty but that didn't change Atith Rattanak's plans for lunch. Outdoors in the Impala rain or no rain. He was a creature of habit and besides he wanted to keep a close eye on the FNGs Jorge called Problem Child One and Problem Child Two. If Atith kept Alexander Finster outside it meant simply that much less chance of a lunchroom brawl with Crazy-Chester's gang. As for Augustus Valerian Tessario: Atith was still awaiting the chance for a confidential chat to find out if the kid was staying clean and off drugs.

Though how he was supposed to do that and casually bring up the topic he had no idea. Janey had texted him encouragement again on the way to work. Pretty much the same message as the night before: "U gotta say sth. Counting on u! Thanx ♥♥."

Well thank *you* Janey Evans. He wanted to reply "I appreciate the double hearts but how about some suggestions?" then decided not to bother. *Let's just see what happens today.*

His opening came at lunch. The three sat in his Chevy—doors closed because of the rain—Gusto in front beside him, Alex moody and glum in the back. Both the young men wore hoodies against the unseasonable chill.

To break the silence Atith said brightly his assistant foreman had reported Alex was doing good spray work and showed real promise on the job. "And Jorge Ramirez is a hard guy to please. If he says you're doing good that means you're super-fine."

Through a mouthful of food, Tagger said something back but it came out half-strangled, could have been "So?" or "Sure" or even "Shit." Whatever it was, it didn't qualify as a conversation-sparkler.

Sort of like chatting with Vasuki the dragon-snake: *Ask it how it likes its elixir-churning job and it replies by belching up puke or bile.*

The thought was making Atith lose his appetite. He tried a different topic. "What'd you guys get from the food trucks today?"

One word from Tagger. "Hoagie."

Gus was a bit more forthcoming. "Fried baloney and cheese. It's good."

Back to chewing in silence. Just as they had the day before, both Gus and Alex fussed with their phones as they ate.

But the reference to food had apparently stirred a thought in Gusto Tessario. "Rain seems to be keeping the pigeons away. Too bad. Feeding them was fun."

Tagger surprised Atith by saying something in reply. "Dude, you want something to feed, today's your lucky day. Look under that first truck. No, not that one. The one selling tacos."

Sure enough. Cowering under one of the trucks, seeking shelter from the rain, crouched a dog—white fur, very small, very wet.

"Hey." Gus looked up from his phone. "It's looking right at us. Like it wants our attention."

It certainly seemed to. It wagged a damp tail and stared straight at them with eyes full of woe.

The tail wags had an effect. Gusto sat up straight and laid his sandwich aside. Gaze no longer vacant; instead he grew suddenly purposeful, alive. "Be right back."

A sprint across the gravel, splashing through puddles in the rain. In a moment he was back.

"She jumped right into my arms." The dog was licking his face.

"A shorthaired Chihuahua," said Atith. "From the size, I'd say not much more than a puppy."

"She's shivering," said Gus, real concern in his voice. "Cold and soaked through."

Alex Finster surprised Atith again by offering a helpful idea. "There's an old towel in the back seat here." He turned to the supervisor. "Is it okay we use this to dry her off?"

Atith said sure and watched the two teens towel the dog.

"Short-haired the way she is, she must be cold all the time." Gus lifted her up in his arms. "She needs a sweater maybe to keep her warm."

Atith suggested what she needed was a human to keep her warm.

Gus said good idea and unzipped his hoodie and stuffed the dog against his chest and zipped the jacket back up. The Chihuahua poked out her head and recommenced licking his face.

"Probably hungry," said Alex and offered her a piece of hoagie.

Which she snapped up, along with Gusto's fried baloney and cheese.

Alex asked what was he going to name her.

Gus said if he gave her a name that meant for sure he was going to keep her. "Which might be hard. I'm staying at that halfway house on Mathewson Street downtown. Called Safe Anchorage. It's a shelter for homeless guys on rehab. Don't know if they'd allow her."

"Dude. The dog's homeless too. That means she qualifies."

"Did you see how she liked the cheese from my sandwich? That's what I'll call her. Cheddar. Yeah."

For a moment all three men thought about the same thing at the same time: how best to fuss over a lost-child dog and make it feel at home.

The moment didn't last long.

The rain was just easing off. A car wheeled into the lot beside the food trucks. A black Honda Prius. Atith knew the cars from first shift and this wasn't one.

Three individuals emerged. A young woman and two young men. All dressed alike, in gray polo shirts and gray chinos. All with shoulder-length hair. They turned and gazed about the lot as if searching for someone.

Wordlessly Alexander Finster withdrew his attention from the dog and hurried from the Impala. Atith watched as he approached the trio by the Prius. The three—especially the young woman—hailed him with glad-hand greetings as if they were friends. And Alex Finster did something in reply Atith had never seen him do before. He smiled back. The smile transformed Tagger, lit him from within, suggested depths and possibilities beyond a grim surly facade.

The young woman motioned to her car and the trio got in and sat with Alex in the Prius. Atith wondered what they were chatting about that filled Tagger with such evident warmth. The thought was replaced by another: here was his opening. What Janey had asked for. A chance to talk with her nephew.

"Got a text last night," he began. "From your aunt."

"Aunt Janey? Funny you mention her." Before Atith could say more, Gus Tessario launched his own stream of chatter. "Other day she texted me and told me something cool. She does that Riverglow thing you know and says her boat has someone new on the crew. A guy with a long scar on his jaw and some weird tats on his arms. Wears a coat to keep 'em out of sight. At first she couldn't see too good. All she could tell was his arms were inked with a string of words. My aunt says it was like those tats were the key to some secret past life and so of course she just had to see. Anyway after a while he gets careless and then she gets a pretty good look. Or at least a look at one arm. And you know what's inked on it?"

Atith said he had no idea.

"It said 'Girlie you look like—.' That's all she saw."

Atith asked what was that supposed to mean.

"Same thing my aunt said. But I knew the answer just like that. I knew those are the words to a pretty famous song. I mean famous here of course. Here in Providence. See I follow this local tribute band. Called Treff and the Raptors. They do golden oldies and covers of hits, especially pieces by anyone from Rhode Island or New England who ever makes it big in any way. So as soon as Aunt Janey tells me those words I know it's from a song I've heard the Raptors play. The line goes like this." He sang the lyrics in a thin high voice:

> Girlie you look like the Queen of Diamonds
> Burning your cigarettes right down to the bone.

Gus crooned the words again as he rubbed the dog's ears. "Cheddar, ain't that a cool song?"

He turned back to Atith. "So I tell my aunt you got a celebrity on your boat. She says no way. I say I swear no shit you got yourselves a rock star. Front man, lead singer for a band called the Fox Point Punks. Used to play Rhode Island years and years ago, way before my time. His name is Joey something-or-other. Used to go by the stage name of Joey B. She says yeah yeah Joey Bonaventure and I go that's the one."

More patting and tugging at the dog's ears. "Man I been a big fan of Joey. Always have been. I mean I love his music but it's not just that. Truthfully I love the way he made it kinda big and escaped from Rhode Island and had a career in California. Gigs in L.A. Looked like he might have a big career. Huge. Looked like he might be all set."

Meditatively he rubbed Cheddar's ears. "Course everything changed after the Bacchanale business."

Atith asked what was that.

"West Coast nightclub. Pacific Bacchanale I think was its full name. Or maybe Golden Bacchanale. Something like that. Thing is Joey's Fox Point band was playing there the night of the big fire. Place was packed. Exit doors not marked right or opened the wrong way or something. Buncha people got hurt. Fire marshals blamed management. Blamed the band too. Pyrotechnics on stage. Whole place went up. Yeah. People got hurt. Including Joey. Got his face burnt some. Course that fire and the bad publicity meant the end of the band. He dropped outta sight after that. Bad shit all the way round."

He squeezed the dog to his chest. "But now Joey's back in Providence and that's gotta be good news. Sounds like he's still incognito for now but I bet before you know it he'll play the New England circuit. Shit it'd be cool to see him live playing 'Queen of Diamonds.' "

He crooned the song lyrics again to the dog. Atith's intuition was that the kid's chatter was meant to deflect talk on awkward topics. He decided this was his now-or-never chance to bring up the subject assigned him by Janey Evans.

"Been meaning to ask"—*here goes, hope I can phrase this right*—"what you've been looking up online on Google." *That sounds stupid. Probably just going to offend him.*

Gusto didn't seem offended. At least not at first. "This doggie likes me." Cheddar was studiously applying her tongue to his face. He turned in his seat toward Atith. "Sorry. Didn't catch what you said."

"Just asking what you've been googling online."

A guarded expression came into his eyes. "Why you come at me with a question like that?"

"Your Aunt Janey asked me to ask you. She's worried for you."

"Well tell her she can stop worrying. I'm doing okay."

"What about redrum?"

"Well what about it?" The teen's face darkened from guarded to suspicious.

"Or whatever you want to call it. China white. Apache. China girl."

"You mean fentanyl." This in a flat, lifeless tone.

"Yeah. I mean fentanyl."

"I'm doing research, okay? Composition of different forms of opioids. Which ones are stronger. The effects they have on users. Kind of a game for me. It's like I'm doing it without really doing it. Loading up but not quite. Can almost feel it. Even just looking at pictures of the junk on the screen. It brings it up close. Brings it all back."

The dog ceased licking his face and from within the hoodie studied the boy with her enormous brown eyes. Gus gazed out the car window, spoke again.

"You know some people at Safe Anchorage say I shouldn't do that it's just another sort of addictive behavior but truthfully I'm thinking my research is building a vocational skill. Yeah. Thinking maybe I could be a counselor."

He patted the dog's head. "See, people on rehab can be the best counselors because they know what it's like. Tim Fitzgerald he's my probation guy he says half the counselors at Safe Anchorage are ex-junkies. Tim says they're in a position to help because they been in the shit. Says that all the time. They been in the shit. So maybe I can help too. So me going online that's just doing research. Opioid effects. Bring it all back. Recapture the moment. Do it without really doing it." The words swelled up and then faded, incantatory, dreamy, distant. "Bring it up close. No harm in that. Recapture the moment." His voice trailed away.

The Chihuahua cocked her head, nudged him with a quivery, pleading nose.

Atith nodded at the creature nestled in the hoodie. "I think she's asking you to notice her."

Gusto Tessario snapped back to attention, wrapped his arms round the dog. "Okay, little kid. If we're gonna call you Cheddar, we'd better feed you more cheese. Here, hold her a second, okay? I'm gonna get her another sandwich from the truck."

Her oversize ears cocked and alert, the Chihuahua sat upright on Atith's lap and stared after her new human as the teen exited the Impala. Gus splashed across the rain-puddled lot but before he reached the trucks the Prius driver's-side door opened. A hand waved and hailed the youngster and he stepped aside by the open door. He stooped, head bent as if in conversation.

Atith saw someone inside the car—he thought it was the young woman—reach out from within and offer him something. Gus pocketed whatever it was and then dodged around more puddles to get to the trucks. A minute later he was back in the Chevy.

"See, baby, another sandwich. And just what you ordered. More fried baloney and cheese." He welcomed the Chihuahua back into his hoodie and zipped up the jacket.

Without needing to be asked, Gusto said it was funny when he walked by the Prius the trio talking to Alex had waved him over real friendly. "And the girl sitting behind the wheel hands me a ten and says my new dog looks hungry so go buy it more food. Just like that. Ten bucks. Pretty nice."

"She say anything else?"

"No. Wait. Yeah." Gusto was breaking off baloney-and-cheese bites and feeding them to Cheddar. "She did say something else. Something a little weird. She said 'Maybe you can be useful too.' And then she gave me a big smile."

"Huh. Was that all she said?"

"Yeah. Kinda weird. 'Useful for what,' I wanted to say. But I could see she wasn't in the mood to explain. Still in my world ten bucks is ten bucks so I ain't complaining."

Cheddar interrupted him with an I'm-still-starving gaze that urged, "More baloney please." As the teen complied, Atith watched the Prius. The passenger-side door opened and Alexander Finster stepped out. The car sped away across the gravel and out of the lot.

As Tagger neared the Chevy he swaggered and pumped a fist, then bounced into the back seat, aglow with elation and triumph. Atith said he sure looked happy.

"So would you man if someone just showed you a way to bust out. And also promised you a whole new life. Yeah."

He turned away from Atith and from the Impala's rear seat leaned in toward Gus. "Dude. Got an idea for a cool thing to do tonight. How'd you like a close-up look at that thing the losers around here call the Big Blue Bug?"

"Man, that'd be awesome." Gus said he'd never seen it up close. "I'd love it." He lifted the dog from the hoodie and asked if he could bring his new friend. Then he glanced over at Atith and added in a glow of generosity, "And how about Stubby? Maybe he'd like to come too."

Alex frowned a second but then shrugged. "Sure. Bring the dog. And if the boss here wants to come, why not—no one's gonna get in the way of tonight."

Atith's first instinct was to boom a loud No. If he remembered right from the piece he'd read in the *Providence Journal,* when Tagger had gotten arrested for spraying "RMH" on the bug, the court had issued a restraining order that forbade the graffiti offender from going anywhere near the city's prize termite for the next umpteen million years. Plus Atith didn't like the look of that trio in the Prius—he mistrusted anyone who went around handing out tens to teens and telling them they might be "useful"—and he wondered if the trio had planted this nutty Blue Bug thought in Tagger's head.

But then he saw the eagerness in Gus Tessario's eyes and said to himself *Well at least this will be one evening where the kid's not obsessing over opioids online and instead is taking an interest in things outside his head and Janey Evans did say pry him free from his phone.*

So he gave a cautious okay. "But no climbing around up close. We'll just get a quick view from across the street. Or even better from way down the block. That way we'll stay out of trouble. A fast in and out."

"Deal," said Tagger promptly.

So at nine that night Atith Rattanak left the reassuring quiet of his Arcade apartment and got into his Impala and drove south on 95. Alex Finster had said meet at nine-thirty and it would take only ten minutes tops to get to the place but Atith wanted to be there first and plenty early. Early enough so if things looked wrong and likely to get them in trouble he could do his best to call the business off.

Should never have agreed, he chided himself as he drove. *You are one stupid egg. But Gus looked so delighted to be asked on a venture and Janey's been saying help the kid get away from his phone.* Atith shook his head as he drove. *One stupid egg.*

Route 95 south. Exit 19, Borden Street to Eddy. Atith parked the Chevy near the corner of Eddy and O'Connell.

He sat in the car a moment, studied the nighttime street. A wind blew trash and dead leaves along the gutters.

Behind him and to the east, the tunnel-darkness of the highway overpass and the passing rush of cars on high. Across the street, a shuttered garage and auto-parts shop, beside a chain-link fence and a vacant lot where the concrete had cracked and given way to thick weed-trees.

And directly in front of him, tonight's destination. The four-story cinderblock mass of New England Pest Control, its office windows unlit, all its workers long since gone for the day.

All its workers save one: the Big Blue Bug.

From the ground Atith could see a floodlight positioned to shine on the termite so its fifty-eight-foot bulk could be seen from 95. Tonight the Bug was costumed with giant neon-red sunglasses. Propped before it was a seven-foot-tall waxed-cup mock-up serving of Del's Lemonade—in Rhode Islander tradition the way to mark the start of summer. The year before, the Bug had posed with another summer drink that was sacred to Rhode Island: an ice-milk-and-flavored-syrup concoction served up by the Newport Creamery and revered statewide via its trademark name of Awful Awful.

The street was silent. He stepped from the car and at once heard a roll of wheels on pavement.

From the dark of the overpass tunnel emerged a silhouette on a skateboard. Augustus Valerian Tessario, in jeans and hoodie. From just under Gusto's chin, above the half-zipped jacket, poked the head of his new-friend Chihuahua. The dog caught sight of Atith and yipped.

Gus stopped, tucked the board under his arm, said Cheddar had reminded him she had permission to come. "Anyway the Safe Anchorage staff are giving me grief about keeping her. Better if she's with me tonight."

He gazed up at the display. "So that's our Big Blue. Never seen it this close. Awesome. That Del's Lemonade looks good. Makes me thirsty. But where's Tagger?"

"Not so loud, you dork." The voice made both Gus and Atith flinch. From the shadows by the Pest Control building stepped a figure in black—black running shoes, black jeans, black tee, and—fastened at the throat—a black cape with a cowl. He loomed beside them with a swirl of his cape. The dog yipped in fright and squirmed against Gus' chest.

Tagger hissed at the Chihuahua and its human. "Make that hairless maggot shut up."

"She ain't a hairless maggot. Why you call her that? I thought you liked her."

"I like dogs that know when to shut up."

"She barked cuz you scared her. Shit. You scared *me.*" Gus laughed, but Atith could tell it was more nervous-jangle than sense-of-fun. "But what's this getup? You some kinda crime fighter?"

"Me?" Alex Finster extended an arm and gave his cape another swirl. "More like some kinda criminal." His feet sketched a dance step and his lips mouthed a tune:

They call me Devil Dog
and Busy Bee
But mostly I'm known
as the Master Thief.

"Hey," exclaimed Gusto. "I've heard that before. Played by Treff and the Raptors. But written way back when by Joey B for the Fox Point Punks."

Their voices echoed loud in the empty street. Cheddar yipped again. The dog was nervous.

And now so was Atith. He didn't like how close the three of them were standing to the out-of-limits building. *Better scale this back now before things spin out of control.* "Don't you have a restraining order barring you from the vicinity of anything you've tagged?"

Alex Finster flicked him a cold dismissive glance. "Ask me if I care. Tonight ain't no one can touch me. I'm riding high. Cuz I got the word. Be on top of a certain specified rooftop tonight, keep my eyes on downtown, look out for a signal at 9:45. That's what she told me. And the rooftop in question just happens to have something I tagged. Which is cool. Very cool."

Atith stepped forward. "You're not going up there. You'll get us all—"

Tagger spun about to Gus with a sweep of his cape. "Dude. Live a little." He gave a sly wink, nodded toward the roof. "Come on to the back. I'll show you something that's a hyper-natural high."

He turned and ran to the back of the building. His cape billowed behind him.

"Hyper-natural high." Gus licked his lips. "I like the sound of that." Cradling Cheddar he ran trailing after Tagger, calling out "Hey wait for me."

"Gusto. No." Atith watched the teens vanish around the building's corner. *This will end badly.* He thought of Janey and knew he had to follow.

At the rear of the building, away from the highway floodlights, a ladder leaned against the wall in the dark. Tagger was already halfway up. "Come on." Atith saw him motioning Gus to follow. "It's easy."

"We need a permit," pleaded Atith, "before we go climbing up people's roofs."

From the ladder Tagger twisted his head and paused in his climb long enough to reply. "Permits and permission slips. That's for the dorks and losers that use hand sanitizers and antibacterial wipes and hope they can stay all nice and safe." He waved down at Gus. "You can sanitize your way through life, or you can crash on through and tear up shit. Dude. What's it gonna be?" With that the sprayer vaulted himself up atop the roof.

Atith called out to Gus to stop—he was still keeping his voice as low as he could, worried some watchman or passing police patrol would spot them and arrest them and put them in jail—but Gus paid him no heed. "Crash on through," he laughed. "Hyper-natural high." Then he clambered up the ladder one-handed—with his other hand keeping the frightened Cheddar pressed up close against his chest.

"There. Ain't it worth it?" Alex Finster opened his cape wide and bowed as if to take full credit for their rooftop vista.

Atith had to admit the view was splendid. To the north, the office buildings of the nighttime downtown skyline, the Statehouse with its gilded statue of the Independent Man, and Superman's own Industrial Trust with its tower beacon that glowed red every night. To the east, factory smoke stacks, 95 with its highway rush of freight trucks, and the lights of a cargo ship by the wharves of Narragansett Bay.

But he gave it all only a glance. For close up before him, over nine feet in height, crouched Providence's Big Bug. Floodlit from below, it glowed a deep metal blue and bristled with appendages and feelers that shook in the breeze.

Atith stepped forward to join the teens and noticed at once the texture of the roof on which he stood: thick layered tarpaper, soft, spongy, eerily yielding beneath his feet. Would it buckle under his weight? He reminded himself this same roof bore up under the heft of a fifty-eight-foot Bug.

Gus and Alex were sitting beneath the termite's thorax. He joined them and peered upward at the underside of the Bug's fiberglass wings. Arrayed in a dark yellow-brown, the appendages made him think of a butterfly's patterning or the stained glass he'd seen once in the Catholic cathedral downtown. The steel rim of each wing was corroded and pitted with rust. *Even things of metal*, came the thought, *are subject to Time the Devourer.*

And that's when the Bug surprised them all three by beginning to hum.

That's the word at least that Gus used as he sprang out with a start from under the termite. "Didja hear that? Swear to shit it's starting to hum." Cheddar the Chihuahua whimpered in sympathetic woe.

The other two humans stood too and listened.

Atith heard it now. A variable thrum. First near, then afar. Felt it as much as heard it. In his gut, in his ears. What was it?

He glanced up at the nine-foot-tall insect. The imagination runs fast, outpaces daylight logic in moments like this. *Winged termites approaching, in swarms from the north? A billion bugs munching, under command of their king?*

That's when he saw something he hadn't spotted before. Surrounding the Pest Control icon on all sides were guy wires and support cables, each fastened to the Big Bug and pegged to the roof. Like restraint ropes round a circus-tent attraction, they kept the giant beast fixed fast in place.

The night wind rose and the cables thrummed, first loud and then soft. Thorax and wings bucked, groaned, held taut by the cords.

"It's like it's alive," gaped Gus Tessario and backed away in awe.

And at that Atith noted something else as well: one more backward step would suffice to flip the boy and his dog off the roof and down a sixty-foot drop.

"Whoa." Atith caught his arm just in time.

"Jeez. Hey. Thanks, Stubby." The teen shuddered. "That wouldn't'a been too good for my Cheddar." He patted the Chihuahua's head in apology.

"That wouldn't have been too good for you either. Your aunt wants you to take care of yourself."

But Gusto went back to enthusing about how alive the Blue Bug looked as it rocked in the wind.

"Alive? That's all shit." Arms folded, black cape around his shoulders, black cowl shielding his shaved head, Alex Finster surveyed the fifty-eight-foot object with an artist's appraising eye. "What we got here is just a big surface in a high-profile spot that's ideal for tagging. That's why I came up in the first place all those weeks ago. Spray my 'RMH' and leave my mark. 'Cept it's gone now cuz some shit-ass removal crew came up and took it all away and repainted the thing with this boring blue."

"Course it's alive. Or nearly," said Gus in defense of the Bug. "And no wonder, when you think of the way people in Providence have been showing it love. They dress it up with costumes and leave it hundred-gallon cups of lemonade and Awful Awful ice milk. You think it's never been tempted to take at least a sip? Who wouldn't come alive, with a sugar rush like that?"

"Dude." A world of scorn, squeezed into that one word. "Those opioids of yours have screwed up your brain but good."

Gusto's words apparently disgusted Tagger but they stirred a memory in Atith. Siem Reap in the good years, the time before the Khmer Rouge. His father conducting a morning tour of Angkor, leading visitors along the temple galleries. Nine-year-old Atith trailing the crowd, proudly saying to a Frenchwoman beside him, "C'est mon père." His father smiling and hushing him and gathering the group before Atith's favorite wall-length frieze: the gods and demons tugging and twisting Vasuki the serpent in the cosmic ocean. One day his father concluded with a philosophical afterthought of the kind he often favored: "We must be careful what images we choose to carve. If we put sufficient energy into them we may awaken a longing for movement. What if corporeal creatures of mortal clay aren't the only ones alive? What if our actions stir up life in what we think of as inanimate? What if we haven't been attentive enough to all the forces in the ether that press in on us? It may be, my friends, that flesh and blood are merely pinpoint marks on a continuum of life. A continuum that ranges from angels to iron and stone."

His father drew a similar lesson one evening in reading aloud to young Atith an episode from a storybook brought him as a gift by an American guest: *The Wizard of Oz*. Dorothy and her friends have to cross a meadow of red poppies—beautiful but somniferous, inducing sleep that lasts forever and puts an end to all quests.

Atith remembered how his father told the story. "Dorothy and the Lion yawn and fight hard to stay awake but can't. Human and beast crumple and curl up in defeat. Luckily the Scarecrow and the Woodman-made-of-metal don't have this weakness, don't have to inhale. So they're the ones to save the girl and the Lion from the field. There's a lesson here, my Atith: Things we might look down on, supposedly inferior in rank, might be our means of rescue. Straw and tin have mercy on us when blood and bones fail. Be alert to the nonhuman. Be gracious to what seems beneath us."

The memory of Cambodia and Oz broke off at an angry yelp from Tagger. "Where's my signal?" The young man paced back and forth beside the Bug. "It's past 9:45 and she said get up on the rooftop and face downtown and get ready for a signal. Well I done what she told me and I got 9:49 so where is it?" His cape whirred in black swirls around him.

Atith asked if it was the young woman in the Prius that had made him this promise.

"Dude. It wasn't just some young woman in a Prius. She called herself Lady Alicia. Baroness of Yog-Sothoth. Or something like that. She said I do what I'm told I can have a title too. I don't know what Yog-Sothoth is but it sure sounds cool. And way better than what I got around here."

He checked his phone: "9:51. No signal. Nothing. Hell with it. While I'm up here may as well leave my mark." He reached within his cape and brought out a can of spray paint. "Krylon. Jungle green. Cuz I'm in a jungly mood. Gonna mark up that thing with another big fat 'RMH.' "

But before he could spray, Augustus Valerian Tessario jumped at him and yelled something—"Don't squirt the Bug" or maybe "Don't hurt the Bug," Atith wasn't sure. The two teens grappled at the roof edge and the black cape swirled and the Chihuahua howled and for one second a horrified Atith thought of a tattered old Frank Frazetta pulp-art poster that for years had been pinned up in a back room of Guild Metal: Dracula vs. Wolf-Man.

Then he shook off his paralysis and jumped forward to try to keep teens and dog from falling off the roof.

Alex Finster was far stronger and was just about to spray Gus in the face when Cheddar popped out of the hoodie and nipped Spray-Man in the wrist. Now it was Tagger's turn to howl. The can plunged and bounced on pavement a dark sixty feet below.

Atith had just leaped atop Tagger's back and was forcing him away from Gus when an interruption made them all stop.

Interruption in the form of a flare. A great flashing light in the north.

Welling up from the red beacon tower of the Superman Industrial Trust, then rippling down from the heights of the skyscraper.

A cascade of red radiance, urgent and pulsing. Again and again and again. A brief pause of darkness. Then the red cascade resumed. Again and again and again.

Nine times in all it did this, until the light ebbed and ceased.

"That was my signal." Alex Finster still gasped from the fight. "That was meant just for me. They haven't forgotten." He kept his gaze on the north, spoke low to himself. "I can be Baron of Yog-Sothoth. Or Lord of it. Or something."

He turned round in triumph, glared up at the Bug. "Ain't nothing can touch me. Not now." He sprinted across the roof and disappeared down the ladder.

From within Gusto's hoodie the Chihuahua cried in a soft whimper. Atith stepped forward and patted her head. "How's your Cheddar doing?"

The teen said he thought she could use another fried baloney-and-cheese sandwich. "And truthfully so could I."

"Me too," said Atith. "I know a diner downtown that's still open. Come on."

At the top of the ladder he cast a last glance at the roof. The guy wires and cables thrummed in the wind. The Blue Bug bucked against its restraints.

24

Another night of troubled sleep for Joseph Bonaventure. As always the dream had to do with the fire.

Back—yet again—at the Pacific Bacchanale. Club packed, as it had been each night. Bodies shimmying on the dance floor. Lots of booze, smell of weed. Music loud—too loud really, he could hardly hear himself sing—but Max the manager liked it cranked up and claimed the public liked it that way too.

The band had gone through a string of their own songs the fans wanted most—"It Must Be True Love," "Fox Point Girl," "Someone I Used to Know"—and now the evening was ending with a flourish and their best-known all-time number-one quasi-hit. "Queen of Diamonds." Easy to see the crowd was having a good time: everyone was on their feet, dance dance dance. Bonaventure turned his head, saw Tibbett the drummer. Tibbett normally frowned in concentration the whole evening through but there he was all lit up with a grin. A good sign. A good gig.

And then the pyrotechnics. Max insisted on setting them off at the end of each night. "Give 'em something to remember. So they'll tell their friends about Fox Point Punks and how good our group is." Bonaventure thought it all a bit much. *And I should have said so, or said something at least.*

Sparklers flaring up. Ruby-red arcs. Firecrackers, fizzy and glowing. *Pop-pop-pop.*

Afterward the fire safety inspectors said the ceiling tiles melted. Styrofoam, plastic, whatever they were: not built for the heat.

Pop-pop-pop, then a crackle and *whoosh.* Flames in a ripple from the roof to the floor.

Pop-pop-pop spooked him right off the stage.

No backward look to check on anyone else: in a fright he just jumped for his life.

But—tonight in the dream—instead of landing on top of the crowd and ignobly clawing over them to get to the door, he flopped into water.

Into the Providence River. Cold, green, opaque. Thick taste of sludge. Ugh.

Underwater; dark. Even subsurface he could see the braziers midstream. Stoked up with wood, for the Riverglow show.

Pop-pop-pop. Braziers alight, wood nicely aglow. People on shore must be enjoying all this.

He'd been spilled from his canoe. Yes of course. He'd been paired with that kid Tagger. He was just about to lift his head from beneath the water when he saw movement through the murk.

Coming toward him, and fast. Rubbery undulating *S*-curves. Some kind of swimmer, six feet in length. What had someone called it? Spike-Head. Eyes glowing ruby red.

And details he'd forgotten from his first sighting the night of the tipped canoe: This swimmer had a long tail that writhed as the thing swam. And gray-green paws or maybe hands almost human with sharp curving claws. And along the top of its head and its long rippling back, a spiny spiked crest.

And in its mouth, a sphere of some kind, being borne underwater, to be delivered just to him.

He backed away in fright: frightened by the creature swimming at him, by the murk, by the fire in the braziers that would burn him if it could as the wood went up in nightclub flames that echoed *pop-pop-pop.*

Louder and closer came the sound. *Pop-pop. Pop-pop-pop.*

Joseph Bonaventure sat straight up in bed.

"I've been knocking for five minutes." In the doorway stood an impatient Fay MacConnell. In one hand she held a thick sheaf of papers.

Bonaventure said he was sorry. "Thought the knock was just a sound in my dream." He scratched his head. "Come on in." He had hastily pulled on nothing more than jeans and a tee and realized now with a jolt his arm-length tats stood exposed. "Girlie you look like the Queen of Diamonds." Too late to hide 'em and in any case Treff Boudreau the other day had already blown that concealment sky-high. Luckily Fay MacConnell chose to say nothing for the moment and simply followed as Bonaventure welcomed her in.

He yawned, made an attempt to smooth his hair, gave it up. "What time is it anyway?"

"Six-thirty or so."

"Oh. No wonder I'm not really awake." He decided not to ask the reason for this visit. *Must have something to do with those papers she's holding. Let her tell me when she's ready. Don't want to risk irking her or scaring her off.*

He plucked a sweatshirt from the only chair in the room. "Whew. Need to clean the place a bit. I start the day with coffee. All I got's instant. Taster's Choice."

"Taster's Choice'll be fine. This early in the day I'll eat it with a spoon if I have to. I just need to mainline caffeine."

He glanced about his living space, imagined it through her newcomer's eyes. Cramped space, narrow bed, tiny desk. Books in cardboard cartons. Sink, hotplate, micro-fridge. All in one room. Clothes flung at random.

"Sorry. Place is a mess."

"Hey. You should see mine." She stepped to the window. "But wow look at this view. Nice."

"Yeah. Westward, facing downtown and the skyline all the way to Federal Hill." He said it was almost the same view H. P. Lovecraft must have had in his own College Street digs. "Good inspiration for a guy writing a dissertation on Cthulhu-Man. Or trying to." Another plus he said about this one-room apartment was that besides being cheap it was just two blocks from Lovecraft's old house and close to Brown's library and the Athenaeum. "So a great perch for research."

He swept his desk free of books, plopped them on the cot. "There. Clear space, thereby constituting kitchen table and breakfast dining spot."

With a wave of his hand he invited her to sit. "Choice of seats. Folding chair, or messy bed."

"I'll take the bed."

He took a hissing kettle from the hotplate and poured water over mounded crystals in two cups. With an opener he punched neat *V*'s into a can of Borden's condensed milk. "I like mine sweet."

"Same here. Pour me some."

From the fridge he took a box of Drake's Coffee Cakes. "All I've got handy in the way of grub. Sorry."

"Are you kidding? I love those things."

She unwrapped a mini-cake. "Can I ask a big favor?"

He guessed aloud it probably involved lighting up a cigarette.

"You read my mind."

He said the landlord listed smoking as strictly forbidden but the place already stank of two centuries of smokers and one more Camel wouldn't hurt. "I'll just open the window is all."

He watched as she dunked a Drake's cake in her Taster's Choice and added more condensed milk to the coffee and drank a grateful gulp. He realized he liked looking at her. She wore her blond hair cropped short but aside from that she looked a little like her namesake Fay Wray. Moxie. Enough to climb aboard a freighter and sail far away and survive a grab by King Kong.

She ate a second Drake's, drank more coffee, inhaled a long deep pull on her Camel. "Ah. This is heaven."

He smiled and waved a hand at the cramped, untidy room. "Dunno about that. Maybe heaven's messy discount trailer annex. Sorry."

"Stop saying sorry. I should be the one apologizing, considering I just crashed in on you with no warning at six-thirty in the morning."

She had nice blue eyes. What was also nice was that she didn't seem sore at him the way she'd been when Treff the Raptor showed up and blew their pizza picnic to bits.

Her glance suddenly traveled up and down his tats. "Can I ask you something maybe way too personal?" He braced himself with an inward *Uh-oh* but before he could reply with an "okay" or "sure" or "I guess so" she continued straight on. "I can't help the question cuz it's been bothering me. 'Girlie you look like the Queen of Diamonds.' Setting aside the sexist vocab, what's that supposed to mean anyway?"

"Hard to explain." He scratched his head. "Not sure I understood it myself when I first wrote the piece back when." He paused but his thoughts tumbled on. *What I'd like to tell her but I just don't know how the hell she'd take it: Queen of Diamonds—glitter, ornament, all surface, turn the card over, you don't see any more from the back than you do from the front. The way I like to keep things in life. Or used to. Used to. Used to keep it all simple. No entanglements, just good-time laughs, no hard feelings, time to leave, another gig, gotta go. Course all that was before the fire.*

"Hard to explain," he said again. "A long time ago now. My head was in a different place. Lots happened since then. Let's just say old

Queenie was inscrutable and I liked that because it meant I didn't have to put much in."

"Inscrutable," she repeated. "Now there's a word you don't hear often anymore."

"Yeah." He shook his head, self-conscious, thought maybe she'd be angry at how he flubbed about with words. But the gaze she leveled at him seemed sympathetic rather than critical. *Or maybe she's just feeling good from that Drake's Coffee Cake.*

Desperate urge to change the subject, get off the topic of his past before he irked her. He spied an opportunity as he returned her gaze. "Hey. I just noticed. You're wearing the stud earring I was stupid enough to knock off your ear." He added he just wanted to tell her how bad he felt about that whole horrible incident.

"I told you already. Stop saying sorry. But funny you mentioned the earring because that's part of the reason I'm here. The earring. Plus this."

She waved the thick sheaf of papers she'd brought.

"What's that? More journal entries by Novalyne Price?"

She said it was something even stranger. "But before I show you I'd better give you a little background." She said that the night before, she'd gone from the Athenaeum to her apartment in the Westminster Arcade. "I put the stud back in my ear because I was feeling good about having it back again. So I'm sitting at home on my couch with Dupin, that's my cat, and we're flipping through a paperback Poe and watching TV and eating Cheerios and tuna and Wonder Bread."

"That was supper?"

"Don't laugh. Some nights we have blueberry pop tarts."

He gestured at the desk and the Drake's Coffee Cakes. "Your secret is safe."

"So anyway we eat our Cheerios and stay up late and fall asleep on the couch. All typical for me. And I have these strange dreams which again is typical because I never really sleep that good."

Another pull on the cigarette. "But get this. About five I wake up. Dupin's awake too and he's staring at me. Or more like he's staring at *this*." She tapped the stud she wore in her ear. "So naturally I go to the mirror. I want to know why my cat's giving me a look like I've sprouted two heads."

"And?"

"Well get this. I look in the mirror and I'm ready for anything. I mean at five in the morning I never look good and like I said I never really get a decent night's sleep and mirrors are never my best pal anyway but I tell myself *Okay girlfriend take a peek, see what your cat's trying to say.*"

Eagerly Bonaventure leaned forward from his seat on the cot. "Yeah. Yeah. But what did you see in the mirror?"

"Hold on. I'm getting there." Another bite of Drake's and a sip of Taster's Choice. "So I look in the mirror and my face is okay and everything and I go well that's a relief and I turn around to Dupin and start to say 'Hey furball thanks for shaking my already shaky self-confidence' and then I suddenly notice what musta caught his attention."

"Which was?"

"Which was—and you're not gonna believe this—which was that my silver stud earring, the one you gave back to me, the one you said some wriggly thing in the Providence River had in its mouth, what was it you said its name was?"

"Janey called it Spike-Head."

"Yeah. So that very same ear-stud, which I'm wearing as I'm standing in front of the mirror at five in the morning, is glowing red. Red, with a kind of pulse. Bright, bright red for a second, then fading away back to silver again. A pulse, every few seconds. Bright red, and then fade. Till finally after a minute or so it stops for good."

"Wow. The same piece Spike-Head had in its mouth."

"And get this. Dupin's staring at me with a look as if to say, and I know this sounds nuts but sometimes it's like me and my kitty we've got this telepathic exchange, as if he wants to say 'I've been trying to tell you that thing's been pulsing all night ever since you fell asleep on the couch.'"

"No wonder you had strange dreams."

"It gets stranger." Another sip of her coffee. "I turn around from the mirror and I see these sheets of paper scattered all over the couch. The ones I'm holding now in my hand." She unfolded the notes as she spoke. "The pages were torn from a notebook I always keep by the couch. In case I want to jot thoughts while I'm reading at night. And the handwriting on all these pages is definitely mine. But boy my wrist is plenty sore. I mean look how much I wrote. Dozens and dozens of sheets." She slowed as she spoke, as if unsure how to phrase what she felt compelled to say next.

"But if this is just something you jotted for yourself last night, why are you spooked about it this morning?"

"Because A, I have zero memory of writing this even though it's in my handwriting, and B, the stuff that's written on these pages describes people you and I know about and care about from a century or two ago. But this stuff involves intimate and personal details and crazy shit, I mean crazy, that I couldn't possibly know yet here it is all written up in my own handwriting. Almost like psychography."

"You mean automatic writing, someone's ghost temporarily taking over your hand? Spirit writing? Jeez."

"Yeah. Exactly. And that's scary." She stubbed out the last of her cigarette, lit another. "I know I gotta limit myself to one a day but what the hell. I mean my nerves are shot. So I skimmed through the pages and as soon as I finished I knew there's only one person in the city of Providence who I could show this to without being told I'm looney-tunes or having people just laugh in my face. So that's why I'm here. I mean you've had some strange stuff happen to you too. That thing swimming up to you in the river. And here I was thinking *you* were nuts."

"That's always still possible," laughed Bonaventure. "But now you've got me intrigued." He held out his hands. "Let's take a look."

"I need just one little thing first," she said. "Or make that two little things."

"Name 'em."

"Another cup of Taster's Choice. And one more Drake's Coffee Cake."

"Coming right up." He leapt to the hotplate, put the kettle back on.

"There." He handed her a fresh cup. "Coffee. Sweetened condensed milk. Plus a side order of Drake's Coffee Cakes."

"Like you said. Heaven's trailer annex. Now let's start with page one of whatever this is."

25

Providence, Rhode Island, June? July? (not sure), 1936

My eleventh day in this glass cell. Or is it my twelfth? Hard to keep count.

My fellow prisoner is dozing on a heap of pebbly earth and torn grass. Propped against the cell wall is a Mercury dime, almost the same height as either of us. Our jailer tossed it into the enclosure some time ago by way of taunt: *since acclaim in the form of wealth was what you craved all through the folly of your life, here's a token to apprise you of just how much you're worth.*

Looks like another torture session is being readied for us today. Readied with diabolic care by Giant-Face. Whom I also name Wizard Tuzoon, foul foe of noble Atlantean Kull. To pass the hours I think up more names for our captor. Mesmer of Stygia. Khemsa the Sorcerer, dread spinner of spells. Every necromancer that's ever been skewered or stabbed by Conan the Barbarian. Or by Solomon Kane, or Bran Mak Morn, or any other old friend of mine.

They'd know what to do. Crush Mesmer of Stygia.

Crush Khemsa the Sorcerer.

Crush Wizard Tuzoon.

A wizard known to the world by a soothing and less sinister name. Born of a fine New England family, so he tells us. From distinguished Old World roots. One Howard Phillips Lovecraft.

There. He's looming above our cell now, looking in. Ol' Giant-Face.

"Say." I yell up at him. "Say you. Pale Corpse-Bag. Hey you."

"Ah. Two-Gun Bob." His favorite name for me. I can hear him but he can scarcely hear me. I still can't accept, can scarcely believe, I'm no more than three-quarters of an inch in height. Okay maybe seven-eighths.

"Beg pardon." He cups a hand to his ear. "You're almost inaudible. Unintelligible. Not that you've much of worth to say." His lips turn up in a smile. "You're too tiny. Insignificant. Both of you. Too trivial."

"Trivial?" My cellmate scrambles to his feet. "You dare call me trivial? The finest versifier ever known to this nation?" He struggles over to that Mercury dime. I've been telling him "Partner just let it be" but he has to have at it again.

"Mister Howard. Come help me. I'll tap out a rebuttal."

Doesn't feel worth the effort. Nothing much does. "Eddie," I tell him. "Sit down. Take a break."

"Sir. I have instructed you already." He stamps his foot, stirs the leaf mold all about us. "I resent the temerity with which you hail me as 'Eddie.'" He says such familiarity is unwarranted from a backwoodsman. (He means me.) "Have the goodness to address me as you should. With the deference due to the late correspondent of the *Southern Literary Messenger.* Someone who should have been hailed as a scintillant peer in the Aristocracy of the American Intellect. Someone who should have been rewarded with the emoluments befitting the most creative genius known to these shores. Someone who should have been ..."

"Okay, Mister Poe. I'll help you with the damn dime." Anything to divert him once he starts recalling all the slights he endured in his life.

The thing is heavy, not easy to handle. Takes the two of us to grip it and tap it against the wall of our cell. *Tink-tink*, until Edgar Allan Poe begins to get tired.

The glass is dark, smoky, allows us to see out but gives back no reflection at all. Probably just as well. I haven't shaved, haven't combed my hair, haven't had a chance to sort myself out. Not since that river-ride in the cream-soda bottle. Not since that final moment in Cross Plains, when I took that three-eighty and ... No. Don't want to look at myself now. Just as well the glass is smoky and dark and reflects nothing back. What would it reflect? The face of a failure. Ol' Corpse-Head was right. I'm too tiny to matter. Too trivial.

I stop tapping. Easy to get discouraged when you're dead. Or three-quarters of the way. What's my new label? "Vespertine." Caught between worlds.

Eddie looks glum too. We ease the dime against the wall. Thing weighs a ton. Could crush us both bad. We stand it with the god Mercury facing us. We don't like the look of the ax on the back.

"Now. If you're quite through with your little display." My cellmate and I know what's coming next. We sit slumped in the sod. Giant Corpse-Face Tuzoon the Wizard places a chair by our prison. He sits beside us and unrolls the manuscript on which he's been laboring. That crow of his (damnation it is big, bigger than I remember from my last day in Cross Plains—the first time it fluttered about Lovecraft's room I thought it'd swoop in and pluck one or the other of us prisoners up and gulp, down the gullet, as a quick little snack), that crow flutters onto his shoulder and flaps and fusses and then settles down as if it wants a good listen.

And sure enough: we're slated to hear another recitation of his latest work whether we want to or not.

Which Eddie Poe clearly doesn't. He grabs a clump of twigs and dirt and flings it skyward at the open top of our cage. It all drifts back as always and just falls on our upturned faces.

"Gentlemen." Our warden is enjoying himself hugely. "Relax and listen. The latest installment from my new composition. A draft of what I'm thinking of entitling 'Buried Alive Among the Mummies.' Appropriate, perhaps, considering where the two of you may well be dispatched."

At this the crow emits a loud *graack*.

"True enough, Kavva. But let's not discuss the Portal now. No need to upset our guests."

The crow on his shoulder eyes him a long moment as if wishing to resume a discussion—or a disputation?—that's arisen between them before. It opens its beak wide but Lovecraft's hand shoots forth and clamps the bird-mouth shut. Sounds gurgle from within the clenched beak. "Wrn . . . m . . . fuvrs."

I'm not fond of this critter—how could I be when the sight of it reminds me of that awful last morning in Texas?—but clamped mouth and all it's staring at the two of us in prison as if it has a message it knows we need to hear.

I shout as loud as I can—maybe it hears better than its master: "What do you want to tell us?"

Corpse-Face still keeps the beak clenched. Kavva tries again, squirms in his grip. "Wrn ... m ... fuvrs."

"What?" Poe and I are both shouting now.

The crow jerks its beak free. A fast squawk: "Warn them of others."

"Others? Other what?"

But that's as much as we learn. Lovecraft mutters something—sounds like "Don't make me call on Abdul Hazred and bind you fast for a week"—which is enough to put the bird to frightened flight. It alights atop the corner coatrack and hides its head beneath a wing.

"As I was saying." Lovecraft brushes a feather from his shoulder. "'Buried Alive Among the Mummies.' You'll recall from yesterday's reading that our hero has ventured to Egypt, where he is taken captive by the ruffian dregs of Cairene alleys, ruffians who prove to be henchmen-minions of Great Cthulhu. They plan to punish him for seeking the location of forbidden Yog-Sothoth. Yog-Sothoth, which can reveal the true and foul nature of our world. Yog-Sothoth, the gate and the bridge. Which must be kept guarded against unspeakable intrusions from beyond. A fortress gate that you yourselves will help strengthen. That you yourselves ... But enough of Yog-Sothoth for now."

He pauses, peers down at us, resumes. "These Egyptian servants of Cthulhu bind their prisoner and by night take him to the vast Gizeh plateau, with its pyramids and Sphinx of Khephren. They blindfold their captive and fasten to him a rope of impossibly great length. Then with this rope they lower him down the mouth of a hidden well."

Cadaver-Head looks up from his manuscript. "Thus far yesterday. If I may say so, I rather fancy what I've written to date." From its coatrack the crow mutters a surly *grrrick-grrrick*.

"Yes. Well." Lovecraft's lips move in what may be a smile. "How much aesthetic discernment can one expect from a crow? Whereas you two—even if now miniaturized—you two are men of letters, albeit overrated. Two-Gun Bob and his pitiful pulp fictions. Little Eddie and his displays of neurasthenia that he dares to call art."

"Neurasthenia!" My cellmate shakes a fist at the world.

"You do no more than deplete yourself with these agitations. And now to resume." Corpse-Face pats his lips with a handkerchief and begins to read aloud:

Bound and helpless, I was lowered on the rope, down, down, ever downward, plunging through the depths of a limitless abyss. Beyond my power to articulate was the experience I endured. Into what eldritch realm I was being cast I was powerless to say. I swooned at blind thoughts of the terrors that awaited me below.

Swooned, only to revive, at a smell that made me gag—the stench of embalming oils gone putrid, of canopic jars gaping open to disclose liquescent organs, of wrapping cloths torn loose in a funerary ritual gone awry. Yes, a stench such as only the dead can breathe forth. Stenches wafted to me on winds that made my blinded inner vision conjure visions—visions of thousands upon thousands of the mummified deceased, all marching at command of foul Cthulhu in a procession ever subservient to his malevolent will, a will more omnipotent than the pharaohs at their worst.

These visions forced my reeling consciousness to gain cognition, thrust upon me the horrid thought: I was to be deposited in the very maw of Yog-Sothoth.

Lovecraft clears his throat, again pats delicately his monstrous lips. "There. The result of my morning's labor. I had to break off, because I have an appointment in these quarters to receive a guest a bit later in the day. But I think you gentlemen will agree my efforts are not altogether without merit."

From within our smoked-glass cell I nod at Poe. "Pretty good. I'll give him that."

"Give him? Give him nothing, blast the man!" My fellow prisoner seems none too pleased with my critique. "You call it good? In fact 'tis superlative—but he stole it from me. From me! The villain! Don't you have the wit to recognize what he's done? He's merely Egyptianized my 'Pit and the Pendulum'!"

I can guess what's coming next. Poe stands before me and summons my attention with a magisterial wave of the hand. "Listen to my declamation of the terrors of the Inquisition, terrors evoked in the story just travestied by this larcenous Love-Crude or what do you call him—and tell me if you are or are not in the very presence of a true master." He struts within the confines of our cage and declaims his own work from memory:

These shadows of memory tell, indistinctly, of tall figures that lifted and bore me in silence down—down—still down—till a hideous

> dizziness oppressed me at the mere idea of the interminableness of the descent. They tell also of a vague horror at my heart, on account of that heart's unnatural stillness. Then comes a sense of sudden motionlessness throughout all things; as if those who bore me (a ghastly train!) had outrun, in their descent, the limits of the limitless, and paused from the wearisomeness of their toil.

Poe himself pauses for breath and I use the chance to tell him Corpse-Head's Egyptian tale isn't all that similar to "The Pit and the Pendulum" and maybe Lovecraft hasn't really stolen anything from him.

But Poe's not listening to me. He's standing absolutely still, taut as strung wire, his head cocked as if capturing distant voices. I know the feeling—it's like old times, when friends like Conan and Kull and Bran Mak Morn used to drop by daily and talk and all I had to do was give an ear and take dictation and type away at my machine. Old times, before I took the Colt that morning and—but let's shelve that thought for now.

Poe's been saying something. "... if you compare the juvenile and jejune efforts of my rival with what I achieve in the first paragraph of my tale. Instead of limply bleating that a horror is 'beyond my power to articulate,' as *he* so weakly does, behold how I convey the emotional effect of the sentence of death pronounced in the courtroom by the shadow-draped judges of the Inquisition. I render the *effect* of that death sentence in what follows:

> And then my vision fell upon the seven tall candles upon the table. At first they wore the aspect of charity, and seemed white slender angels who would save me; but then, all at once, there came a most deadly nausea over my spirit, and I felt every fibre in my frame thrill as if I had touched the wire of a galvanic battery, while the angel forms became meaningless spectres, with heads of flame, and I saw that from them there would be no help.

"And that," he concludes in triumph, "is how you convey the frisson of true perdition."

"Bravo." I clap, give the man what he wants: a full round of applause. Poe places a hand over his heart and bows. It's the first time since being dumped in this cage with him that I've seen his countenance touched by anything approaching a smile.

But he's not quite done. He whirls and declares (and he's getting louder and faster as he talks, and Corpse-Face frowns down on us as if he's had enough for one day and wants us to lie down for a nap like good children): "You want to show yourself, if you're *serious* about your art"—and here my cellmate sneers up at our captor—"you want to show yourself as next of kin to Cervantes and his Quixote, who proudly tells the mob, 'I think thoughts no mortal has ever thought before.' In your art, show your heart is a lute with its strings finely tuned and wound up tight: if touched ever so lightly by a Muse, it resonates, resounds." Poe's getting so loud I imagine even with his three-quarter-inch frame his lungs may be delivering a message Ol' Corpse-Face can hear.

And I'm right. "Don Quixote. High-strung lutes. Enough. As I said, I have an appointment I must tend to." Lovecraft turns to Kavva and nods. The crow flaps its way over from the coatrack and alights on the table. Not too much visibility through this smoked glass, but I see the bird hop its way across the table-top to a bowl containing some type of liquid. It dips its beak in the bowl. I hear a long slurp.

A quick jump and Kavva is perched on the upper rim of our prison. The bird stoops so its beak projects directly over my cellmate.

Who's still declaiming. "Virgil tells us 'Nobler spirits breathe a purer air.' And so it is. You must show you belong to a higher order of being. A finer creature made of finer stuff. With every portion of your soul thrilling to the touch ... to the touch ..."

From the crow's beak drips a golden liquid drop. The soft splash, well targeted, lands directly on Poe's defiant upturned face. The scent drifts to where I'm seated. I'm no drinking man but I know brandy when I smell it and this here's the best.

In Cross Plains Texas in times of drought I've seen horses lift their heads to greet a sudden welcome rain.

It's just like that with Edgar Allan Poe. Declamation: halt. He opens his mouth and extends his tongue. From the crow's beak drips another fat golden drop.

Direct hit. Poe smacks his laps. "Cognac." A groan of pleasure. "Rémy Martin. I know that savor."

Kavva offers another drop. And another. My cellmate opens his mouth wider, drinks deep as from a trough. He weaves on his feet, staggers, recovers, shouts defiance at the ceiling. "So, Mister

Love-Creep, or whatever your name is. You've heard of my reputation. You think me a drunkard. Well sir I am not. You've heard nothing but unfounded slander from my foes." He interrupts himself to catch yet one more drop, chokes on the big mouthful, swallows.

"No. I am not. I do no more than accept an occasional glass when so offered in the spirit of Southern conviviality. In Richmond I took the pledge and became a loyal member of the Sons of Temperance. So. My habits are as far removed from intemperance as the day from the night. Ergo ..."

Again he staggers. I spring to my feet and prop him up. I try to drag him from his cognac-drip (we're right below that corvid beak) but he's obdurate and can't be budged.

The next splash soaks us both. He gulps another mouthful, coughs and gasps. "Your crow seeks to tame me with inebriation. But I defy thee. 'Take thy beak from out my heart, and take thy form from off my door.' Deuced if I remember the rest ... Something something 'Nevermore.'"

But even with this brave talk Poe is making a poor show of resistance. He simply stands there, mouth lifted, and gulps, as the crow hits him with yet one more shot.

Getting hard to hold the man up. I've gotten splashed enough I'm feeling tipsy myself. Could use some help at this moment from Conan or Kull.

As for my cellmate: now he's slumped to the floor of our glass cage, sinks into the sod. Mission finished, the crow flaps back to its coatrack.

A knock on a door, somewhere far away, on a floor below perhaps. Corpse-Face peers in on us, says we must excuse him but he has to welcome his guest. "A young lady. My appointment." And with that he lowers over our glass enclosure a mass of burlap.

Darkness. But through the burlap cloth I can hear voices. Howard Phillips Lovecraft. And someone else. A gal I know well. My best friend in the world. Or used to be.

The last person I'd ever want to come within reach of Wizard Corpse-Face.

Miss Novalyne Price.

What's she doing in Providence? What's she doing in this apartment?

Hard to think. Woozy from those cognac fumes. I shake my head, stand up, unsteady on my feet. Try to find my way in the dark across our enclosure.

First thing I do is trip over Poe, who snores and mutters in his sleep. Regain my footing, then off to the far end of our prison, where a scooped hollow holds a pool. I kneel and drink and splash water frantic-fast on my face. *Snap to it boy you've gotta warn her.*

Can't see a thing in this shrouded dark but from across the room I can hear Lovecraft all right. Unctuous, oily, polished. What's he want from her?

I stumble to the wall, try to peer through the glass. No good. Burlap's too thick.

Gotta warn her. With what?

I shout her name but quickly quit. Three-quarter-inch frame with lungs to match: *No go.*

The dime. It'd been stacked against the wall but it must have slid and now it's lying flat atop a damp dirt-and-brandy sludge.

Use it to signal her, get her attention.

I squat and grab, heft the coin in both hands. Funny to think. In my old life (the one I shot to hell) I could call on the two-hundred-pound brawn of a body strong enough to go six rounds with prize-ring champs from Del Rio to Abilene. Now I grunt and strain and can't manage to lift a crummy ten-cent piece.

"Eddie." I rush to my cellmate and give him a shake. "Wake up. I need your help. Snap out of it."

His eyelids flutter and drunk though he is he musters dignity enough to rasp would I please have the goodness to eschew familiarity and address him as I should.

"Sorry, Mister Poe."

"That's the trouble with you backwoodsmen. Lack of decorum. Question of breeding." His head flops and he sets in to snore.

I shake him again. "Mister Poe. There's a young lady to rescue. Where's your gallantry?"

"Gallantry?" He blinks, shakes his head. "Well, in that case ..."

I help him to the pool, splash him with water.

Outside the burlap I hear Novalyne ask about the crow on the coatrack. She exclaims over how impossibly still it appears, as if it's a stuffed specimen. "Is it preserved, or alive?"

A big raucous caw from the crow. I hear her gasp in surprise. A chuckle from our warden. "You must forgive Kavva. He has a streak of mischief. Impish, for one so old. So very old."

By now I've dragged Poe to the dime. The cognac sludge is knee-deep here and slippery, gives us little purchase for our feet. But we lift the coin together and ram its edge against the wall.

There. *Tink-tink. Tink-tink.*

I put my whole soul into this dime, into these taps. I want to tell Novalyne *Sorry: Sorry about neglecting you, about the waste of promise and opportunity, about separating us by suicide, about leading you however inadvertently into the clutches of Corpse-Face, about being reduced to communicating via ghostly taps on a glass.*

Poe and I pause. My heart pounds. In the dark I listen to the voices outside our burlapped cell.

Lovecraft is asking if she's come here about the position.

Position? She's seeking work in this foul den?

I've published plenty in the pulps. I know the story. *Innocent Beauty Kidnapped: In the Cruel Embrace of Slavers and Plunderers and Brutes of Every Stripe.* But this beats all.

If Corpse-Face can shrink me and snatch Poe and keep us in a glass tub, who knows what he has in mind for Novalyne Price?

I wipe the sweat from my face, rub my hands, nod at Poe. He nods back gamely and we have at it again. *Tink-tink. Tink-tink.*

Still no sign she's heard.

Lovecraft's telling her she's the very first to apply for the housekeeping post. "Commendable. This suggests an ethic I approve. A willingness to be useful."

Try again. We bang harder. *Tink-tink. Tink-tink.*

I hear our captor ask her something. No reply. He asks again, more loudly. "I said you must have a name. If you would be so kind as to introduce yourself."

Don't tell him, I try to shout. *Any information you give he'll just use against you. Every fairy-tale heroine knows that.*

"Harriet Hopkins." She announces her fake name with all the confidence in the world. "My friends call me Hattie."

Atta girl. Wily enough to be the pal of any highwayman you'd care to write about.

I nod again to Poe. He's sweating too. *Tink-tink. Tink-tink.*

Still no sign she's heard.

Lovecraft's saying something about how dark-complected her skin is, how black her hair. Can't catch it all; must have his back to us. But I hear the next bit clearly.

"You will serve quite well. You will do ideally. Consider yourself hired. You're now in my employ."

My heart hammers at that. I remember something he wrote months ago in his letters to me, how he praised Signor Mussolini for extending Rome's empire over barbarian hordes in Africa from Libya to Abyssinia. How when I wrote back objecting to Mussolini and putting in a word for the barbarians, he called me a "foe of civilization." Explained for my benefit how "a certain excess in execution may be pardoned for the sake of a higher cause." Concluded with a dictum he announced he always used in his personal "Cthulhu Campaign": "Employ everything to your own advantage, and then dispose of those things later as you will."

"Employ to your own advantage"—and now here he is welcoming Novalyne to his employ.

My muscles are aching up and down, trembling all over. But I have to keep trying. "Mister Poe." He nods across to me in the dark. *Tink-tink.* Another good slam against the glass. *Tink-tink.*

"Perhaps before you leave"—our jailer's voice approaches; he must be crossing the room—"you'd like to see my vivarium?"

And with that our burlap shroud is whisked away.

From dark to light. Dazzlement; confusion. We cellmates blink.

Maybe it's the sudden brightness, or because our hands are so sweaty: we lose our grip on the dime. Before we can stop it the metal knocks us both flat.

Whew. Lucky. We're lying in soft mud. No limbs broken, even if we're trapped under the coin. Just enough light to see the god Mercury and his wings. I ask Poe if he's all right.

"Stunned. But enjoying the comforting fragrance of Rémy Martin." Good for Poe: any man who can joke about cognac while pinned beneath a dime is okay in my book.

I hear Lovecraft urging his new employee to step closer to the vivarium, to get a good look.

Now or never. I breathe deep, tense my arms, push up against the coin. Poe's much slighter of build than I and from the way he's wheezing it's clear he's all but spent. But he pushes too—"For the pride of the South," he gasps—and the thing begins to budge.

Done. It's upright. We're out from under, on our knees, slipping in the sludge.

Cadaver-Head points at us as he watches Novalyne try to make sense of what she sees. He rests a finger on the enclosure's rim. "Laborers. Toilers." He points again at us. "Yes. Workers struggling to who knows what end."

My first glimpse of her since my suicide-shot. Maybe—probably—the only glimpse I'll ever have again. She's still lovely as ever, vivid dark eyes, rich mass of hair, a gaze of intelligence, quickness, and wit. But she's ill at ease now, puzzled, unsure what she sees.

And who wouldn't be? What could I tell her even if I had a megaphone that could somehow reach her ears? *Those little stickmen below you, scarcely larger than the dime they're holding upright: One's a big-shot poet from a hundred years ago, currently nourished on brandy supplied by a crow. The other happens to be your boyfriend—or was in the once-upon-a-time. Now I'm just a Vespertine on the other side of the Divide.*

She lowers her head, comes closer. Stares hard at us. Can she tell? A spark of recognition, of love? I swear she stares at *me.*

I stare back. Stare with steadfast gaze. Mouth the words loud though I know she'll never hear: *Yes. Just a Vespertine now. But if I could I'd find a way to make it up to you. I'd find a way to work something out. Work my way back. To a life back with you.*

Life. Life that I wasted. With a three-eighty Colt.

Even as she gazes at me, and I gaze back, my hands grip the dime harder and I bellow at Poe: "Let's do it again, our distress call."

He too grips the silver and we drive the thing at the glass. *Tink-tink. Tink-tink.*

As we do this I'm confronted with the coin's reverse surface. The sculpted relief of an ax. The blade bulges out bright and sharp. When I stood five foot eleven and weighed two hundred pounds I'd jingle a dozen dimes in my pocket and never give 'em a thought. Now this thing looms up at me as if it'd like to bite wood—or maybe human flesh.

Our warden's still watching Novalyne as she watches us, as she watches me. "The insect world is underestimated, I think, in its strivings, in its torments, in its dreams. Do you ever wonder, Miss, ah, Hattie, of what do insects dream?"

Why's he calling us insects? I feel my temper rise. *It's insulting, and there's no call for that. True, we did ourselves in, me with the pistol, Poe with the bottle, and I know we're Vespertines and have more or less passed over and can't ask for much in terms of honor, rank, or title. But by Odin a fella alive or dead has still got some pride so don't call us insects call us men that's not asking too much.*

A madness sets in. I tap faster and faster. *Tink-tink. Tink-tink.* Poe's getting weaker. He's doing his best but he just can't keep up.

Faster and faster. *Tink-tink. Tink-tink.*

Which leads to disaster—and all of it my fault. The dime's wet with sweat, slips from my grip. Poe tries to help, stands by my side.

Strength all spent. Can't hold it up. The silver weight bears down on us: ax-edge poised right above our heads.

We slip in the sludge. A spray of liqueur.

Bam. We fall flat on our backs. The sharp blade cuts straight into my face. I feel my blood spurt and hit the glass of the cage.

From outside, a scream. From beneath the coin I breathe "Forgive me, Novalyne."

Darkness. Cadaver-Head must be refitting the burlap shroud atop his vivarium. "Ah well. Such is aspiration. In the insect world as in the human, not always crowned with success."

Damn it, we're not insects, we're men.

That's my last thought. And then I guess I black out.

26

Don't know how long I'm out. Must have dreamed. I remember fleeing for my life, twisting my head for a peep over my shoulder, running from the cops, running fast, but never fast enough to escape. I remember saying in the dream *I can't do nothing but keep moving. That's all that's left for me.*

And then I'm awake. My head hurts. Bad. Scalp sticky and matted. Blood. That dime-blade. Head hurts bad.

Beside me my cellmate is curled up and weeping. I try to get his attention even as I look about the vivarium for something to stop the bleeding. "Mister Poe."

He groans, face wrapped within his arms. Keeps weeping.

There. Torn grass and mud on the floor of our cage. Esau Cairn used some such mix as a poultice for his wounds on the planet Almuric. Or was it Kull the Atlantean after being scimitar-slashed in Lemurian combat? No matter. I scoop grass and mud, apply the mix to my head.

"Mister Poe." For answer he groans louder, extends an arm to point at the wall of our prison. He whimpers two words. "The glass."

I turn where he points. Propped against the vivarium wall stands something that wasn't there before. A smooth silvered surface of metal. A mirror.

More moaning. "I took a look. Mistake. Saw myself."

Puzzled, I ask what's wrong but he keeps his head hidden. "Don't look. Stay away from it. Far away."

So naturally I have to see for myself. I step to the mirror, expect nothing pretty. I already know I've been through a lot, so am prepared for a reflection that's this side of shabby. But Poe's a peacock. Has been telling me for days how Eastern Seaboard society ladies from Boston and Providence down to Philadelphia and Richmond used to flock to his readings, found him an object of fancy. "I did them proud," he's been telling me in quiet cell-moments these past few days. "I justified their fancies." So he's told me how at his best he likes to keep his thick curling hair combed carefully back, how he keeps his cravat neatly knotted, how he prides himself on his massive protuberant forehead, how the phrenologists say its ridged bulk portends a temperament both choleric and profound. "Profound," he's often told me. "A matter of undisputed fact. My imaginative and intellectual faculties are nonpareil."

Profound, nonpareil, but it seems my weeping peacock's been brought low by a glimpse in the glass.

"Don't look," he groans again, but I'm game for self-assessment. I already know I need a shave and a trim.

But what I see in the mirror won't ever be cured by a turn in the barber's chair.

There's my mud-grass poultice, freshly applied. That much I recognize. But instead of being daubed on my head, the mud-grass mix is fixed to a waving green stalk. I stare in the glass and the green stalk stares back. I feel my mouth drop in shock. I see a red maw agape. Plus beady orbs topped by feelers. A green head-stalk on a segmented tube. The tube rears in a flexed rhythm and flow. Appendages, many, ripple in the glass.

I see green pus ooze from the top of the stalk. "It's bleeding," I cry softly. I step back, recoil. Can't help it. Shock.

"That's not blood, Mister Howard." The voice comes from just atop our cage. "It's haemolymphatic fluid. What the Greeks knew as ichor. It flows in the veins of the gods. And in members of the realm we know as insects."

"Love-Crude. You villain." A tone of rising wrath. My fellow prisoner uncoils himself from concealment. Now in the vivarium's half-light I can suddenly see: the cellmate I knew as Poe is possessed of the same form as the shape I've just glimpsed in the glass.

I look down, palpate my own form. A tube, wriggling, green, segmented. Once hailed as Pulp-King Robert E. Howard. That's me.

"You villain." Poe's wail rises high to a howl. "You've transformed us to caterpillars. You've destroyed us."

"Oh no. Not I." Our captor brings a chair and calmly sits by the cage. From the coatrack comes the crow and alights on the table. "You destroyed *yourselves*, each of you quite handily, each on your own."

He reminds my cellmate of the events of late September 1849. Of his disembarking from the Norfolk steamer at Baltimore. "As always you were thirsty, weren't you, little Poe, as you stood on the wharf? Athirst for recognition of your literary genius, athirst for vengeance against all those who mocked you in the press. And you tried to drown that thirst as you always did when acquaintances abruptly espied you on the dock and invited you to join them for a sociable tipple."

"The custom of conviviality. I could scarcely refuse."

Lovecraft reminds him the convivial tipple lasted six days and six nights. "An unceasing stagger from tavern to tavern. Quite disgusting. Undisciplined. Until on a cold raw October night a colleague found you face down in a Baltimore gutter. Which is where Kavva also found you, useful Elemental that he is, when I dispatched him on his errand to track you."

A loud *graaack* as the crow outside the glass flaps his wings. My cellmate flinches, says his wretched recollection returns. He gazes out at Kavva. "Men took me to the charity hospice. But 'twas with you, O dread raven, 'twas with you I held vacant converse as I saw spectral objects on the hospital walls." His green tubular form writhes with the memory. " 'Take thy beak from out my heart, and take thy form from off my door!' "

The black crow eyes him grimly, squawks a comeback: "Nevermore." A mirthless *grrrick-grrrick*, and the bird adds something else: "They took your shell. I snatched your soul."

"But why?" The Poe-bug's onyx orbs glint with what appear to be tears as he turns to confront Lovecraft. "By all that's dark in Hades, to what end did you contrive all this? And if you must snatch us from self-destruction, why cast us low once more, but now in caterpillar form?"

"Spare me your self-pity. At least you're alive, even if in only a shadow-form of life." An imperious tone from Captor Corpse-Face. He says—with what I think is the faintest trace of embarrassment—that the caterpillar embodiment was unplanned. "I implemented the spell. I cast it but cannot take credit for creating it. I simply recited what I found in Abdul Hazred al-Majnun's *Necronomicon*: 'Instructions for harvesting the spirits of the freshly self-slain.' "

The freshly self-slain. As he says this I wilt with regret and shame. But Edgar Allan Poe wants to contest the point. "*He* may have shot himself"—a green appendage waves at me—"but as for *me* I merely drank myself into delirium. Even if"—a grudging concession—"perhaps just once too often."

"Did you or did you not say as your colleagues tried to revive you, 'The best thing you can do for me is blow out my brains with a pistol'?"

Tubular agitation in response. "That was no more than a moment of cerebral congestion. Of stupor, nothing more."

"A moment sufficient for the spell to work. You laid yourself open, in your thoughts and drunkard deeds, to have your soul harvested. If you fail to value your life, if you throw it in the gutter, then others will cull it for their own purposes. I say others but of course I mean someone with the lofty rank of magus. Someone such as myself."

Eyes aglitter, Lovecraft adds, "Which is why I dispatched Kavva to the Baltimore of September 1849. He scooped up your ectoplasm just as you breathed it forth."

At this my cage-mate gets freshly upset. I'd laugh to see a caterpillar sputter in protest—except I remember I'm in the same vermicular condition as Poe.

Lovecraft raises an imperious hand. "I solemnly command and adjure you not to interrupt. All—or at least a bit for now—shall be made clear."

Solemnly command and adjure. The same preening, pompous air I remember from his letters. To think I once admired him as a mentor. And now: I'm confronted with a self-declared magus. Except he's a magus who's managed to get hold of the works of Abdul Hazred.

With evident self-satisfaction he says he discovered a copy of the *Necronomicon* here in Providence. "In this very neighborhood. In the private library called the Athenaeum. Not that the librarians themselves, those unenlightened innocents, have any awareness that the volume rests within those walls. No. In their ignorance they misfiled it. Their catalogue lists it merely as an untitled treatise by the sixteenth-century heretic Giordano Bruno. When in fact what they have, all unknowing, is Bruno's translation of the *Necronomicon* from Arabic into Latin. A unique treasure, if a deadly one."

The bird flaps its wings, emits a low *grrrick-grrrick.*

"My Elemental is right. It's tea-time. Excuse us for one moment."

Poe and I slump glumly while our warden retreats to another room.

"There. Crushed walnuts for Kavva." The crow eats with greedy jabs of its beak from a plate on the table. "English tea for myself. Would I could offer you each a cup, but it's too fine a refreshment to waste on your present forms. However." Lovecraft stoops over our prison with something clenched in his hand. "Here. Dinner." His hand opens, and a drift of crushed leaves flutters down around us.

Leaves. Crushed greens. What I wouldn't give for a hamburger and a Royal Crown Cola. Which is another way I guess of saying, what I wouldn't give just to have my old life back.

Lovecraft's been lecturing us while my thoughts drifted. "Abdul Hazred's genius was to blend two branches of occult science: Hermeticism and psychometry. Zosimus and other Greco-Egyptian alchemists of Panopolis learned from Hermes Trismegistus the doctrine: 'As above, so below.' All things in our world are connected via cosmic *sympatheia*, a hidden tissue of harmonic convergence that can be accessed by the spiritually attuned."

"Why, I said much the same thing," interrupts caterpillar-Poe, "in my discourse on the finely strung lute."

"No one cares," sniffs our host, "about insights from a bug." He sips his tea and shrugs as if to dismiss whatever either of us prisoners might have to say. "Corollary to Hermetic wisdom is the science of psychometry. It teaches that we may 'measure' or contact or even captivate the souls of those with whom we're linked by great passions, whether of love or of hate. And it matters not if we're separated from such souls by barriers of space or time or death. How to burst such barriers? Through physical contact with an object that's been handled by the target of our passion."

Another sip of tea. "But I needed more than contact. I needed enslavement. Complete control over entities whom I could dispatch back through the dim corridors of the ages, for the purpose of fetching long-lost treasures in the service of my very special project."

This can't be good. I start to ask "What project is that?" and "I sure hope we're not the ones you're planning to dispatch." But he talks right over my squeaky insect-voice.

"The *Necronomicon* explains that once psychometric contact is made, the easiest entities to enslave are the self-slaughterers, those who yield up their own volition and surrender their sense of purpose. Abdul Hazred's text includes the spells for harvesting the souls of suicides. He learned such things on his long journeyings—he was one of the great medieval travelers, in the league of Ibn Battuta and Benjamin of Tudela and even Marco Polo—and whilst in Rajasthan, and southeast Java, he found the very charms he needed. Charms, yes, and incantations. Wondrous what can be done by night with a candle and length of thread and the flight path of a moth."

Candle, thread, and moth? But I don't get a chance to ask. Lovecraft has turned his attention to my cellmate.

"You, O infinitesimal Poe, were relatively easy to ensnare. I'd felt a psychic bond with you since first reading your tales of horror as a child. As I aged I sensed you increasingly as a rival, someone to be bested—a rivalry that grew to be an obsession. So the emotional link was certainly there. And you'd laid yourself open to culling by drinking yourself to death. All I needed then was a psychometric link—objects you once had handled. And here I had good fortune. For the selfsame library I frequent, that Athenaeum mere footsteps from my door, is one that you yourself once did haunt. Again and again you took the train to Providence for assignations with that poetess. What was her name?"

A groan from my fellow caterpillar. "Sarah Helen Whitman. I called her Helen. Helen, who launched a thousand poems in her honor."

"Of course. Sarah Helen Whitman, of Benefit Street. Repeatedly you held your trysts in the Athenaeum's alcoves. And while there you handled many a volume on the library's shelves. I checked the circulation files and discovered which books you'd withdrawn and pondered and read. And I in my turn handled these very same books and thus began to weave my psychometric spell. But that was not all. For in your folly you left behind in Providence an even more agitated trace of your presence, a trace that gave me great advantage."

He sets aside his teacup and from a jacket pocket withdraws a square of sheer cotton fabric. "Do you recognize this, little Poe?"

A frantic wave of appendages and feelers. "It's from the muslin dress my dear sweet Helen wore!"

"Indeed. One day—not many months before your untimely end—you held a rendezvous with her in the Athenaeum's reading room. One week prior to that she had agreed to your impassioned suit for marriage, but only on condition that you foreswear all drink and vow yourself as abstemious forevermore—a condition to which you fervently pledged your honor. Nonetheless the very morning of your meeting, while you proclaimed to her your mellifluous mouthings of love, a messenger stepped into the meeting room, bearing a note addressed to Sarah Helen Whitman."

Our jailer's voice loudens, and Poe shrinks smaller, as the recollection continues. "The note was penned by an anonymous spy. It announced that Helen's paramour had already violated his vow of eternal abstinence. The missive contained the malevolent but entirely accurate intelligence that you, little Poe, had been seen imbibing to inebriation at a soirée only the night before. It added further information to the effect that you had begun your breakfast that very morning with a half-bottle of champagne. Son of Temperance, indeed. The anonymous letter-writer suggested Helen should address you rather as an Orphan of Orgies or true Bastard of Bacchus."

Lovecraft sips a virtuous taste of his tea. "An understandably distraught Helen Whitman fled to her mother's residence on Benefit Street. You for your part, O thou drunken Hop-Frog, hastened to the nearest taproom, where you downed six shots of whisky. You followed this up with a draught of laudanum. A half hour later, albeit unsteady on your feet, you appeared at your beloved's door. You had in mind some addled thought of renewing your proposal of marriage, with the aid of liquor and tincture of opium to give you courage. Needless to say the proposal fell flat on its face—as did you, my dear sir. A distraught Helen Whitman made note of it all in her journal. 'He hailed me as an angel sent to save him from perdition. He clung to me so frantically as to tear away a piece of the muslin dress I wore.' "

Smugly Lovecraft brandishes the square of fabric. "And here's the muslin in question. Obtained by me from a dealer in antiques down on Wickenden Street. Cost a pretty penny, but very much worth the price." Lips pursed in a smile, he turns to Poe. "For this bit of cloth was drenched deep with the sweat of all your confused hopes and frustrated longings. What better homing device to track a spirit through the twisting corridors of time? With this in its beak, my Elemental had no difficulty tracking you to the Baltimore alley where you sweated and wallowed in a stew of the same confused longings."

A dejected caterpillar wilts beside me in the cell. "Why not just crush me now," he moans, "beneath your triumphant shoe?"

"Because, O little, little Poe, I have a special use for you and your colleague both."

"Hey. Corpse-Head." I'm feeling bad for Poe and pretty sorry for myself and also very hungry—in fact those greens and scattered leaves are starting to look good—but a question's nagging at me and only Lovecraft has the answer. "I've never been to Providence before this or met you face to face. How'd you get the drop on *me*? How'd you pull this off?"

"You will address me respectfully and by my name. Or by my title of Magus, a title I'm now prepared to fully own."

"All right, Mister Magus. How'd you manage your psychometric stunt all the way down in Cross Plains Texas with a fella you'd never met in person?"

"Ah. Little Two-Gun Bob." From another pocket he produces a thick sheaf of creased envelopes and folded sheets of paper. Sheets scrawled with writing. In my hand. "Did it never occur to you to wonder why for three years I troubled to maintain correspondence with a writer of such inferior skills as yours? It was to establish a psychometric thread, and to thicken that thread and tighten it with every exchange of the post. These various items you sent me—the paper on which you wrote, the envelopes you addressed, even the postage stamps you affixed—were all handled by you. More than enough to build the link I needed."

He places the correspondence on the table, takes up his teacup. "But I needed more. To activate Abdul Hazred's spell for harvesting souls, I needed you to engage in self-slaughter so you could accompany little Poe on the task to which I'll assign you. How to do that? Well. I sensed already from your publications how mercurial and tenuous your attachment to this world was. Ripe, ripe for the culling, I could see. Hence my taunts of 'Two-Gun Bob.' My aspersions on your art. My deluge of news clippings that I sent you, all headlining losers and criminals and no-goods who shot and hanged and stabbed themselves and did themselves to death. To heighten your own whispered doubts of failure. And I triumphed. You let yourself slip into suicide, while my Elemental was poised on the wire to cull. All so you might be conscripted for a higher purpose. A purpose assigned by me."

"So that's what you did. Why, you ... you ..." I feel the rage boil up. How dearly I'd love to pound that smirking Corpse-Face, to hammer his head with blow upon blow. But to do that takes fists. All I can do is wave indignant feelers.

The Magus sits undisturbed. But nonetheless at least the bird takes the hint, squawks, bobs away. And says something too, after its *grrrick-grrrick* of fear: "I had no choice. You and Poe aren't the only ones here who's a slave."

Lovecraft levels a cold glare at the crow. It opens its beak to say more, seems to think better of it, flaps away to the coatrack by the wall.

The Magus turns back to me. "You forget, tiny Two-Gun, how predisposed you had already been to play the role of Atropos and snap your own thread of life. I simply handed you the scissors. You were the one who went snip-snip."

Poe's been muttering all this time. Now his voice rises. "Beat Love-Crude, pound him insensible? That would be too kind a punishment. I know the perfect penalty. Perfect. I describe it all in my 'Cask of Amontillado.' Wall him up slowly. Brick by brick. While he's chained in a crypt and helpless. Brick by brick. Slowly. Yes. Yes."

As he catalogues the tortures he'd like to uncork I admit to myself I'm damnably hungry and stoop to the leaves on the floor. I mouth one, then another. Juicy succulent green. Not bad. Of course what I'd really like is a burger and fries and a shake. The thought stays with me as I mouth another leaf.

"Gentlemen." Lovecraft interrupts our broodings. "I know well what you're thinking. Two-Gun Bob here yearns to flex his muscles and best me one on one with sword or spear in some form of primitive duel. Little Hop-Frog would like to play Torquemada and rack me with torments in some underground pit. Well."

He drinks the rest of his tea, sets down the cup. "But let's put aside your pitiful fantasies. You cannot enact them without corporeal frames, and I have a proposal for you. One that will allow you to regain your bodies and unleash your every impulse, whether for violence or torture. And what greater pleasure is there, after all, than to indulge your appetites and enlarge them and watch them grow bloated, as Callicles of Athens once preached in defiance of Socrates?"

"Regain our bodies?" The orbs on Poe's tubular stalk pivot toward our jailer. I stop chewing my leaf and eye him as well. The man has our attention.

"Just so. You see, for some reason, after harvesting a self-slaughterer's soul, the *Necronomicon*'s spell can encase it in a frame no larger than that of a vermicule. With the passage of years your present larval forms might metamorphose into something bigger, perhaps even a lizard, but never into the shape of a human. Unless ..."

"Yes?" We caterpillars voice the hopeful question as one.

"Unless a skilled magus propels the Vespertine larvae backward in time. Thereupon the self-slaughtered enter a period that predates the moment of suicide. At which point you regain a human body—and you become useful to me."

I'm not surprised there's a catch. Still, here's a chance to escape this chomping of leaves.

Poe asks how in Hades does our jailer propose to propel us backward in time.

"Via something you may have noticed, my bombastic poet, in your frequenting of the Athenaeum. Something in the reading room known as the Egyptian Cabinet."

"Of course. I saw it often. But scarcely remarked it, I confess, what with my attending on dear Helen."

"More's the pity. Which confirms my conviction that your powers of ratiocination were always overrated. But stop your indignant sputtering and pay heed to what I say."

Sure of our attention now, he speaks in a sweeping, confident tone. "You may or may not be aware that for nigh on a century the Athenaeum's Egyptian Cabinet has housed a twenty-five-volume work called the *Description de l'Égypte*. The dozens of French scholars who contributed their expertise to the writing of this tome were all veterans who had joined Bonaparte's invasion of Egypt. And each of them, each of these savants, was a man who risked his life to explore the Nile valley's ruins and temples firsthand—and this at a time when hostile tribes and Mohammedan zealots opposed them at every turn. Many of these Frenchmen died, whether slain in battle or laid low by disease; but nothing discouraged them in their restless quest for knowledge."

As he speaks he looks away from us, out the westward window, as if envisioning what Napoleon's scholar-corps once uncovered. "Think of it. These men were the first to open tombs, to handle amulets and figurines, to touch the lids of royal coffins that had lain undisturbed for three thousand years. And through the artifacts they touched, they came in contact with the longings and subtle thoughts that had once graced the owners of those tombs. What psychometric energies the French savants must have amassed!"

Lovecraft turns back from the window as if recalling himself to the task at hand. "Well. The particular copy of the *Description de l'Égypte* now owned by the Providence Athenaeum was once the property of a Parisian nobleman named Count Jules de Polignac. The count was a personal friend of many of Napoleon's savants. A man of eccentric habits—at least as reckoned by the ignorant—he frequently held psychometric séances in his palatial home. After dinner, amid the coffee and liqueurs, he would open the *Description* and invite his guests to meditate and visualize with him the ancient treasures depicted on its pages. And whenever the guests happened to be scholar-veterans of Bonaparte's expedition, he beseeched them to lay their hands atop the stacked volumes of his personal copy of the text—the very same hands that had once caressed the scarab amulets and mummy pectorals of the august pharaohs themselves. Polignac continued this practice until—or so my antiquarian sources attest—he had contrived for each and every one of the surviving savants in turn to lay hands atop his text. A total that reached the number of ninety-nine. A satisfying sum, as far as students of Egyptology are concerned. For nine is the digit symbolizing infinity in pharaonic thought, and the number ninety-nine mirrors infinity back onto itself."

Our captor eyes us to see if we've understood the implications of what he's just revealed. "Imbued with the psychometric energies of the ninety-nine savants, Polignac's copy of the *Description de l'Égypte* was now fully primed to serve as a bridge between worlds, between times. Of an evening, after his servants and family members had retired for the night, he often sat alone by lamplight in his study and leafed through the pages of his text. This sufficed to induce in him waking dreams that wafted him on royal barges down the Nile. And more: in a letter he wrote to his sons, unread till after his death, he swore one night a portal opened which, had he entered, would have transported him whole—spirit, self, bones and blood—to what his epistle calls 'a rich strange life midst sand and palms beyond the pressing cares of this our present day.'"

Lovecraft nods. "Odd. A few short years later, the good count had reason indeed to wish he'd accepted the portal's invitation. He labored as a minister in the government of Charles the Tenth, until the July Revolution in 1830 toppled the monarchy he served. Forced to flee the revolutionaries, Polignac wandered the wildlands and forests of France, only to be caught, imprisoned in a fortress chateau, and finally expelled to England. Stripped of possessions and wealth, he missed most sorely his library, especially the *Description de l'Égypte*, with the comfort it once afforded him and its glimpse of 'a rich strange life midst sand and palms.'"

I nose among the greens, mouth the freshest leaf, and between bites ask how Polignac's *Description* made its way to the States.

"Just the point to which I'm coming. Immediately after the count's death, agents of the Athenaeum purchased his twenty-five-volume set at auction. To celebrate the acquisition, and to house the texts in a way that might do them sumptuous justice, the library's directors arranged for the construction of what we now call the Egyptian Cabinet. And this arrangement had a most curious effect. Had the volumes been merely left untended on an open shelf, their psychometric virtue, I am sure, would have gradually ebbed and faded, like an abandoned shrine to the gods in some ancient pagan glen. Instead they were kept closely confined, stacked one atop another, in the narrow drawers of the Egyptian coffer. My hypothesis—not yet wholly confirmed, mark you, although the two of you will shortly provide confirmation—is that Polignac's books, even after a century, still possess enough strength to function as a psychometric bridge, but only when they repose, one atop another, tightly packed in the coffer. Their force seems to dissipate in the outer air. I know this because on several occasions I've asked the Athenaeum's staff to let me examine the individual volumes; and when I do so, no matter what spells I recite or talismans I secretly apply as I sit at a reading room table, nothing at all happens. Oh, I get glimmerings, true; dim stirrings, half-visions. But half-visions won't do."

He studies us each in turn. "Which brings me now to you. What I need are individuals who can traverse the psychometrically charged drawers of the closed coffer, who will do so by making their way across the surface of the tomes that lie stacked within the cabinet. Of course given the narrow confines of the enclosure—no more than an inch of headroom between the stacked books and the roof of the drawer—I require individuals who are quite small of stature."

I pause in my leaf-chew. "Which makes me and Poe here suddenly useful."

"Useful indeed."

Poe states what's on my mind. "And the risk?"

"I won't say there is none. My previous attempts with Vespertines before you have not been, shall we say, altogether successful. But think of it. Recall you do not have much to lose. Little Poe, in your present form the most you can hope for is an occasional drop of cognac from the beak of a crow. Humiliating, as you think on it, and far beneath the status to which you know yourself entitled. And Tiny Two-Gun: You do realize, don't you, you'll never see your Novalyne Price ever again? She beheld you as you are and fled screaming, leaving you to your wormy fate. I know you from your published stories, Two-Gun. Your Conan shouts in his barbarian fashion: 'Cut loose. Bust out. Smash heads.' Well, here's your chance. A chance to have your life back. Or at least some form of it."

Cut loose. Bust out. Smash heads. Odin knows I wrote often enough about all that. Yet the truth was—although my fans never knew—I always stayed pretty close to my family's home and minded Mom and Pop. But now: now Corpse-Face is offering me a kind of chance after I threw my life away. Is he deceiving me and Poe in some way, hiding the awfulness of the tasks he'll have us do? Knowing him, I'd say probably. But what's the alternative? Chewing caterpillar greens, wishing I could have a Coke?

Easy enough for Lovecraft to guess what we're thinking. "Agree to serve me as Vespertine slaves, bring me the apotropaia I seek so I may buttress the mouth of Yog-Sothoth, and in exchange you'll come as close as you ever can to the old lives you crave. Consider well. You can linger as oddments in a vivarium, or each of you once more can be a man among men. Vendetta, revenge, anger, assault: whatever you want, glut your lusts to the full."

My cellmate's tubular stalk eagerly bobs in assent. "Deal me in."

For me, hesitation. *If I go through that drawer, step backward in time, it means definitive parting from Novalyne—the closest I ever had to a friend who understood me.*

"Little Two-Gun?" Lovecraft pulls a watch from his waistcoat, consults the hour. "If we leave now, we can slip into the Athenaeum just before it closes."

It's not so much the parting that hurts—I know I ruined everything when I put that gun to my head—it's just I wish so much I had the chance to tell her I'm sorry.

"Your decision, Mister Howard?"

Well, as Corpse-Head said, she saw me and ran screaming. Can't blame her; couldn't really offer her much companionship in this current caterpillar-life.

"Mister Howard?" Rising impatience.

Just wish I could see her sweet face one more time. Say goodbye.

I get stern with myself. *Hey fella: enough.*

I grunt with as much dignity as a man can muster in vermicular form. "Count me in."

"Splendid. And now let's make our preparations."

Stoppered in a flask—which reminds me of my Ten of Swords voyage in a Moxie Cream Soda bottle along the Providence River, a thousand, feels like ten thousand, eons ago—but this time I've got a shipmate, a wriggling Edgar Allan Poe. Glad of the company: I'm scared of what's coming next.

Our warden places the flask in his waistcoat pocket and quickly exits his apartment. Hard to breathe in this confined glass; the two of us are gasping so hard we can scarcely tell what's going on in the world outside the coat.

The sound of footsteps on the street. We must be outdoors. But only briefly: now we enter a building. Voices: murmured conversation. A key turned in a lock. A squeak as a door is opened. The sliding forth of a drawer.

A woman asks if Lovecraft is sure he won't need further assistance. He thanks her and says he's certain he'll be fine. He promises he'll close up everything when he's done. An exchange of pleasantries as the librarian wishes him success with his research. The click of heels. Retreating footsteps.

Silence. Sudden light as the flask is extracted from the coat. A glimpse of the Egyptian Cabinet and a half-opened drawer. Fresh air as the stopper is removed, then a sudden tumbling fall as we're shaken from the flask.

Only to land atop a vast expanse of grainy surface.

"The cover of volume one of the *Description de l'Égypte,*" explains Lovecraft. He says his tests have shown it was the most frequently handled—and hence most psychometrically charged—of Polignac's twenty-five-volume set. "Once I close this drawer, simply trek across the book's surface to the far end of the coffer. After you recover the treasures I seek, you'll be enabled to bring them to me."

My fellow factotum asks the same question I have in mind. "What exactly are these treasures we're supposed to be seeking?"

All will be made clear, our Magus assures us, once we reach the other side.

A wailing query from Poe: "But what about the human bodies you promised us we'd have?"

For answer the drawer is slid shut and we hear a key turn in a lock and we're left in the dark.

Stygian dark. I raise my tubular head, and my feelers or antennae or whatever they are brush the coffer's roof. Whew. Narrow space. Coffer? Call it coffin.

Poe must be thinking similar thoughts. "You know, I once wrote a story called 'Premature Burial.' I confess to some lingering abhorrence of confinement." He's trying for a jaunty tone but I can hear the fear in his voice.

I can hear it because I feel the same way. To take our minds off the feeling I say I always thought that story was exceptionally well written.

"Why, thank you, sir." He says if we survive this he may rewrite the tale in light of this fresh experience. I say that's a good idea. He agrees: "Assuming I can teach this vermicular form of mine to hold a pen."

At that we both laugh. The laughter resounds in the dark, echoes off the coffer's roof as if we're in the depths of a cavern.

Still can't see a thing in this midnight black. Which way is forward? As our laughter dies, the fear comes bounding back.

And then a sudden light, and a voice I swear I know. "Gentlemen."

It's Kavva the crow. Somehow the same size we are. He says he's been miniaturized to serve as our guide. Around him cluster a dozen insects. Light radiates from the abdomen of each of them.

"Glowworms," says Kavva. "To serve as torchbearers."

"*Hoo.* I never thought I'd say this"—I let out a sigh of relief—"but I sure am glad to see you."

A tremulous Poe—I can see he's still grappling with his claustrophobic "Premature Burial" fright—asks if Kavva will guide us all the way through.

"I can take you as far as the Wayside Warning. No farther."

"Wayside Warning?" From his tone I can tell my jailmate doesn't like the sound of that. I know I don't.

"You'll see. We'd best go."

The worms lead the way. Their glow lights the pebbly surface over which we trek. The cavern roof overhead gives off a smell of wood. Kavva bobs and walks stoop-shouldered. The crow's in a hurry but it's hard for us to walk fast. Especially since for Poe and me, walking consists of *crawl-inch-arch-lurch, crawl-inch-arch-lurch.* I guess if you're born a caterpillar you can make good time in movement but Poe and I are new to this and it's not easy to keep up.

The two of us start to lag. The glowworms hasten as if they want to get the job done and go back home. Kavva stoop-shoulders his way forward and I guess he has the same thought. I'd love to ask the crow a thousand questions about where we're going but I'm panting hard and out of breath. I concentrate on keeping up. *Crawl-inch-arch-lurch. Crawl-inch-arch-lurch.*

Poe's having trouble too. Can hear him breathing hard. He gasps he could use a glass of cognac about now. "Rémy Martin. Just one drop."

A turn of the crow's beak towards us. "No cognac where you're going. But I can tell you there's good strong wine."

"Oh?" This rallies Poe. "That puts fresh heart in me." He tries to laugh again, but it comes forth as a gasp.

Crawl-inch-arch-lurch. Crawl-inch-arch-lurch.

My cellmate and I are lagging farther behind now. Poe's gasping harder. I don't want to leave his side.

I'm just about to ask Kavva to slow down for us when I see in the distance, beyond the crow's bobbing beak, some object bulking in the path dimly outlined in the glow.

I call out, ask what's that.

A terse answer: "The Wayside Warning."

A long moment later the two of us straggle up to where Kavva and the glowworms have come to a halt beside the bulky object.

Which turns out to be what's left of an insect. A big one. A beetle. Upside down, on its back. A great rounded shell. Stiff and dried out. Legs curled in the air.

But its head: the head is what draws my frightened fascination, with its suggestion of a facial physiognomy almost human.

I recoil and ask what's this.

Kavva says, "It would be more polite to ask *who's* this. Like you, it's a Vespertine, or what remains of him. But the Magus claims it happens to be, and I quote, 'A literary figure of some eminence, with whose name tonight's two servants will undoubtedly be acquainted.' "

"Okay," I say, "so what's this thing's name?" I'm still gasping and catching my breath.

The crow turns on us an eye I can just see in the worm-light glow. "His name is Herman Melville."

Poe and I both gasp afresh. We gape and speak as one. "Melville? What's he doing here?"

The crow explains that like us Herman Melville was an author who labored mightily but suffered from lack of recognition and continuous financial woe. "Which made him embittered, so that his soul dried up most aridly. His stories brought him rejection and mockery rather than wealth and acclaim. He was reduced to working as a scrivener and clerk in some government bureau. For twenty long years he did this, even as he sought and failed to find readers who might appreciate his epic tale of the white whale."

Poe asks but how in Hades did Herman Melville end up here?

Kavva says the bitterness within this writer's soul grew so acrid that its scent reached both forward and back along the corridors of time. "Until it was sensed by our Magus. And he dispatched me—after securing some articles of the poor man's clothing that put me on his psychometric track—to find him in his government bureau and make him an offer."

"An offer?" I interrupt. "You didn't just pluck him, the way you did me in Cross Plains?"

"I couldn't. He didn't shoot himself or do himself in. Not like that at least. He was simply plunged into despair. Which made him vulnerable. Vulnerable to suggestions, and an offer."

In the glowworms' sheen the beetle's carapace gleams a deep rust-copper. The shell is brittle, seamed with cracks.

"I did as the Magus ordered." It's clear the crow isn't proud of its part in what happened. "I offered Mister Melville a complete change of life. At first the poor wretch resisted, said his loathsome bureaucratic job must have finally driven him mad, for him to be receiving temptations brought by a bird through the window. But I persisted and kept repeating, 'Change of life, exotic climes.' Until one day he flung aside his account ledgers and inkpots and cried out, 'Call me Ishmael. Let's away. Tropical palms and perfumed airs. Let's escape to the South Seas of my voyages of youth.' "

Kavva pecks once at the carapace, tentatively, gently, and eyes it like a man contemplating the framed oval portrait of a friend now long lost. "Greatly enthused he was initially, willingly undergoing the metamorphosis, the reduction in size, taking it in good spirit, even joking that his 'insect-scaled living quarters' as he termed them were no more compressed than his old berth on the *Acushnet* and the other whalers on which he'd once sailed. He acceded without murmur when I explained this miniaturization was needed so he could make the Vespertine trip through the drawer even as you two are doing now."

The bird flaps a wing, lowers its head. Before meeting Kavva I wouldn't have thought crows could show compunction and experience remorse; yet now I think I'm proved wrong. "But then Mister Melville found out he wouldn't actually be going to his beloved South Seas at all. The Magus hadn't been altogether honest about the destination—or to put things bluntly, he'd lied. He'd allowed Mister Melville to imagine what he wanted while concealing that his actual mission lay in most ancient Egypt. It was only as we were traversing this very passage, here within this cabinet, that I felt the burden of the deception so strongly that I decided I must tell this Melville-beetle the truth."

A pensive *grrrick-grrrick*, and Kavva resumes. "I no sooner said 'Egypt,' right at this point where we're standing now, than the man balked and jibbed and came to a halt. He said what he wanted was a return to his much-missed islands. Hikokua. Tahuata. The balmy isles of Polynesia. 'Send me there,' he pleaded, 'even if only as a beetle. Better a bug in Nuku Hiva than a scrivener in New York.' Of course I couldn't do that, told him he had to conform to the Magus' master plan."

Kavva flutters feathers in what I take to be an avian shrug. "So what happened next wasn't really my fault. Not really. Melville heaved his beetling exoskeleton up and reared on his hind legs. 'I would prefer not to,' he proclaimed, and rolled over onto his back. I entreated. He simply said it once more. 'I would prefer not to.' And those were the last words he ever spoke, to man or to crow. So I had to return to the Magus, who as you can imagine was not at all pleased. He said, 'We'll leave that useless scrivener in the drawer as a wayside warning for any future Vespertines who might think to jib or balk.' "

Abandoned weathered beetle hulk: a sad sight. To think: all of *Moby-Dick* was once housed in that bug husk.

The glowworms have lined up and are all facing the way we just came. Kavva makes an announcement. "Gentlemen. This is where I must bid you adieu. I may proceed no farther. My fellow Elementals and I must return to our master."

With a pained cry Poe asks, "But what about us?"

Kavva says we simply have to keep going all the way to the end. "Just don't try to turn back. If you do that you'll end up as simply two more dried bugs in the drawer."

The light from the glowworms recedes as Kavva leads them back the way they came. A last caw from the crow. "Don't worry, gentlemen. You'll see me again."

The light dwindles and Poe and I are left alone in the gloom.

"Now what?" His voice is close to a wail. He peers down the far end of the tunnel. "That bird says we have to keep going. Yet it's nothing but unyielding darkness. What if it just goes on like this forever?"

I confess I'm having the same doubts but decide to keep them to myself. I try to say something calming but don't succeed in doing my jailmate any good.

"This is nothing but ambulatory entombment," he shrills. "What villainy!" He calls frantic curses on Love-Crude. "This coffer is truly our coffin. What confinement! What horror! And what indignity, to consider that my corpse will be tubular, vermicular."

Plain to see he's having another "Premature Burial" anxiety attack.

Poe's doing a good job of making me anxious too. *Got to somehow distract him before he drives us both nuts.*

"Say," I suggest. "How about you compose a fresh poem? Could be useful where we're headed. You know, enthrall the masses."

At first he reacts poorly. Says my suggestion proves I lack the aesthetic refinement to apprehend the dire circumstances of our straits. Calls me a backwoodsman. A barbarian.

Yet only a minute later he asks, "Must it be heroic, in dactylic hexameter?"

I say not at all. "How about you create a verse in honor of your poetess? You know, what's her name. Something-Something Whitman."

He rears up to his full vermicular height. "You mean, sir, my dear sweet Helen."

"Yeah. That's the one. Sorry. But just make it a poem that's bright and jolly. I could go for something cheerful in this here gloomy tunnel."

"Cheerful? My good man, you talk as if we're having a sunlit promenade on Benefit Street instead of stumbling on insect legs through the pits of Erebus."

"Hey. Remember the phrenologists told you your imagination is second to none and nonpareil. Go ahead. Show them all."

"Nonpareil. Yes." He mutters as if pleased and then starts mumbling words to himself the way I used to when I composed stories and was still King of the Pulps.

A moment's silence as we make our very tentative way forward. Then: "I misspoke in calling you a backwoodsman. I think in these circumstances we may forgo formalities. My friends call me Eddie."

I say "Okay Eddie" and tell him my friends call me Bob.

So: Caterpillar Cognac Poe and Bug-Wort Bob Howard. Not very heroic figures. We stay close together, *crawl-inch-arch-lurch*, as we march through the long dark.

27

College Hill, Providence, Rhode Island, present day

Fay MacConnell tossed her scribbled notes on the cot. "Imagine. All this going on inside that Egyptian bookcase, in the very same place where I work every day. Fantastic." Her eyes shone.

Impatiently Bonaventure snatched at the sheets. "But what happened next? Is that it? Is that all? Does it just break off there?"

"Hang on. There's more." She snatched the sheets back, held out her coffee cup. "But I need topping up."

He poured her a hasty splash of Taster's Choice. "*Hoo.* Melville, Poe, and Robert E. Howard. All ending up as captive bugs. The kind of situation your Edgar Allan pal would call 'Grotesqueries of happenstance, befalling seared and writhing spirits.'"

"You want grotesque and writhing?" She gulped her coffee, put aside the cup. "Wait till I read you the next bit. Just listen to this."

28

City of Syene, Roman province of Egypt, Year 5 in the principate of Gaius Octavius Imperator Caesar Divi Filius Augustus

What I remember of before. Comes back in bits I prefer to suppress. Confinement. Larval subsistence. Shreds of leaf. Long dark tunnel. Almost airless. Small cramped existence. I know I lacked a corporeal envelope—save for a wriggling tube no longer than a nail.

But now: I'm robed in flesh. A real body. Human.

I stretch my arms, hold out my hands. Study them.

It all feels good. *Good.* A marvel. I jump. I shout and dance.

Poe tells me to stop doing that. Says I'm drawing attention to us. Says people here will think us strange.

Which makes me laugh. "Strange? We *are* strange, and out of place. There's no hiding that. But so what? We've got a new life."

Peasants found us—naked, exhausted, filthy, unconscious, but indisputably full-sized *human*—sprawled by the mouth of a cavern not far from the Nile. They told us no one ever enters that cave. They said it leads to the realm of the dead.

Or so Poe explained to me later. At the time, some six weeks ago now, when the peasant folk found us they spoke and we understood not a word. They revived us, gave us water, jabbered something. My companion proved himself quicker than I at responding.

"They must be speaking some form of Egyptian."

I asked if he had any notion what they were saying. He frowned, shook his head. "Well, let's essay what may be the region's lingua franca." He struggled to his feet, staggered a moment, then to the most venerable of the lot—a bald mahogany-skinned wrinkle-faced elder—he declaimed a long improvised speech. I could make out only the end: "Si tibi placet da nobis refugium."

I was impressed. "Are you speaking Latin?"

"It appears to be the only language we have in common with the natives." In response to Poe's speech the old man was talking excitedly with his fellow peasants.

I told my companion he seemed to be doing a bang-up job with the lingo. "Me, I had a year of Latin back in Texas as a kid. But that was it."

Poe replied haughtily—and it seemed easier for him to put on airs now he was no longer a caterpillar—it was the height of misfortune I had no more than the rudiments of an education in the classics. "My own attainments include studying the finest works of Greek and Roman literature."

I didn't mind his snobbishness. His speech seemed to be getting results. The old man was smiling at us. So were his friends, all bobbing their heads and rubbing their hands. They gestured as if they wanted to guide us to a welcome destination.

Hey, not bad, looks like we're getting somewhere.

I asked Poe what he'd said. "I caught just the last part, 'refugium.' Were you rustling us up some shelter, a place to stay?"

"Precisely. And I thought I phrased it rather elegantly."

But the quarters to which they brought us weren't exactly elegant: a high-walled mudbrick fort at the outskirts of a town. Over the gate was an inscription: "Legio Vicesima Valeria." A knot of men—non-Egyptians, outlanders, from the look of them (*a bit like us*, I thought)—stood by the entrance. They wore breastplate armor and thick leather belts from which dangled swords.

Old Baldy approached the soldiers and began a rapid harangue. He pointed at us. One of the soldiers nodded and stepped through the gateway to the interior of the fort. I guessed him to be a man of some rank, sergeant or maybe lieutenant. In a moment he was back.

The sergeant handed the old man something. Whatever it was made the elder grin. I heard an unmistakable clink of silver.

The old man scampered away, and so did his peasant friends. Poe and I stood about, in front of the fort. The sergeant spoke to us in a voice of command. A single word: "Venite."

Even I with my Cross Plains Latin could savvy that one. This was a succinct summons. "Come."

That's when Poe and I figured out the score. Baldy had just collected himself a commission for bringing in recruits. To wit, two fresh conscripts for Rome's imperial legions.

Which proved to be not at all bad. At least not for me. (My companion moaned and moped.) In fact I'll say it loud: I love this new life. Of course having escaped the state of bug-hood makes even a harsh existence feel swell.

We're assigned to the third cohort of the Valerian Legion. Daily before dawn we do a route march, a fast twelve miles. Full field gear and weapons. Back in camp for breakfast, then training all day. Javelin toss at stake posts fixed in the ground. Combat with wicker shields and wooden swords. One-on-one fighting with *caestus* battle-gloves (simple leather, not the spike-tipped or iron-knobbed versions: we're to refrain from murdering each other). I'm good at this, Poe not so much. I keep an eye on him so he won't get crippled or killed.

And Poe looks after me. For six weeks at night in barracks he's been my tutor in Latin. I'm getting better. And I have a Roman name now. Me they call Rufinus Crassus. Poe styles himself Fulgens Nitidus Splendidus. He improvised these tags our first day in camp at parade-ground assembly. The centurion passed through the ranks and asked us our names. Poe thought fast and came up with these handles. I whispered "What does Fulgens Nitidus Splendidus mean?" Without turning his head and while still at attention, Poe whispered back, "The man who is glittering, shining, and brilliant. That's me." "Modest, too," was my reply. "Don't forget modest." And I couldn't help laugh. Which earned us a beating with the centurion's vine-wood swagger-stick and extra guard-duty in the sun. He calls the two of us *Hyperborei pallidi*, the unit's Pale North-Men. Conan would love it.

Poe complains he's too tired come night to think or reflect or compose any poems. Me, I don't want to reflect or remember. Last week at drill some muscled lout punched me hard in the mouth. I spat broken teeth, had to ask the camp barber to pull the stumps. Hurt like the blazes. But through it all I grinned, my spirits undampened, because I still recalled that caterpillar-crawl and the ax-blade gouge in the top of my stalk and the way I bled vile ichor-fluid in a trail the whole length of the cave. So a couple of smashed teeth? That's nothing. At least now I'm five foot eleven again and that's better than three-quarters of an inch. No, nothing good of the past to remember.

Come evening in barracks we sit and we drink. I like the beer. Poe likes the wine. (Of course he drinks too much. Says he has serious catching up to do.)

Third cohort, Valerian Legion: the insignia on the standard shows a wild boar. Our mates salute the standard as they swill. One belches forth a declaration: "We're nothing but pigs with extra-big snouts." I nudge Poe: "Hey, better boars than bugs." Poe gulps a draught and shouts "Huzzah, I'll drink to that."

If I think of the past, and I try my best not to, what comes back at once is confinement, all airless, and a giant Cadaver-Face that kept us hemmed in. A glass box. No escape from the prison. Hammering with a big coin to get someone's attention. Someone forgotten. *Peer into the past? Unh-uh, no thanks. I'll just have more beer.*

Poe sits beside me, says we're supposed to remember, we were sent on a mission, something we're supposed to fulfill. I could care less. I've got my human frame back. Even the ache of smashed teeth tells me I'm truly alive. Let me tingle and spark with the blood, real blood, that flows through my veins. For me that's enough. No thought for the past, no care for what's next.

Things are tougher for Poe. He's the shortest and frailest recruit in our squad. The other soldiers say the Legion would never have taken him except an expedition's coming up and we're undermanned and the cohort can't be choosy. They don't like my companion's name. They say Fulgens Nitidus Splendidus is much too grand. Especially for someone it'd be more fitting to call Shortie. So they dub him Pumilio Nanus. I'm afraid to ask what it means but I can see it makes him brood. Finally he tells me: Dwarf-Runt. "Almost as bad as 'Hop-Frog,' from my old life," he says. I tell him to forget his old life and just enjoy our new one. "Forget?" His lip curls in scorn. He says his specialty is mournful remembrance. That, and brooding on vengeance.

All such thoughts get momentarily scattered, six weeks into our conscription, when a tribune assembles our cohort on the parade ground and announces a deployment. "To the Nubian-Kushite frontier," is the order. We're to march at dawn.

Most of the legionaries use this last night in Syene to seek out women and drink in the tavern huts along the Nile. But I'm in a strange mood and want to be by myself. So I stride along the riverbank far from the crowds.

It was something Poe said that made me feel strange. Yes, his going on and on about being sent on a mission, about mournful remembrance. But I don't want to remember. Every time I turn my thoughts back, comes the memory of confinement, and of things even sadder.

Good evening air. I breathe deep. To the west, across the river: distant cliffs and vast sunset skies that burn red.

Faint shouts and revels from the cantonment huts. But here, simply quiet. Unusual for me to seek this out. I stoop and pluck a stone and toss it idly in the river. Ripples form and widen in the water.

Even idle actions can trigger epiphany visitations. Bubbles bloom within the rippling circles. Then something emerges from the Nile.

A head. A pair of eyes. Eyes large, dark, expressive, that gaze most thoughtfully at me.

I blink, stand transfixed. What manner of creature is this?

It gazes, opens its mouth wide a moment, then disappears beneath the surface.

Nothing but a river dweller, I realize, then laugh and call myself a fool. For a moment the eyes looked familiar, reminded me of something, made me almost remember—and it turns out I was just frightened by a fish. And all because of Poe and his talk of mournful remembrance and my walking out here by myself when I should be in town drinking loud with all my mates. I tell myself *Now's the time to make up for lost time* and in the fading light I hurry toward the noise without a backward look at the water.

Dawn finds the cohort assembled and headed south. A few hours' marching sweats out last night's beer.

I find a place in the column just behind Lucius Regulus. He's our unit's centurion. A patient, slow-spoken man, getting up there in age. I can tell by the stiffness, the slight halt in his walk. Experience shows in his gaze and his face, seamed as it is with fighting scars and bronzed by countless suns.

Our barbaric Latin amuses him. We're lucky: he says he likes Hyperboreans. He's known many men from the cold climes beyond the Empire's reach. And he surprises Poe: he says he heard him declaiming verse back in Syene the other night and he hopes our poetically minded recruit will entertain us when we make camp tonight. Plus Lucius addresses him as Fulgens rather than Dwarf-Runt. This rouses Poe from his moody ruminations. He says he'll be honored to create some entertainment.

An under-officer trots forward from the rear of the column, an earnest youngster called Caecilius Agricola Facilis.

"Sir?" He salutes Lucius. The centurion waits for his lieutenant to regain his breath after running in this heat. Caecilius says he thinks the men are getting nervous.

It has to do with the omens, he says, that have been following us the length of the Nile. Yesterday at noon thunder sounded from a cloudless sky while we were still at the fort. At twilight an owl circled overhead and called once as it flew past the cohort's left flank. And at first light, as the unit traversed a farmstead, a peasant emerged with an ax and butchered a pig. Everyone, says Caecilius, knew that had to be a warning, considering the wild-boar insignia of our legion.

The sight of that pig squealing under the ax made the men mutter. The lieutenant says he heard one soldier say something like: "A bad sign. Why did Rome send us on this pointless mission?" The centurion asks Caecilius if he reprimanded the man or made a note of his name. Caecilius says no he didn't think it'd be good for morale. Lucius tells him he did the right thing.

Poe and I exchange glances. *Pointless mission?* We've been told nothing of our deployment except we're marching south.

The two of us keep close behind Lucius Regulus as we march so we can discreetly listen. He's chatting with his lieutenant, says he knows despite the grumbling the unit's a good one. "There are men in this cohort from every province imaginable. Dacia, Thrace, Hispania, Hellas, you name it. Even from beyond the frontier, like those two newcomers from Hyperborea. No matter. The Empire makes use of them all. We've taken this raw rabble and trained it to cohere as a team."

He says in an hour's time we'll reach a settlement called Neb-Ta-Djeser. There we're supposed to rendezvous with a guide for our wasteland mission.

But before we reach Neb-Ta-Djeser we witness something strange. The cohort is marching past a temple. By the entrance is a statue, massive in height. Shaped like a man, but with a falcon's face. Must be one of the gods of the Egyptians. As we pass, tears trickle in a stream down the limestone face.

A soldier points and shouts. "It's weeping."

"It's angry," says another.

A third cries it must be lamenting the foul fate we're off to meet.

I exchange looks with Poe, wonder how Lucius Regulus will deal with the troops. Caecilius whispers a suggestion I can barely hear. "Sir, perhaps a sacrifice to honor the resident deities? Just to reassure the men."

As soon as he says this a crowd of camp followers presses forward. I recognize many of them as hangers-on from the fort at Syene. Entrail readers, sand diviners, stargazers, scorpion women: all of them prepared to make money by casting fortunes for the cohort.

But Lucius Regulus says he's unwilling to call a halt before he reaches the rendezvous with the individual who's supposed to be our guide. "Don't get me wrong," he says in a low voice to his lieutenant. "The way I make it through life is by respecting whatever gods inhabit any land where the Empire happens to send me. Nonetheless we've been given a job to do—even if this particular one impresses me as stupid—and as centurion in charge of this unit I'm responsible for seeing to it the job gets done with no unnecessary lingering."

A half hour later something happens that makes our commander change his mind about calling a halt.

We're marching through one more village, a settlement like countless others we've passed on the shore of the Nile. Lucius tells Caecilius to keep the ninety-six legionaries of our unit clustered together. Formation marching, fast and tight. Impress the locals, minimize the chance of any hostile incident.

Then we come upon the crones.

A trio of old women they are, standing by the road. Black gowns, black veils, nothing of them showing except pairs of withered hands. But those hands are busy with work. In the roadway are cages full of squawking chickens. As we draw closer we get a good look at what the women are doing.

One reaches into a cage and extracts a chicken. She grabs its head and stretches its neck. The second woman grips the bird's feet and pulls them taut. The third produces a knife and saws at the creature's outstretched throat. She mumbles as she works. Probably a chant of some kind. A pile of slaughtered chickens twitches in the dust.

"The Three Fates." Poe speaks in a low voice so only I can hear. "Let's hope they don't decide to snip the threads of our lives while they're at it."

"How very poetic of you, Fulgens Nitidus Splendidus." The centurion must have heard him. "But for the sake of group morale I suggest you save your versifying effusions for our campfire entertainment tonight."

My effulgent friend Poe replies with a hasty "Yes, sir" but I can tell he feels slighted and is beginning to sulk. I hiss at him to keep his mouth shut before we two Hyperboreans get slapped with punishment duty like digging latrines.

Just as we pass the crones they reach for another victim. I avert my eyes as the blade flashes in the sun. The corpses underfoot twitch by the roadside. Lucius says to his lieutenant it reminds him how the battlefield looked after the Harz Forest campaign in Germania.

Then comes a surprise. Blood spurts from the victim's throat and spatters the centurion's cuirass.

The men gasp. Poe mutters this is worthy of "The Masque of the Red Death." I tell him to keep his aesthetic insights to himself.

"Not a problem." Lucius Regulus laughs and talks loud, does his best to make a joke of what's just happened. "As long as it's not *my* throat or *my* blood." Easy to see he's trying to reassure his troops.

But a murmur runs through the cohort. No need for a diviner to read this particular omen. This one is bad. Period.

The centurion turns, gazes at his men, abruptly announces we'll halt at the next crossroads for a quick augury. As we march he contemplates his blood-smeared breastplate and says to Caecilius, "When it comes to *prodigia, ostenta, monstra*—all the signs Nature provides to guide us in this journey we call life—I learned my lesson the hard way about the need to heed portents." He says he had his stern schooling twelve years ago, when he was deputy centurion in the fourth cohort of the Legio Duodecima Ferrata. Far northern duty, he says. Deployment in Sarmatia. "It was winter, it was raining a freezing sleet, and forest tribesmen harassed us as we marched."

His unit bivouacked one night by some nameless river. A camp sorcerer came forward with a wicker cage full of divinatory pigeons. "The ritual's simple enough. Place a barley-meal cake before the bird cage and open the door. If the pigeons emerge to eat: you've just had a favorable augury. The gods will emerge from Olympus and fight beside you in your next battle." A grim grunt as the centurion describes this. "But if the birds skulk in their cage and won't budge: you've got a problem."

"Well," continues Lucius, "that night twelve years ago the pigeons did nothing but skulk. No appetite. I remember the roar of the current from the river as we all stood around. Made me feel cold. The sorcerer poked and coaxed and tried to get his prize creatures to take an auspicious nibble. My men got more and more jumpy, exclaiming about the bad signs."

The centurion confesses at that point he lost his temper. "I said if the birds didn't want to eat then maybe they'd prefer a drink. So I grabbed the cage, pigeons and all, and chucked the thing into the river."

He notices Poe and I are trying to listen too, includes us in the punch line. "And of course later that same night ten thousand Sarmatians attacked our camp and followed that up with a month-long winter siege that nearly killed us all." He barks a short dry laugh. "And that's how I learned not to lose my temper when confronted with omens."

We reach the crossroads and halt. Lucius Regulus says anyway this is near our rendezvous point where we're supposed to meet our guide. He has a servant wipe the chicken blood from his cuirass. "Now let's do that augury."

Poe and I watch as the diviners crowd forward. They elbow each other and shout at the centurion, each hoping to be hired for the job. Glad I don't have to be the one to choose among them. They wave amulets and wands and sticks wrapped in animal hides. All things of power of course. Important to pick the right diviner, after all these ill omens. Lucius Regulus closes his eyes. I see his lips move. Probably praying to his gods for guidance.

Then he opens his eyes, sees something, frowns as if startled. He stares at someone on the fringe of the crowd.

There, on the far side of the crossroads. I see the individual at whom the centurion is staring. A tall man, a Nubian, standing motionless on a rock. Naked except for a neatly plaited linen kilt. Around his neck is a collar of ivory; in his hand, a lance. None of this I notice as much as what's perched on his shoulder: a crow, a big one, that caws and flaps its wings. In the sun its feathers gleam blue-black against the man's blue-black skin.

A crow. Glaring fixedly at me. And glaring, as far as I can tell, even more fixedly at Poe.

A crow. Important, but not sure why. Once played a role somehow. Hard to think straight as I look at it. Puts me in mind of something. Of life before emergence from that cavern. Of life as something weak and small. That crawled in cramped confinement. Of even greater shame before that, things I can't bring myself to recall.

My companion beside me says something. "Love-Crude. Love-Creep." Back in the Syene barracks I heard him gibber these same words in his sleep. Never understood what they meant. They stir recollection but my mind shies from such thoughts. I ask Poe now what he means but he pays no heed. Instead he hisses, "At last memory begins to revive more fully. He gave us license. Glut your lusts." He repeats the last phrase fiercely. "Glut your lusts."

The Nubian raises his lance as if to command attention. We legionaries turn and stare. The crow caws and rises from the Nubian's shoulder and suddenly flies straight at us. It skims right over the head of our unit's *signifer* and settles abruptly on the crest of the cohort's standard.

The *signifer*, Quintus Remigius, is one of the unit's most experienced men. Scaevola, his buddies call him: Lefty, from a sword thrust years ago that crippled his right arm. But he impresses me as a reliable individual. He holds the standard steady in his good left hand while the crow perches on its crest.

The legionaries hold their breath, studying the omen. The crow eyes the wild-boar image on the crest. Then it bobs its head three times as if offering homage to the image.

Quintus Remigius Scaevola scratches his beard and laughs. "It's acknowledging the power of Rome." Our *signifer* fancies himself an amateur augur. "It's acknowledging the luck of the legion."

The crow lifts itself from the standard and returns to the Nubian's shoulder.

"A favorable venture," announces Scaevola, before any of the professional diviners can get in a word, "and a safe homecoming."

The men grin at each other. This is the omen they wanted.

The Nubian approaches, the crow still perched on his shoulder. He speaks. His Latin's not bad, in fact much better than mine. He says he seeks Lucius Regulus, centurion of the third cohort of Rome's Valerian Legion.

Our commander tells him he's found his man.

The Nubian says his name's Butaana. "I am your guide. I have been waiting for you."

Behind me I hear Scaevola tell Caecilius this really must be the unit's lucky day: the source of our morning's good omen turns out also to be our scout.

Butaana asks the centurion about our destination. Poe and I crowd closer. This is what we've been wanting to learn.

Lucius announces he received his orders directly from a legate in Rome: reach a place called the Temple of Mesu Aapep and retrieve from it a certain artifact of value to the emperor. "I understand this temple is supposed to be somewhere in the desert southwest of here," he adds. "Fourteen days' march from the Egyptian-Nubian frontier."

"Mesu Aapep." The Nubian frowns. At first he says nothing further. He scans the ranks of our cohort. This Butaana carries himself well. The air of a chieftain, rather than a simple scout.

Up close I see his face is marked with deep scars that notch his face in parallel lines from nose to jaw. Tribal markings, maybe. Flesh-work artistry, elegant and neat. But his forehead is marred with a deeper scar in a jagged, crude gash. That scar doesn't look like artwork at all. That one, I think, was done by some enemy. That one is a mark of war.

The Nubian is saying that Mesu Aapep is deep within the realm of the Kushites. "If these are all the soldiers you have, then you lack sufficient men for the task."

I watch Lucius Regulus. He hesitates and I wonder if he too doubts he has enough men. Then he explains. The other five cohorts that were supposed to accompany us have been reassigned for the emperor's new campaign against Arabia. "In any case," he says, "the Kushites have just signed a treaty of submission acknowledging the suzerainty of Rome throughout this part of Africa."

Butaana says nothing in reply.

Lucius asks if he knows this Temple of Mesu Aapep.

"I know it. No one goes there. It's an evil place." On his shoulder the crow caws and flaps its wings. The Nubian asks, "You have no choice but to go there?"

"That's right. I just follow orders."

"Then let us not waste time." Butaana says curtly we'll begin by heading due south along the river the length of a day's march. With that he turns and lifts his lance and moves off at an easy trot, away from the crossroads, due south, the riverbank on our left. The crow rises and circles above the scout as he runs.

Evening twilight. Our last encampment by the Nile. At daybreak we'll head southwest deep into the desert.

I figure tomorrow we'll face sandy wastes so now's my last chance to walk along the river. I squat and watch the light fade. Wind rustles shoreside reeds. Without thinking I toss a pebble. A soft plop and just as I did at Syene I watch ripples form and widen in the dusk.

And just as happened at Syene I see a face rise from the depths.

The mandible opens, the mouth gapes wide, fins flap back and forth. Scales ripple gold in the last of the light.

Eyes intelligent, communicative, gazing up at me. Gazing as if with urgency.

The mandible trembles, the mouth gapes and shuts. Ready to speak. To remind me of something.

My mouth goes dry. A sign of fear. In my heart I'm not sure I'm ready to hear. I feel a chill. I can't help but shiver. I want to run but part of me also wants to know what it is this thing has to say. I feel my heart pound hard.

And then a voice. But not from the river. From right at my elbow.

"Her name is Hat-Mehit." It's Butaana. I consider myself an alert individual but somehow he's crept up without making a sound. "The goddess of water-life."

I study the Nile. A last glimpse of the eyes, intelligent, expressive: urgency. Then the face is submerged. A last pooling of ripples on the river's dark surface.

"You have been honored." He says it's rare to be granted a sighting of the goddess.

I'd ask more but I'm interrupted by a harsh caw from his shoulder. The crow flaps its wings. Butaana says we're being summoned to dinner. Which gladdens me. The night air grows cold.

Firelight. Companions. Food and good strong drink. I need these safe familiar things after that *whatever it was*, that fish-mouth gaping open, that revelation from the river. A goddess, desperately needing to speak? A thought wells up within me in reply: *Maybe I don't want to hear whatever's supposed to be revealed. Maybe I don't want to be made to remember. I recall some things but not others and would prefer just to leave it all that way.*

I sit by the fire, squeeze myself between Scaevola and Poe. I tell them to pass me that flask of wine.

Food, and drink. Laughter. Joking and chatter.

There. That's better.

Lucius Regulus stops by our fire. "Fulgens Nitidus Splendidus. Perhaps you might entertain us with a poem?"

The soldiers cheer the idea. They're sprawled at ease, heads propped on their packs, toes toward the flames. "But make it cheerful this time," says a big brute who goes by the name of Pugnax. I know him well; he's the bruiser who broke two of my teeth.

Poe glowers, strikes a pose of dignity most injured. "I cannot answer for cheerful. Too often my muse leads me down byways all dreary."

"Well tell her," says Pugnax, "we're heading into the desert tomorrow and we'll have a bellyful of dreary so how about something sweet and sweaty to remind us of our lively lady-friends we've had to leave at home?"

A chorus of "Yeah lively lady-friends" from around the fire.

"Lively lady-friends. Very well then." Poe stands so he's backlit by the flames, a cloak wrapped against his tunic to ward off the evening chill. Diminutive he might be among these men. Still he's graced with a commanding voice. "But first. Rufinus Crassus, if you would be so kind." I hand him the flask. He drinks deep, wipes his mouth with the cloak, throws back his head and declaims:

My evanescent love, my Dom'na Thume
Her ghost flits all about me in the gloom.
I'm condemned to march forever 'cross these dunes
And flinch from moonlit terrors as they loom.

Death with bony fingers interlaced
Flaps vulture wings and asks us for a taste.
We legionaries say: No need for haste.
On hell's horizon, grant a moment's grace.

The Worm impels us 'cross the sandy wastes.
It doth choose our fate, it chews our face.
Condemned are we to die—some foreign place;
Condemned to drop and croak without a trace.

When Conqueror Worm next bars my way in deepest gloom
I'll ask it: Bear a message with this tune
Salute her when you're next within her tomb
My evanescent love, my Dom'na Thume!

Full stop. Hand over his heart, Poe gives a deep bow. He pretends to be dismissive of the effort, says the meter is ragged. "A mere bagatelle, a *jeu d'esprit.*" But he's clearly pleased with himself. I clap and cheer. Some soldiers join me. Poe nods at me in return.

But there's also hooting and booing. "Damn it, Dwarf-Runt." That's Pugnax. "I said something cheerful. Sweet and sweaty. Lively ladies. We already know we're hell-bound. We don't need ghosts and tombs!"

Fulgens Poe may be little but he looks ready to hurl himself at Pugnax. "Sir, how dare you address me as either dwarf or runt?"

Pugnax hoots again and laughs, finding all this very funny. He nudges the pal at his side, a lout by the name of Vorax. Vorax is squat and thick and built like a mudbrick stove. He picks up the Dwarf-Runt tag with jeers of "Pumilio the Puny" and "Nanus the Natterer."

Poe's hand darts beneath his cloak. After all this time I know him well and I also happen to know he keeps a dagger concealed about his person.

I spring to my feet to intervene but the centurion motions me to sit. "I like your versifying, Fulgens Nitidus Splendidus." He pays Poe the compliment of using his full effulgent name. As Lucius speaks he addresses my companion but directs his gaze to the rowdy audience. "Especially that line, how does it go? 'It doth choose our fate, it chews our face.' Gruesome, but well chosen."

Pugnax and Vorax bellow good-naturedly that actually they like the poem too. "It's just we don't get the chance too often to have a laugh at a runty Hyperborean. No offense intended." Pugnax snatches a wine flask, offers it to Poe. "Here. Go ahead. Have a drink."

In reply Fulgens Poe tilts back his head in haughty refusal and stalks away out of the light. Pugnax shrugs and helps himself to the drink he offered Poe.

Me, if I know my fellow former-insect aright then I suspect this isn't the end of the affair as far as he's concerned.

And I'm proved correct. Fires die low, the night grows colder, soldiers huddle sleeping in their cloaks. I pick a spot to snooze where I can keep watch on what's likely to happen next.

Sure enough. Midnight darkness. Red embers glow. No one astir, save a slight movement: a shape sliding belly-flat along the sand. Making straight to where Pugnax and Vorax lie snoring plenty loud.

I leap and land on Poe. Grab his wrist and squeeze the dagger from his hand. Clamp a palm over his mouth to stifle protests and lift him up and haul him some distance from the camp. (Glad he doesn't weigh much; grateful for my own two hundred pounds of heft.)

I'm afraid when I set him down he'll fly right for my throat. But he merely sits chin in hand and sulks. "Primitives. I will have neither my honor nor my verses impugned. I'm a Virginia gentleman."

I tell him primitives yeah but Pugnax and Vorax actually don't mean any harm. "They were just having fun."

He clutches a fistful of sand from the desert earth and flings it away on the wind. "You and I were promised. 'Glut your lusts to the full.' That's what he told us. That's what he promised."

"Who was it that promised?"

"Our captor, you fool. Love-Crude. Love-Creep. Whatever he called himself. He said 'Get your body back, glut your lusts to the full.' "

Love-Crude. Captor Corpse-Head. One among many memories I've wanted to block.

I toss Poe back his dagger. I make a suggestion. "You want to glut your lusts, don't go stabbing people. Especially squad-mates in their sleep. Gratify yourself with this." I pass him the flask Pugnax offered him before. Poe pouts a moment but there's never been a drink he doesn't like. He takes a long swig and gradually relaxes. "Or"—I follow up with another suggestion—"find yourself a fresh young lady and write her a fresh new poem."

From behind us: "And may I interpose one thing further." A rasping utterance startles us as it arises from the sands.

Poe spills the wine and fumbles for his knife.

We turn and find addressing us a bird that eyes us each in turn. A crow. Butaana's pal.

"Don't you know me?" It speaks in a low throaty hiss. Like us, it seems not to want to awaken anyone in the camp.

The two of us stare stupidly, saying not a word. It's not just the shock of crow-talk. For me, and I suspect for Poe, this is opening up memories of incidents left forgotten.

Another low squawk. "Don't you know me?" Impatience aplenty in that voice.

Finally I manage a reply. "Well yeah. You belong to that Nubian scout."

The indignant crow tilts back its head—much like an indignant Poe in fact—and says it belongs to no one of this era. "My current form is merely the role I assume for this present age. I'm an Elemental. I'm enslaved and indentured to our Magus. I say 'our' because he's your Magus too."

A memory stirs but it's not one I welcome and so I try to say something defiant.

The crow cuts me off. "You're both Vespertines, which means you answer to him just as do I. And I have a message from him, and I quote." It lifts its head to declaim. " 'I've arranged for you to have bodies on loan. By all means use them to glut your lusts to the full. Indulge your appetites and angers—but only when indulgence doesn't jeopardize the mission. Heed Kavva, my Elemental, and obey orders. Retrieve the apotropaion as you've been ordered.' "

More pouting from Poe. "But if the Magus says we can glut our lusts, how come I can't stab idiots who insult me and thereby slake my thirst for vengeance?"

Kavva squawks a dismissive *graaack*. "Forty years of life, a drunken death, then revived, and still all you do is babble like a child." It stoops and bobs its head. "Do you two want to keep your current envelopes of flesh and bones? Or do you want to go back to doing a caterpillar-crawl?"

We both blanch in real terror. *Not a hard choice to make.*

"Very well then. As our master says: 'Glut your lusts to the full.' But be sure to obey orders. Retrieve the artifact." It gives us a final admonition. "I will be watching, and through me, the Magus."

Silently it rises and flaps its way back to the camp.

29

Next day we make good progress as we head to the southwest. Nothing hinders us. No barbarians, no sign of any enemy. The land is empty. It seems the Kushites really have accepted the terms of their surrender to Rome.

Feels good to move. Kavva's words remind me. This body's just on loan. Enjoy it while I can. Could be forced back to bug status at any time.

I breathe deep of desert air, feel the wind and the silence. Dry streambeds, acacia and tamarisk shrubs. Once, in the heat-haze of noon, we see a scattering of gazelles.

The men are in a fine mood and match strides by their singing. Bearded Scaevola the standard-bearer tells me it's a marching song freshly composed for the cohort this morning by my Hyperborean friend:

Lemme tell you what's nice
You come back from a fight
And surprise hey surprise
You're alive, still alive.

They sing this bit three times and then go on to the next:

Nasty cockroaches are we,
with nasty cockroach teeth;
We eat and we excrete
Then die off on the street.

After which the legionaries improvise an addendum. As they march, Pugnax suddenly shouts "Vee-Vee, Vee-Vee." Vorax picks up the cry, and soon the whole column is chanting: "Vee-Vee, Vee-Vee."

This goes on for the length of a mile, and then Pugnax roars a line from last night's poem: "It doth choose our fate, it chews our face."

And the column sings this same verse over and over.

A puzzled Poe turns to young Caecilius the lieutenant. "What's all this infernal prattle of 'Vee-Vee, Vee-Vee'?"

"Sir, it's from your poem." Caecilius says "Vee-Vee" is short for "Vermiculus Victor." He says it's the men's new nickname for Poe. "The men like your versification. It's a kind of homage."

I whisper helpfully to Poe, "That's their way of translating 'Conqueror Worm.'"

Poe whispers in return he needs no help from any backwoods Texan in making sense of Latin. "Confound it all," he hisses. "An epithet like 'Vermiculus' makes me sound damnably diminutive." He adds it's too much of an echo of our wretched former life.

I tell him to brighten up. "Think of it as a compliment from the legion."

He tries to scowl, but I can see he's secretly pleased.

A brief halt for rest, and the men try out the new cognomen on Poe, hailing him as "Vee-Vee" and "Vermicule" and "Victor" till they settle on "Li'l Vic."

On the afternoon march the cohort bellows once more what seems to be their favorite verse from the morning. "It doth choose our fate, it chews our face."

They must really like it. They sing it right up through sunset, keeping cadence as we march.

The dust from our column rises behind us.

Until we're twelve nights out from the last Roman outpost at Syene. Tonight the Nubian asks for details about the mission.

Poe's poems have given us Hyperboreans good status. We're invited to sit at the fire with Lucius Regulus and Caecilius and the other officers. Butaana suddenly squats beside us. The crow is there, perched on his shoulder. My fellow Vespertine and I watch it warily.

"Hey. Grim-Beak." Quintus Scaevola salutes the bird with affection, says it's guarding our luck. I see why he says that. Every day the crow circles far overhead, then settles by Butaana's ear as if to convey intelligence of everything it's seen. Anadj-Kemet, the Nubian calls it. He says the name means Black-Claw.

I ask Scaevola if he knows how our guide acquired the bird. Says Butaana told him one day it flew out of a cave by the shore of the Nile and settled on his shoulder. It's stayed with him ever since. I watch Kavva as the legionary tells me the story and Kavva returns my contemplation with a black-eyed gaze that says "Spill no secrets. Stay focused on your mission."

I look away. No good ever comes of provoking a crow. Especially not this one. I don't want to go back to that caterpillar-crawl.

Butaana's asking why the Empire feels the need to send its soldiers on a hazardous quest so deep into the territory of a people as hostile and dangerous as the Kushites.

"Well may you ask," says the *signifer* gloomily, as he throws more wood on the fire. "A pretty foolish business, this is. We're going after a severed head."

The Nubian raises his eyebrows.

Lucius Regulus explains that the severed head in question is from a bronze statue of the emperor that once stood as a guardian figure at the southern frontier of Rome's dominions on the Nile. "I've seen this bronze," recalls Lucius. "I know it well." Larger than life the statue stood, a frown on its metal face, its arm outthrust in warning to those thinking of invasion: *This far and no farther. Turn back.*

For years the statue served its purpose, held the barbarians back. But the last time the Kushites swooped out of the south and raided Rome's outposts in Egypt, they lopped off the thing's head and took it back with them as a prize. "They've kept the head captive," says the centurion, "and they subject it to indignities and perform rituals over it to weaken the emperor's power."

"Strong magic," comments Butaana.

Scaevola rubs his beard and says he wouldn't want any likeness of himself held captive like that.

Young Caecilius argues it's a matter of honor. "These barbarians have surrendered. Recovering the head is a way of reminding them who's in charge now." His voice quivers with energy. "Teach the Kushites a lesson."

"My lieutenant here makes me feel old." Lucius sighs and says he too used to think like that. "Matter of honor. Who's in charge. Teach a lesson." I study the centurion's lined face as he talks. He sounds tired.

"I know these people of Kush." Butaana reminds us his land of Nubia lies between the Kushite realm and the southern border of Roman Egypt. "They've waged war on Nubia many times. It's not so easy to teach the Kushites any kind of lesson." Scaevola tosses breadcrumbs to Black-Claw Kavva. The crow bobs about in the firelight pecking at the bread and hops back onto Butaana's shoulder.

"Recovering a stolen head of bronze," says the Nubian quietly. "I hope it will prove worth it to you. I know these Kushites. They're a fierce people." The light from the flames illumines the tribal scars on his face and the jagged faded gash on his forehead.

"If they're so fierce and all," young Caecilius wants to know, "why did you volunteer for the hazard of scouting for the Legion on this mission?"

"We each have our reasons for what we do." That's all Butaana has to say for the night. The crow tilts its head and gazes beyond the fire into the darkness as if scanning the night for omens. Or maybe for more breadcrumbs.

Thirteenth day out from Syene. Early in the morning we sight a range of cliffs on the southern horizon.

"Our destination," says Butaana. "The Kushite stronghold. There you'll find the thing you seek." He trots ahead of the column, then turns and waves us on with his lance. The centurion orders us to quicken our march to a double-time pace, but with the water donkeys and baggage camels we can't keep up with our scout.

It's noon before we reach the cliffs. Butaana and his crow are waiting for us at an opening in the cliff face—what looks to be the mouth of a canyon. Flanking the canyon mouth stand two statues of stone.

"These," says Butaana as we approach, "mark the entrance to the Kushite stronghold."

The statues depict Nubian captives, kneeling, their arms bound behind their backs. Surmounting each captive is a lion. The lions crush the Nubians' skulls in their jaws.

Butaana points to the figures of the Nubians. "This is what the Kushites did to my people. And what they did to my family too."

We advance into the canyon. The gorge is narrow. Rock walls tower above us to right and left. The midday sun glares down on us. The glare makes it hard to scan the cliff top for foes. I find myself hoping the Kushites all know they've surrendered. Flies buzz about seeking the sweat on our faces.

An hour into the gorge, the path bulges into a natural amphitheater. Lucius calls a halt to let the men drink. We stand about, remove helmets, splash water over our heads.

Scaevola the *signifer* reminisces as he drinks. "I served as adjutant once for a punishment battalion in the Egyptian desert. Quarrying alabaster from a pit in the Wadi 'Allaaqa. Plenty hot. Almost like this."

He stops talking to gulp water. That's when the silence presses in on us. Not a sound except the buzzing of flies and the hiss of wind through the canyon.

Butaana is contemplating something in the cliff face. Poe and I join him. He's studying another sculpture, a carving chiseled in the rock. The carving shows a winged snake.

"The imperial cobra," says Butaana. "The pharaohs' symbol of kingship. Now that Rome has overthrown Egypt, the Kushites claim the old royal insignia as their own."

The carved cobra has its fangs exposed. Venom spits forth from its mouth. Its wings are feathered with insets of lapis lazuli and gold.

No question this is ill omened. Worse is what lies heaped at the base of the sculpture. Torn corpses of birds, their wings bound, their necks wrung.

Poe contemplates the scene and asks what primitive rite is this.

"Offerings to the Mesu Aapep." Butaana explains the name means "offspring of Apophis."

Beneath the fresh bird corpses lie older offerings: a sun-whitened mound of bones and skulls. Some animal. Some human.

I tell the Nubian I've never heard of Apophis.

"Apophis is the Shadow-World Serpent."

I ask what the Shadow-World Serpent is supposed to be.

"Pray you never learn."

Butaana's crow flutters to the ground and pauses before the strangled birds.

"He will want vengeance," explains the Nubian, "for his kin."

Black-Claw Kavva flaps its wings and alights atop the cobra carving. The crow pecks once at the stone eyes. Then it launches itself upward, above the canyon walls, atop the cliff face, riding the heat drafts of noon. It hovers a long moment and then caws a quick cry.

Butaana turns to the centurion and says, "He has seen them."

Lucius shouts for us all to take cover.

Just in time. Stones from above hurtle among the cohort. I see an arrow part the horsehair crest on Scaevola's helmet. I crouch not far from Lucius Regulus. Caecilius runs up to him amid the enemy fire and asks for orders.

The centurion turns to Butaana and asks if there's a path up these cliffs.

Our scout nods and says he knows these hills. "I can find a way."

Lucius tells his lieutenant to have the men form a *testudo*.

Back in our bug life, before Poe and I emerged from that cave, I'd have had no clue what a *testudo* was. But six weeks of barrack-yard drills have taught me well. The legionaries scramble to form up and unsling their shields. I look for Poe and see him standing about unsure what to do. (His mind must have been busy composing poems while we were in Syene rehearsing precisely this drill.) A stone hurtles down and just misses his head. Pugnax yells "Come on Vic," grabs him by the shoulder, tugs him along.

In no time the ninety-six of us have ranked ourselves into a *testudo*: a closely packed turtle-shell formation, six across, sixteen deep, with interlocked shields arranged over our heads and backs to protect us as we climb.

Lucius asks his lieutenant if the men are ready. Young Caecilius shouts back an eager "Yes, sir."

I hear the centurion tell Butaana "Well then show us the way up."

Scaevola and Caecilius bellow like hell: "Heads down, climb fast. Heads down, climb fast."

I thought I'd be scared but no time for that now. I'm in the middle of the *testudo*, got my left arm raised to arch my shield overhead. I keep Poe on my right, feel him stumble beside me. With my right hand I steady him. From the other side Vorax steadies him too. My shield thrums as an arrow strikes with a *thwock*. Followed by a rock that smacks the shield's metal boss and bounces off. I grunt and strive to keep pace with my squad.

A cry from above. We're at the top.

Now I can see the enemy. *So these are the Kushites*. I get an impression of ostrich-feather headdresses, spears, animal-hide armor. From somewhere near I hear Lucius Regulus roar: "Shoulder shields.

Unsheathe swords." At once the turtle shell becomes a battle line. Now we rush the foe.

We're supposed to keep phalanx formation as we fight but that's easier said than done. Boulders on the summit make it hard to stay in line. We break into clusters, fight side by side in twos and threes. Somehow I get separated from Poe. Vorax and Pugnax flank him to keep him safe.

I'm five paces forward of my squad, which makes me a terrific target for the foe. A volley of spears hurtles my way. Four stick fast in the wood. Each lance is heavy, weighs the shield down bad.

Someone rushes me close. Big brute with a mammoth hardwood club in his hands.

Crazy the things one notices: palm-tree tattoos pinpricked on both his arms. With a whirl, Tattoo-Tree strikes hard with the club, aims it right at my head.

I raise my over-weighted shield, barely lift it in time. The blow tears the thing right out of my hand.

The man's stomach: exposed. I stab, plunge the blade deep into his gut.

He drops the club, wrests the sword from me even as he falls.

Shield and sword both gone. I stoop and seize the club, brain him as he tries to sit up. He flops back and that's that.

Another rush of foes in a swarm. I grasp the club two-handed and leap atop a boulder to meet them as they come. I swing the club and crack bones and smash skulls. I'm stabbed and struck and slashed I don't know how many times. Doesn't stop me a bit. I catch one Kushite in the jaw, another on the chin. Corpses mound up.

Through all this something hypnotic plays in my mind. Like a tune or a chant. *Glut your lusts to the full.*

One more wave comes at me. I pivot to meet them. What did the Legion's song say? "Nasty cockroaches are we, with nasty cockroach teeth." Yup that's me. I grin with the rushing pulse of it. *Glut your lusts to the full.*

Life simplified. Survive and smash heads.

What I think I've always wanted. *Glut your lusts to the full.*

Toothy cockroach. That's me. Survive and smash heads.

Glut your lusts to the full.

Screams and shouts to left and right but it all feels far away.

Then I realize someone's calling. "Rufinus Crassus, Rufinus Crassus."

Which is my name in this new life.

"You Hyperborean war-dog." A friendly bellow in my ear. "It's pretty much over."

The hypnotic pulse gradually eases in my ears. *Glut your lusts to the full.* Dwindling voice, not as loud now.

Enemy dead lie all about me. Guess those lusts are glutted to the full. The club falls from my hands.

I'm unsteady as I step down from my rock. Pugnax is there and steadies me and says something like "You did good."

I shake my head to clear it, look about. Vorax and Pugnax are still protectively flanking Poe. The two legionaries are joking about how they've given themselves the job of safeguarding the cohort's Vermicule poet. Meanwhile Poe's pointing at what's left of the enemy forces.

On the topmost crest of the cliff, a Kushite in a red cloak, howling something. Must be the chieftain, trying to rally his men. Beside him is someone in what looks like a crocodile-skin headdress. Definitely an exotic getup. The two seem to be quarreling while the Kushite forces waver.

And there's our scout Butaana. He's shouting in some unknown language. His shouts seem directed at Red Cloak and Croc-Skin. He tries to slash a path to these two through the foe. But then the Kushite forces break and the enemy scatters in a hundred directions among the cliff paths.

I hear Caecilius yell across the summit to Lucius Regulus. "Sir, pursue and annihilate?"

The centurion replies with undisguised weariness. "Let's save our strength, lieutenant."

Butaana's crow caws and settles hungrily among the enemy dead.

Our commander announces we'll camp here tonight in this big canyon-walled amphitheater.

Butaana shows us a basin bubbling with fresh water hidden behind a jutting pillar of stone. "The Kushites say this pool springs from an underground river that flows directly from the Nile. And in turn the Nile flows out into all the world's rivers." He watches as the legionaries cup their hands to drink and fill their flasks. "For in truth there's only one river. It's all connected."

I'm worn and stiff from a dozen criss-cross cuts. The sun has long since retreated from the high cliffs. Cool evening light fades from the sky overhead.

I sit by the pool after the others have gone. I splash water on my arms. It stings cold on my wounds. I lie flat on the basin's rim, dip my head, drink deep.

And that's when I see her.

What did the Nubian name her? Hat-Mehit. Fish goddess.

Fins flapping gently. Scales ripple, beaded gold.

Large intelligent eyes. Familiar, from long ago. Gaze of urgency, of summons.

Bubbles streaming from her mouth.

Mandible gaping open. Message forming.

Not that any fish can talk, even if a god or goddess.

But a message, in the form of recollection. A clearing of what's been blocked.

My time before the tunnel has been more or less a blank. But the mists are starting to recede.

Glut your lusts to the full. (Which in that cliff-top fight just felt so good.) Who said that to me once?

Love-Crude, Poe's been calling him. Love-Creep. Yes: Cadaver-Face. Also known as Howard Phillips Lovecraft. Of Providence. A different world. A different age.

Glut my lusts. (Which felt so good.) It's all been a distraction, encouraged in me, to cloud my memory and judgment.

But the gaze from this fish, or whatever it is, so full of compassion, conveys a message: "Don't be forgetful. Know where you came from."

Which jolts me with the memory of what I've been trying to forget.

I'm here because I'm a failure. Because I shot myself.

Which turned me into a Vespertine night-crawler, under the command of Captor Corpse-Head.

And because I shot myself (and this is what I've been trying hardest to forget) I cut myself off from someone now I know I loved. Novalyne Price. Eyes of compassionate longing and radiant warmth.

Eyes that are gazing at me here in the pool. A goddess, a fish. With scales that ripple gold.

"Novalyne?" I sit up at the rim, say her name aloud. Repentance pierces me. Remorse.

The mandible gapes wide. Bubbles stream forth, each one doubtless a word. The creature's appendages flap frantically. If those fins were hands, I can tell she'd reach up and hold me tight in her arms. But however this happened—*Did Corpse-Head catch her in a spell?*—now she's simply a fish. And fishes can't hug humans, just as caterpillars have trouble signaling their personal problems via a Mercury ten-cent piece.

Well maybe she can't hug me but her fins keep flapping and she keeps gazing at me to make sure I get the message. "Don't be forgetful. Know where you came from."

Fins slowing down. Getting tired I can see. But it's a fish with moxie. One last look from those dark and knowing eyes, one last reminder—*Don't be forgetful*—and with a last deep sigh it dives and dips from view.

I return to the camp just in time to see Caecilius escorting a group of Kushites to the fire by which Lucius Regulus is seated. "A delegation from the barbarians, sir."

I recognize two of them: Red Cloak and Croc-Skin, the leaders from this afternoon's ambush. The centurion motions for them to sit and summons Butaana to serve as interpreter. Poe's seated nearby and I quickly join him. I don't want to miss this.

"Taharqo is this man's name." Butaana nods toward Red Cloak. He explains that Taharqo is chief of the Kushite stronghold.

"And this"—Butaana gazes a long moment at the other man—"is Temsaah. He serves as counselor to Lord Taharqo. Also court magician and necromancer."

The counselor's crocodile-snout headdress overshadows his face and makes it impossible to see the man's eyes. But he seems to be staring at Butaana. Butaana stares right back. This is not a friendly exchange.

From beneath the lizard mask Temsaah says something. Butaana makes no attempt to translate but instead replies in the sorcerer's own tongue.

The centurion asks what all this talk's about. Neither man says anything. Chief Taharqo surprises us by addressing Lucius Regulus directly in Latin.

"My counselor Temsaah says this Nubian scout of yours is an escaped slave. He is the property of the kingdom of Kush." The Kushite wizard in his crocodile headdress holds a staff of some kind and points with it at Butaana's face. The staff is carved with a likeness I recognize: the winged cobra our guide showed us here in the canyon.

Taharqo says the jagged gash on Butaana's forehead is a slave brand. "This is the mark we give our prisoners of war. The mark shows they have been consecrated as offerings to our gods. This Nubian of yours must have fled our altar."

The wizard Temsaah says something further and laughs. The teeth on his crocodile snout shine white in the firelight.

The Kushite chief translates. "The gods never forget a slave that has been promised them."

Lucius tells Taharqo the Nubian is a servant of Rome now and under the Empire's protection.

"The Empire. Yes. Rome is the new power here in our land. One must acknowledge such things. That's why I've taken the trouble to learn something of your language."

Butaana and Temsaah are still staring at each other. Lucius tells Taharqo what the cohort is here for: the severed bronze head of the emperor.

Taharqo says he's aware of our mission. "You will find the thing you want in the crypt of our Mesu Aapep temple. It's two hours' march from here, deeper within the valley. We will not hinder your passage."

At that the crocodile snout turns to the Kushite chief. The wizard mutters something. Taharqo says something in reply. The reply sounds sharp and angry.

The Kushite chief withdraws with his escort but the wizard Temsaah lingers. He, too, knows our language. He says he has a gift for Rome, and he motions one of his men forward. The man presents us with a ram haltered with a coarse hemp rope. The sheep is pure black in color, with tightly curled horns. It bleats and trembles. I see Caecilius and Scaevola trade glances. I'm sure they're thinking the same thing I am: *Why this gift?*

Temsaah is saying something about good-will gestures. "Rome is the new power, just as my lord Taharqo said. But there are older powers in the land, powers of the Earth, powers that must be propitiated if a traveler wishes good fortune and a safe passage home."

Good fortune. Safe passage home. In the mouth of this wizard the words ring like a curse.

"When you reach the temple crypt tomorrow," Temsaah is saying, "sacrifice this beast in honor of the Mesu Aapep. Ask the offspring of Apophis to grant you safe passage through their realm." He lifts his staff and presses its winged-cobra insignia against the ram's flank. The creature trembles anew. "There. Now your gift is consecrated."

Our commander asks how we'll find this temple.

The wizard nods at Butaana. "He knows the way." Laughter from within the crocodile mask. "He has seen the entrance. He will not have forgotten."

Morning, and the Nubian walks at the head of our cohort. He moves slowly, with effort, a heavy, reluctant tread. A man in deep memory, a dream-trance. The crow paces back and forth on his shoulders.

Since last night I've been minding the sacrificial ram. Ever since Temsaah touched it no one wants to go near the poor thing. Now I'm leading it by its halter. It bleats and follows behind me. I pluck leaves from shrubs where I can and give it something to eat.

Abruptly from the Nubian's shoulder Black-Claw Kavva arches its wings and caws.

Butaana turns to Lucius Regulus. "There."

Carved into the rock face before us is the doorway to a temple, its pillars chiseled from the sandstone of the cliffs. Statues stand on either side of the entrance. We've seen the design: lions mauling bound captives.

Butaana contemplates the doorway and points to the ground before the entrance. Fifteen years ago, he says, while still a boy and a prince among his people, he was captured in a Kushite raid, he and his family, together with all the members of his clan. The Kushites branded them and marked them as slaves and brought them to this temple. The Kushites were led by a man in a crocodile-skin mask. Temsaah.

"A day and a night I lay out here in the dirt," he says, "trussed like a chicken in rawhide cords. I lay here awaiting my death. One by one my mother and father and kinfolk were taken inside this place and I never saw them again. Finally I was the only prisoner left alive. The crocodile told me I was to be offered as a sacrifice at dawn. But in the night some god gave me strength and I fought free of my cords and fled."

The centurion interrupts with a question. "Is that when Black-Claw decided to become your companion?"

"No, the crow joined me only after I returned to the valley of the Nile. It flew out of a cavern by the river. The place they call the Cave of the Dead. It prompted me to go to Syene and become a guide for the Legion. In a dream it told me service as a scout would benefit both the Empire and me."

Beside me Caecilius coughs discreetly. "Sir?"

Lucius smiles. "You're right, lieutenant. Let's complete our mission."

Inside the temple we find torches and light them and hunt about for the crypt. From the rear of the sanctuary, Effulgent Poe shouts he thinks he's found something.

We bring our torches close. A massive marble trapdoor. Fixed to its surface is a big ring made of iron. Poe tests it with a tug, gasps, "Too much for me."

"Li'l Vic, allow us." Bruiser Pugnax shoulders him aside and looks about for Vorax. His squad-mate lumbers over and the two each grab the ring. With a grunt they heave and pull and the door comes rearing up.

Which reveals a steep stone staircase descending into darkness. We breathe a smell of stale, dank air.

"Let's get this over with," says Lucius. "Rufinus Crassus, you be ready with that sheep."

In the crypt we find what we've been assigned to recover: a severed bronze head, larger than life-size. A youthful face, thick wavy hair spilling over the forehead. A blank gaze greets us from the glass eyes: ivory white, grayish blue. The lips close in a frown meant to warn off interlopers and repel intruders.

"Hey," says Scaevola, "the emperor's got a goddamned big noggin."

Caecilius shows a look of wounded piety.

Lucius tells the *signifer* to curb his irreverence. "At least till we're out of here."

"Yes, sir. Sorry, sir." A grin from Scaevola.

The head's been positioned on a marble altar of some kind. The altar's surface is scored with grooves that lead to run-off channels in the floor to carry away the lustration water and life fluids.

Lucius Regulus details a couple of legionaries to put the head in a sack. Then he glances at the ram, motions me forward. "May as well use this here altar," he says. "Let's see. Where's Sennefer?"

Sennefer's an Egyptian priest who's followed us all the way from Syene. He steps from the rear of the cohort. Bald and hairless, elderly and shriveled, he hurries forward with impressive eagerness. He knows he'll earn a nice gift for his service.

"Give us an auspicious sacrifice," says the centurion, "and I'll see you get a good bonus."

The priest smiles happily and sets to work. He wipes clean the altar top and adorns the ram's horns with ribbons and wool tassels to offer the local gods a pleasing sight. With his back to the animal he sharpens the offering knife on a whetstone.

"No." An agitated Butaana intervenes at the altar. "I think it's wiser to omit the sacrifice and leave at once with what we came for. I don't know what will come of offerings made within this temple."

Privately I agree, if not for the same reason. The sheep's done nothing but gaze at me the whole time we've been in the crypt. The look is confiding, intimate: "I've put my whole trust in you. I know you'll let nothing harm me." The creature baas and bleats. Strange pity wells up within me.

A scandalized Sennefer is protesting. "Omit the sacrifice? And risk offending the resident gods?"

Someone in the cohort says, "Yeah, he's right. We're gonna need all the good fortune we can get if we want a safe passage home."

"These gods are thirsty," declares Sennefer. "Their thirst must be slaked." He ignores the Nubian, goes back to sharpening the blade on the whetstone.

Butaana looks troubled. No wonder, considering the memories this place must hold for him. The crow paces restlessly on his shoulder. He whispers to the bird and suddenly it flies across the chamber and up the stair and disappears from the crypt.

Meanwhile the ram keeps gazing at me. A trusting gaze, but one filled with longing. A longing for life and for freedom to wander in verdant fields with its kind. *The same longing for life and freedom,* comes the thought, *that I myself once had as a bug*. But something else is conveyed in those intelligent animal eyes. A message: "Beware of glutting lusts."

The Egyptian's done with the sharpening. He points to the ram, beckons me forward.

I step forward all right but instead of offering him the sheep I twist the knife from his hand and push him aside. I stoop and slice the rope and free the creature from its halter.

An indignant Sennefer shrieks the altar must be wetted. "The gods are thirsty. They have to have their blood."

"Fair enough. I'll just pour them a drink." Stepping up to the altar, I take the knife and nick my arm from the palm up to the elbow. Blood drips onto the marble surface. "There. That should slake their thirst a bit."

I look down at the sheep and smile. I swear the critter smiles back.

Of course few good deeds go the way one would like them to.

The blood from my arm flows from the altar and along the run-off channels on the floor and then down a series of drains into the earth.

And that's when I get my *uh-oh* moment.

From the mouth of one of these drains I see something emerge. Something with wings, that flutters about the altar.

My first thought is: a bat. Must have been startled awake by our torchlight. A second creature emerges from the drains, then another, and a fourth.

Then I get a clearer look. These aren't bats at all. They're cobras—cobras with wings. Wings that glint in the torchlight with colors of lapis lazuli and gold. I recall Butaana's warning: "Beware the off-spring of Apophis, Serpent of the Shadow Realm."

That's when one flies at my face. I see gaping jaws and fangs stained red with my newly shed blood.

A blow from a lance butt strikes it down. Butaana has stepped between me and the thing. He skewers the snake with his spear and cries, "The blood feeds them."

More of the winged nightmares emerge. The cohort steps back, forms a circle facing outward, using their shields to keep the Apophis-spawn at bay.

Beside me Sennefer cries out. A serpent has fastened its teeth on his neck. Leechlike it swells as it feeds on his blood. I wheel with my sword and slice it in two. I stoop and scoop up the ram just in time to save it from attacks by the swarm.

Worse is to come. A volley of arrows and spears announces the arrival of another menace. In the torchlight I glimpse a figure in a crocodile mask on the stairs of the crypt: Temsaah the wizard, surrounded by what must be hundreds of Kushite warriors.

He shouts something to his men. Another volley from the stairs. Our shields bristle with arrows and broken lance-heads. Dead and wounded legionaries lie bleeding at our feet. And as their blood runs into the drains around the altar, more Apophis-snakes emerge to assault us.

If one has to die in battle, it's good to do it with friends. I scan the chamber for Poe. He looks understandably scared but Pugnax and Vorax have got him protectively wedged in between the considerable bulk of the two of them. A crazed thought comes unbidden: All this grisly ghastly death could give him fresh inspiration if he decides to rewrite "Rue Morgue" or "House of Usher."

Lucius Regulus nods to Caecilius and orders a charge. We surge across the crypt, slash and stab and force a path up the stairs. We kill one after another of the Kushites. They kill one after another of us. The stairs run wet with blood.

More serpents emerge from the altar drains. They spiral upward to the vaulted ceiling like leaves caught in a whirlwind. Then they dive and strike us with their wings and fix their fangs on face and neck and limb. I shield the sheep with one arm and with the other whirl my sword overhead.

The Apophis-plague attacks everything human in the room, Kushite and Roman alike. Temsaah the wizard stands atop the stairs and stretches forth an arm as if to consecrate the slaughter. He laughs, and I see the teeth of his crocodile snout gleam in the torchlight.

I feel the same hypnotic urge I felt in the cliff-top fight. *Glut your lusts. Glut your lusts.* But this time I sense the ram looking up at me, which reminds me of what the fish tried to say: "Don't be forgetful. Know where you came from."

Which jars me free of the glut-lust. In the roar all about me I shout out a warning we should stop fighting each other. "They feed on human blood. They feed on us all."

But just as in nightmares no one hears what I shout. Temsaah goes on laughing. Kushites and Romans continue killing each other. More serpents rise up out of the drains.

As the killing continues, the snakes swell larger. More Kushites and Romans fall. We'll all die here.

Commotion at the top of the stairs. Someone else has entered the crypt. Red-cloaked Taharqo, lord of the Kushites.

Taharqo steps behind Temsaah and drives a lance through his back. The point comes out his chest. The wizard and his mask drop down the stairs.

Taharqo shouts a command at his warriors. The Kushites break off combat against us and instead stand shoulder to shoulder with us in slashing at the horrors from the crypt.

Taharqo calls to Lucius Regulus, "If we have to die, let us die together as men, fighting off this foul swarm."

The centurion nods. He and Taharqo, Roman and Kushite, fight back to back.

Too few of us left to win. Looks like the emperor's never going to get back his foolish head. Nor is Lovecraft going to get his precious apotropaion.

But then come reinforcements.

The Nubian's bird returns, leading a black turbulence of crows. They fill the crypt and caw and peck and claw at the flying cobras.

More crows come, and more, till the snakes retreat down the drains and vanish back into the earth. Those that remain are torn to pieces by the crows.

Black-Claw Kavva alights on Butaana's shoulder. Its eyes glint at me. I understand what it's signaling: "Nothing will prevent this artifact from reaching our master."

A weary march back to Egypt, and the Empire's frontiers. Once more in the fortress at Syene.

With raised lance Butaana gives us a farewell salute and trots south through the desert in search of what's left of his tribe.

A puzzled Lucius Regulus tells us the legate in Rome has fresh orders. The newly recovered head will be given as a gift to someone known as the Magus. "With a name like that, must be a foreign potentate of some kind. Hope he enjoys it, whoever he is, considering all the lives it cost." The artifact is to be left untended at the mouth of a cavern by the Nile called the Cave of the Dead. The sole sentry and escort posted beside it is to be the crow called Black-Claw.

"Just hope no one tries to steal the head before this Magus picks it up," says the centurion. "Especially after all the trouble we went through to retrieve it." If I could I'd tell him "Don't worry. Kavva will miniaturize the thing in a flash and whistle up a horde of Elementals from the cave to bring it home to Corpse-Head."

In the barracks Poe eyes me dubiously, asks me if I'm sure I've made the right decision. "You know if you go back through that cave, you'll be busted down to bug-rank again."

I say I know but maybe back in Providence I'll get promoted to lizard size. "With luck, I might work my way someday up to iguana."

"And all for the sake of this Goldie?" Poe says he understands better than anyone about infatuation with females and *femmes fatales*. "But my dear man, really. To fall for a fish?"

I tell him her real name's not Goldie. "It's Novalyne. Anyway, she kept faith with me when I was a caterpillar. I'm not gonna give up on her now just because she's got fins."

He asks where do I think I'm going to find her.

"Back in Rhode Island. She delivered her message here in Egypt of the emperors and then she swam all the way back to 1936." I tell him I felt sure I could sense this when we communicated face to face.

I add something else I discovered. "Remember, the Nile flows into the Providence River. All waters are connected. That's what I learned from Butaana."

The other legionaries are crowding around to wish me luck on my journey. A puzzled Vorax turns to Pugnax. "He's gotta take furlough cuz his girlfriend's a goldfish?"

I entrust the black ram to the two bruisers. "Take good care of this critter. I carried him on my shoulders all the way back from that Kushite temple."

Pugnax says they won't let anyone harm him. "He's a survivor. Like us."

I turn to Poe, ask him if he's sure he wants to stay on here in the Legion. He says absolutely. "I thoroughly enjoy having a human frame again. And if the only way I can retain it and its attendant pleasures is to be at the beck and call of that infernal crow and fetch the occasional apotropaion for our Magus, then so be it. A small price to pay." He motions to Vorax, who's guzzling from a flask. The soldier passes him the drink. Poe takes a long swig. "Ah. Now *that* I couldn't do as an insect."

He passes the flask to Pugnax. "You know, my phrenologist in Baltimore once imparted to me a bit of wise counsel. For aesthetes of a temperament at once choleric and tinged with melancholia, the best tonic is life lived as constant pageant. A whirl of distraction, sensation, and color, tempered with odd moments in which quietly to compose verse. And life in the Legion, I suspect, will afford me pageantry aplenty."

He stands, claps his hands to get his squad-mates' attention. "Speaking of verse. Let's show Rufinus Crassus here the latest song I just taught you." Turning to me he whispers in a confiding voice, "It's in my new vulgarian meter."

Cooperatively Pugnax and Vorax both rise. They reel a bit from their drink but willingly bellow out Poe's latest tune:

Gloomy worms
When they rust
Cry: Prop me up!
Cheer me up!
Give me wine
Cuz I must
Glut my lusts,
Glut my lusts!

When I'm knifed
With a thrust
And I'm dead,
I won't fuss
Just inscribe
In the dust
Glut your lusts—
It's a must!

Use my skull
For a cup
Pour me wine,
Fill me up

So in death
I can say:
It's a must—
Glut your lusts!

I applaud their singing, compliment Poe on the poem. No sense telling him "Glut your lusts" is exactly what ol' Cadaver-Head wants him to do. Politely I add, "But my favorite's still the piece you recited at our camp in the desert. You know, the one about the Conqueror Worm: 'My evanescent love, my Dom'na Thume.' Has a way of sticking in the mind."

"Yes, I rather outdid myself there, didn't I?" This with quiet pride.

I bid farewell to everyone in the barracks, tell them to look after my Hyperborean brother. Pugnax says he and Vorax will see to it. "I mean, we have to. Li'l Vic here, he's the squadron's poet."

I embrace Poe last of all. "Eddie. Fellow Vespertine."

He says gallantly if things don't work out in Providence just pop through that cavern tunnel again. "We'll keep a slot open for you in the cohort."

Poe has the men sing in my honor as I stride south from the fort. I can hear their distant words on the breeze blown from the Nile:

"It doth choose our fate, it chews our face."

The chant follows me all the way to the mouth of the cave.

30

"And that's it," concluded Fay MacConnell.

"Wow." Bonaventure looked up from the notes he'd been taking as the librarian read aloud.

"So what do you think?" A note of anxiety, a desire for reassurance, in her voice.

"Dunno. If nothing else at least I can see why you said your wrist is sore. You did a ton of writing overnight."

"That's the weird thing. It wasn't really me that did the writing." She shrugged, made a face. "Well I mean it *was*. That's my handwriting, like I said. And I've got the aching wrist to prove it. But none of this really came from me."

"Are you sure? I mean, is this for real?" Even as he said it he realized he shouldn't have. A wounded expression flashed across her face: he'd bruised her with his doubt.

"Look. I trusted you, coming here like this." Indignantly she snatched up the scattered pages, rose from her perch on the cot.

"Sorry. I'm a jerk. Always have been." He raised his hands to signal his surrender. "And I'm the last guy to have any right to play Mister Skeptic, what with my believing I saw a spiky six-foot something wriggling down the Providence River." She watched him warily as he spoke.

He paused, tried again. "Please. Please stay. Let me make it up to you. How about another Drake's Coffee Cake?" He bowed low, presented her the cardboard box of pastries.

That made her laugh. She had a nice smile. "Oh. Well. If that's the case." She sat back down on the narrow bed, leaned back against the wall.

"And I'll throw in another fresh brew of Taster's Choice."

"I give in." She slapped the sheaf of papers. "All I can say is, I could never have made up all this on my own, asleep *or* awake. Not in a million years. It's for real. It's gotta be."

He spooned mounded crystals into a mug, added hot water. "There. Plus another round of Drake's, as promised in my clumsy bribe."

"Works for me."

As she dunked the cake in her cup, he marveled aloud over the implications of this latest find. "Think about it. You had this psychographic episode last night, but only after putting that silver stud back in your ear. The same stud that had been mouthed and brought to me by our river-dwelling Spike-Head."

"Which means"—she paused with the Drake's halfway to her lips—"that my sudden ability to write down the thoughts and experiences of Robert E. Howard is all because the earring I was wearing last night had been slobbered over by that six-foot thingy in the river."

"An inelegant way of conveying a psychometric experience. But yeah."

"Wait." She slurped coffee, waved a hand in excitement. "That psychometric-transmission theory works only if this red-eyed river-crawler of yours happens to be Robert E. Howard."

"And that's exactly what I'm saying. Mister King of the Pulps no longer has the bodily configuration to sit down with pen and paper or bang away at a keyboard and type out his memoirs. So he does the next best thing. He scoops into his mouth whatever treasure he can find in the river and imbues it with the whole weight of his fevered recollections and longings. And then he spits it out at the feet of the first goofball to fall splat in the water."

"But you forgot something. It says here"—she leafed through the pages—"that because he was going to return from Roman Egypt to Providence and the world of 1936, Howard would lose his human body and—how does his pal put it? Yeah, here it is—get 'busted down to bug-rank again.' Which means becoming a three-quarter-inch caterpillar once more. Not a six-foot-long whatever-it-was you saw."

"Hang on." He snatched the pages from her, leafed through the sheets. "It says here somewhere, wait, wait, I made a note of this while I was reading. One second."

"Let me see too." She leaned forward in her perch on the cot. He scooted the folding chair closer. Their heads almost touched as they peered at the text.

Up close she smelled like tobacco and coffee and caramel sugar crumbs. He'd never noticed before: her eyebrows were a thin penciled pale brown. Looked good with her cropped mane of blond hair. From mere inches away he saw brunette roots, metallic tones. She squirmed and seemed suddenly uncomfortable. *Maybe she doesn't want her dye job revealed.* He felt an urge to reassure her, blurt something. *Hey. You look good. You look good. It's all right.*

But before he could speak she turned her gaze on him. That's when he realized he was getting distracted.

"Here," he said. He fumbled, found the page he wanted. "See, Howard thinks maybe once he's back in Providence he'll get promoted to lizard size. 'Who knows, I might work my way someday up to iguana.' His exact words. Or yours, except you were channeling him. Anyway. That's exactly the type of creature I saw that night with Riverglow when I fell out of the canoe. Long tail. Long rippling back with a spiny crest plus spikes on its head. Not to mention paws that seemed almost human in appearance. Except they're gray green with big curving claws. Which nixes any chance for him of ever getting comfortable again with a writing implement."

"So you're saying you saw some kind of iguana." She said this in a flat, inquisitorial you-must-be-daft tone.

"Not just any iguana. But yeah."

"A six-foot tropical lizard."

"I know it sounds nuts."

"Right here. Downtown. In the Providence River."

"Yeah. Like I said. But let me expl—"

"Hundreds, no, make that thousands, of miles from the Caribbean or Costa Rica or the Galapagos or wherever that kind of thing is supposed to live."

"I already said I know it sounds nuts."

"And it's an iguana that happens to be the twenty-first-century Vespertine remnant of one Robert E. Howard."

"Yeah. Though when I hear you say it out loud like that, I start to think I'm truly out of my mind."

"You know what?" A note of suppressed excitement in her voice. "I believe you. I think you're right. But then what does that make the two of us?"

"Either a pair of crazies unfit for human society, or . . ."—and here his tone grew from diffident to defiant—"or a couple of super-smart rebels that have just made the most exciting literary discovery in the history of Providence."

"Of Rhode Island."

"Of the world."

She laughed. "Super-smart *and* crazy, maybe both at the same time." Her laughter ceased as she sprang from the cot and paced the small room—a space too cramped for her excitement. "But if that part's real, then I guess all of it is. Including those new poems by good old Edgar Allan."

She wheeled to face him. "For a Poe fangirl like me, having the chance to discover a trove of his unknown verses: I mean, life doesn't get better than that. Wow. Can't wait for the next Goth poetry night at the Ath. I can recite these new pieces, blow the audience's socks off. I'll get that stuffed raven they keep in the basement, use it again as a prop. This'll give a fresh twist to 'Nevermore.'"

He wondered aloud what the Athenaeum's membership would make of Roman-legionary Poe's "new vulgarian meter." "You know, 'Glut your lusts, it's a must.'"

"So okay," she conceded, "it's a tad different from anything else we've ever seen from Poe. But that will just make the shock of impact all the more pleasurable." She rubbed her hands as she paced.

Only to stop abruptly. He could see she'd been overtaken by an unexpected turn of thought.

"What is it?"

"Novalyne Price. Goldie, they called her. That poor woman. Transmogrified into a fish. How did that happen? Was it all because of something awful done to her by your horrible Lovecraft?"

"Hey. Don't say 'your.' Don't blame me. He's not really mine."

"Well who else does he belong to? You're the one writing the dissertation on him."

Best not to argue the point, he decided. Aloud he said, "I wonder if we'll ever find out what happened to her." He said this was one of many unanswered questions posed by the text. "Like how come Robert E. Howard is still swimming in the Providence River decades after Lovecraft's death? Is he still on some unfulfilled quest? I guess we'll never know."

"Nevermore," agreed Fay moodily. She lifted her head, snapped her fingers. "Unless ..."

He asked unless what.

"Unless I wear the earring stud again tonight and maybe get another psychographic jolt. It might give us the next installment. Assuming my wrist can take it." She chuckled. "I mean I'd really like to know what happened to those two. Bob and Novalyne. Iguana and Fish. Did they ever find each other again?"

"You could try. But I don't think it'd work."

"Why not?"

He reminded her of what the savant Polignac had written about the tendency of psychometrically charged objects to lose their aura over time. "I suspect that last night's usage drained the batteries, so to speak, in your ear-stud. To get it recharged, I bet we'd have to toss it back in the river and hope Iguana Howard finds it again and rolls it around in his fevered mouth some more."

"Yuck. Sounds a bit dubious." Reluctant agreement. She paced the cramped room again. "You got any better ideas?"

He sat and thought and pulled a small glass object from his pocket, rolled it back and forth in his hand. He muttered they needed fresh clues to have any hope of resolving these mysteries. Back and forth he rolled it.

Idly she asked what was that.

He opened his hand, showed her: a diminutive flask that housed the husk of an insect. A dried-up beetle. "Remember? We found it the other day when I came to the Athenaeum and talked you into opening the drawers of that Egyptian Cabinet."

She smiled at the memory. "Yeah. I gave you a hard time about fussing over that bug, didn't I? Of course that was before last night's psychographic extravaganza. Which just happened to reveal the identity of the bug husk in the drawer."

"Yeah." He breathed a sympathetic sigh as he eyed the insect. "To think. This little flask is the burial mound, such as it is, of Moby-Dick Melville."

He broke his meditation with a shout. "That's it!"

"What?"

"Burial mound! Swan Point! Why didn't I think of this before?"

She said irritably she had no idea what he was going on about.

He said if they needed fresh clues there was one place that so far they'd overlooked. "Swan Point Cemetery. It's Lovecraft's burial site."

"You think it's worth going there?"

"It just might. For years Cthulhu cultists have been leaving things there in his honor. All kinds of stuff. We might luck into a lead."

She checked her phone for the time. "Oh crap. I've gotta get to work."

"Hey. Come on." He said Swan Point was close by. "Blackstone Boulevard. Not far at all from College Hill. I can get you there and back to work inside of an hour."

She said she couldn't afford to show up late for work yet again and try her supervisor's patience any further. "Besides, I've got a clue of my own to check, right in the stacks of the Ath."

He asked what was that.

"The *Necronomicon*. Remember? Our overnight iguana-revelation claims that Abdul Hazred's long-lost book has been lurking on the shelves of the Athenaeum lo these many aeons. If that's the situation then I aim to find it."

He said in that case they each had a quest. "You in the library. Me at Swan Point." He suggested they rendezvous later in the day at the Athenaeum. "You know, just like Eddie Poe and Helen Whitman used to do."

Oops. As soon as he said it he recognized this might not be the most felicitous comparison to make.

Which of course fangirl Fay pointed out right away. "Uh, you do realize that the whole Whitman-Poe-at-the-Athenaeum thing didn't exactly end well."

"Yeah. Shoot. Sorry." He flushed hot as the thought overcame him that what he'd blurted also inadvertently hinted at the notion that he was starting to like her. In fact like her a lot.

Whereas he had no idea what Fay MacConnell made of him, aside from the fact that he knew he often exasperated her, and she didn't like his ancient tats—"Girlie you look like the Queen of Diamonds"—and she sometimes gave him a look like he was one of the lowly creatures in that vulgarian poem of Poe: "Gloomy worms when they rust."

By now she was halfway out the door. He called after her—in an attempt to make light of it all—a promise that when he saw her next at the Ath he wouldn't tear off a swatch of any muslin dress.

"You try any tearing," she countered, "and I'll knock you flat on your ass."

"Oh."

"By the way." Her parting comment. "I favor jeans over dresses. In case you haven't noticed."

To which he could only append another "Oh."

How to make hasty amends? He fumbled about for the cardboard box of pastries, had some idea of asking "Would you maybe like a Drake's Coffee Cake for the road?"

But she was already out the door and down the stairs.

31

Of course he had been here before. In fact many times. Everyone who researches the life of Howard Phillips Lovecraft goes to Swan Point Cemetery, whether to express psychic kinship with Providence's own man of cosmic dread or to breathe inspiration for writing a tale in Lovecraftian mode or simply to imbibe whatever aura can still be sensed at the grave. On one visit Joseph Bonaventure had seen a cluster of devotees run about crying in chorus "We too feel the vertiginous call of the abyss."

Yes. Bonaventure used to come here often. But not for some time now. Not since the night of . . .

Not since (one way he tagged it in his mind) the Incident . . . the Fire . . .

Not since the fear and the shame that showed him just what kind of ne'er-do-well knothead confronted Joseph Bonaventure each day at dawn in the mirror . . .

Not since . . . Not since . . .

Stop.

He stood hesitant at the cemetery's entrance, listened to the fountain, its play of water a flow that was engineered to reassure, to soothe.

Doctor Cartwright had a voice that soothed. Guess if you're going to be a therapist you'd best develop your vocal assets as one of the tools of your trade. Doctor Cartwright often reassured him no one else had been all that badly burned that night, that it was Joseph Bonaventure who'd gotten it worst (the drips of smoked ceiling tiles on his face), that his fans didn't blame him for panicking and jumping . . .

Stop.

Ever since that night, he'd been doing his best to block such memories, such thoughts, to throw up walls, build bulwarks.

And ever since that night, the night that divided his life into Before and After, he'd had a new perspective on Lovecraft (not that he'd necessarily want to confess this in his dissertation), a new lesson from (what did Bob Howard call him?) Ol' Cadaver-Head.

To wit: all the things that loom up in stories by Corpse-Face—the Lurkers, the Haunters, the Horrors, the Rats—such things always find a way to gnaw through the walls one throws up as bulwarks between one's frail self and the world.

Swan Point Cemetery. Why go visit the dead when the dead keep coming to you?

And yet here he was once again. Stupid maybe to have volunteered himself to journey here this morning. He'd forgotten how badly his thoughts could behave when he put himself in the wrong spot. But he'd done it as a way to try to keep things going with Fay MacConnell, and he felt like Fay was someone who might understand how thoughts can chew away at one's mind (she was a disciple of Poe, after all)—or she *would* understand if he could ever find a way to put his thoughts into words that might make sense to someone else.

He grimaced as the memory returned of what those groupies had been crying as they ran about Lovecraft's grave. "We too feel the vertiginous call of the abyss."

He grunted, shook his head to shake the mood. *Abyss. Yeah. I know the feeling.*

But by luck Swan Point this morning seemed restfully quiet. A pleasant breeze blew among the tombs and granite memorials. Birds sang from carefully manicured shrubs. Leafy trees offered welcome shade from the sun. A crow cawed as it winged overhead. Lovecraft's headstone, one among hundreds, stood undisturbed.

Or nearly. As Bonaventure passed the entrance and approached the spot consecrated to Lovecraft, he saw a solitary figure kneeling on the grass. A young man; the face was shrouded by a cowl that obscured this individual from view. Abruptly the kneeling figure prostrated itself, forehead touching the earth, as if in token of worship. *Okay. Maybe some Cthulhu-cultist. With Lovecraft you never know.*

Stepping softly—he didn't want to disrupt Cthulhu-Man's meditation or prayers—Bonaventure crouched before Lovecraft's headstone.

Nothing of particular interest. Not at first. Stubs of black candles. Bouquets of flowers. Stones heaped in a cairn. A rock painted with an image of a tentacle-sprouting blob. Bonaventure wondered if any scholar had ever catalogued the votive offerings left for Lovecraft by his latter-day devotees. *Could be included as an appendix to my dissertation. Assuming I ever finish it.*

He sat on the grass by the headstone. Nothing useful here. Nothing that could serve as a clue. Not that he'd had any clear idea what he might find. He'd come with no more than a hope that the gravesite might yield a pointer, a sign. Something that might somehow signal: "Look here, go there, follow the arrow, follow the thread."

He didn't like the thought of disappointing Fay, wanted to keep their quest going. To find fresh material? Sure. But also to have an excuse to keep seeing this self-described Poe fangirl. Miss Moxie, the private name he'd made up. He liked thinking about her.

No signal. No sign. Too bad. *Still,* he told himself, *once you get a grip on your thoughts this is not a bad place to be. Outdoors on a pleasant June morning. Soft breezes. Birdsong in the shrubs. Crow cawing overhead.*

The crow settled on the topmost branch of the nearest tree. Must be a whole colony resting up there. Caws and croaked cries greeted the new arrival as it settled on its perch.

A different kind of sound arose from close by. Muttering of some sort. Cthulhu-Man, some ten or twelve feet away, swayed as he knelt.

No. Not muttering. Mister Cthulhu was humming a tune. Familiar. Bonaventure had heard it before. He didn't want to intrude on other folks' devotions but he glanced at the kneeling figure. Face still obscured by the cowl or hood he was wearing.

Gratingly familiar, that tune, that hum. Something he once knew well. He imagined telling Fay—he liked thinking of conversations they might have one day, if he could manage to stop irritating her with comments that sparked her the wrong way—*You know how sometimes you half hear something you're sure was once a big part of your life? And you know that when you finally remember you're going to feel like a complete idiot for forgetting something that had once been so integral to your sense of who you are?*

And he imagined her saying in reply "No, you're not an idiot. I understand. It happens to me too. All the time in fact."

Of course she might also just say "Shut up" or "Get lost" or "Drop dead." But he liked imagining chats with her that actually turned out well.

Burst of caws from the crows overhead. Almost like a reproof: *Hey human snap outta your dream.* He blinked, looked about once more.

That cairn of votive stones by the grave. Something protruded from beneath the bottommost stone. Bonaventure stood up, stepped closer, crouched before the pile, tugged at the protrusion.

A clump of papers, damp with morning dew. Handwriting on each sheet. *Petitionary prayers to Lovecraft's shade? Random effusions from some Lovecraftian passerby?*

Joseph Bonaventure was, among other things, a scholar and lover of archives, and nothing pleased him better than a newly discovered text—whether found on a library shelf or under a pile of rocks. He plopped contentedly back onto the grass and began reading the topmost sheet.

Had he been paying attention he might have noticed two things.

The first was that the humming from the hooded figure had come to a stop.

The second was that the crows overhead in the tree were cawing more loudly than ever. Cawing in bursts: *graaacck—urgent—graaacck.*

Both things went unnoticed. Joseph Bonaventure bent his head over the topmost sheet from the pile.

The first ten or twelve lines were in a language he scarcely knew. Latin. Intriguing. Yet for the moment something he couldn't decode.

But below the lines of Latin script was writing penned in a hand he could read plain and clear:

"Promises twain we make to you, O Magus. We will rediscover Yog-Sothoth; we will reinforce it and strengthen it anew—Prov GGCG."

Yog-Sothoth; GGCG. Where had he seen that quadriliteral cluster before?

He was just telling himself *Now here's a real clue, here's something I can share with Miss Moxie* when a cawed *graaacck* overhead finally snapped him alert.

Which made him look up in time to see a hand clutching a stone—a stone from the cairn beside Lovecraft's gravesite—hand and stone descending in a swipe at his head.

He ducked fast to one side. But not fast enough.

The stone—and the hand propelling it—grazed the side of his head. Bonaventure crashed to the grass, lying helpless and stunned.

And in that stunned state he heard the hum resume and burst forth into song, a dance of triumph as his assailant jigged a kind of two-step and sang:

They call me Devil Dog
And Busy Bee
But mostly I'm known
As the Master Thief.
I work the night shift
I work it all night long.

His head hurt like hell and he felt dribbles of something—sweat and most likely blood—flow down the side of his face. But Joseph Bonaventure was still plenty conscious, enough for the thought to pop: *Of course I know that tune. I wrote it for the Fox Point Punks. We played Devil Dog that last night of the gig.*

The gig in question of course was at the Pacific Bacchanale. And as the cowled figure continued its two-step, yelping its proud boast of being a Master Thief, the Bacchanale roared over Bonaventure as he lay stunned on the grass. The fire, the panic, the way he jumped blind from the stage and clawed and flailed for the exit without even looking to check if everyone else was okay.

"Bacchanale Panic," had flared the news headlines next day. Bonaventure always felt that this title had been aimed expressly at him. For he certainly had panicked. Fire and flames and the end of his band. No one wanted anything to do with the Fox Point Punks after that. Panic and failure. Nothing to show for that night but a scar along his jaw from when he dived off that stage.

He might have wallowed in the past for who knows how long but then he sensed a shadow stoop over his face. A bellowed repetition of a line from the song—"Mostly I'm known as the Master Thief"—and then the prostrate researcher felt something torn from his hand. The shadow paused to snatch something else and then vanished.

That cleared his mind. Bonaventure forced himself upright, put a hand to his head—*Damn does that hurt*—and lurched to his feet. *I ain't gonna let some jerk—especially one singing a hit from my own past—make off with my hard-earned clue. A clue I want to show to Miss Moxie.*

But it seemed Mister Master Thief was going to make off just fine with every one of the clues. Bonaventure glanced at the ground, saw all the papers were gone from under the cairn. The thief was running and leaping along a row of headstones, still bellowing that song, and no way was Bonaventure—with blood dripping down his face over the line of his Bacchanale scar—ever going to catch that cowled clown.

But someone else did it for him. The fleeing figure passed beneath the tree that stood nearest to Lovecraft's tomb. And as he passed, there dived at him a flight of birds that cawed and croaked as they swooped. Bonaventure remembered a phrase from Robert E. Howard's Vespertine Egyptian text: "a black turbulence of crows."

Cthulhu-Man flailed and cursed as the crows swooped and pecked. Which gave Bonaventure a chance for a good look at the Devil Dog thief. Shaven head, tattooed neck, that night on the Riverglow canoe: the assailant was none other than Alexander Finster. Better known as Tagger.

The crows still bombed and pecked. Tagger saw Bonaventure come stumbling up. With a yelp of frustration—"Take the frickin' things then"—Tagger flung the papers at the whirl of birds. And with that they let him go.

And so did the blood-streaming researcher, who felt too wobbly and faint for even the thought of pursuit. He sank to the grass, sprawled with his legs flung apart, pressed a hand to his head.

The abandoned papers tumbled and fluttered in the breeze. Some fetched up against headstones. Others drifted to the base of the tree.

As for the crows: they spun up in a spiral and then flapped away toward College Hill and the Providence River.

All the crows except one. With a *graaacck* it made its way to the ground. Bonaventure paid it no attention. His scalp was still bleeding. Blood dripped to his jaw and trickled over his scar and made him grimace at the memory of the Pacific Bacchanale.

What with his messed-up head it took the man a moment to realize: *This crow is acting a bit odd.* With a purposeful stride it bobbed its way to one of the papers and lifted it up with its beak. A muzzy thought floated up: *Material for a nest?*

But no. Quickly the crow fetched one sheet, then another, until it had plucked them all and gathered them in a neat pile.

Bonaventure fumbled in his pockets, found a bandanna, held it against the side of his head. The crow was stooping over the pile and fussing with it as if sorting the lot into some kind of order.

Came a dim thought: *This is all deeply strange.*

And it got stranger. Pages clamped in its beak, the bird bobbed its way over to him.

A metallic tang of blood dribbled on his lips, just as the crow came up to where he sat.

So weak now he felt his focus go in and out. The next thing he knew, the creature perched on his knee and dropped the pile in his lap.

He glanced down. Somehow the sheet on top happened to be the one he'd been studying when he'd been smacked by Tagger. Latin text plus "O Magus" plus "GGCG." Through his banged-up brain came the thought: *Miss Moxie will love this.*

He lifted his head, felt the blood drip some more. Crow talons gripped his knee and gripped hard. Onyx orbs eyed him. The beak opened wide.

Bonaventure expected a conventional *graaacck.*

Instead what he heard was a voice, and corvid speech.

Or at least he thought he heard. His head hurt so much he just couldn't be sure.

Another thought floated up—*I'm in Howard's pulp-world*—and he gave the crow a weak but companionable grin. He mumbled—or tried to—"Funny I thought you were trying to speak. Thought I heard real human speech from a simple bird's beak. Funny."

Which the crow must have heard. An impatient flap of its wings. Onyx orbs eyed him once more. The beak opened wide and grew vocal again.

But this time the claws dug into Joseph Bonaventure's knee good and deep, enough to clear the man's mind and make him listen up.

Which he did, and he heard the crow say: "Yog-Sothoth."

And again: "Yog-Sothoth."

With that it rose up and flew fast through the sky on the path of its friends.

32

Janey Evans tried phoning Atith Rattanak but he didn't pick up. Then she called Guild Metal but the assistant foreman said he'd just clocked out for the day. "Said he wanted to go pray. Not sure where he went."

But Janey knew Atith's habits well enough to guess where he'd be. So she got in her car and from Providence took 295 for Cranston.

The machine she drove wasn't much. A '92 Ford Escort with a hole in the muffler that produced a roared *pock-pock-pock* every time she floored the metal. *Like you paid extra to install strobe exhaust pipes. Cool. Way to go, Aunt Janey.* That's what her nephew sometimes said to tease her.

Her nephew. Augustus Valerian Tessario. That's why she was out looking for Atith. Gussy was worrying her. Worrying her a lot.

To push the fear aside a moment she gave herself a quick once-over in the mirror. Eye-shadow and lipstick daubed on dense the way she liked it. Sparkly fingernails: unnecessary maybe, but today her mood really needed a lift and nails that flared fine always gave her a boost.

A glance at the road ahead, then back to the mirror. Just had her hair done and it looked good. Teased out and long and dyed a pale platinum blonde. *Touch of glamour* was what her beautician said and Janey had laughed. *Honey at my age I can use more than a touch. Lay it on thick.*

She glanced down at her outfit such as it was. Tight leopard-print Capri pants and a white tee from the Tiverton Casino Hotel. Inked on the shirt was a spread of cards, all hearts, ace-king-queen-jack-ten, and the words "I'm flushed red-hot from my Royal Flush." Not that Janey Evans had ever been dealt anything better than an inside straight, not for as long as she could recall. *But so what.* These days she and Barb would watch the play at the blackjack table, do a few turns at the slots, keep the losses down between the two of them (this was their deal, and they stuck to it) to twenty-five bucks tops. She had a head on her shoulders, knew when to quit.

And aside from that, have a smoke and a drink, chit-chat with the players. She liked the fact men still looked at her. Liked it even better she didn't have to take any home. As she often told Barb, "Been married twice. Been there, done that." And as Barb often said in reply, "Leave the trash in the casino. No need to bring it into the house." Which always made them both laugh.

Laugh, and she smiled now at the memory. Except the smile faded as the thought of her nephew came back. She needed to talk to someone about Gussy, and casino-mate Barb just wouldn't do. The last time Janey had asked for advice all Barb offered was "Tell 'im to stay straight and stay sober or else he'll get dead." Then she'd barked a harsh snort like she'd said something wise to settle the whole case. End of talk. Back to discussion of their odds at the slots.

Which was why Janey Evans was grateful for Atith, glad to have met him at Riverglow years ago the first time his *Persephone* docked near the *Icarus*. Not that he always said much of anything at all. But he listened, actually listened, and what were the odds of finding *that* in a man? Talk about being dealt a royal flush. Plus he'd gotten Gussy a job at Guild Metal just like he'd promised.

Which in a way now made Augustus Valerian Tessario almost as much Atith's problem as hers. So—and now she smiled again—she had every right to go pestering him when he was trying to pray.

Janey knew the route. From 295, exit 6 to Plainfield Pike. She liked this part of Rhode Island, less congested than Providence, with traces of the state's old rural life. Grassy meadows, horses grazing, barns and bales of hay. She drove west a few miles, pulled over at a roadside stand that bore a sign saying "Pezza Farms," told the clerk to give her a couple of pounds apiece of whatever was fresh. While she waited she petted the ponies that ambled up to the fence.

And right across the road was the place she wanted, a new arrival in this old landscape. Wat Dhamagosnaram. Cambodian Buddhist temple.

She walked to the entrance, bag of groceries in hand. No need to go searching. Right in front stood Atith Rattanak.

Not that he saw her at first. A knot of visitors chatting in Khmer obscured her from view. She was happy to stand quietly and watch.

Joss sticks in hand, he bobbed and bowed in worship. But he was performing his prayers not within the main temple itself but rather outdoors before a sprawling replica model, three-and-a-half feet tall, of a distant and much more famous shrine. Diminutive domes and spires and pagodas, carved in marble and jade. Midget staircases rising to towers within which reposed miniature seated Buddhas. Pillared galleries leading to halls that housed smiling bodhisattvas. And, surrounding the replica's outer wall, a deep water-filled moat. Leaves and wind-drift grass floated on its surface.

"An evocation of Angkor Wat," Atith had explained on her first visit, "to help us remember. Cambodia comes to Cranston Rhode Island." Refugees by the thousands had fled to Providence and outlying towns after the Indochina wars. This hand-carved Angkor model, Atith had told her, helped Cambodians connect with something precious that was now half a world away.

On Janey's first visit he'd pointed to the moat and said, "That water is linked with the Tonlé Sap, which pours into the Mekong. Which in turn flows into the South China Sea. And that's the route my sampan took. That's what brought me here. Which means"—and Janey remembered he'd chuckled when he said this—"the Mekong and the Providence River are directly connected."

And he'd said something else on that first visit of hers. "Think of all this as a map." He'd leaned forward and stretched out an arm and pointed to a tiny statue-filled alcove in the midst of the shrine. "Here's where the monks hid me, when I was a boy"—he'd lifted up his mutilated hands—"after I got the chop-chop."

And (this was what Janey Evans recalled more vividly than anything else from that visit) as he'd told her his tale he'd given her a huge goofy grin, "like everything was okay now," as she'd told Barb later, "and losing five fingers wasn't such a big deal."

To which Barb had replied by saying something like "Hunh if it'd been me I woulda gone back to my homeland and kicked ass. Forgive and forget? No way." Janey's thought in response had been *Lady maybe that's the difference between you and Stubby*, but she'd decided not to voice that thought aloud.

Now here she stood with her groceries. Atith Rattanak bowed once more, then carefully placed the burning joss sticks in a sand-filled incense urn. Turning, he saw her and smiled as she handed him the bag.

"Here," she said. "Courtesy of Pezza Farms. Tomatoes, red pepper, corn on the cob."

He hugged her. "You mean my favorite lady drove all the way to Cranston just to make sure I stay fed?"

"Truthfully, Stubby, not exactly. I got someone on my mind."

"You mean Gusto."

"Yeah." She said it'd been four, maybe five days since she'd last heard from him. "And that's not like Gussy. I mean we're close. He's constantly texting and calling. Technically he's my nephew but he's more like a son or maybe grandson. I mean what with his mom and dad splitting up years ago and both moving out of state and leaving him on his own here in Rhode Island. Not good for a kid."

Atith asked if she'd tried the halfway house downtown. "You know, the one on Mathewson Street."

"Safe Anchorage. Yeah. I been there. You know I visited him at that place just last week and right then he was doing all right. We went for a walk outside and he had his Chihuahua with him bundled up inside his jacket and it's licking his face and he's loving it and looking so happy. And we're walking down Mathewson and I'll tell you something interesting we saw. There's a humongous outdoor painting filling up the whole wall of some old brick building next door to an empty parking lot. You know the one I mean? The painting shows some young guy with his pet mouse and the mouse is perched on the guy's shoulder like it's talking in his ear. And Gussy points to the picture and says 'Aunt Janey I know you worry about me but you don't have to cuz Cheddar here she gives me advice all the time what to do just like that mouse advises the dude in the painting.' So I come back at him and say 'Well then I hope your Cheddar is advising you now to stay clean and stay off dope.' And he just laughs and gives me a kiss. Gave me the feeling he didn't have nothing to worry about. Like he was on top of things. Like maybe he was gonna be okay after all."

She paused, ran a hand distractedly over the nearest marble and jade pieces in the scale-model temple. "Lookit all the detail. God these things are teeny. But nice." Atith agreed they were.

"*Hoo*. Could use a smoke." She clawed at her hair, pushed it back from her face. "Anyway. Last night I went back to see Gussy again and he's gone. Cleared out. Just like that. I asked the staff what gives. Quite a story they told me."

From the sleeve of her T-shirt she unrolled a pack of Camels. "I talked to a counselor there. Timothy something. Didn't catch his last name. Anyway. Says the other night they confiscated Gussy's phone cuz they had their suspicions just what he was up to. Checked his web searches, turns out all he's been doing is clicking on sites linked to opioid habits. Sites selling products with names like redrum and Apache. China girl, China white."

"In other words," said Atith softly, "fentanyl."

"You got it." She pulled a cigarette from the pack, offered him one. He shook his head no. "Anyway. This counselor Tim tries confronting Gussy, says clicking on drug sites is strictly off limits. Violation of house rules. The counselor told me Gussy comes back at him saying he was just doing research, keeping up to date, no harm in that, recapture the moment. Loada crap, as the counselor told me, and he was right. Long story short the two of them have words, my nephew gets pissed off, he snatches back his phone and picks up his dog and he's outta there."

She studied the cigarette, rolled it about between forefinger and thumb. "Really oughta kick this habit someday. Anyway. The counselor tells me just as Gussy is going out the door he gets cocky and says something like 'No more halfway house. No more factory shifts. I don't need either no more cuz I got myself a brand-new home and a brand-new job all wrapped up in one.' Whatever that means."

She tapped the unlit cigarette against the pack of Camels. "Needless to say no forwarding address. I been texting and phoning but I just get no answer."

A big sigh. She stared down at the ground, drew a deep breath. "You know I see you pray, Stubby, and I realize I don't pray enough. Not sure I'm religious but I do believe in God and I know he wants to help if we'll just give him a chance and if we'll just stop screwing up our own lives. Anyway. All day today I been praying and asking God please keep my nephew safe."

Another sigh. She looked at Atith, tried a smile. "Anyway. Just thought I'd drop by and bring you some groceries and check out these tiny statues you got on display. And while I was at it maybe just ask. By any chance did Gussy show up for work this morning at Guild Metal?"

He said there'd been no sign of him. "I was planning to call you once I finished here at the temple."

"I was afraid of that." She blinked, rubbed her eyes. Her hand came away wet. "Damn. I'm ruining my makeup. I must look a fright."

He reassured her she looked great. "You always do."

"You're very sweet, Stubby. You always know what to say."

He reached in a pocket and offered a Kleenex.

She wiped her eyes, said she was fine. "You know this whole business is basically one hundred per cent my fault."

"You mean the business with Gusto?" He said she shouldn't go blaming herself. "What he's doing to himself, no way is that your fault."

"Oh yes it is. You don't know the story of how he got started." She patted her eyes again, put away the Kleenex. "Truthfully it all has to do with the RIPTA tunnel on the East Side of Providence."

"RIPTA tunnel?"

She said the acronym stood for Rhode Island Public Transit Authority, and she explained about the tunnel. An old subsurface roadway, built a long time ago, that burrowed from South Main Street straight up through College Hill, with an exit mouth on Thayer Street right by Brown campus. "Big signs at both ends. Restricted use, buses and emergency vehicles only, everybody else keep out."

She took out a hand mirror, studied her face. "Aargh. I really do look like crap." Atith said again she looked fine.

"Anyway. That bus tunnel's steep. I mean serious steep. And you know how Gussy loves skateboarding."

"Oh no. You mean to tell me ...?"

"You got it." She lit her Camel. "Some of the youngsters that hang out on College Hill, kids from Hope High and who knows where else, they always got an eye for anything to shake up the boredom. From time to time some'a them try what they call 'shooting the tunnel'."

"You mean skateboarding downhill through that subsurface roadway?" He said that sounded both insane and dangerous.

"You got that right." She said one night a couple of years back her nephew decided if other skateboarders were doing it well he had to shoot the tunnel too. "And you know what the worst thing is? He even told me about it in advance. Course this was back when he told me everything, when we were really close. He comes home one day from the hill and he says 'The other wood-pushers say I gotta try shooting the tunnel sounds really awesome sounds really gnarly.' Course I tell him no is he outta his mind and make him promise he won't try anything like that no matter what the other skaters do. When what I *shoulda* done was just take the damn skateboard away and never let him get on the thing ever again. But I didn't. I didn't think far enough ahead." She inhaled on her cigarette, breathed a long plume of smoke.

"So Gusto broke his promise and tried to skateboard the tunnel?"

She nodded, blinked some more. A streak of black eyeliner leaked down her face. "And the night he tried it, of course the exact same moment a bus is coming up through the tunnel. A rainy night too, just to make everything worse."

Atith handed her another Kleenex. She wiped her eyes and continued. "And you wanna hear something strange? Turns out the bus driver that night was someone I know. Tony Caparella. My cousin Mikey's ex-brother-in-law. That's Rhode Island for you. Everyone knows everyone. Anyway. Tony had RIPTA Route One that night, which meant he was coming through downtown from Kennedy Plaza, crossing at South Main and then straight up the tunnel. Just as my nephew's shooting straight down the slot."

She flicked ash from her smoke. "I can't tell the story too good. I get emotional. But I remember Tony the driver telling me later 'So I'm in the bus and I'm driving up through the tunnel and I got some passenger behind me asking where does he transfer for I don't know what and I'm looking through the windshield and all of a sudden I got this batshit-crazy kid on a skateboard showing up in the headlights waving his arms and yelling and diving straight at my bus. Scared? I about died. I pulled the wheel hard hoping I wouldn't hit the kid.' Poor Tony." She grimaced.

Another long drag on her cigarette. "Tony says he still has dreams about it. 'Kid in the headlights coming at me, me trying to turn the bus.' No wonder he's got nightmares."

Atith offered another Kleenex. "So what happened?"

She shook her head to signal she didn't need another tissue. "I'm good. Well the bus lucked out. Sorta. Tony managed not to hit Gussy. But Gussy lost control of his skateboard and slammed smack into the wall of the tunnel."

"Bad?"

"Coulda been worse, considering. Didn't bang his head, thank God. Took the impact on his shoulder. Wrenched his back wicked fierce. All of which coulda been avoided if I'd just taken that skateboard away from him."

"And that's how his opioid habit got started? For the pain?"

"You guessed it. First it was prescriptions to ease the constant ache in his back. Vicodin to start with. Then Oxycontin. Then Percocet. And pretty soon things are spinning out of control with him taking really nasty dope, and before I know it my nephew's in rehab and living on the street and I'm feeling grateful the city found him a bed at Safe Anchorage. Well until last night anyway."

A last drag on the cigarette. She dropped the butt and ground it under her foot. "Anyway." She blinked through the tears, managed a smile for her friend. "So we know he's not at the halfway house, and he's not showing up at Guild Metal. I'm gonna tool around and see what I can do to find him."

Atith stepped up and hugged her as she waved a goodbye.

She patted his arm, said, "Stubby, do me a favor."

He said sure.

"Light one'a those incense things for Gussy and say a prayer for him."

"I'll light more than one. I'll light lots."

She got in her Ford Escort and turned the car back toward Providence. Her last glimpse of him, he was holding a cluster of joss sticks as he bowed before the six-inch bodhisattvas.

33

Zahra Shahbaz Beheshti, museum guide and docent at the Rhode Island School of Design, was having yet another contentious day on the job.

Not that she disliked her work. Far from it: she loved it. Being paid to give tours of lovely art, in a lovely historic building on historic old Benefit Street, one block down from tree-shaded Brown University on College Hill, across the street from an exquisite private library called the Athenaeum: "*Bil-kull pagal, hay na*?" as she often said in calls to her mom back in Lahore—"Completely crazy, isn't it? They actually pay me to do my favorite thing in the world, studying superlative art, and talking and thinking about the lives of creative and risk-taking visionaries. Making visions from the past come alive for the people of today."

To which her mom always replied with an exasperated wail: "It's exactly those risk-taking visionaries of yours, and all that talking and thinking of yours, that have gotten you into so much trouble. That's why your father hasn't been willing to say a word to you, ever since the *fatwa*, and ever since you ran away from here and fled the country in a hurry. And don't even ask, he's still angry and still won't speak to you. And the same for your brothers and uncles and cousins: you've brought all of us into disgrace. And all because of some worthless impious *kafir* you fell for who happens to have been dead for five hundred years. I hope it was worth it for you"—this last bit with an impassioned sob, before her mom hung up on her as she usually did.

"Hope it was worth it for you." Once a week at least her mom found a way to convey this bitter jab, whether by email or text or call from Lahore.

How to reply? Her mom never gave Zahra a chance to articulate her arguments. So for six months now, ever since arriving in America (and what better city than Providence in which to seek asylum, given its foundation by one Roger Williams as a haven for nonconformists and "those distressed of conscience"?), she'd been wandering the streets of College Hill, rehearsing all the arguments she'd present to her family—if they'd just give her a chance—as to why it was worth reviving the memory of a South Asian *kafir* now five hundred years dead.

She carried these suppressed arguments around in her head, carried them all the time. The burden was with her, rode on her back, hissed in her ear, even as she marched up College Hill for classes at Brown and hurried back down for her job at the museum.

Arguments that sometimes spilled into the tours she gave as she guided groups around the galleries of the Rhode Island School of Design. "Small points of clarification," was what she said in self-defense, when head curator Heather Kirkwood reprimanded her for her recurring quarrels with guests. "Avoid hectoring them."

I am not hectoring. Fortunately Zahra managed to bite back the words. Her mind appended a silent addendum of defiance: *If I can't combat ignorance in the Punjab, at least I can confront it here in the States.* Heather Kirkwood doubtless sensed this recalcitrance but to her credit didn't push the point.

"Don't go getting contentious," was what co-worker Gabriela Teixeira kept urging. "If the visitors say stupid-ass things, just nod and smile along. Don't go correcting them and telling them they're dumb shits."

"I do not call them dumb shits," fumed Zahra with a defiant tilt of her chin. But she knew Gabby was right, was worth listening to. It was Gabriela Teixeira more than anyone who'd shown her around and helped her settle in when she first arrived in Providence, when phrases still floated to her lips in Urdu instead of the U.S.A. English that she needed. (And now, six months in, she dreamed in English every night—except when her dreams took her back to Lahore for more quarrels in Urdu with her folks.)

It was Gabby who took her to the Newport Creamery to sip her first coffee cabinet (not, to Zahra's confusion, a piece of furniture but a milkshake ultra-thick). It was Gabby who introduced her to quahogs and clam cakes and Del's Lemonade.

And it was Gabby who explained how to refer to her place of employment. "Rhode Island School of Design. You know what to call it for short?"

"Certainly." Zahra thought sure she had this one covered. "R. I. S. D."

"Nope. Don't spell the letters out. That takes forever to roll off the tongue. Definitely uncool. Say Rizz-Dee. That way you won't sound like you're from out of town or out of state."

"But I *am* from out of state. Very far out of state. Pakistan out of state."

"Well say Rizz-Dee anyway," was Gabby's firm reply. "Rizz as in Fizz. Got it?"

And here she was this morning on the job at the Rizz-Dee museum, trying to avoid quarrels with the customers but nonetheless plunging headlong into contention.

The worst of it was that today's outburst came just as the curator happened by.

Her fourth school group of the morning. Which one was this? East Greenwich High? West Warwick? Cranston East? They all just merged in a blur.

Whatever. (A handy American word.) She guided the students through gallery after gallery, each a site consecrated to refinements of the spirit. Decorative Arts. Modern and Contemporary. Europe, Medieval and Renaissance. Ancient Greece and Rome.

And the teens' response? They yawned and chewed gum, sniggered and checked their phones. All this she'd endured before, didn't mind too terribly much, even if she privately regarded such behavior as desecration in a shrine to things she revered.

Didn't mind too much till they got closer to home. The gallery of the arts of Asia. She gathered the students round a sculptured portrait of the Buddha. "From Gandhara," she said proudly. "From what is Pakistan today, but what was then a subcontinent not yet divided into two countries clawing at each other's throats. The Buddhist legacy, something India and Pakistan share in common. Third century B.C. Gandhara. Full of lessons for today, if only ..."

"Who cares about all that ancient stuff?" The interruption came from a pimply lout in the back who popped his bubble gum. "History doesn't matter." Appreciative titters from the crowd.

"History doesn't matter?" She hissed the retort so loud it nearly snapped the kid's neck. "My dear friend, history all but killed me. I'm here to testify, it almost did me in. You need to learn to care about such things before history rears up to bite you in the crotch."

The kid gulped, must have swallowed his gum. She'd caught people by surprise like this back in Lahore. Zahra Shahbaz Beheshti: a hunched young thing, small and thin and frail, with long thick black hair that all but hid her face. *Chhota chiriya,* was what her father used to call her when he'd still bestowed on her some affection: Little sparrow. (These days he referred to her distastefully as another kind of bird—*cheel*: pariah-kite.) Studious, with big round spectacles obscured by all that hair. It'd taken her folks some time to learn this was a child with one fiery mind.

"History all but killed me," she said again, and she began to explain just how. How back at Punjab University she'd been writing her dissertation—a thesis she'd never been allowed to finish—on Dara Shikoh, crown prince and eldest son of Moghul emperor Shah Jahan. How Prince Dara had been a Sufi mystic whose idea of spiritual and intellectual pleasure was hobnobbing in chitchat with Jesuit priests and Brahmin pundits and naked Jain ascetics. How he'd written a treatise to harmonize Islamic and Hindu wisdom. How for his pains he'd been declared a *kafir* unbeliever and put to death. How she for her part had been writing about Dara Shikoh's life in hopes of sharing his seventeenth-century message of tolerance until the dean and provost and all the weak-kneed staff at Punjab U had gotten scared and squealed on her to the religious thought police. How they in turn pronounced the *fatwa* branding her a freethinking infidel. How—

"Miss Beheshti?" Right there at Zahra's elbow, tugging on her sleeve: an unsmiling Heather Kirkwood. "Might I have a word with you?" The chief curator dismissed the students, told them they might find food three floors down in the museum café. They charged away as soon as she spoke the word "food."

"Sorry. I know." Zahra waggled her head. "Got carried away again. Flew off the griddle."

"You mean 'flew off the handle.'"

"Whatever. Sorry."

"We talked about not getting contentious with the visitors."

"Yes. I know. Sorry."

"Tell you what." Heather Kirkwood's tone was sympathetic. "You look like you could use some food yourself."

A proud tilt of the chin. "I am not hungry. My moods have nothing to do with food."

"Of course not. But take a break anyway. And after lunch you've got only one more group for the day. With any luck they'll be easier to deal with than gum-chewing high-schoolers."

Heather Kirkwood was right. The afternoon tour was with the Golden Donors Circle, big spenders who spent big bucks to support the RISD museum. A senior citizens crowd in their sixties and seventies and eighties, white-haired and serious, quite obviously ready to listen appreciatively to every word she might utter. Not a gum-snapper in sight.

"Thank God: adults!" gasped Zahra aloud in relief, raising a hand to the ceiling. Gold bracelets jingled along her arm. "My gratitude to all of you, for your air of gravitas!" That made them smile. And she smiled too. This would be a good tour.

Exceptionally good, as it turned out, because among the attentive and solemnly nodding elders there was one young woman—about her own age, late twenties, early thirties—who offered a lot more than just nodding along.

Zahra didn't notice her especially until they reached the tour's last stop, the gallery set aside for ancient Egypt. Until then the young woman had simply been one of the crowd. But in the Egyptian Gallery she politely but energetically elbowed her way to the front.

Mummies, sarcophagi, ibis figurines. Fayoum portraits and statuettes of Ptah-Sokar-Osiris: this visitor had intelligent questions about them all. And not just idle queries. She clearly knew her stuff.

Which in turn made Zahra Beheshti more engaged and energetic. She answered the young woman's questions in the kind of detail that normally made Zahra feel a bit guilty: *Maybe I'm indulging myself, showing off my knowledge, boring the poor customer to tears*. But no. This was one visitor who smiled and thanked her for every response and bit of info and who even laughed appreciatively at the witticisms Zahra inserted to ornament her replies. For once the Lahori refugee didn't feel she was talking too much or boring a guest or simply showing off. For once—*how rare!*—she felt she was actually making a connection, mind to mind, heart to heart, with another human soul.

She wondered if this individual would like to hear about her hero Dara Shikoh.

Twenty faces in the crowd, but she felt she was addressing only one. Even as she lectured the group she studied her new friend—Zahra Beheshti was impulsive, she made her judgments fast—and marveled how someone so young could be in the Golden Donors Circle. Each member pledged per annum fifty thousand dollars and up, generally the province of the well-established and senior and very comfortably retired. To judge from her clothes this youthful woman didn't seem wealthy; far from it. Gray chinos, gray polo shirt. Inconspicuous plain shoulder-length hair. Nothing by way of jewelry or ornamentation.

Unless one counted two little tin buttons this guest wore pinned to the collar of her shirt. Some sort of logo or motto inscribed on each one. Lettering too small to read from this distance. Zahra strained to see.

Last stop in the gallery, last artifacts of the tour: a pair of canopic jars, sixth century B.C. Her new (and as yet nameless) friend stepped away from the group and approached the vitrine, nose all but pressed to the glass protecting the display. *Like a child, in her eagerness. Really quite touching.*

Zahra suddenly realized the crowd was staring at her, awaiting in white-haired patience whatever wisdom she might wish to impart. "Oh," she stuttered. "Yes."

So she delivered her standard bit on these jars. (By now she had the delivery down pat, which was just as well, because she was feeling distracted.) "Each was meant to hold the internal organs of those fortunate enough to afford mummification. One jar boasts a human-headed stopper, the god Imseti, who guards what's contained within: the mummified liver of the deceased. The second ..."

Even as she heard herself say the words, Zahra watched her friend at the display case, waited for her to turn just a tad so Zahra could read what her two buttons said.

"The second jar is topped by the likeness of Qebehsenuef, the raptor-avian god who keeps the mummified intestines cool and intact throughout all eternity."

Eternity. The crowd was getting tired; Zahra knew the signs. Discreet sighs, furtive checking of the time. Politer than those dreary high-schoolers, but with the very same thought in mind: time for a snack, time for a rest.

But her unnamed friend was still energetic, called out a question from where she stood by the vitrine. "Don't these canopic jars normally come as a foursome?"

Zahra replied yes, said the two missing jars had been stolen from the museum many years ago, said there was a plaque beside the display explaining what had happened. "I can read it aloud if anyone is interested."

In fact no one—or almost no one—was interested this late in the day. One elderly gentleman peered right and left, quavered, "Where's the closest toilet?" Another asked about refreshments and the Donors Circle lounge.

Time for dismissal. Zahra thanked them for their interest, pointed out the nearby restrooms and the elevator down to the donors lounge. The seniors shuffled off as fast as they could manage. She permitted herself an inward smile. *In the end not all that different from West Warwick High or Cranston East.*

Which left one guest remaining. Her unnamed friend. Who stood reading the display plaque beside the canopic jar vitrine.

Zahra had of course studied it before. What it offered was the text of a newspaper article dated August 31, 1936 and reprinted from the local *Providence Journal.* She stood beside the young woman and read through the article again to keep her company:

"LIZARD HEIST" AT FAMED MUSEUM
MARS RI TERCENTENARY

Yesterday throughout our state, celebrations were held to honor the three-hundredth anniversary of the founding of Rhode Island and Providence Plantations. For it was in 1636 that a fugitive Roger Williams paddled his canoe to Slate Rock and was hailed by friendly natives on the shore with the tidings "What cheer, Netop?"

And yesterday, massive Sunday throngs in downtown Providence offered their own cheer to hail the parade that marked our Rhode Island Tercentenary. Led by drummers in uniform and Red Cross women proudly bearing our Stars and Stripes, naval cadets from Newport marched smartly in formation, followed by serried ranks of soldiers who presented arms as they passed the reviewing stand where presided Mayor James E. Dunne and members of the Providence City Council. Thereafter came horse-drawn buckboard wagons, and floats to tell the story of great events in U.S. history. Many a black-clad Puritan could be seen in that march, many a bonneted lass. The crowd cheered and clapped to greet all the marchers as they passed.

An Intrusion

But little did the frolickers know, amidst the rejoicing and general merriment that continued well into the night, that a crime was underway on the slopes of fabled College Hill in the very groves of academe—a crime doubtless timed to coincide with the frivolity downtown, when the city's prudent guardedness might be expected to be less than its very best.

For sometime on Sunday the 30th, whilst the downtown parade was at its height, intruders broke into the upper floor of the museum of the Rhode Island School of Design. The only objects missing were two items from the Egyptian gallery, described by the curator, Professor Worthington Harker, as funerary jars meant to contain the inner body parts of the mummified dead. One jar is surmounted by a figure in the shape of the head of a jackal; the other features the face of a baboon. In an exclusive interview with the *Journal*, Professor Harker explained to members of the press that the jackal and baboon represented gods whose job, as the professor phrased it, "was to ward off hostile demons with unblinking and unceasing vigilance."

The means of ingress and egress have yet to be determined. No door was forced. All locks and fastenings were examined by Chief Inspector Patrick Malone of the Providence Police Department, who declared them undisturbed and untampered with.

An Unlikely Clue

The watchman on duty in the early evening hours of the 30th, when the theft is believed to have been committed, a Thomas Smith, declares that he was making his rounds as usual when he entered the Egyptian Gallery, "about a half hour after sunset," as Mister Smith reported, "about eight o'clock or so." According to his police testimony, the two jars were already missing, and no one was in the gallery. Nonetheless he states that he saw a "shaking movement" in the overhead air duct directly above the display cases. He came closer to investigate and reports that he saw something disappear up into the duct. "Like a snake, maybe, or a lizard," is how he describes it. Under police questioning Mister Smith admits he cannot be sure. "The light was uncertain, that time of evening. But it sure gave me a turn, that I can swear."

Slimy Trail of the Perpetrator?

Leaving no clue uninvestigated, no matter how improbable, Inspector Malone, with the assistance of Professor Harker and other museum staff personnel, examined the air duct in question. It is of standard sheet metal, twenty-two inches in diameter, and unlikely to afford entrance or egress for trespassers of any kind. Of some marginal interest is that the lower interior surface of the duct was found to bear traces of water and river mud, although as one museum staff member jocularly observed, "Many explanations for that could be put forward without invoking a reptilian intrusion."

Inspector Malone nonetheless pursued his inquiry with commendable persistence, sufficiently to discover a similar slick of water and mud on the eastern facade of the building, leading from the external mouth of the duct, down to the pavement, and then north on Benefit Street until it reached the nearby intersection with College Street. At College the mud slick veered right and proceeded uphill, only to vanish halfway up the street.

An Unsettling Reminder of Other Such Incidents

Local residents when interviewed observed that this is not the first such recent theft of its kind. Antiquarians on Wickenden Street and dealers in rare objects in the vicinity of Fox Point note that in the past five weeks there have been at least three other break-ins involving the loss of ancient objects from Egypt and elsewhere in the Orient.

Compounding the sense of unease is that in the very neighborhood of the RISD museum, on Benefit Street, a junior staff member of the Providence Athenaeum has been missing since July. The staff member in question, a Miss Novalyne Price, had been employed in the capacity of assistant file clerk. She neglected to give notice of termination at either the Athenaeum or the Benefit Street boardinghouse at which she had been lodging.

There is some speculation she may simply have returned to her native Texas. Police are continuing to pursue inquiries in this matter.

The RISD museum has announced a reward for information leading to the apprehension of the culprit or culprits involved in the theft of the missing Egyptian jars.

The young woman finished reading and turned to Zahra Beheshti. "Were those two canopic jars ever recovered?"

"No. An ongoing mystery." Zahra smiled. "'Lizard Heist.' Pretty wild, isn't it?"

"Yes. Pretty wild." The friendly stranger smiled back.

"Where I grew up we'd call such intruders djinns." Zahra knew she was taking a chance by referring to her homeland, but this young stranger somehow managed to make her feel at ease.

"Oh. Where did you grow up?"

"Pakistan." Zahra let the word dangle in solitude, half-defiant, half-afraid. She braced for revulsion, misunderstanding, questions about ISIS, extremism, bin Laden, al-Qaeda, wanting this woman to like her, wanting to be liked for what she was no matter where she came from.

"Oh, how *interesting*!" The visitor had a charming way of crinkling her nose when she smiled. "You must have so many unusual stories."

"Why yes I do." Zahra's instincts had been right. This *was* a new friend. She started in on a favorite anecdote. As a little girl after school she used to play until dusk on the streets of Lahore's Cantonment district. Her mother's strict command was that Zahra absolutely had to come home as soon as she heard the mosque loudspeakers sound the *azaan*. "Because if I stayed outside after the evening call to prayer, djinns would drop from the trees overhead and entangle themselves in my big bushy hair. *That* propelled me home in a hurry!" The stranger laughed at her story, and Zahra laughed too.

"My name's Alicia. Alicia Wheatley." The stranger crinkled her nose again, still smiling from the story. *How nice*, came the thought to Zahra, *that a customer enjoys my anecdotes. Makes the whole workday worthwhile.*

Up close, it was easy enough to read the lapel pins on Alicia Wheatley's collar. One offered a quartet of letters: "GGCG." The other propounded a terse assertion: "HPL was right."

Zahra was about to ask what the mottoes meant when Alicia turned back to the plaque and read aloud a sentence. "Ward off hostile demons with unblinking and unceasing vigilance."

"Yes," agreed Zahra eagerly. "That refers to the apotropaic function of these canopic jars. 'Apotropaic' means having the ability to keep dangerous things from entering a spot you're trying to defend. You know, like—"

"Actually, I have *quite* a good idea already just what 'apotropaic' means." From anyone else—like the countless grad-school colleagues back at Punjab U who'd shunned her once the religious thought police slapped her with a *fatwa*—such a reply would have really stung. But her new friend softened what she said with a smile and a wink and a pat on the arm that seemed like an invitation to join an exclusive new club.

To show she hadn't taken any offense at Alicia's curt remark, Zahra burbled on about the jars. "Of course, for those who take the realm of magic seriously, these apotropaic objects are fully effective only when you cluster together the full set of four. Ever since that theft in 1936, we're left with only human-headed Imseti and Qebehsenuef the hawk. But if we could somehow retrieve the other two jars—Duamutef the jackal, who watches over the stomach, and Hapy the baboon, who guards the lungs—why then we could repel just about anything that might try to come through the door. Djinn, demon, you name it." She shrugged to show she herself wasn't sure how seriously to take any of this magic talk.

As Zahra spoke, her new friend was staring so intently at the jars it was unclear whether she'd been listening at all. But then Alicia Wheatley repeated word-for-word something Zahra had just said. "Repel just about anything that might try to come through the door." A tone half-dreaming, as if Alicia felt herself called by the jars to some distant mission.

The visitor returned to the placard, read aloud another phrase from the *Providence Journal*. "A crime doubtless timed to coincide with the frivolity downtown." She turned to Zahra and said forcefully, "Now *that's* what I call smart tactics. Wait till everyone's distracted with some kind of festivity. Perhaps along the river. I like that. I like that a lot."

The tour guide was just puzzling over what her new friend might mean by this comment when Alicia came up and stood close and took her by the hand. "Here I am introducing myself and I forgot to ask you what's your name."

Zahra told her and then followed this up with a question of her own. "If you don't mind my asking, what's GGCG stand for?"

"Oh yes. Gnostic Guardians of the Cosmic Gate."

"Wow. Cosmic Gate. Gnostic Guardians. Sounds impressive."

Alicia said it was a service organization. "You get promoted according to the service you provide. Stay in long enough, you can earn a pretty high title."

Zahra impulsively asked if she herself had a high title.

"I think I might say so." This with just a touch of pride. "Lieutenant of the Magus, Baroness of Yog-Sothoth."

"Wow. Way cool." (One of the first Americanisms Zahra had acquired when she'd initially landed in Providence.) "It's like you're royalty."

"Well"—again the note of pride—"we like to think of ourselves as constituting a spiritual aristocracy."

Zahra hesitated a moment, then asked another question. "But wait. What's Yog-Sothoth?"

"Why, that's the cosmic gate in question."

"Maybe I should already know this"—Zahra put the question apologetically—"but where's the gate located?"

Alicia Wheatley gave her a shrewd measuring look in reply that conveyed "I wouldn't tell just anyone but I think you're special enough to be entrusted with what I'm about to reveal." "We know it's in Providence. We know it's nearby. In fact *very* nearby. And, confidentially, we're on the track of someone now who just might lead us to precisely where it is. And then, at that moment, we will finally fulfill—"

The visitor broke off as if to rein in her thoughts. "Zahra. What a very pretty name." Alicia smiled once more. She really could be vivacious when she chose. "Zahra, did you know that GGCG is a major donor to your museum?"

Zahra said no she hadn't been aware.

"Oh yes. Not just Donors Circle. Platinum-Level Corporate Sponsor."

Zahra was still processing this—*Donors Circle is fifty thousand dollars a year, so Platinum must mean a hundred thousand in contributions, maybe more*—when in the sweetest voice Alicia asked if she could confide in her and share a family problem she was having.

Wide-eyed Zahra said sure.

Alicia said she had a nephew who'd been in trouble from time to time but a darling boy still in his teens, a kid with a good heart, which could easily be seen by the way he looked after a puppy he'd just adopted. "And he needs a job but you see he has difficulty sticking with things unless they intrigue him and really pique his interest. Do you know what I mean?"

Zahra said absolutely. "I'm the same way."

"I just *knew* you'd understand." The visitor said her nephew simply loved Egyptology and all things Egyptian and was just the other day saying how great it would be if he could somehow get a job at RISD's museum—"the best Egyptological collection in the state of Rhode Island"—and spend his free moments contemplating the museum's artifacts and thereby feel inspired to make a fresh start and maybe even go to college some day and begin a real career. "So I was thinking it'd be grand if somehow the museum could find him a job here as say maybe a security guard."

On impulse Zahra blurted, "I can help with that."

"Really?" Radiant smile from Alicia.

"Yes, really. One hundred per cent. Absolutely." Which Zahra knew at once she probably shouldn't have said. *I mean I'm pretty much near the bottom of the museum hierarchy myself and I have completely nothing to do with hiring or Human Resources.* But she'd wanted to help her new friend and she felt sorry for Alicia's nephew and her heart went out to any teen who was kind enough to adopt a puppy.

Should she find a way to back out of her blurted one-hundred-per-cent offer? Too late. Alicia was already hugging her and saying how perfect it would be if Zahra could help find the darling boy a job.

In an attempt at caution Zahra said she actually wouldn't be able to do more than talk to her supervisor. "That's Heather. I'll ask her to speak to the head of Personnel."

"Delightful. My nephew's name is Augustus Valerian Tessario. His friends call him Gus or Gusto."

Alicia Wheatley pivoted once more to gaze at the vitrine and its pair of canopic jars. "Reunite the four," she breathed, barely loud enough for Zahra to hear, "to maximize the apotropaic effect."

The pause allowed Zahra to begin to collect her own thoughts. She was just about to ask Alicia "What about your other button? Who was HPL, and what was HPL right about?"

But Alicia Wheatley wheeled and squeezed her again in a hug and hurried off to the exit.

Well. Didn't matter. HPL and HPL's rightness could wait. Zahra Shahbaz Beheshti finished her shift and left the museum that evening in an upbeat mood. Making a new friend, feeling appreciated, having the chance to tell stories about her childhood in Lahore: all in all a good day at work.

She descended the hill—destination her apartment downtown—mingling with the swirl of Brown undergrads and RISD art students lugging portfolios and sketch pads. *A happy energy*, she thought; *everyone's glad to be done with classes.*

As she crossed the College Street Bridge over the river, she counted off in her mind the names of nearby waterfront alleys and lanes she'd found in her wanderings these past few months. India Street, Packet Street, Merchant: all testifying to a bygone time when great sailing ships had set forth from Providence to bring trade to the Indies.

Well it's a two-way trade now. They sailed west to east, and I've flown east to west, on my own voyage of discovery. And what have I brought to trade? Intellectual cargo, I guess you could say: lectures about canopic jars and whatnot, and—if I can get anyone to listen—thoughts about Moghul prince Dara Shikoh.

Her oceanic musings continued as she entered downtown and turned her gaze skyward a moment to the Turk's Head Building at the intersection of Westminster and Weybosset. Carved at third-floor level above the entrance was a stone image of a Saracen: scowling visage, drooping mustache, turban topped by a crescent moon. Some of her peers from overseas complained it was unflattering, insensitive, culturally inappropriate. But she liked the thing for its backstory.

She'd heard various versions of what originally inspired the stone carving. The one she liked best claimed inspiration had come from a ship's wooden figurehead that once graced the prow of a merchant vessel called the *Sultan*. Laden with cargo on a return voyage from the Orient, the *Sultan* had sailed into rough coastal weather and foundered in a storm in Narragansett Bay. Amid the wreckage that washed up in the mouth of the Providence River was the turbaned head of the Turk. *A survivor, in other words, a kind of east-west refugee, like me—and if a wooden Saracen can bob safely ashore and find a new life, well then I guess so can I.*

She was smiling privately over her twilight fantasia when the thought of shipwrecks and refugees and new lives made her recall a line from that newspaper article dated 1936 on display beside the jars. "A junior staff member of the Providence Athenaeum ... missing since July ... employed in the capacity of assistant file clerk."

What was the name of that missing employee? A Miss Novalyne Price. Yes, that was it.

Zahra had read the article so many times on her tours she knew much of it by heart: "... neglected to give notice of termination at either the Athenaeum or the Benefit Street boardinghouse at which she had been lodging ... some speculation she may simply have returned to her native Texas."

As Zahra left behind the Turk's Head Building and walked along Westminster she regretted she hadn't mentioned this Novalyne Price to her new friend Alicia Wheatley. Zahra's own intuition was that the Athenaeum staffer had never made it home to Texas, that her disappearance had been tied up somehow with the stolen canopic jars (also never accounted for) and all the other antiquities that had vanished in the summer of 1936.

Could Miss Novalyne Price have been the thief who made off with all these treasures? Zahra didn't think so. Funny how Alicia Wheatley had gotten so obsessed with the jars and never seemed to spare a thought for the long-missing assistant file clerk. *Is it just possible my new friend Alicia isn't quite as sweet and sensitive as she appears?* In which case Zahra—impulsive as always—perhaps shouldn't have offered so quickly to find Alicia's nephew a job as a security guard. *Well,* she told herself, *you have to keep your promise, and I'm sure—more or less—it'll all work out fine.*

Novalyne Price—a woman who had found work in Providence after coming all the way from Texas. Texas to Rhode Island: a pretty far distance, which meant that Novalyne had been kind of an immigrant up here, a bit like Zahra herself.

Had the clerk been kidnapped by the lizard-djinn that so skillfully slithered up air ducts? As Zahra Beheshti walked along Westminster Street she shuddered at her own fancy and breathed a prayer for the lost woman's soul, reciting *al-Fatihah* and other sets of short verses from the Koran. *The mullahs may have declared me a heretic but they can't stop me from petitioning God.*

Still pondering lizards and vanished abductees, Zahra walked from Westminster to Union Street. She had an apartment in the Peerless

Building, a one-time department store now converted to studio-loft rental units. The Peerless stood in the midst of the old downtown shopping district. As a student of history Zahra liked noting the surviving traces of Providence's former status as a thriving market town: the tall Shepard's Clock still keeping time outside a long-gone emporium; the weathered Tri-Store Bridge that once funneled shoppers from Shepard's to Cherry & Webb and Gladdings.

Sweaty, humid, hot: a typical Providence evening in June. Not ready to confine herself to her room, still restless with her own thoughts, Zahra took the elevator to the top floor, then climbed a short flight of stairs and stepped out onto the roof.

This was better: a restful twilight breeze, and a view that dissipated troubled thoughts. She paced about the rooftop garden plantings and enjoyed the sunset downtown skyline—city hall, the Statehouse dome, the Biltmore Hotel with its name that glowed neon red.

As she strolled she saw only one other person on the roof—Dieter Konrad, a neighbor with whom she exchanged occasional hellos in the elevator and lobby.

She knew it was best to approach Dieter with caution. Occasionally chatty, more often surly and rudely taciturn, long since retired from an on-again off-again job shelving secondhand tomes at a downtown shop called Cellar Step Books, he gave himself to odds and ends of hobbies and what he called "notions of how the world really works and what no one else has ever been sharp enough to think of."

Dieter seemed not to have noticed her yet. He was hunched over one of his hobbies now, a telescope perched on a tripod, its lens aimed at the biggest building on the skyline: Superman's own Industrial Trust Building.

Dieter straightened, scratched his gray, stubbled goatee, waved her an offhand welcome. "Come have a look." So: apparently tonight he was in a mood for conversation.

Zahra asked if he was studying the decorative friezes on the skyscraper's exterior.

"No, no. Friezes are frivolous. Today I've got something more interesting than that. Way livelier. Have a look."

Glad for the distraction, she bent to the tube, adjusted her eye to the lens. He stooped beside her. "There. Do you see? Do you see the movement?"

At first nothing all that interesting. The telescope seemed simply aimed at an upper story of the building just below the massive beacon tower. She saw windows, a stone ledge.

But then something on the ledge. An oblong structure of wood perhaps two-and-a-half feet in height, transverse beams atop supporting vertical planks, a shelter perhaps, open at the front. She asked what was that.

"A nesting box," he said, "for peregrine falcons. Set up by the local branch of the Audubon Society."

"It's empty," she said, "except maybe for some feathers and twigs. Nothing to see."

"Keep watching."

Then she saw. A blur in the lens, a flash of talons: something in flight, aimed straight at the building. "There's two of them!" she cried. "Two birds."

"Peregrines. A mating pair."

"But what are they up to? Looks like they're diving at the windows."

He said that was exactly what the birds were doing. "They're trying to drive something off. They must've seen movement through the glass right behind their nesting box. It's making them nervous."

For the second time that day Zahra Beheshti felt a shudder. "But there can't be anyone moving around in an upper story of that building. It's been abandoned and shut up for years."

"That's right. Ever since Bank of America moved out. Years ago, as you said. Which is what makes these birds' behavior so intriguing."

As he spoke the falcons swooped once more at the upper story windows behind the box. Then they broke off in a long dive, deep among the cement canyons of downtown, trailing a shrill, angry cry of vexation as they flew.

Zahra confessed she didn't know what to make of it.

"You don't know because you haven't been watching." He scratched his goatee, scratched his belly. His thick flannel shirt concealed an ample paunch—a girth acquired, he'd told her one morning while sharing the elevator, through many years of shelving books and munching Dunkin' Donuts. "In case you haven't noticed, lately downtown there've been lots of funny things going on."

"Funny?"

"Not funny ha-ha. Funny strange."

She asked for an example.

"Like lights rippling down the sides of the Superman Building at night. Pulsing, like they're sending a signal."

"A signal? To whom?"

"To whom, or to what." He blinked, gave her an owl-shrewd look. "To answer that question, you've got to triangulate, extrapolate, navigate the beam. From origin to target."

She said she wasn't quite sure what he meant.

"Well, it doesn't seem to have occurred to anyone yet, but"—he darted suspicious glances on all sides, although they were entirely alone atop the roof—"those beamed pulses have an intended audience. And by extrapolation with this telescope I've determined what that is."

His fixed stare, his tone of utter confidence, reminded her of half-mad dervishes she used to chat with in the marble porticoes of shrines like Data Ganj Bakhsh back in Lahore.

He was waiting for her to prompt him. So she provided what he wanted: "And the audience for those pulses?"

"A big old building a ways from here called New England Pest Control."

"What?"

"That's what most people would say. What? As in 'Dieter Konrad, you make no sense.' But consider what squats atop that particular building: the Big Blue Bug."

She said she had to admit she had no idea what was the Big Blue Bug.

"Not your fault. You didn't grow up here. It's a fifty-eight-foot metal termite, a proud icon of our state. But nobody should be beaming unauthorized pulses at our Bug. Nobody. Trying to stir it up, trying to do who knows what. Nobody. That Bug's sacred. That Bug's Rhode Island."

Fully dark now. The Biltmore neon glowed a deep blood-red. The air blew chill. She rubbed her arms.

The owl eyes bored in. "You're getting cold. I won't keep you long. But I have to tell you one last funny thing."

She wanted to go in now, retreat to the four walls and familiar soft light of her own apartment, but politely she asked what was the one last funny thing.

"I don't have too many acquaintances, don't talk to too many folks since I retired. But one person I keep in touch with, name of Janey Evans, she used to stop by Cellar Step Books. I'd offer her a doughnut, I buy them by the dozen, naturally they're cheaper that way though of course they're not really healthy for you or at least that's what people say. But they taste good. Fantastic. Janey she always likes honey-glazed and she'd always eat one with me. Sweet lady."

Zahra rubbed her arms some more, wished she'd brought a sweater.

"I won't keep you but a minute. So just yesterday I see Janey and she tells me these days she's with Riverglow out volunteering on those boats. Me, I don't make it down to watch that often because in my old age I get phobic around crowds. Sometimes I just stay up on the roof and watch it all through the scope. But get this. Yesterday she stops by the Peerless and she says hi and she says she's got a bit of news she knows will interest me on account of in my youthful days I used to spend time in the clubs downtown, Lupo's, the Mouthpiece, you name it. And she says there's a new guy on the Riverglow crew name of Joey Bonaventure. She says do you recognize the name and I say whaddya think I am of course I do. Big-hit local star of the Fox Point Punks, one of the best bands Providence ever had. Years ago of course. I was a lot younger then."

Zahra was starting to feel tired and hungry. *Getting hard to pay attention.* She didn't want to be impolite and just walk off.

Dieter Konrad apparently hadn't noticed she was beginning to tune out. "Joey Bonaventure coming home from the West Coast, that's interesting you might say but not really all that unusual. But do you want to know what's truly, deeply strange?"

Zahra drew a breath, steeled herself to patience, gamely asked what was it then that was so deeply strange.

"Well I'll tell you. He gets out on a boat, falls into the river, and underwater he sees the same thing Janey says she's seen before. Ol' Spike-Head, she calls it. A big reptilian thing that she says has been slithering and swimming around the neighborhood."

Now he truly *did* have her attention. "Reptilian? Like a lizard?"

"Yeah. Yeah. Like a lizard."

She thought at once of the museum's break-in all those years ago, of Alicia Wheatley's questions, wondered if she should mention the missing canopic jars, realized if she did he'd keep her out here all night.

Dieter Konrad was working himself up to a conclusion. "But my point is this. Falcons diving at windows where there shouldn't be anybody in residence. Someone pulsing lights at our sacred Big Blue Bug. A rock star coming home and going eyeball-to-eyeball with a six-foot slimy something. Well I tell you I got a theory."

"Oh?"

"Yes I do. Everything's building up to something big. A climax. A revelation."

"What kind of revelation?"

"That I haven't figured out yet. But you heard it from me first. Apocalypse. Revelation." He slapped his paunch for emphasis, scratched his beard as his speech slowed. "Well, you'll be wanting to go inside now. It's gotten dark. Really starting to get a bit chill."

She hurried away to the lighted stairwell and the elevator that would take her to her floor. Before she left the roof she turned to wave a goodbye.

But he was already hunched again over his telescope, spying on the sky.

34

Nighttime, downtown, on Dorrance right by City Hall and the bus stop at JFK Plaza. Home to Rhode Island's most famous food venue on wheels: the Haven Brothers Diner. *How many times I used to come here,* thought Joseph Bonaventure, *one A.M., two A.M., for something to eat and a place to hang out just to work off the buzz after an amped-up gig at some waterfront club. Been how long? Years and years since I last set foot in that diner. With luck maybe no one will remember my face now.*

Fay MacConnell asked how come James Cypriano wanted to meet them here instead of in his home parish at Saint Francis Xavier Church. "I mean, he knows we're asking him to translate the bit of Latin you found on that sheet of paper at Swan Point Cemetery. Wouldn't he be more comfortable doing that kind of work in a quiet comfortable setting like his rectory study instead of an all-night eat joint?"

"My thought too," said Bonaventure. He repeated what he'd told her before. The Jesuit's email reply to his request for translation help read simply "Let's meet tonight 9pm Haven Bros. Have network of informants with whom I need to check in."

And here he was now, waving and smiling with a hug for them both. James Cypriano asked if they'd stopped by Haven Brothers before. Bonaventure muttered tersely, "Lifetime or two ago," suppressing the urge to add, "Always bad luck to return to old haunts." Fay said she'd walked by the place once or twice but that was all. "Figured it was just another food truck."

The priest said this was far more than a food truck. "A real Rhode Island legacy. This diner on wheels has been setting up shop right here on Dorrance every night since the late nineteenth century. Back then the trailer was towed by a pair of horses. These days they have a pickup truck to tow the trailer. Late-night eats in the very same spot for over a hundred thirty years."

Knots of customers waited their turn to climb the short flight of metal steps up into the dinette trailer. James Cypriano took his two guests each by the arm and propelled them to the staircase. "Let's get in line."

Inside, amid jostling customers, they found themselves surrounded by mirrors and steel counters and bright electric lights. Pink neon tubing pulsed out "Big shakes." Black and white wall tile, silver bar stools topped in red vinyl. For décor, a movie poster of Marlon Brando from *The Wild One*; a picture showing McDonald's Golden Arches surmounted by a stop sign and the warning "Don't eat that crap"; and a sign saying "Try our Triple Murder Burger—as seen on TV in Man vs. Food."

A server at the cash register hailed them as soon as they came in. "The usual, Father?"

Cypriano waved back. "The usual, plus two for my friends."

"Half a sec till I deal with this crowd. Just grab some seats."

They found three stools together. Fay asked, "Not to spoil the surprise, but just what are we having?"

"Coffee cabinets. They make them good here."

Beside them sat a pudgy man in his fifties. Big-bellied, stubbly goatee, thick flannel shirt. Cypriano nodded and smiled. The barest head-bob from the man but no smile in return. The unsmiling customer drummed his fingers on the counter and fixed his gaze on the server. A cluster of high school students claimed the clerk's attention. The customer called out "Hey how about my hot dogs?" and the server replied with a patient "Half a sec."

The high-schoolers paid for their food, looked around the cramped interior, decided to make theirs take-out. With the diner less crowded now, the server grabbed a plate from a woman at the back, hurried forward to the man in the flannel shirt. "Three hot dogs. Mustard. Meat sauce. Celery salt. Just the way you like 'em."

The man grunted. "Gimme a ginger ale to go with that, and a side of pickles."

The server turned to relay the order. From the back the woman yelled she was on it.

The customer wolfed half his first hot dog by way of opening bite, tilted his head to Cypriano, spoke through a mouthful of meat. "I understand this is on you."

The priest nodded agreeably and said indeed it was.

"Cheers then." Without the distraction of further talk the customer went back to his food.

The server lingered by the stools until the woman appeared with the ginger ale and pickles. Once she had set them beside the hot dogs the two workers turned to Cypriano, said it was too long since they'd last seen him. "And I see you brought friends."

James Cypriano made the introductions. "Tommy and Gina Deluca. My Dorrance Street Irregulars. They keep me informed of any sightings of interest."

"Easy enough to do, Father," grinned Tommy Deluca. "Feels like everybody in Providence stops by here at some point from one end of the week to the other." Tommy stood five foot five, thick muscled biceps, with a high-and-tight buzzcut and a youthful face that creased easily into a smile. Mid-thirties in age. Tattooed on one arm was an M4 carbine framed by the words "Weapon of choice" and "3 tours of duty: Afghanistan/Iraq."

The tattoo on his other arm was differently themed. A curvaceous fleshy female, nude but for nylons and go-go boots, waving a checkered Indy 500 race-flag. Tommy saw Fay stare, her lips curled in a frown, at which he grinned and said by way of explanation, "My wife in her glory days. Luckily she's still gorgeous." By way of riposte Gina swatted him with a menu and punched his back and barked, "Oh shuddup about those tats."

As further commentary Gina Deluca tapped the logo on the baseball cap atop her head: "I'm with Stupid. Please don't hold it against me." Short, amply figured, in black jeans and black tee (which bore its own motto: "I'm the brains of this outfit"), she wore gold hoop earrings and a half-dozen gold necklaces and thick expansive hair tied back in a ponytail.

The priest raised a hand to ask for peace. "I understand you have some fresh information."

Tommy Deluca said yes he did. "The wife tells me 'Honey just text him, easier on the botha youse' but me and Father Jim we both like face to face."

"Hey." Gina swatted him again with the menu. "I like seeing him too. I never said don't invite him."

He ducked as she rained more blows on him. "Okay. Okay. Anyway, Father, you come in here, we get to chat, plus you get to relax with a beverage. Speaking of which. Let me fix up those cabinets."

He hurried back to the kitchen. They watched as he scooped vanilla ice cream from a big carton, slapped it in a blender, then added milk. From a bottle labeled "Autocrat Coffee Syrup" he poured a long shot of the dark, viscous fluid. A press of a button, and the blender whirred up the mix. As they waited, James Cypriano pointed out the logo on the bottle: "A swallow will tell you," together with the image of a cheerful red bird atop the name Autocrat.

The priest said when he was young—"I must have been five"—he was so pleased to discover a word could mean two things at the same time. "My mother and father told me 'When you swallow something you can taste that it's good; but a swallow is also a type of bird, like this little one on the bottle that's telling you about Autocrat.'" He smiled at the memory. "Two meanings rising out of the same word simultaneously. I was so pleased, I hugged that thought all day. Must have been the first clue in my life I would turn into some kind of scholar."

He smiled as Gina set the shakes before them. "There you go, Father, for you and your friends."

"Bless you." The three of them had barely begun to sip their drinks before being hailed by the man in the thick flannel shirt. "Hate to interrupt, Padre, but I just might happen to be a swallow myself. One that's in the mood to tell *you* a little something. Something worth your attention more than that coffee syrup gunk."

"Sorry, Father." Tommy stepped forward. "This here's Dieter Konrad. Lives in the neighborhood. One of the fresh information sources I was telling you about when I invited you to stop by."

Cypriano smiled. "Mister Konrad. A pleasure. I think we met once when I stopped by Cellar Step Books. But you look as though you could use a bit more food."

"As long as you're paying, Padre." Dieter Konrad held up his empty plate, thrust it at the servers. "Gimme a couple more. This time with a side order of fries. And another ginger ale."

"Coming right up." Gina went to the kitchen to fill the order.

Cypriano turned interrogatively to the informant. But the latter now seemed in no mood to hurry, chewed a toothpick, said he'd wait till he had a second helping before making the effort to talk. "You folks just go ahead and have your drinks for now."

The priest nodded unperturbed and turned to his two guests. "You said you had some Latin for me?"

Bonaventure nodded, pulled a sheet of paper from his shirt pocket. As he did so he saw Dieter Konrad stare at him hard. Konrad muttered as if startled, scratched at his chin, stared at him more. *What's bothering him?* Bonaventure was sure he'd never seen him before.

"Hey. Dumbo." Fay MacConnell was tugging at his sleeve. "Give Father Jim the paper."

Bonaventure said sorry and handed over the sheet. Flannel-shirt Guy was still staring. "This, ah, this is something I found at Swan Point. Part of a pile of papers left in front of H. P. Lovecraft's headstone. You can see it's torn at the corner. So some of the text is missing. It's just a fragment. But here's what I think makes this valuable." Hard to talk, hard to focus, what with that man on the red vinyl stool keeping his gaze fixed on him. *Pretty unsettling.*

Bonaventure told himself *Just concentrate on what you've got in front of you,* then gathered himself to speak aloud. "I've studied quite a few Lovecraft manuscripts in the archives up at Miskatonic U and I'm pretty sure this is in his own handwriting. So whatever this Latin passage says, it must have been something that meant a lot to him, enough to make Lovecraft want to transcribe it from the original source."

Cypriano smoothed the sheet and read through the text:

> Ab alia vero parte tam valide cuncta conflagravit ut amnis finem inponeret. Verumtamen ecclesia cum domibus suis non sunt aduste. Aiebant enim hac urbem quasi consecratam fuisse antiquitus ut non ibi incendium prevaleret non serpens non glerus aparuisset. Nuber autem cum cuniculum pontis emundaretur et coenum de qua repletum fuerat auferetur serpentem cleremque aereum repererunt. Quibus ablatis et cleres ibi deinceps extra numero et serpentes aparuerunt et postea incendia preferre coepit.

The priest studied the page in silence. Finally Fay said, "We both worked on it but our Latin's none too good and the best we can say is it has to do with a fire and a bridge."

"Right on both counts." The priest sipped his shake, said from the style and the spelling it had the feel of ecclesiastical Latin, sixth century A.D. "Probably Gregory of Tours. I'd guess this is from his *Historia Francorum*. The city of Paris suffered a massive fire during his lifetime, and this might be part of the description of what happened. If you don't mind an inexcusably loose translation, I'll give it a whirl right here on the spot."

Tommy Deluca, who was listening in even as he served other customers, called out encouragement. "Go for it, Father."

"Then go for it I shall." Another sip of his shake, and he improvised a translation:

> From the other side, however, everything had gone up in flames so fiercely that only the river could impose a boundary and a limit to the fire. But the church and its buildings weren't even singed.
>
> People used to say that in ancient times it was almost as if this city had been consecrated, so that fire would never prevail there, nor would even one snake or rat ever dare to show itself.
>
> But recently, when the tunnel under the bridge was being cleaned out, and when the filth that had filled the tunnel was being hauled off, they uncovered a serpent and a rat made of bronze. Once these things were taken away, immediately swarms of rats and snakes beyond counting began to appear, and fires began to break out.

"So that's what had been keeping Paris free of snakes and rats," marveled Fay. "Guardian images made of bronze."

"That's right," agreed the priest. "There were elaborate rituals to empower the images. Then they'd be placed anywhere that was considered a vulnerable entry point for unfriendly spirits. Tunnels under bridges at the periphery of a city might provide a way for a demon to find a way in. So you had to shore up those weak points. The practice in antiquity was that you always set up the guardian image or statue so that it faces forward, so it's looking out and glowering at the thing it's supposed to deter."

"Yeah," enthused Tommy Deluca, who was serving Dieter Konrad one seat over even as he listened in. "Like the way you follow instructions when you plant a claymore mine. 'Front Toward Enemy,' it says nice and clear on the thing. After that you back off and wait till unfriendlies come charging in at you. Then hit the clacker and *boom*.

Problem solved." He frowned to himself, shrugged. "Well, sorta like that I guess."

"Hadn't thought of it that way," conceded the priest. "But yes."

Up to now Dieter Konrad had kept his gaze on Bonaventure as if doing so would help him nail a thought he was trying to recall. The grad student kept his head down, prayed no one would cry out 'Hey don't I know you?,' say anything to remind him of a past life he wanted to forget.

But the arrival of a second round of food deflected Konrad's stare. "Two more hot dogs," announced the server, "plus fries and a ginger ale."

Dieter Konrad asked where was his malt vinegar. "You can't expect me to eat French fries without vinegar. What kind of joint is this anyway?"

"Sorry." Tommy pivoted to the kitchen and was back in an instant. "There. Salt. Ketchup. Vinegar. Now you're in a position to do justice to those fries."

Konrad sullenly said that was more like it.

The priest was explaining that the artifacts found under the Parisian bridge were good examples of objects serving an apotropaic function. "To ward off terrifying forces that might otherwise come slithering into your house ..."

Dieter Konrad paused, hot dog halfway to mouth. "Now there's a coincidence. 'Apotropaic.' "

Cypriano smiled and asked how so.

"Because it says right here"—Konrad put down his food, used his flannel shirt to wipe his fingers clean of vinegar and ketchup, pulled a grease-stained notebook from a pants pocket—"right here, here we go, notes I took so as to be a valuable informant, valuable enough at least to justify a free meal at Haven Brothers, says here in the conversation I had just the other day that the person I happened to be talking to also used the word 'apotropaic.' You have to admit this is not a word you're going to hear every day of the week."

Cypriano admitted that was true.

Konrad finished his hot dog in one big bite, picked up his second. "Tommy here tells me you're putting out the word you're interested in tidbits of information from the street on several disparate topics." He studied the remaining hot dog, held it up at eye level, applied a judicious layer of mustard. "One. Valuable antiques that have gone missing in the vicinity of Providence. Two. A group calling itself Gnostic Guardians of the Something Something."

"Cosmic Gate."

"That's what I meant to say. Three. Young woman goes by the name of Alicia Wheatley. Have I got that right?"

The priest said yes he had.

"Well in that case I got a data point for you that combines all three and just might sock you right between the eyes." He finished his hot dog in one last gulp and devoted himself to his fries. "Got a downstairs neighbor over at the Peerless Building likes to come up to the roof at night and catch the breeze. Sorta like me except in my case of course I've got serious projects I'm pursuing with my telescope."

"Of course."

Konrad sprinkled vinegar atop his fries, added ketchup and salt. "Well this neighbor she's a young lady from overseas, has a job in a museum up on College Hill. Last week she stopped by, looked to see what I was doing, I showed her my falcons, she didn't have too much to say for herself. But the next night she stops by again and this time she seems more in the mood to talk. Tells me about two pieces in her museum's Egyptian gallery, she calls them, let me just check my notes here, yeah, calls them canopic jars. Supposed to be four in the collection, but two have been missing for years and years. Since 1936, I think. Yeah. That's what my notes say. She says one of the missing jars has a baboon's head. The other one's a jackal. Says if the four are ever reunited they'll have greater apotropaic strength or something." He took his time as he talked, manifestly savoring his brief authority as dispenser of sought-after knowledge. *Much like many a professor I've known*, thought Bonaventure, *who like nothing better than holding forth.*

"The young woman who told you this," interjected James Cypriano. "Is she from Pakistan? Is her name Zahra Beheshti?"

Konrad stopped in mid-bite. Ketchup-tipped French fries bristled half-eaten from his mouth. "Sounds like I'm wasting your time here, Padre. You know all this already." His chewing slowed to a grumpy, gloomy halt.

"Not necessarily," Cypriano reassured him. He said he'd met Zahra Beheshti one Saturday night some weeks earlier when she stopped by the dock to watch the Riverglow skiffs as they set off to light the braziers. "We got to talking and she simply mentioned how much she loves showing visitors the Egyptian artifacts and the other galleries at the RISD museum. But I'm unaware of any connection between RISD and the Gnostic Guardians group."

"Well in that case maybe the cash you expended on my hot dogs isn't entirely misspent." Konrad jammed a final fistful of French fries into his mouth. "So this young lady tells me in our most recent conversation she had a curious visitor at work just the other day. Someone wearing a lapel pin that says 'GGCG,' someone by the name of Alicia Wheatley. I know I got that right because I wrote the name down. And this Alicia gal shows a strong interest in those two missing canopic jars, spends time at the museum reading up on the details of the theft. 'Lizard heist' is what the papers called it back in 1936."

"That *is* interesting," mused the priest, "considering that Alicia Wheatley is the selfsame person who dropped by the rectory for a visit on behalf of those Gnostic Guardians not so very long ago."

"And that's all I got," announced Dieter Konrad with a belch, standing up from his red vinyl stool. "Hope it was worth your while." He took a step toward the dinette's door, then halted in front of Bonaventure, snapped his fingers in triumph. "*Now* I've figured it out. I know who you are. I've been working on this to the point of indigestion."

Oh no. An unvoiced groan from the grad student. *Here it comes.*

"Of course. You're Joey B. Joey B, in the flesh."

The Haven Brothers Diner is a small establishment. Conversations get overheard. Tommy Deluca was on this in a second. "Joey B? Fox Point Punks? Here? Are you shitting me?"

"No," replied Konrad in smug certainty, "I'm not shitting you."

"Sweetie," yelled Tommy toward the kitchen, "it's Joey B."

From the back Gina yelled something like "Well dummy get his autograph."

Bonaventure couldn't hear clearly because by now the stool where he sat was being swarmed. Dinette customers surged forward. A guy with a razor on a neck chain. Another with pink frizzed-out hair. A girl in a sleeveless leather vest with a gold wishbone through her nose. Things came thrusting for him to sign. Napkins, paper plates, Haven Brothers take-out menus. The girl with the wishbone had him sign her arm.

Presiding over the flash mob was the triumphant man in the flannel shirt. "Hah. And you thought you could slip back into Rhode Island and skulk around incognito. Not when Dieter Konrad's on deck. No sir. Especially when I'm tanked up with good nutrition and hitting on all eight cylinders. Not that the average citizen could pick you out. No more long hair, no trace of those tats you got inked on your arms all covered up by that tweed coat you're wearing. But a disguise like that, it's not gonna last more than ten minutes around a super-sleuth like me. No sir."

Gloomily Bonaventure penned his signature. Paper plates, menus, napkins.

Konrad bobbed his head at Fay and Father Jim to include them in his oratory. "Folks you ever been to any of his concerts back when he was hot stuff? Woulda blown your mind, the excitement, the way they cranked the music up loud. And the way the girls dressed when they turned out for his gigs some of them not wearing much more than this lady here." He jabbed a thick forefinger at Tommy Deluca's arm and its tattoo of the nude female with the checkered flag. "Boy howdy on that dance floor what a collection of tits and ass. All howling for Joey B and Providence's own Fox Point Punks. Me and my buds we'd show up and stand off to the side just hoping for some bycatch. Hoo-ee."

Bonaventure didn't dare look at Fay to see what she was making of all this. But he could guess. *Some people's frowns you can feel from blocks away.* Followed by the thought *Why doesn't this diner come equipped with trapdoors to drop me out of sight and plop me in the river?*

By now most of the other customers had gotten their signatures and exited in cheerful chatter. Konrad leaned over confidingly, held out one last paper plate, asked as a special favor—"Since I was the one that busted you out of obscurity just now"—if he could just jot along with his autograph the most famous line from his most famous local-hit song.

Bonaventure wasn't feeling particularly grateful at the moment to have been busted out of obscurity, in fact was fantasizing about apotropaic devices, especially of the kind Tommy Deluca described, the kind that say "Front Toward Enemy" and then when unfriendlies come you hit the clacker and *boom,* end of problem. At which point Bonaventure chided himself *Doctor Cartwright would say this is unwholesome and unproductive thinking* and miserably he wrote out for the flannel-shirted man what he wanted on his precious paper plate. "Girlie you look like the Queen of Diamonds."

"Am definitely taping this up on my fridge. This is a keeper." Konrad tucked the plate carefully away inside his shirt. He turned to Fay and Cypriano, nodded to the priest. "Those hot dogs weren't too bad. But gotta get back to the Peerless and my scope up on the roof."

He snapped his fingers again. "But wait. One last thing. I got a man-to-man question for you, Mister Joey B, and I want a truthful response. Janey Evans, you know her, she tells me you fell into the Providence River a little while back and had an encounter close up with an aqueous Godzilla. Is that true? Is it? No, don't bother answering. The look on your face tells me what I need to know."

Shrewd owl eyes surveyed everyone in the diner. "I've got an announcement for all of you in the general public. Aqueous Godzilla: that's not our only urban aberration. Laser-pulse dot-dot-dots from the Superman Building. Message of some kind. Plus our fifty-eight-foot termite is being perturbed. Stabbed by unwarranted arcs of light. It won't stand for much more. So I've been putting together the pieces of our very own Providence puzzle. And I can tell you this. We've got apocalypse coming. Believe you me. Revelation. You heard it from me first."

He slapped his paunch by way of salute and valediction. Konrad repeated the warning: "From me first." Then he stepped from the diner's door and out into the night.

"Joey B." Now it was Fay MacConnell's turn to stare at Bonaventure. She repeated the appellation aloud as if assessing what it meant, added a few more phrases from Dieter Konrad's declamation. "Tits and ass. Hot stuff. Fox Point Punks. Joey B."

Embarrassing to have his past burst out like this in the confined space of the diner. "That's what they called me. My stage name back then."

She said nothing further, continued to stare. He couldn't read her look. *Not sure if she's disgusted or amused or just generally dismissive of my general worth.* He scratched at the scar along his jaw. "Sorry. It was a long time ago. Brings up memories, most of them not so good."

"Hey. Hey." She tugged his jacket sleeve for his attention. "You look like crap. You look like someone just stuck a knife in your guts and jerked the blade back and forth but good."

"Well thanks a lot." He wrung his hands, twitched and knotted his fingers.

"Sorry. That's the Poe fangirl in me talking. Knife in guts. Always the lurid lurch." She surprised him by laying both her hands atop his twitching fingers. "What I'm trying to say is, it's okay. If someone came up to me and slit open my own past for public display, I'd feel crappy too. And Mister Super-Sleuth wasn't exactly delicate in announcing your greatest hits."

Her hands felt warm, felt good. *She just told me it's okay.* He took a deep breath. *She just told me it's okay.*

She patted his sleeve, withdrew her hands. "But listen I wanted to tell you and Father Jim I've got a bit of investigatory news of my own, even if it's largely negative." She explained to Cypriano about the Athenaeum's copy of the *Necronomicon.* "Well the last couple of days at work I've been using every spare minute to see if I can find it. But not a trace. Nothing, except a note in the Ath's catalogue system. The note classifies the volume like this: 'Lost, possibly stolen. An extensive search has been made throughout the building, to no avail.' And get this." Her eyes gleamed. "The note's dated July 1936. And inscribed underneath is the name of the file clerk who made that extensive search. Can you guess who that was?"

Bonaventure roused himself from his agitated twitching enough to make the requested guess. "I'm betting Novalyne Price."

"Smart student. A-plus."

"Seems like a lot happened on College Hill in the summer of '36." James Cypriano sipped the last of his coffee shake. "A book of magical spells goes missing. A pair of canopic jars are stolen. And Novalyne Price disappears from view."

"And the last word we have of her," added Fay mournfully, "she apparently becomes a supersized goldfish trying to reunite with her Bob Howard."

She looked so distraught Bonaventure thought hard—or tried to at least—of something he could say that might cheer her up. He drew a blank.

The Jesuit intervened by setting on the counter a thick accountant's ledger with faded inking on the cover. "Folks, there's another reason I asked you to come here tonight. I've got something here I found just the other day in the FX parish archives. Journal jottings by the priest who happened to be the pastor in 1936, a Monsignor Emile Bergeron. I want to show you an entry he wrote in July of that year. I think it'll shed light, well some at least, on the mysteries we've been probing."

"July 1936?" exclaimed Fay. "Just like you said. That's when everything happened."

"Indeed. Just listen to this." And listen they did, as customers went in and out of the Haven Brothers Diner, and Gina yelled out orders to Tommy in the kitchen for burgers and fries and jumbo onion rings. Through it all James Cypriano took them back to the summer of 1936.

35

Journal of Monsignor Emile Bergeron

July 1936

July 28

A long day out and about in the parish. Many house calls to families with children who are ill. Performed Anointing of the Sick for Mrs. Anita Agnelli, knelt by bedside with family to say Rosary together with supplemental Pater Noster and Ave Maria Gratia Plena by request. I pray there not be another influenza outbreak this year on Federal Hill. No opportunity to pause for lunch in my rounds, so that I returned to FX frankly famished and looking forward to a bite of supper. In which state of mind I was therefore taken aback upon arrival to be greeted by young Father Damien, who reminded me that members of the Sacristy Committee were awaiting me (in fact, had been waiting for some three-quarters of an hour). When I asked what was their business and could it not abide until the morrow he pointed out it was I who had commissioned the sacristans to raise money for new vestments and now that they had succeeded they wished simply to show me their recommendations for possible choices of chasubles and stoles.

Weary though I was I had presence of mind enough to say Yes of course and met with the committee and thanked them for their fund-raising and listened as they argued with each other over which robes would look smartest on me when I say Sunday high Mass. Kept my patience throughout all this and did not lose my temper once. (Irritability: a weakness of mine, and a temptation I fall into, and at the end of the meeting I whispered a quick *Domine gratias maximas tibi ago* in thanksgiving for not having succumbed to anger or impatience.)

Relief that was unfortunately premature. For no sooner had I escaped the sacristy, pausing by the altar to genuflect and breathe a groan of gratitude, than Sister Mary Alcuin, vice principal of our FX grammar school, intercepted me with an entreaty for two minutes of my time. A discipline problem with the seventh graders, and might she consult with me? I fought off the urge to point out this was beyond my purview, consulted with her by the altar rail for two minutes and much longer (fifteen, in fact: I confess I sneaked glances at my pocket watch to signal I was tired). I did my best but found my thoughts seduced by the hope that some of yesterday's beef stew might still be left in the icebox and attendant on my pleasure. Man does not live by bread alone to be sure; but I was finding it hard to gnaw on these dry crusts of discourse concerning middle school rowdies. Finally, with apologies for the claim on my time, Sister Mary Alcuin took her leave, departing for the convent, even as I all but sprinted for the rectory and refuge for the night.

But all in vain. For no sooner had I slipped off my jacket and loosened my collar than there came a knock on the rectory door. One moment of temptation (yet another!—which testifies to my inherent weakness) and the wild thought of lying low with lights extinguished hoping all callers would think me away or fast asleep, and then, with the words "Just give me strength" upon my lips, I tugged the door open.

And almost closed it straightaway upon my visitor's face. Oh no not him again. Please dear God, no.

But there it was, in the flesh and irrefutable: another visitation from Howard Phillips Lovecraft.

"Won't take but a moment of your time, Monsignor." And with that he stepped inside. "Really no more than a moment." Which hadn't been true of his last dropping by, and wasn't true on this occasion either.

Bare hospitality required I bid him sit and offer him a cup of coffee. Remembering how he likes to sweeten his brew, I stationed an oversized bowl of sugar beside the pot.

He came to the point rapidly—I'll give him that at least—asking if perchance I'd reconsidered his earlier request. I said absolutely not, hoping to foreclose discussion and whisk him out the door.

But of course no such luck. So he reprised the arguments he'd made before in trying to persuade me. "Monsignor, once again I am offering you the privilege of contributing one or two consecrated objects from your church to add their deterrent power to my collection of apotropaia. I need all the magical artifacts I can find to strengthen the gates of Yog-Sothoth and prevent the inrush of the foul forces of Cthulhu."

"Why do you keep insisting?" I asked, with what I have to acknowledge as uncharitable irritation. "I thought you're militantly anti-Catholic."

His thin lips moved in the driest mockery of a smile. "I am. I hate the Church. I hate the whole Papist lot of you. But I recognize raw power when I see it and I want to harness it. To combat hateful strength with hateful strength."

"Christ's strength is in weakness, and love," I reminded him. "He will not serve in hate." As I'd done before, I tried to explain that crucifixes and statues of the saints, whether blessed or unblessed, weren't magical paraphernalia and weren't intended for strengthening the gates of Yog-Sothoth, whatever that was supposed to be.

But it seemed he hadn't heard me. He was set on boasting of his latest acquisitions, of the latest persons he had induced to become what he called his "indentured followers." "Could you but know their names, my dear Monsignor, you would be thunderstruck to see what a distinguished roster of literary figures has entered my employ. Oh of course their appearance might seem a touch odd." He reached for the sugar bowl, removed the lid. "Yes, you might smile to see my followers, vermicular of mien, Vespertine by fate, by turns and twists reptilian. And yet withal not unuseful."

I told him I had no idea what he was going on about. It was all I could do to keep from saying "I'm uncommonly hungry so drink your coffee and just get out."

But my visitor was in no hurry at all. He measured a heaping teaspoon of sugar into his cup, then a second spoonful and a third. "No, not unuseful at all. For recently my servitors have retrieved the bronze visage of a most august emperor, retrieved it from a distant land. And as reward one servitor in particular has been allowed to grow and is now a full six feet long. And he disports himself now and again in the company of a fish of a pleasing golden hue. Why, even now I am plotting an enterprise whereby this selfsame Vespertine servitor will bring me a pair of... But soft, I talk too much." He sipped his thrice-sweetened coffee.

"Yet enough of badinage. Potential entry points for Cthulhu's astral hordes are dotted throughout our planet, and as grim chance would have it one such point—the *Necronomicon* names it Yog-Sothoth—exists right here in this city. If the unhuman hordes win entry they'll contrive to breed with us and dilute our good Yankee stock. You see, Monsignor, I love Providence, and I intend to defend it against invasion. But my task is made harder because foul worshipers of Cthulhu swarm in secret cabals the world over. Jews and Negroes. Slavs and Arabs. Asiatics from every part of the Orient."

He sipped his coffee. "Three teaspoons. Mmm. Quite fine." Setting aside the cup, he put more urgency into his tone. "In their rituals and cults these worshipers strengthen Cthulhu and bring ever nearer the day when the astral hordes may finally achieve their barbarous wish and burst through the gates of Yog-Sothoth. Fortunately there are bearers of civilization in Europe who are struggling to beat down the barbarians. Mussolini bestrides Africa from Libya to Abyssinia and is taming the dark tribes. In Germany, Herr Hitler has come to power and is even now contriving to protect the purity of the Aryan race."

"Hitler?" Lovecraft had angered me on his last visit with talk of this kind; now, tired and hungry, I couldn't sit through any more of it. "Do you have any idea of the persecution to which he's subjecting the Jews? Do you have any idea of the savagery he represents?"

He raised a hand to silence me. "The preservation of Germany as a coherent cultural and political fabric is of infinitely greater importance than the comfort of those who have been incommoded by Nazism." He sipped his coffee, patted a napkin to his lips. "Oh, I grant you there's more than a touch of crudity to Herr Hitler. I for one deplore his book-burning, his theatrics, his plebeian taste for opera-bouffe posturing. But what distresses you—in your Christian idealism and soft humanitarianism—the savagery, the persecutions, why these are the very things we need to keep our culture pure. Herr Hitler may be crude and a bit of a clown, but my word, I *like* the boy!"

He waved his sugar spoon for emphasis. "In my fiction I've tried to warn of what will happen if we allow foreigners to enter our New England with their alien Cthulhu-cult. You'll see how I sounded the warning klaxon in 'The Horror at Red Hook,' 'The Haunter of the Dark,' and sundry other tales. These nameless immigrants with their primitive half-ape bestiality, these swart and insolent prowlers who bring a hybrid pestilence concocted by the astral hordes beyond the stars, these bearers of spiritual putrescence, blear-eyed and pock-marked: all of them will contrive in their wild-beast mindlessness to tear asunder the gates of Yog-Sothoth and welcome their cosmic master even as I struggle mightily to keep those gates sealed against all contagion!"

I interrupted to say his railing against immigrants sat poorly with me since I too am an immigrant to this nation.

"Oh, but of a different quality, to be sure." He pointed out I was refined, educated, European, French, hence Aryan or very nearly—"not part of the swart ruffian swarm."

French-Canadian, I retorted, and not so refined or educated by background. My parents and grandparents had been landless laborers in Quebec. And as for ancestry: family lore claims intermarriage with native Indian tribes—likely Algonquin, perhaps Cree and Huron too. "So you see, Mister Lovecraft, I too am part of that ruffian swarm."

Finally I'd found a way to sting him into departure. Hastily he put down his cup, stood up abruptly from his chair. As parting shot he proclaimed there to be no such thing as a benevolent God in our world. "There's nothing out there but howling cosmic wastes populated by chaos-lords like Cthulhu and the Old Ones and the lumbering brainless Shoggoths. They and all their ilk are implacably hostile to men. And should they succeed in breaking through the gates of Yog-Sothoth, and should their half-ape minions—the swart and slant-eyed foreigners you pamper with the name 'immigrants'—should they continue to swarm our shores, well: that's the end. The end of Providence, and of everything I've grown up with and hold dear."

Famished and tired as I was, nonetheless now I perversely wanted him to stay a moment longer. I had something else to say even if he didn't want to hear it. "You say you love Providence but you see so do I. I too have had the intuition of Providence as a cosmic entry portal, as a gate whereby powers beyond our daily ken may enter and make contact with us in a profound and stirring way. But you mistake the nature of these powers. My own research suggests these beings do not wish us harm at all. In truth they wish to help us."

Unintentionally I had conjured the fastest possible means to shoo Lovecraft out the door. He shot me a glare, shrugged on his coat.

I kept speaking. "Evidence for what I claim can be found in the annals of this state of Rhode Island we both profess to love. The evidence I have in mind concerns none other than Roger Williams." I recalled for my visitor Williams' exodus from Massachusetts in the winter of 1636, and how some historians assert that a young English-born servant named Thomas Angell accompanied him on his trek. "And as you know, Mister Lovecraft, you with your superior knowledge of all things Providence, College Hill boasts a street that bears this very name of Angell, supposedly in honor of this young Thomas."

Lovecraft had his hand on the doorknob and stood poised to bolt. I spoke faster. "Through my own research into the unpublished correspondence of Roger Williams, I've discovered that an 'Angell' did in fact accompany him on his wanderings when he first approached Slate Rock, but rather than English-born it was an exile from the very realm of heaven. Little do the good citizens of Providence know that this Angell Street of ours is named not for a human but a penitent seraph. So you see Roger Williams may have been the first to welcome to Rhode Island an otherworldly 'foreigner' from the vast cosmic wastes you so abhor."

"In that case," snarled H.P. Lovecraft, "Roger Williams was a fool." And with that he stalked out the door and slammed it shut behind him.

That door slam echoed through my evening. As is often the case in quarrels, I continued the argument in my own mind for hours after he'd rushed forth from the rectory. From the icebox I removed the longed-for stew and heated it on the stove, even as I rehearsed what I would have said had Lovecraft lingered.

The Bible tells us of "angels who have sinned against God." Origen of Alexandria writes of "angels who transgressed the limits of their nature." Did they find themselves consigned eternally to hell? I wonder. Saint Catherine of Genoa in a mystical vision beheld the entranceway of paradise, uncovered a secret known to few before their death: the gates of heaven stand always open, always welcoming to all. There is no door that bars us. God waits in love to hold us in His arms. It is only our own consciousness of sin that makes us blush and hesitate to enter. "It is not God who casts us into fire," says Catherine, "but rather the soul itself, eager to burn itself free of all sin from its past life, that retreats from heaven's entrance and gladly plunges of its own volition into the blaze of purgatory for a time, until through purity of longing it knows itself ready to ascend from the fires and step through the gate that stands always open for reunion with the One who has always loved us. In the smithy's furnace, fire does not destroy gold but simply purges it of all impurities and alloys. So too with the precious metal of our soul, till all dross of distraction is burned away and we know ourselves ready for the Beloved."

I sat rereading my Catherine, put the book aside to ladle my stew into a bowl. I searched in the breadbox, found that Mrs. Navarino—bless her!—had brought me a fresh loaf. So I cut myself two slices and dipped them in the stew. As I ate I got up from the table repeatedly (something one can scarcely do if one has company) and gathered together jottings I'd left on scraps of paper scattered about the rectory parlor. Herewith a copy of these jottings, relevant perhaps to this evening's flow of thought:

God bars no one from heaven—neither humans nor angels. Nor does He expel anyone therefrom. As Christ Himself tells us, "I came not to judge the world, but to save it." Rather, as Catherine demonstrates, both angels and humans may feel themselves unready to enter the Presence. Then they voluntarily depart, descend, seeking ways to purify themselves so as to know themselves worthy. Some seek out the element of fire for purification. Some come to Earth to expiate their sins in service, and many are the disobedient angels, once tempted by distracting pride, now mindful of what grief they caused, who wish to make amends.

Foremost among these fallen angels are the penitent seraphs, who in token of their penitence have plucked white-hot brands from the very paving stones of hell and with these fiery irons have stamped onto their own souls these words of Scripture they mean never to forget: "Are not they all ministering spirits, sent forth to serve and help?" And from the regretful stony floor of hell—which in truth is the first stage of purgatory—these seraphim come to our Earth, to expiate their sins in service, helping earthly creatures, human and nonhuman, however they possibly can.

Thus Earth for them is a site of penitential pilgrimage. As it is for us—a beautiful place to sojourn, but in the end not our final home. And throughout this pilgrim's world of ours, there are certain gateway points, where—if one's own spirit is hushed, if one has the skill to remain still—one can hear a numinous flutter of wings, as seraphs descend to join us.

Curious and strange—and I do wish Mister Lovecraft had stayed, so that, now I've articulated the thought, I might share it with him—to think that this Yog-Sothoth he fears, wherever it's located, might in fact be an angelic entrance-port for these angels that wish to help us. By filling it and stuffing it full with works of black magic all Lovecraft may have accomplished—sadly—is to send a frowning signal: "We don't want you. We don't want your help."

Who knows? If the penitent seraphs felt welcome, their petitions and prayers might just release a new outlet of grace into our world of exile. Could it be that this very instant they're trying their best to reach us and signal that if we let them they stand ready to help?

Amen. Enough for one night. Now back to bread and beef stew.

36

"Wow. So glad you shared this with us." Fay MacConnell was the first to react. She speculated about how Edgar Allan Poe might have reacted to the pastor's depiction of Lovecraft striving to stuff Yog-Sothoth with baleful artifacts to keep out the hordes of Cthulhu. "I suspect my man Poe would've said 'Yeah yeah that makes sense.' I mean look at all the stories where his heroes secrete themselves in fortresses to keep out monsters and build walls or dig pits and plaster them over to confine the dead and smooth them out of sight. And does it work? Not often. The scary things keep breaking through. You see it in his 'Masque of the Red Death' and 'The Black Cat' and 'Tell-Tale Heart.' What do you think, Joey?"

But Joseph Bonaventure scarcely heard. He was thinking of the fallen seraphs. *"The regretful stony floor of hell." Sounds like me. "Tempted by distracting pride." Yeah, that was me. That was me. As Dieter Konrad and Treff Boudreau both said in their own way: it was quite a kick to be a star, to be fussed over with all those fans fawning over me. But it all just fed my buzz; all those kids out there at the gigs: they were nothing to me but ciphers and blanks. They just fed my ego and I just fed them noise. And when the crunch came the night of the Pacific Bacchanale I just dived off the stage and clawed to the exit without a thought for any of those kids, any of those fans, who had fed me all that buzz.*

"Some angels seek out the element of fire for purification." Well the fire sure sought me out but it wasn't by any choice of mine. No purifying moment for me. Just a bunch of regrets and the regretful stony floor of hell. And people here back in Providence come up and say "Man you lived the life! I envy you." Shit, if they only knew.

He realized dimly Fay was saying something. He caught two words from her. "You okay?"

"Oh yeah. I'm fine. I'm fine." A picture came to him of Robert E. Howard in his Vespertine state. *Aqueous Godzilla. Keeping out of sight.*

Swimming in the dark. Swimming on a river bottom, out of sight and out of reach. Ill-suited for daylight worlds. Ill-suited. Moodily he tapped a straw against the glass of his empty shake.

What snapped him out of this—if only briefly—was an enthused slap on the back from Tommy Deluca. "Say guys I almost forgot! Father Jim calls me and Gina his Dorrance Street Irregulars but an important piece of intelligence, well I hope it's important, interesting at least, all but slipped my mind."

James Cypriano had put away the FX parish archive journal and was just standing up to leave. "Intriguing. Let's hear it."

"You remember that punk troublemaker they call Tagger? The one who got arrested for spraying graffiti on our Big Blue Bug? I forget his name."

From the kitchen Gina yelled, "You mean Alex Finster."

"That's the one. So get this, Father. The other night, pretty late, must've been two in the morning, he comes in here to buy something. Can of soda I guess it was. All I can say is he's got a lot of nerve showing his face downtown after what he did to our Bug."

Gina supplied a comment from the back. "Give the kid a break. He wants to come in here to buy something, he's got the right. It's a free country."

Tommy agreed but said it still ticked him off. "Anyway the thing is this. He buys his Coke or whatever and he sits down, right where you were just sitting, Father, and he starts talking. Place was deserted that time of night on a weeknight, not sure if he was talking to us or to himself or what. Anyway what he had to say, and he said it over and over so no way I could forget, well what he said was pretty weird."

Patiently Cypriano asked what was it that Alex Finster had said.

"Something about how 'The Blue Bug can't sleep at night and I can't either.' Kept saying that. 'The Bug can't sleep and I can't either.' Something about the Bug being restless. And he had a look on his face like I don't know, like maybe he was feeling sorry for what he'd done spraying it with that graffiti shit. And then he takes a big slurp of his Coke and he changes his tune and he's saying 'But I'm gonna be big.' Baron of something. Not sure what."

Fay prompted him. "Let me guess. Baron of Yog-Sothoth."

"Yeah. That's it. Then he says something like 'We just have to find the gate and the Baroness thinks she's got a way to do that.'

Something about being 'on the track of someone who can lead us to it.' "

Cypriano asked was that all.

"Yeah, Father, that was it. He got up to go after that."

"There was something else, you dummy." Gina came out of the kitchen, wiping her hands on a towel. She swatted him with it and as he ducked he said, "Yeah, yeah. He did say something else. Something weird. What was it?"

Gina said she remembered. "Tagger said it just as he left. 'We're in a race, and we're gonna win.' Race to do what exactly, that I'm not sure."

"I think I know." This from Bonaventure, who in his thoughts was still swimming in the wake of that aqueous Godzilla. "A race to find the gates of Yog-Sothoth."

"*Hoo*. Heavy shit." Tommy Deluca blinked and looked impressed. The go-go girl on his tattooed arm waved her checkered flag.

37

She liked to keep people waiting.

In fact even now a lackey in the antechamber awaited permission to enter.

So much the better. It made all the more delicious her current moment of leisured contemplation.

Thus she lounged on her throne (for so she deemed any chair on which she deigned to sit), reveling in the knowledge her lackey had no choice but to wait, feeling it only appropriate given that this particular subordinate had failed her in his latest assignment.

But she deferred thought of this displeasing failure for just a moment. Instead, to refresh her mind she contemplated a framed manuscript page upon the wall—an excerpt from *Il Penseroso* that had been transcribed many years ago by HPL himself:

> Or let my lamp at midnight hour
> Be seen in some high lonely tower
> Where I may oft outwatch the Bear
> With thrice great Hermes, or unsphere
> The spirit of Plato, to unfold
> What worlds, or what vast regions hold
> The immortal mind that hath forsook
> Her mansion in this fleshly nook ...

Yes, this was yet another trait she shared in common with HPL (for so she invoked him in her private musings, though she strove always to refer to him more grandly as "the Magus" when she spoke in public). Both she and Lovecraft—he in the twentieth century, she in the twenty-first—esteemed this bit of verse by Milton, with its evocation of sages and magicians who considered themselves worthy of keeping company with Hermes Trismegistus himself, the "thrice great," patron of alchemists and wizards. She had found these handwritten verses the first time she ecstatically leafed through the pages of the *Necronomicon*, on the day she was appointed Grand Duchess (youngest ever to receive this honor!) of the New England branch of GGCG, with the supplementary titles Baroness of Yog-Sothoth and Eldritch Heir of the text that HPL himself had stolen from Providence's Athenaeum.

She'd been quietly shocked to find that Lovecraft had casually scrawled these Miltonic verses on the back of one of the manuscript sheets comprising the sacred text of Abdul Hazred, as if this ancient volume were no more special than some well-thumbed high school textbook. And then came the thought *Why not? What better way for HPL to show that he was not only the heir but also the master of the legacy of the* Necronomicon *itself?*

Whereupon she had challenged herself to find a way to prove she too was a master and not merely a cowed and trembling follower of the Mad Arab's sorcerous path. Greatly daring, she'd torn out the manuscript page containing Lovecraft's transcription, half-fearing Plato's spirit might unsphere itself, as in the poem, and descend to reprimand her, dreading even more that she might unwittingly unleash some Shoggoth from Cthulhu's wastes. But all had gone well, and there it hung now, a trophy on her wall, a page from the *Necronomicon* with jottings by HPL himself.

Her favorite two verses of course were those that pertained most peculiarly to her present habitation:

Or let my lamp at midnight hour
Be seen in some high lonely tower

Perfect. Eerily perfect. For here she was now, camping out in a concrete robbers' cave on the topmost floor of Superman's abandoned Industrial Trust Building, making occasional use of the skyscraper's tower beacon to beam signals to minions far and near. She knew Rhode Islanders wondered why this twenty-eight-story landmark had stood empty and useless for so long. Well in fact it wasn't empty—at least not certain upper floors—and it was being put to good and very important use, even if it wasn't a use that many in this puny-minded New England region had the wit to understand.

The GGCG was pumping out plenty in monthly private payoffs to keep the public in Providence ignorant of the Superman Building's newest tenant.

The slightest of tappings on her throne-room door. One of her courtiers, no doubt, announcing the arrival of this disappointing lackey who had failed her in his quest. She already knew of course. Her closed-circuit cameras had picked him out as he stood uncertainly in the deserted ground-floor lobby beneath the chandeliers and ceiling roundel of Zodiac gods outlined in Pompeian red. Nervous he looked as security guards appeared from behind a scrolled Corinthian column and bade him enter a golden-doored elevator. Nervous, as well he might after fumbling his mission. *So then let him wait.*

His nervousness and uncertainty reminded her of when she too had felt such feelings, when she'd been just a child.

Childhood in California, in a Bay Area city called Sunnyvale (complacency enshrined in a name—*ugh!*—as if the very town itself took no account of shadows). Her parents were both well-paid techies, one at Google, the other at Cisco Systems. Both described themselves as "comfortable materialists." As her dad cheerfully said, "If you can't write code for it and can't measure it then it probably doesn't exist and in any case it's not worth thinking about." No books anywhere cluttered up their house. Another aphorism from her father: "If it's old enough to be bound and printed then it's already outdated and long since past its sell-by date, so ditch it."

Whereas she, for as far back as she could remember: she'd grown up with a strong sense that the life around her wasn't big enough to contain her vision. As if the material world provided the only horizon she could see! She didn't realize at first how big the differences were between her parents' world and hers. This came out only at age nine when in a secondhand bookshop (she bicycled there secretly on her own after school—she knew better than to ask Mom and Dad to take her) she found an old paperback of tales by HPL. She slipped it in her saddlebag and pedaled home and smuggled the contraband indoors and read it by flashlight under her blankets that very night. Neither parent noticed: they'd both been at their laptops coding till time for bed.

The story that grabbed her right away: "The Rats in the Walls." Wealthy man buys a moldy, crumbling old castle, spends big bucks fixing it up. He's warned of fearsome legends that come with the castle but pays no heed. He bricks up old punched-out walls and buys pricey furnishings and he paints and refurbishes and drapes sumptuous hangings everywhere. All that effort gives him the feeling things are under control, and they are, for all of a night or two. But then comes rustling and scurrying from behind the freshly painted and bricked-up walls. And in the end, a chomp-chomp swarming of rodent teeth to chew through the barriers the rich man has thrown up to fend off the shadow side of his tidy life.

A story set in gloomy, cloudy England, not in cloudless Sunnyvale. But no matter. Nine-year-old Alicia Wheatley made the mistake of showing the story to her mom. "Sweetie, we don't have any infestations. Nothing to worry about. There's nothing in our house."

"There's nothing in our house." Alicia's silent reply had been: *How right you are*, and that was the last time she ever tried sharing with her parents the awareness she had of larger always-encroaching realities. As she put it to disciples in later years: "You can either hear the rats in the wall, or you can't. You can either detect the encroaching threat, or you can't. And those who can't are useless. Some people are just too comfortable to listen up for looming shadows."

Ignored by parents, scorned by classmates: she spent junior high in misery, just her and HPL. The first three years of high school were likewise bad. She thought of herself as an observer, stayed quiet, watched everything, said nothing. She wore a hat with a big floppy brim to keep her face hidden from the world. Steel pins held the hat in place against her hair as a safeguard for those times when mindless classmates snatched her headgear to torment her for fun.

At recess outdoors while the girls around her shrieked at each other or played Pokémon or otherwise amused themselves with their electronic devices, she sat alone in the far corner of the exercise yard and found refuge in verses from *Samson Agonistes*. (By freshman year of high school she'd discovered the consolations of Milton.) She took comfort in imagining herself as the blinded captive hero, struggling for a moment's peace as the triumphant Philistines, drunk with gloating, allow him to emerge ever so briefly from his dungeon labors to feel daylight for ten minutes:

> A little onward lend thy guiding hand
> To these dark steps, a little further on;
> For yonder bank hath choice of sun or shade.
> There I am wont to sit, when any chance
> Relieves me from my task of servile toil,
> Daily in the common prison else enjoined me,
> Where I, a prisoner chained, scarce freely draw
> The air, imprisoned also, close and damp,
> Unwholesome draught. But here I feel amends—
> The breath of heaven fresh blowing, pure and
> sweet,
> With day-spring born; here leave me to respire.

A spring morning, March of her senior year at Sunnyvale High, sitting outside alone as usual in a break between classes, hidden beneath her floppy hat, hiding from the world. *"Where I a prisoner chained ... the air imprisoned also": what an apt description of school-year existence.* And as if to confirm the thought, up strode Tiffany Heatherington with an entourage of hangers-on. Alicia winced as the group hailed her the way it always did: "And what have we here? Little Miss Nobody, all by herself."

Tiffany Heatherington: a sturdy cherub-cheeked exemplar of sun-kissed Californian health. At six-foot-one she sneered down at the hunched and seated Alicia. Well-muscled, this Tiffany, captain of girls' softball and volleyball and this and that. As if to compensate for her strong-limbed dominance (her awestruck clique called her "Goddess"), the softball captain sported a child's baby-pink backpack as if to say "I'm so cool I can flaunt what I want." Clipped to her pack was a keychain from which dangled a big pink plush squirrel.

"Whatcha reading, little Miss Nobody?"

Alicia knew better than to answer. Since absolutely anything she said was always deployed against her, for years she'd followed a policy of saying nothing.

"Hey, I'm talking to you."

Alicia had gotten so good at tuning out abuse it sounded as if it came from far away. *Keep still, a little patience, they'll get bored and look for fun elsewhere.* That's how it usually went.

But for whatever reason things went differently today.

"I asked you whatcha reading." Tiffany grabbed her by the wrist and wrenched the book from her hand, tearing the paperback cover as she did so. "Samson? What shit is this?" The entourage tittered and added their own pile-on verbiage.

What normally got Alicia Wheatley through incidents like this was the rule she tried to stick to: *Keep still, a little patience*, what she'd been telling herself only half a minute ago. But the sight of her half-torn Samson in this Philistine's hands: that made something snap.

Sometimes the best responses happen without any planning.

Alicia plucked a six-inch steel hatpin from the crown of her floppy headgear, reached up to her foe's backpack, and neatly pierced the pink plush squirrel. She glared up at them as she did and rasped out one fierce sentence: "All of you just die."

The entourage ceased their tittering and simply gasped their shock.

Tiffany Heatherington stood openmouthed for a count of three—a long stretch of silence in that young lady's world—and then she was all over Miss Nobody, slapping her face and calling her "bitch" and yanking off her hat and pulling her hair, until Prefect of Discipline Mister Norris pulled the Goddess off still screeching.

But Alicia Wheatley didn't need the hat anymore. She never wore it again. Word of the fight got around, just in time for the yearbook staff to enter beside her photo the nickname Voodoo Doll. But she understood quickly enough that the name implied not only her classmates' scorn but also their fear and a best-to-step-around-her-lightly dread. Freshly-hatless Alicia walked about boldly, still quiet as ever, but with a gaze in her eyes part basilisk, part Gorgon. Tiffany Heatherington and her clique shunned her of course but never risked a confrontation with her again.

Which in the waning weeks of senior year led to a curious phenomenon. Alicia Wheatley attracted her own little clique.

Not by her design. She'd survived childhood needing no one and she wasn't about to change that habit now. But she took to wearing a lapel pin that read "Oderint dum metuant." Venturesome students—nerds and flotsam lonely-heart types (there were surprisingly many), individuals who'd known themselves unwelcome in the Heatherington crowd—asked her what the Latin meant. In a muttered I-could-care-less tone she tossed out a casual translation: "They can hate me as much as they want—as long as they run scared." Someone braved her cool indifference to ask where she'd found the motto. Alicia condescended to bestow a one-word reply: "Caligula."

And suddenly she found herself the focus of a fad. Fellow seniors, quite a few, then lower classes too, sprouted pins that read "As long as they run scared." In the month of May, in the last few weeks of school, Alicia still sat outside at recess as she always had in the far corner of the exercise yard. But now she had company. Some wore collar buttons that boasted "I'm a Caligulite"; others, "I'm with Voodoo Doll." None of them said much; they took their cue from her. They saw her reading so they did too. Some tried Camus, some Tolkien. The most daring took inspiration from her and tried her dearest HPL.

Occasionally she'd test her Caligulites with a riddling utterance. "You can either hear the rats in the wall, or you can't. Some people are just too comfortable to listen up for looming chaos." Her acolytes would check their texts of Lovecraft and argue over her Delphic pronouncement. Those who seemed to get it: why, she'd reward them with a smile.

All this served to harden convictions Alicia had long since formed about human nature. *Most people are followers, looking for a leader, no better than cattle, than sheep. If they don't know what to do with themselves, then they're meant to be used by those who do.*

Like HPL, she sensed hostile presences pressing in on the pale bubble of the world, and she intended to press back. It was her job to keep them out. There were two kinds of people in this world, she realized: those who could smell the horrors burrowing at the Earth's frail barriers and those who couldn't.

Those who couldn't: they were of no interest. Those who could: they were to be used, then set aside.

Come graduation, the first thing she did was to flee—*fast*—from shapeless Sunnyvale, so ignorant of shadows. Her parents were happy to support her and provide a hefty allowance, even if they were a bit puzzled. "Move all the way to Providence? But why? What does Rhode Island have that we don't right here in beautiful California?"

She almost said, "I'm doing it to make an HPL pilgrimage," but realized that to them it would mean nothing. A temptation, very strong, overcame her to shout "I'm Providence-bound because no one out here ever heard the rats chewing away at the foundations of our world and I'm betting there's a greater chance maybe someone there has keener ears to hear." But a voice told her *They'll simply say this girl's got a few screws loose* so she bit back the words and just gave them wordless hugs.

When she reached the city of the Magus at first she was dazzled by how faithfully Providence conformed to Lovecraft's fever dreams. She could stand where he'd once stood and see what he'd once seen. Downtown's domes and spires. The westward sunset view from College Hill and a sky shot through with twilight's promise of unfolding mystery. The Industrial Trust Building at night with its brooding beacon-flare. Federal Hill, site of old Italian churches and mind-rending blasphemies. All there, still all there, just as HPL had mapped it. She embraced it: hers to own.

But what shocked and repelled her was that others also claimed the legacy. Lovecraft conventioneers made Providence their own two or three times a year, bringing in hundreds of Cthulhu fun-lovers (and she was appalled to find anyone could put "Cthulhu" and "fun" together in one sentence). Their idea of dealing with cosmic dread was to engage in cosplay and wear costumes that featured tentacles and teeth. HPL to them meant nothing more than a chance to dress up half Goth, half Shoggoth and treat venerable Providence as a steampunk party venue.

Finally one night near the end of her first year in the city she attended a Lovecraft conference and did so with a mind to making a last-ditch despairing protest gesture. She dressed plainly as she always did, gray chinos, gray polo shirt. She stood in the crowded noisy ballroom of downtown's Biltmore (more Halloween gala than mystic initiation site), amid cheery Cthulhu-costumed merrymakers, surrounded by music and streamers and endless cans of beer. At the top of her voice she shouted, "Hey haven't you ever heard of the Dunwich Horror? Don't you care about locating the gates of

Yog-Sothoth and strengthening them? Can't you hear the rats in the walls? Don't you know they can chew their way through?"

Of course no one heard her. Party noise was designed to make it hard to think.

She retreated from the ballroom, sat slump-shouldered in the hall. *These happy Cthulhu cultists can't sense the shadows any more than folks could back in Sunnyvale.*

But then three silver-haired individuals suddenly stood over her and helped her to her feet. They wore collar tags that read "HPL was right" and "GGCG."

Gnostic Guardians of the Cosmic Gate, they explained. Said they attended these conferences just to pick out the serious, the few. And clearly she was one.

Thus after a probationary period (brief, in her case: she'd come to them already psychically provisioned) Alicia Wheatley became a fully initiated member of GGCG. Quickly she rose within the organization, and in the course of a swift twelve years earned the trust of the Guardians' Global Governing Council. So that tonight (and it comforted her to think on this as she considered what she would say to her disappointing lackey) she sat enthroned in the upper reaches of the abandoned Superman Building: Baroness of Yog-Sothoth, Grand Duchess of GGCG's New England province, Eldritch Heir and custodian of HPL's own purloined copy of the *Necronomicon.*

Another discreet knock on the chamber door.

She raised her voice, said languidly "Let him enter."

"So, Alexander Finster." She made him stand before her as she surveyed him up and down. "What do you have to say for yourself?"

The young man seemed diminished, shrunken, compared to what she remembered. The night that the Gnostic Governing Council had first selected him for her use, when she'd approached him on the dock as he boarded his canoe (not that many days ago, although so much had happened since that evening): then he had come across as cocky, defiant, ready for a fight. Now he looked tired and defeated.

She repeated her question. "I said what do you have to say for yourself?"

He kept his eyes downcast, his face averted. Mumbling came from his mouth. Something about a bug.

This was impertinent of him, if not downright disrespectful. And twelve years with the Gnostics had taught her how to deal with such behavior. She had the *Necronomicon* at her disposal, after all, and she felt an urge to try a light whiplash-spell on him just to snap alert his downcast face. But she also knew from experience how a spell cast in confined quarters could ricochet around a room.

She told him to speak up.

"The Bug. It can't sleep at night. And neither can I." His speech came out thick, confused. He still had his head down. "I mean, sometimes I can, but then I just dream about it, and in the dream it's on the roof and it's restless, wants to fly."

She commanded him to raise his head and look at her.

He obeyed, briefly met her gaze, then looked away to gawk glances at the chamber. "Hey, cool." A faint stirring of animation in him. "Shit. Skyscraper penthouse. What a view."

Well might he marvel. Had she been minded to share (and she wasn't: at the moment she found his diffidence irksome; he was on the verge of becoming useless), she could have pointed out he was standing in what was once called the Gondola Room. Back in the 1920s it had been designed to resemble the passenger compartment of a dirigible like the Graf Zeppelin, complete with observation portholes and bulkheads upholstered in red leather and wine cabinets trimmed in precious woods. There had been talk in those days of airships docking at the Industrial Trust's sky-high beacon tower to take on passengers and mail. She liked the thought: a zeppelin airship to spirit her away at need in case of cosmic crisis.

His chin had sunk once more. Amid her fantasia, Finster had begun mumbling again about the Bug.

"We'll get back to that," she interrupted him. "But first explain to me why you failed to secure the Swan Point papers. They're in the hands now of a librarian from the Athenaeum and some researcher I've seen at Miskatonic. Those two have shown the papers to a priest from Francis Xavier. I've dealt with him, or tried to. He's clever. These individuals will get in the Guardians' way if we're not careful. The loss of these papers is inexcusable, and the Council wants an explanation."

The word "explanation" only made the man more flustered. He mumbled something further, sounded like "Crows coming at me they wouldn't let me go they nipped my skin."

"Crows?" She paused in thought. "We could be confronting some recalcitrant Elementals. I'll have to look into this."

"You know I used to think 'Shit I'm cool I'm on top of things.'" He briefly squared his shoulders, stared at her as if doing so would help him steady his troubling thoughts. "I used to tell myself 'People call me Tagger, I spray what I want where I want, and that includes this city's Big Blue Bug.' I told myself 'Hey I've caught the attention of this cool chick, she's gonna make me Baron of Yog-Sothoth or some deep shit like that.' But now I just don't know."

"Don't know?" Alicia challenged him sharply. Yes indeed: he was teetering on the edge of being no longer useful. She exerted herself to soften her harsh glare, heighten her allure. "Tell me, Tagger," she said more gently, and she leaned forward from her throne. "What's gotten into you?"

"Gotten into me. Funny you put it that way. Cuz that's exactly how it feels. Like something's gotten inside of me. Thoughts that buzz at the back of my head during the day while I'm awake, not sure just what they say. But at night I lie down, they turn into dreams and then I can see them clear." He swallowed, wiped his mouth. "Shit. I sure feel thirsty. Maybe it's the air up here."

She stood, crossed the gondola chamber to the cabinet, offered him a Coca-Cola.

"Hey. Thanks. Hits the spot." He popped the can, drank a deep gulp.

She sat again, crossed her legs, assumed a sympathetic counselor's tone, approachable, inviting. "What kind of dreams?"

He hesitated, Coke in hand. "You'll think I'm nuts."

"No I won't." She put on her softest coaxing-kittenish tone.

He said the dreams were always the same: he was back up on the roof of New England Pest Control. "And in the dream it's always night but I'm up there by myself. Just me and the Big Blue Bug. There's a wind blowing too just like the night I was really there and there's all these guy wires and metal cords holding the Bug in place. And I can hear the wind cuz it's catching the Bug's wings and rocking it back and forth. And I take out my can of jungle green or whatever shit I was gonna spray it with, I forget the brand, Krylon maybe or Kobra or Scribo. But before I can tag the Bug it opens its mouth and looks at me and says something like it's tired of its restraints and it just wishes it had the strength to undo the cords and wires and fly up free the way other bugs do. And in the dream instead of spraying the Bug I pat it on the nose and ask 'Is there anything I can do to help?' Sounds crazy, I know." Another gulp of soda pop. "Oh, and there's one more thing too."

He hesitated again, tapped his Coke.

"Go ahead." This in the gentlest tone she could muster, even as she suppressed her annoyance at his having lost the Swan Point papers to a flight of crows.

"This last part of the dream is what's really dumb-ass nuts." He ventured a glance at her for reassurance. She bestowed her most radiant smile.

"Okay. In the dream the Bug looks at me and says for calories to strengthen its wings and get itself in the air it needs a refill on its drinks."

"A refill?" She started to say "You most certainly are crazy" but caught herself and instead reapplied her smile like lipstick.

"I told you you'd think it's nuts. So in the dream I offer it a choice. Del's Lemonade. Or Awful Awful. Or what they call a coffee cabinet." He added, "It's like a milkshake. Extra thick."

"I've heard of it," Alicia Wheatley said drily. She was making rapid calculations: *Has this loser become too demented to be of further use to the Gnostic Guardians?*

At that moment came an interruption: a whir beyond the windows. A thud and a sudden shudder of the glass. Then a shriek that keened away on the wind.

Finster flinched and spilled his remaining Coke. "Shit. What the hell was that?"

"Peregrine falcons," she said with an air of proud ownership. "Residents with whom I share the tower. Or with whom I dispute it. They seem a bit inconvenienced to find me here. They have a nest just outside the window. I seek to improve my relations with them. They may prove useful."

"Useful? A nest of falcons?"

"You never know." This more to herself than to him. "The *Necronomicon* says it's wise to provide for contingencies, especially in the sphere of the magical arts."

She clapped her hands. Time to be decisive with this bug-besotted youth. Her tone turned businesslike and brisk. "So. Do you still want to be Baron of Yog-Sothoth?"

"Fucking A. Shit yeah." His words faltered. "I mean, I guess so."

"Well then. We may employ you again on that New England Pest Control roof. Until that moment don't let your thoughts be captured by that bug. We have a more immediate task, to locate Yog-Sothoth and shore it up afresh against incursions from Cthulhu. I'll be in contact again with further instructions. Now you may go."

Tagger withdrew from the chamber, still mumbling to himself.

She sat alone in the Gondola Room and contemplated her next move. The race to find Yog-Sothoth: Alicia Wheatley visualized it as a game of chess. The next move she had in mind was risky and involved the deployment of an expendable pawn. She'd briefly considered this Tagger for the gambit but decided against it in light of his bug-ridden mind. Fortunately she had another chess piece that would also serve, one so malleable she could easily shape him to her will. *Him*, she chuckled, *and his little dog, too.*

More tapping at the glass. Wings beat in frustration mere inches from where she sat.

If the museum penetration goes poorly, she mused, *I'll need a rapid means of egress from this perch. The police could easily track me here to my gondola lair. If only a zeppelin airship could dock atop the beacon tower and snatch me away in that case.*

A fresh storm of angry tapping at the glass. Two falcons at it now, both trying to chase her from their perch.

"Or just maybe," she said aloud to the birds, "the both of *you* might be put to use."

At which words the falcons keened and swept shrieking out of sight.

38

"Joey B?"

Joseph Bonaventure didn't want to turn his head, didn't want to acknowledge whoever it was that had just approached him from behind. Early morning, and he'd wandered from his apartment, too keyed up to sleep after last night's encounter with James Cypriano and Fay MacConnell and the crowd at the Haven Brothers Diner. He'd roamed the heights of College Hill, then descended to South Main and finally seated himself on the embankment by the College Street Bridge on the lip of the Providence River. The stone was wet with dawn damp. But it felt good to sit with his legs dangling just above the water and nothing to disturb him and no one for company save a pair of pigeons on the grass.

Again the voice behind him, tentative, uncertain. "Joey B?"

Somebody from the diner last night must have posted a photo of him on Instagram or Facebook. *Now word must be out all over the state: lead singer and cofounder of Fox Point Punks is back in town after many years away.* He quailed, silently berated himself. *Why did you ever come back to Rhode Island, you idiot? Did you really think you could outrun your past?*

A third time. "Joey B?"

Your past isn't going to go away. May as well meet it head on.

He turned, tried to say "Yeah that's me," but the words came out strangled.

Yet whatever he voiced seemed enough to encourage the interloper, who promptly sat on the embankment beside him. The pigeons politely *roo-rooed* in greeting and bobbled aside to make room. Joseph Bonaventure said nothing, didn't move.

The newcomer patted the rough-hewn perch. "Whew. Stone's wet. Kinda chilly." Bonaventure started to say "Well go find someplace drier nobody's making you stay" but just managed to dial back the snub. He told himself *Make eye contact with the guy, that's what Doctor Cartwright would like, let whoever it is ask for an autograph, get the thing over with.*

Beside him sat a thin, stoop-shouldered teen. Pale, narrow face; wispy curls of a goatee, unshaven stubbled chin. Eager, agitated eyes.

Across the teen's lap rested a skateboard. The kid wore a bulging zipped-up hoodie. The bulge squirmed and beneath the boy's chin emerged the head of a diminutive white Chihuahua. "This here's Cheddar. I found her under a food truck at the place I work. Or the place I *was* working. I'm kinda AWOL right now. 'Fraid I'm screwing up in that department."

Bonaventure grunted "Uh-huh" and asked if he wanted an autograph.

"Autograph? No, no. I just wanted, I mean, I just thought it'd be cool if I could tell my pals not only is Joey B back in town but I've actually seen him and I've been hanging out with him a little. And here I am. Here we are. This is so *awesome.* I mean wow." His eyes shone.

Bonaventure said "Uh-huh" again. He was pursuing a chain of thought that had weighed on him all night, didn't want this interloping kid or anyone else to keep him from his thought. *Robert E. Howard. Did he have any idea, when he pulled the trigger on himself back in 1936, that he'd end up as a lizard? And what's he doing now, swimming around in the Providence River? What's this afterlife of his like? Is he trying to make up somehow for the mess he made of things? Is there any hope of doing so as a reptile? And how does he survive these days? How does he get by? What does he snack on? Where does he sleep?*

The kid was saying something. "I mean wow. This is something. The two of us, sitting here, hanging out. Whoops, I mean the three of us. Sorry, Cheddar. Hey do you mind if I take a selfie, get us all in the picture?"

Bonaventure said sure, roused himself to a six A.M. smile for the photo.

"*Whoo.* Thanks, man. So cool. You know I gotta say and no offense but you look a little different from your old publicity shots. I mean the long hair's gone and now you're wearing a tweed coat and I don't remember you in anything like that from your days with the Punks."

That made the man's lips twitch. It was not a happy smile. *Yeah,* came the thought to Bonaventure, *my wear-it-everywhere-these-days tweed jacket. The tattered shreds of my career as a would-be scholar. Also a pathetic attempt to cover up my tats and my whole Bacchanale past.*

Aloud he said, "Do you have any suggestions for what an iguana might like to eat?"

"An iguana? Wow. Do you own one?"

Bonaventure explained no he didn't but he thought he'd seen one recently swimming in the Providence River.

"Wow. That's awesome. But how'd it get in there? Did its owner flush it down the toilet or something?"

"Well yes maybe in a manner of speaking. The owner who did that seems to have had a habit of flushing things or tossing things in all kinds of strange ways."

Bonaventure had caught the teen's interest. "Iguana diet. Let me google that." The kid pulled out his phone. "Website here says mostly herbivore. Tree leaves, vines. Flowers. Fruit." He scrolled down the site. "They eat algae. Green algae. Red algae. Growing on rocks under water at the bottom of the ocean."

Bonaventure said he didn't have any algae on him, or for that matter any flowers or fruit or vines. "Which is too bad, because I just had this impulse, and I get this way sometimes, but I just had the feeling I wanted to toss some food in the water for the iguana as a gesture of solidarity in case he happened to come swimming by this part of the river."

"Hey. Hey. I forgot." The teen reached inside his hoodie, extracted a Dunkin' Donuts bag. "On the way down here I picked up some food for breakfast. The website says iguanas have a certain amount of flexibility when it comes to their diet. Lemme show you what I bought. Two doughnuts, a chocolate glazed and a Boston cream pie. Plus a butter croissant. Which do you think would be healthiest for an iguana?"

"I'd go with the croissant. But don't give it the whole thing. Not sure how its digestive system will handle it."

The teen said he'd break it in half. "That way we can give half to Cheddar. Who happens to love butter croissants."

They took turns breaking off bits of the bread and tossing them in the water. "Gesture of solidarity," exclaimed the kid. "Cool. Now we just gotta keep our eyes open and see if we can spot the iguana that escaped from its toilet flush." In the morning mist they watched the crumbs float on the river and spiral as if breathed on by ascending ghosts of stream and brook.

Penitent seraphs, came the thought from last night's talk at the diner. *Desirous of throwing themselves back into the purgatory of our world, of joining us in our exile, in hope of doing good. On this Earth do we get a crack at second chances? Is there such a thing?* He prayed it was so.

The kid had just said something that caught his drifting attention. "Sorry," he apologized. "Could you say that again?"

"Sure. I was just saying my Aunt Janey was a hundred per cent right. She says if you meet Joey B in person you'll see he's a really decent dude. And she's right. I mean here I am barging in on you at six in the morning and you don't even mind."

"Aunt Janey? As in Janey Evans? Then you must be Augustus Tessario."

"Yeah. That's me." Pride in being identified battled with confusion in his expression. "But you can call me Gusto or just Gus."

"Gus Tessario? A lot of people have been worried about you. Worried sick. Your aunt texted me the other day, told me you might come looking for me. Says you ran away from Safe Anchorage. Not to mention quitting Guild Metal without telling anyone. Where are you staying these days? Are you out on the street?"

"Well, no." The teen looked as if he was trying to project self-confidence. "I found myself a *new* anchorage. High-rise, high profile, even if it's a secret place." He looked as if he wanted to share forbidden information, then restrained himself. "And in fact I even already got a new job offer. And truthfully it could be a fantastic meal ticket for both Cheddar and me."

The ex-musician said Gusto really ought to text his aunt. "And I mean pronto. Do it right away. Like now."

"Oh. Okay." Obediently Gus Tessario tapped a message to Janey Evans. As he did so he watched Bonaventure, who sat rubbing a diminutive glass flask between forefinger and thumb. Inside the flask lay a withered insect husk. Gus asked what kind of thing was that.

"I call it my bad-luck charm."

"Bad luck? Why keep it then?"

"Because it reminds me," said Bonaventure, "of what happens when the meter on your internal hope-gauge, and we all have one inside us whether we know it or not, when that meter drops to zero."

Gusto asked what happens then.

"What happens then is you roll over onto your back, your six legs curl up, you get immobilized, can't budge. Gotta avoid that. See what's inside this little flask? It's a beetle. Named Melville. He got discouraged too."

"Oh." More tapping at the phone, and Gusto announced he'd sent the text to Aunt Janey as requested. He suggested breakfast. "You want the chocolate glazed or Boston cream pie?"

The grad student said he'd go with chocolate glazed.

"You got it. Meanwhile I'll feed the other half of this croissant to the doggie."

Bonaventure essayed a melancholic nibble of his doughnut. Cheddar wolfed whatever she could get of the croissant. Gus Tessario enthused—between bites of the doughnut with the Boston-cream-pie filling—about a plan he had. "Something I've been wanting to run by you ever since I heard about you showing up in Providence. We could sponsor a homecoming gig to welcome you back to Rhode Island. Treff Boudreau, him and his Raptors, they're a tribute band and they already play all your hits anyway. They could be your new version of the Fox Point Punks for Joey B's comeback tour. We could set up as many concerts as you want, I know you don't sing anymore but truthfully all you'd have to do is show up and hop on the stage a second to take a bow and let the fans go crazy. They'd love it. Guaranteed."

"Let the fans go crazy?"

"Sure. I've been thinking about this, planning it all out. I even made up a new song for your comeback. I call it 'Providence Blue,' in honor of the city's metal termite. Did I tell you I met it in person so to speak? A super kick-ass experience. The song starts like this:

I'm a pest
And I'm out of control
I'm big and I'm blue
And I'm just on a roll.

"What do you think? Does it have potential for a gig? I mean like you and me, up there on stage together, singing in honor of Providence's bug?"

"Sure, sure." But Bonaventure had scarcely heard. "Speaking of fans going crazy. When the Punks were in their prime, we used to insist on having our agent list all the perks in the contracts for our gigs. A ridiculously detailed list, let me tell you. Max the manager, he loved Heinekens, so he'd stipulate four six-packs had to be delivered and waiting exclusively for him as soon as we showed up at each club. Ice-cold, they had to be. The contract said so. One time in Vegas the beer arrived warm and he threw a can at the setup crew. The lead guitarist had a thing for Jack Daniels so two bottles had to be purchased by our hosts and set aside to fuel him through the evening. Our keyboardist Nuke Newcomb was obsessed with jalapeño Doritos, so two thirty-six-ounce bags would be waiting for him on arrival and he'd eat his way through both bags on stage between numbers. Me I never ate before a show so I was always starved by the time we finished for the night. At the time I was crazy about quarter-pounders, so the contract said at one A.M. sharp I had to be supplied with hamburgers and cheese plus onion rings and those ice cream parfait concoctions that come with chopped-up Reese's peanut butter cups on top. Anyway a bunch of groupies would hang around outside the door and I mean they'd be waiting there for hours and these girls would pay ten bucks to the delivery guy so they could be the ones to bring me my quarter-pounders and whatever. But mostly they just wanted to make out and I was happy to oblige."

"Dude," gasped wide-eyed Gusto. "You guys were awesome."

"No, we weren't awesome. We were assholes. You get fussed over and fawned over, it goes to your head. Does bad things to your ego. Hell what am I saying. Does bad things to your *soul*. But none of that would have mattered, I mean really it would've signified zilch, we would've been nothing more than rock-and-roll mediocrities like a zillion other self-important mediocre bands. Except for this one thing. Max the manager, he insisted on pyrotechnics on stage to make us stand out. Sparklers, little rockets, fireworks right inside the club. Didn't strike me as particularly safe but I never cared about it enough to check with any fire inspectors or anyone like that ever.

Like everyone else in the Punks I was too focused on the perks and the groupies that loved to cling to us."

He broke off bits of the doughnut and tossed them to the pigeons. They *roo-rooed* in gratitude and nibbled up the food.

"So the night of the Pacific Bacchanale we're up on stage and all I had to do, I mean man all I had to do, was look overhead and I would've seen the ceiling tiles were Styrofoam or some other cheap plastic, I mean how is *that* going to withstand melting if you set off fireworks? But I never gave it a thought and then we had the fire and I panicked and got in this scramble to find the frigging exit door."

Gus offered him what was left of the Boston-cream-pie doughnut. Bonaventure didn't notice, kept talking.

"I shouldn't have been one of the first out that door. I should have stayed behind to help other folks get out. They were our fans, they were the ones who paid to see us Punks. Now, I know my bandmates were just as bad, they ran for it too just like me, but that doesn't make what I did any better. Later they said shit like 'What are you moaning about dude get real it's every man for himself in this world.' Max the manager said 'I had to save my own ass man no time to worry about anyone else I sure as hell don't feel bad about it.' Well that kind of thinking might have been good enough to excuse *them* but it most definitely doesn't work for me."

"My Aunt Janey says—" But Gus Tessario wasn't given a chance to finish his sentence.

"Turns out cheap plastic ceiling tiles melt fast in that kind of heat. Dripped right on my face. The sound of the flames, the crackle in that confined space, I still have dreams about it."

Gus tried again. "My Aunt Janey says when you have bad memories the trick is to do new things and fun things so you can swap out good memories for bad."

"Fun things." Bonaventure rubbed the puffy scar on his jaw.

"If you did a comeback tour with Treff and the Raptors and me it would be a kind of do-over."

The ex-musician went silent. *Do-over. Comeback. Penitent seraphs, seeking entry to our world, to join us in our exile, willing to dive down through the flames to undergo the purgatory of the Earth. Asking for a second chance after having screwed things up in heaven.*

"Joey, I won't bother you with that anymore. Sorry. I'm a jerk for asking. But there's one more thing on my mind and I really need someone to talk to now that I've skipped out from my halfway house. Do you mind if I run this by you for just one second?"

Bonaventure grunted abstractedly. The teen took this for assent and gladly started talking, glad for even the slightest semblance of attention. But in truth the older man was absent. What sat beside Augustus Tessario for the moment was no more than a shell of merest flesh.

"See, I got this job offer, I got it from someone I'm not supposed to say her name we're just supposed to call her the Baroness. She's also the one who found me a place to crash in a room with a real high-rise view. I'm supposed to keep that secret too but everyone knows the place, it's the most famous building downtown. Anyway. The Baroness says she can get me a job as a security guard, it's steady work, even comes with benefits, health care, which would be good cuz truthfully my health these days isn't all that great, I haven't been taking care of myself, which I know I should. But what I like best is this security guard job would be in a museum on College Hill and she says she'd make sure I'm assigned to the floor that has the Egyptology gallery. Which is cool, cuz I've always loved Egyptian stuff ever since I was little and watched *Tomb Raider* movies over and over. And the best part is the Baroness says she'd fix it so I can bring my doggie to work every day. Says the group she represents donates so much money to the museum that if she tells the museum staff Cheddar's a working K9 guard they'll just say okay."

He paused to let the Chihuahua lick cream-pie filling from his fingers.

"So Joey you're probably thinking 'Hey what's the problem? Dream job, dream work setting: go for it.' But here's the thing. The Baroness knows I'm in rehab, knows I skipped out of Safe Anchorage. But somehow when she talks to me, and lately she's been talking to me a lot, even though she's got dozens of people working for her and living in old empty offices up in the Superman ... whoops, not supposed to talk about that. Anyway when she talks to me somehow she always brings the conversation around to dope. Apache, redrum. China girl, China white. Asks me about the forms of fentanyl and would I please go online and look up its chemical composition, where to buy it, shit like that. Exactly the stuff my counselors at the

Anchorage were helping me not to do. I mean I know I can keep it under control and it's just research and completely hypothetical but all the same the way she talks and the things she asks me to think about, it gets my mind going in ways that are kinda scary."

Bonaventure was turned away from him feeding the last of his doughnut to the pigeons. Gusto persisted through the man's silence.

"Course that's what it's always like talking to the Baroness. Exciting, but a little creepy. I'll tell you who she reminds me of. Few weeks ago Safe Anchorage had a group therapy session, co-ed, with gals from the women's shelter on Empire Street. Most of them getting up there in years, worn-out looking, but one my age, maybe just a little older, kinda cute with amazing big green eyes. First group session we were in together when it comes her turn she introduces herself by saying 'Hi I'm Candy or that's what they called me in my New York City days. Now I'm an ex-heroin-addict, uh, but they say "ex" and all that means is I don't happen to be injecting today and as for tomorrow who the hell knows. But if by addiction you mean is it on my mind then I'm here to tell you oh yeah 24/7.' And as soon as she spoke I said to myself 'Oh honey you've nailed it that's how I feel too every single day' and I knew we had something in common. So on the sly for a week or so we started dating. Which consisted mostly of sitting together in a coffee shop in the Arcade on Westminster."

The man he was talking to stared down at the water, seeing flames. Into the momentary silence the grad student offered a perfunctory "Uh-huh uh-huh." But Joseph Bonaventure wanted to be alone again with his own broodings. Just him and his thoughts.

Gus Tessario chattily pushed on through the silence. "So the point I'm getting to is this. One afternoon the week before I ran away I'm sitting in the Arcade coffee shop with Candy. I'm wearing a T-shirt, no jacket, cuz it's so warm outside. All of a sudden she takes me by the hand and turns it palm up and bends over it like she's a fortune-teller or something. But then she runs her fingers up my arm and says 'I love your veins the way they bulge so big sweetie I'd love to shoot you up.' And this is coming from a heroin addict who's trying to quit, or at least she's supposed to be trying. All this talk about shooting me up. *Brr.*" He shuddered. "Creepy and tempting at the same time. Well it's sorta like that with the Baroness too. All this talk about China white and China girl. Things I shouldn't be thinking about." He shuddered again, patted Cheddar's head repeatedly. The dog looked at him with anxious eyes and licked his face.

"So here's where the advice part comes in, Joey. Some days I feel like the Baroness is just using me, I should get outta her orbit, leave the building where I'm squatting, say no to her job offer, get away from her constant fentanyl talk. Other days I say nah, why throw away a fantastic offer when I love the thought of working in a museum. What do you think? Should I take the job?"

Between forefinger and thumb Bonaventure rubbed the flask with its dried beetle husk. *You roll over on your back, your six legs curl up, you get immobilized and can't budge. You're in purgatory, in flames, no way out.*

"Joey? Should I take the job?"

"Huh? Yeah. Sure. Go for it. Take it."

"Thanks." Gus Tessario smiled with relief, said he'd been having such trouble making up his mind it really made him feel better to ask a guy whose opinion he respected like Joey B. He said he'd head off now to the Baroness' lair and tell her "Count me in."

The companionable scavenger birds that had been bumming doughnut crumbs looked from one human to the other on the embankment as if to ask "Are you two sure this is a good idea?" But neither human was paying sufficient attention to the pigeons.

Gus scooted off happily on his skateboard, arms wrapped around his Cheddar.

Bonaventure's fleshly shell stayed seated on the stone. As for his soul: that was another matter. It lay flat, rolled over on its back. Six legs curled up, immobilized, in flames.

39

She was one of the smaller museum guards employed by the Rhode Island School of Design. But she wore with pride the blue knitted vest with its logo that read "Pinkerton Security Systems." She did her eager best to keep up with the person with whom she partnered.

She stood ten inches tall at the shoulder. Her legs were a bare six inches in length, which meant she was always scrambling not to fall behind. Much easier to be carried, but as her partner explained this wasn't always possible.

Her tail curled when she was cheerful and drooped when she was scared. Which was often. Many, many people clogged the halls, unfamiliar scents. Strange large faces stooped over her, peered and showed their teeth. Again, unfamiliar scents. But after three days on the job she realized the hallway faces were friendly and her tail no longer drooped.

Speaking of scents. It was easy to keep track of her partner-human, because his pockets bulged with treats. His Pinkerton jacket, his Pinkerton pants: they contained mini-bags of popcorn, fragrant Slim Jim meat sticks, and sometimes—in a nod to health—sliced apples. Pick him out of a crowd of hundreds? Easy, as long as he smelled so good. No worries: she'd never lose her man.

Day-shift labor, as best she understood it, consisted of following him from gallery to gallery while he checked on visitors, "just so you and I can make sure," as he explained, "that everyone behaves." She knew about good behavior. Guests would see her with him both in uniform and smile—"Look it's a K9 squad"—and she would wag her tail. She took pride in fulfilling her responsibilities.

Other times her partner posted himself in one particular room—"the Egyptian gallery, my favorite"—and she'd flop on her side and take a rest. Being shorthaired, she was generally cold. So in the mornings she positioned herself to lie in the sunspot cast by the fan-shaped eastern window overlooking Benefit Street. It let in good warm light.

She wondered why her human liked this room so much. True, there were faint intriguing whiffs of unguent and gummy resin from the mummified things behind the glass. But she could tell the wrapped ibis and baby crocs were too dried up to chew. And she couldn't understand his exclamations about canopic jars and sarcophagi, yet he smiled and sounded happy. So if canopic jars did that for him it was good enough for her.

As she lay on the sun-touched wood her nose twitched contentedly, tracking her popcorn-and-Slim-Jim human. Idly she remembered where she'd once been: Guild Metal. A place where she'd had to cringe in the parking lot trying not to be run over by delivery trucks while hoping for the merest scraps of food.

She knew the RISD museum was much better. Cheddar the Chihuahua liked her place of work.

Three days passed like this. Put on a Pinkerton vest, just like her partner. Report to work, just like Dad. Roam the halls, sleep in sunspots. All in all not bad.

Best part: nighttime, camped out together in an empty office, high, high up in a building he said used to belong to Superman. They curled up side by side in a sleeping bag and gazed down on the city's lamps and flares. Along the river the lights on a police launch and its radio mast winked red and blue.

Three days passed like this. Three days can be a good rich lifetime, for a dog or for a human, if one spends them well. Spends them to build rhythms, habits, routines to get one past the terrors that crouch waiting in one's path.

She spent them with her dad. Report to work, sleep in sunspots, roam the halls. Her nails clicked on the pinewood. All in all not bad.

But the fourth day at work was different. Began with disruption in routine, which she didn't like. Followed by things that went from scary to much worse.

"Change of hours today," he told her. "Instead of morning and afternoon, you and I are doing the evening shift, four-thirty to midnight. Orders from the boss."

As usual they spent most of their time in the Egyptian gallery. Which was okay, except there was no sunspot. The light had already retreated from the eastern window. She paced about looking for someplace warm to rest.

The museum closed, leaving only the two security guards: the K9 and her human.

Darkness drew in, spread through the room. The mummies lay wrapped in their shrouds. She felt cold.

Colder still when the boss suddenly came through, a woman he called the Baroness. Cheddar had seen her once in Superman's building, had politely beseeched her then for a treat or snack by sitting up on her doggie hind legs while fixing her with a big-eyed hungry-puppy entreaty (which had proved effective with the RISD public). Yet big-eyed puppy had scored zero with the boss in Superman's lair and scored zero again tonight. The woman flicked a glance at Cheddar, then looked away without a smile. Some humans were simply dense and crass, and among them was the boss.

The boss was saying something now that clearly took her human by surprise. Something like "You've been working hard and you deserve a break. Go ahead, take the night off. It's Saturday night and there's a Riverglow show, you can sit by the water and watch the boats."

He didn't seem to care for the offer, didn't care for the break in routine any more than his Chihuahua did. He protested, said he was fine, said the routine helped keep him steady, said he didn't need time off. His dog supported him with an anxious panting whine.

The Baroness overrode him. Four other humans appeared beside her, two female, two male, young folk, all wearing collar pins printed with a cluster of letters. She announced abruptly "We five are going to hold a private meditation séance with this gallery's canopic jars. You're no longer useful here."

Cheddar didn't understand the words but certainly caught the feeling that flooded Gusto's face: being rejected, cast aside. The K9 knew all about that, knew precisely how that felt. She whined again.

Her human made a try at standing his ground. "But I've got this job to do. I'm supposed to stay in place."

Cheddar saw the boss respond at first with a flash of anger. "Job? I said you're no longer usef—" But then the Baroness' expression altered, softened. A cute crinkling of the nose, and then the woman purred, "Gus, look what I've brought for you." She handed him an envelope that was taped and tightly sealed.

Almost odorless, was Cheddar's first impression from where she crouched by Gusto's ankle. No, she could smell something after all, something faintly sweet. *Perhaps sugar?*

He turned the packet over in his hands. Fresh feelings flicked across his face as the Chihuahua watched him from below. Fear, then greedy longing, then horror. He tried to hand it back, but feebly.

The Baroness stepped away, shook her head, crinkled her nose again and smiled. "No, you keep it. It's a special present just for you. China white. Redrum. TNT. Just for you."

A last flounder of refusal. "I've been trying to stay sober. I've been doing good."

"One night off won't hurt you." She coaxed him with a smile that dazzled. "Go ahead. China girl. Apache. Just for you."

Gus Tessario licked his lips. His breath came quick and hard. The envelope trembled in his hands.

No more words. He scooped up the Chihuahua and stuffed her inside his Pinkerton jacket and hurried from the museum.

Night air. A warm evening. She jounced inside his jacket as he hurried down the hill. He trembled and she didn't know why and this made her increasingly uneasy. She wanted to be indoors and home with him, the two of them in the sleeping bag gazing out over the city lights below.

Instead he stopped when he reached the river. "Hey Cheddar remember this place? College Street Bridge. We hung out here on the embankment not so long ago with Joey B. Seems as good a place as any. What the hell."

He lowered himself awkwardly to the stone, sat legs dangling much as he had the other day. Yes, she remembered. But she still wanted to be home with her partner in their lair in Superman's building. A low whine, and she reached up from within the jacket to lick his chin and let him know how worried she was by all this strangeness.

"Hey. Hey. Relax. Chill out." Giddy laugh. "We're gonna have a party. Just you and me."

From downriver came the sound of crowds. Flames crackled from nearby braziers. But the Riverglow action was some distance away and here by College Street all was quiet.

"I've got treats for both of us," he giggled. Again she gave his chin an anxious lick.

Anxiety which was assuaged—at least for a bit—with a Slim Jim sausage stick. He freed it from its plastic and offered her the whole thing.

Joy! Escape from worry! Happily she chewed away.

So happily in fact she paid no heed as he unwrapped his own treat and with unsteady fingers tore it from its packet. She didn't remark the faint sugar smell or see him pop a tablet in his mouth.

She chewed her Slim Jim and didn't notice as his voice slurred and tapered to a stop.

She chewed and didn't notice as his head lolled and his gaze blanked with drowsiness.

She chewed and didn't notice as his breathing slowed and heartbeat faltered.

Didn't notice till he sagged and rolled and plopped into the water.

Taking his Chihuahua with him.

Fright.

She paddled, gulped water, tried to scrabble free from within the jacket.

Panic.

His weight carried her down with him deep within the river.

Terror.

She licked his face to revive him. No good.

Smothered.

She tried to swim, escape, kick up to the surface.

But she was tangled with him, and with him she sank drowning in the gulping murk.

40

"Where's Gussy?"

Joseph Bonaventure had almost talked himself out of attending tonight's Riverglow, precisely because he knew he'd be asked this question—and because he also knew he lacked an answer. For the past three days he'd been mired yet again in his all-too-familiar slump, his mood, what he called (in a fit of self-mocking) his howling pit of melancholia. He'd done nothing on his dissertation, couldn't bring himself to look for new work of any kind, had kept his phone turned off so no one could reach him, had wandered the downtown streets on pointless ambles.

It hadn't taken much to trigger this latest onset of misery. In his aimlessness the other night he'd stepped into a restaurant on North Main, not to eat anything, he had no stomach for food, just to use the men's room at the back. As he left he'd chanced to see the restaurant's rear door and above it the usual sign that said in red neon: "Exit."

Exit—like the door he'd scrambled for the night of the Bacchanale. *Exit*—where he'd abandoned all the concertgoers, all his fans, and left them to the flames. "What are you moaning about dude get real it's every man for himself in this world." True, that's what his bandmates had said afterward to shrug off any blame. "Every man for himself in this world."

He grunted in response to the memory. A thousand times since then he'd pondered what he might have said in reply. "Well guys maybe I just don't want to be part of that kind of world."

Every man for himself. And yet wasn't that what he'd done to Augustus Tessario? He'd been so caught up with his own self-scourging thoughts that when he sat with Gusto by the College Street bridge he'd scarcely heard a word the kid had said. Hadn't Gus asked him for advice, something about a job offer of some kind? Instead of listening he'd left the kid on his own, left him to sort things out solo. *Every man for himself.* Bonaventure twitched his fingers, jammed his fists into his jacket pockets. *I am such a jerk.*

And now to top things off, fail to show up for Riverglow, leave everyone worrying what was wrong with him, leave everyone wondering if he'd heard from the kid? That had spurred him to a decision: *Show up like you're supposed to—that's what Doctor Cartwright would say—face the questions, answer as best you can, take the shit on the chin like you so richly deserve.*

"Where's Gussy?" This time Janey Evans tugged hard at his sleeve to get his attention.

He turned to face her. "I don't know. I just don't know, Janey. Sorry." He gave her what little information he could. How he'd been approached by her nephew a few mornings ago and had sat with him on the river embankment. How Gusto had had his dog with him, a creature to whom he was very attentive.

"Well, that's something," said Gus' aunt. "If he's still looking after the puppy he found at Guild Metal, then he hasn't completely gone to pieces."

Bonaventure confessed there wasn't much more he could offer. "He asked me for advice about a job opportunity. Said he wasn't sure he should take the position. Asked me what he should do. Afraid I wasn't able to help him much."

Janey Evans asked why was that.

Bonaventure stared at the ground a moment, then lifted his head and gazed straight at her. "Because I wasn't listening. Because I'm a grade-A shithead."

They stood on the dock on the west bank of the river, opposite the performance stage and the basin with its ring of twenty braziers. Twilight now, and the *Icarus* was moored alongside, loaded with wood, its crew ready to cast off. Astern in the gathering dark Bonaventure could see other Riverglow skiffs, the *Persephone* and the *Phoebus*. Sightseers ready for the night's show thronged the basin rim.

"And something else," added the grad student. "Something Gus said that I should've responded to, instead of sitting there saying nothing like I was brain-dead. Said he'd love to be in a comeback gig with me someday. Up on stage with Joey B." He shook his head in self-disgust. "Said he'd even made up a song he'd like to sing with me. Called it 'Providence Blue.' A duet in honor of the city's metal termite." Again he shook his head.

Janey asked if he'd ever be willing to do that for her nephew.

"If we can find him before he disappears off the face of the Earth, yeah. The least I can do. 'Providence Blue.' Good title for a tune, for a mood. Not that I have any skill left or the heart for stuff like that anymore. My stage days are done, *fini, terminado, kaputt gewesen.*"

"Joey!" Fay MacConnell waved to him from the *Icarus*. Beside her stood Jim Cypriano the Jesuit, Big Barb in her muumuu, Captain Linda in her pilot's cap. Plus some individuals Bonaventure didn't recognize. He suddenly realized: he had no strength left. No juice for dealing with people, familiar or unfamiliar, known or unknown.

Janey saw him looking. "Those are my friends from Guild Metal. Stubby Rattanak and Jorge Ramirez. Great guys. I'll introduce you. We'd better get aboard. The thing's about to start."

"You go ahead. I'm not up for much tonight."

"C'mon," urged Janey. "It'll do you good." She stepped closer. Strands of hair, dyed platinum blonde, gleamed in the light from a lamp on the dock. "Hey. I don't need no crystal ball to see you're not exactly at peak performance. But I'll tell you something confidential. My pal Barb always tells me 'Girlfriend when you feel down the best thing in the world is for someone to give you a kick in the ass. Failing that, a night out on the town.' And Riverglow's the best approximation of either. So how about it?"

He managed a smile. "You guys go ahead. I'll watch and cheer you on."

Now here was Fay, who'd just scrambled from the *Icarus* onto the dock. "Hey."

He gave her a listless "hey" in reply.

She said she'd been trying to phone him the last three days. "And I stopped by your place once or twice. But it's like you're never in."

I'm truly screwing up on every front, including with this gal I like so much. He almost said it out loud, told himself *It'll sound like shit if I come right out and say it,* fumbled in his mind for a response.

Janey saved him the trouble. "He's having an off night. Says he's gonna sit this one out, wait for us here. You *are* gonna wait for us, aren't ya, Joey? Cuz I want you to help me find Gussy soon's we finish with Riverglow for the night."

He nodded sure. Fay looked at him, said she'd pitch in and look for Gussy too.

He helped the *Icarus* cast off, tossed the crew the mooring lines. He watched the skiffs begin the lighting of the braziers. One stacked-up woodpile after another caught fire and lit the night. Even from this distance he flinched, staggered back from the sight of the flames. *Bacchanale. Exit. Disaster.* Bad memories crowded in. No, tonight was definitely not a good night.

Everything normal at first, a smooth-running Riverglow, no hitches, no glitches. Twenty braziers afire, music soaring and throbbing from loudspeakers, the crowd on shore happily clapping and hailing the show. As so often happened, enthusiasts joined the wood skiffs on the water. Kayaks, rowboats, tour boats, motorboats, all crowding as close as they could to the action, circling the ring of flames in the basin. Astonishing there were no collisions.

There. All the metal baskets were stocked full of logs and kindling. It would be a half hour till the wood burned down and needed replenishment. Bonaventure watched as the *Icarus* idled motionless just outside the basin, in the branch of the Providence River just north of the Francis Street bridge. Linda the skipper must be giving herself a break from navigating the circle of small boats in the basin.

A low rumble in the distance. Against the dark concrete walls of downtown's office buildings, from a tunnel there shot forth a tube of bright electric yellow rumbling on trestle tracks, the ten P.M. Amtrak train on its New York–Boston run. The skipper and everyone else on the *Icarus* hailed the night train as it passed. Linda liked to do that, always told her crew to wave. "Give the passengers a boost, tell 'em hello from Providence."

Which put Bonaventure in mind suddenly of Novalyne Price and how she'd written in her journal of taking the Greyhound bus from Texas, and then the last part of her long trip by train from New York City. Summer of 1936, gazing out the window no doubt as she reached Providence, just as tonight's passengers must be doing now.

And where was Novalyne at this very moment, after having risked transmogrification to journey through the cabinet and help the man she loved? Back from ancient Egypt? Maybe even at this very moment swimming in company with her Bob?

The thought nudged him from his reverie sufficiently to make him study the water hard. Could he possibly be granted another sighting, maybe of the two of them this time?

And that's when Joseph Bonaventure saw something alarming enough to jolt him from his gloom.

A launch of some kind, with twin outboard motors, entering the basin from the south. Painted black like a Riverglow skiff.

Except no Riverglow skiff ever bore a name like the one inscribed on this vessel's stern. *Yog-Sothoth.*

Yes, a jolt to the gut sufficient to lift him out of himself. What was Janey's prescription for melancholia? A kick in the ass. His lips twitched in a smile even as he watched in alarm.

The *Yog-Sothoth* slowed for a moment as it entered the basin and passed by the dock. This close up he could see its crew clearly. Most of them he didn't know. A dozen men and women, dressed alike in gray polo shirts and chinos, with lapel pins on their collars.

But two of the crew he did recognize. The young woman with the button that read "HPL was right," the night he'd tumbled from the canoe. Father Jim had mentioned her name. What was it? Alicia Wheatley. She'd acted then like she was in supreme command of something, and that was her manner now. *Admiral of a warship, going into battle.* She called out some order to the crew, and a half dozen of them scrambled to comply. One was someone Bonaventure knew, had briefly worked with. Alexander Finster. Also known as Tagger.

And Bonaventure noticed something else: the cargo carried in the stern of the *Yog-Sothoth.* A pair of bulky objects covered by a blue tarpaulin. His initial glance disclosed nothing more.

But then a breeze off the river flapped the tarp, gave a brief glimpse of the contents: two large alabaster pots, each topped with a curious stopper, one sculpted in the likeness of an Egyptian nobleman, the other shaped like the head of a hawk.

Canopic jars, he guessed, *from the RISD museum.* His memory flashed to what Dieter Konrad had said the other night in the Haven Brothers Diner. How two of the museum's jars—one jackal-headed, the other featuring a baboon—had been stolen in a "lizard heist" back in 1936. How Alicia Wheatley had visited the museum the other day to chat up an employee named Zahra Beheshti and expressed a strong interest in the remaining pair of jars. What were Dieter's words?

"Says if the four are ever reunited they'll have greater apotropaic strength or something." Yes; that was it.

Movement on the boat. Alicia Wheatley shouted something, sounded like "Cover those up." Two men hurried to snug the tarpaulin back in place. The alabaster was invisible once more.

Not hard to estimate what must have happened. Alicia had somehow acquired RISD's last two canopic jars, and to judge from the way she wanted to keep them under wraps, the acquisition had probably not been all that legal. *Now*, surmised Bonaventure, *she must be hunting for a guide to lead her to the cosmic gate where the other two jars are stored; and what better guide than the Vespertine lizard that had first stolen the artifacts under coercion by H. P. Lovecraft?*

No sooner had Bonaventure thought this than he saw more activity on the boat. Tagger stooped with the other crew members and lifted up something that had been stored in the bow. They lowered the thing over the side of the launch and held it from the top. That's when Bonaventure saw it clearly. A massive fine-meshed net.

They were trawling, in the Providence River, trawling in the midst of Riverglow. No innocent fisherfolk, these. What they had in mind was no ordinary aquatic catch.

And Bonaventure intuited at once what—or whom—it was for which they were fishing. Even as the kayaks and pleasure craft and rowboats struggled out of the *Yog-Sothoth's* way and the rowers yelled "Whaddya think ya doing with that net?" he jumped up and down on the dock to signal the *Icarus* his alarm. It took him a moment to realize he'd best phone Fay MacConnell.

He was still fumbling in his pocket for his smartphone when the *Icarus* came rushing from under the Francis Street bridge and back into the circle of the basin. Clairvoyance seemed in the air that night, for someone on board sized up the scene at once. As the *Icarus* neared, Bonaventure saw one of the crew members holding a gaff at the ready. Someone—it looked like Barb—raised aloft the long-handled boat hook and bellowed forth a challenge.

Perhaps not in time. Something splashed about in the water, directly in the path of the *Yog-Sothoth*. Alicia Wheatley shouted another order to her crew: "Catch it, don't let it get away!" Tagger and a half-dozen others stooped with the net, leaned out over whatever was doing the splashing.

The *Icarus* gathered speed and chugged up alongside the *Yog-Sothoth*. Just as Alicia's minions seemed certain of capturing their subsurface quarry, Barb bent over the *Icarus'* starboard gunwale and hooked the net with her gaff.

At once Tagger and his mates tugged hard to free the net. The gaff was all but wrenched from Barb's hands. She snorted defiance, yelled for help.

Fay sprang forward, grabbed the gaff by its long wooden handle. Then Stubby Rattanak and Jorge Ramirez and Father Jim: they too grabbed and pulled.

Victory for the *Icarus*: with one big tug, Barb and her friends yanked the net from the *Yog-Sothoth*. Yanked another prize too: Alex Finster. Unable to free his hands from the net in time, he tumbled overboard and fell face-first in the river.

He sputtered, gasped, and cursed. But he didn't have the chance to say much. Even as the *Icarus* backed away, its opponent vessel picked up speed. Alicia Wheatley gunned the motor and aimed her launch straight at the Riverglow skiff. The forgotten Tagger had to scrabble aside from the vengeful *V* of the oncoming prow.

Bonaventure heard Tagger shriek "Hey what about me?" But the Baroness seemed to pay him no mind, so fixated was she on ramming the *Icarus*.

Linda the *Icarus* skipper timed her next move well. At the last moment she swung the nose of her boat away. The *Yog-Sothoth* passed within inches but never struck its target. The Riverglow skiff rocked in the wake of the waves.

Alicia's launch swung about as if for another try. But instead of assault this time it sped off with reckless speed along the river, making for the mouth of the bay. Within moments it vanished from view. A sudden fierce *bang* in the distance—as if it had collided with something metal—and then there was simply the receding roar of the twin outboard motors as the *Yog-Sothoth* escaped into open water.

Joseph Bonaventure hadn't stayed to watch. Something else had caught his attention. For just as the *Icarus'* gaff had hooked the net and lifted it free of the water, he saw an apparition—no more than a glimpse—that glistened gray green in the murk. An apparition that had avoided capture by the *Yog-Sothoth*; a flash of red eyes from beneath the surface. Eyes that sought him out where he stood on the dock. Eyes that beckoned and signaled "Follow me." And then the entity swam away south, away from the basin, away from the crowds, in rippling undulations.

The ex-musician had done no serious running in years. Now he sprinted pell-mell enough for his soul to burst—*Gotta keep up, gotta keep up*—along the shore, past Confluence Point, out to the quieter reaches of the river. Still the glistening ripples, still in view.

Just before the College Street Bridge he saw what Alicia's boat must have struck. Two braziers were askew in midriver, their contents spilled and adrift. Logs, kindling, balled newspapers in plastic bags, all soaked in Duraflame lighter fluid, all ablaze on the water. To his panicked gaze the whole Providence River seemed on fire.

And then something else. For he arrived at the College Street bridge just in time to see someone seated on the embankment on the other side of the river. Just in time to catch sight of who it was: Gus Tessario and his Chihuahua. Just in time to see Gus' head nod and sag. Just in time to see teen and dog tumble into the water.

Which is when Joseph Bonaventure—failed musician, failed student, failed counselor for Gusto—remembered what it was the kid had asked him for help with. Trying to escape the temptations of dope. "Constant fentanyl talk. Gets my mind going in ways that are kinda scary. What should I do?" Now Gusto's plea came back. Now it all came clear.

But pretty much too late.

Bonaventure stood paralyzed in fright upon the shore. The river seemed alive with fire, a flickering of flames. It exhaled heat that singed his face, just like the hot ceiling tiles that had melted on his jaw. A confined roaring bowl of heat that promised endless pain.

Purgatory gaped up at him, opened wide its maw.

At that moment he saw something move under the surface. The dog, still struggling. *Alive? Still alive?*

That shook him free. Clumsily he leapt out and dove straight down into the purgatorial cauldron.

Murk. Cold. Confusion.

Nothing. No one visible. *Where are they?*

Then he saw, a bare arm's length away. Two corpses, sinking.

He kicked and swam to them. Not corpses, not one at least, not yet. The dog, tangled in the boy's jacket. Kicking, still struggling.

He tried to lift the two of them. Gusto was unresponsive. The teen sank down upon the failed musician, bore him down. The dog writhed, frantic, about to slip away. Hard to grip them, keep them together. Bonaventure had never done any lifesaving, didn't know what to do.

And then from beneath him a sudden buoyancy: two presences.

Two entities, that pushed up on either side of him. One with a studded spiky crest, the other of a yellow-orange hue.

They nudged and lifted the boy and the dog and steadied Bonaventure as they did this. They wriggled and heaved and with the human's help raised both castaways clear of the water.

Which is when he realized that a Riverglow skiff was alongside him. The *Icarus*.

Stubby and Father Jim hauled the dripping Augustus Tessario aboard and placed him in the arms of his Aunt Janey. Fay MacConnell scooped up the trembling Cheddar, who insisted before anything else on licking the face of her Pinkerton Security partner.

Gusto suddenly sneezed and blinked his eyes.

Bonaventure heard Janey Evans cry "He's alive my Gussy's alive let's get him to the emergency room" and it sounded like she was weeping. But from where he was, still in the water, the voice came from far away.

Fay leaned down and extended him a hand. He heard her say "Joey, are you all right?"

Yet before rising up he lingered. Still beside him, iguana and golden fish. They eyed him, understandingly, forgivingly, as their tails flicked in the murk.

Then many hands lifted him up and out and into the boat.

He gasped, panted, pointed back into the water. "See them? 'Dja see them?"

But the pair had already vanished up the river.

41

Ushers handed copies of the freshly printed program to all the guests as they entered.

Fay MacConnell didn't really need to look it over—after all, along with head librarian Nancy Clayton, she was co-organizer of the evening's event—but she reviewed the program anyway:

The Providence Athenaeum
cordially invites you
to an evening of entertainments both musical and literary:
Treff and the Raptors
playing some of Li'l Rhody's greatest hits
(featuring the mystery guest appearance of a newly rediscovered Son of Providence)
—&—
A discourse and discussion
of some serendipitously acquired (and psychometrically retrieved)
poetic fragments of
a celebrated 19th-century visitor to our very own Athenaeum
To wit, none other than:
Mister Edgar Allan Poe

"Not a bad turnout, Feef. Not bad at all." Coming from managing director Tristram Schaefer, this was high praise indeed. He nodded at her but quickly moved on. Clearly he wanted to greet and thank every donor and high-status sponsor in the room.

"He called you Feef?" Joseph Bonaventure was staying close beside her, darting nervous glances as he sipped a cautious cup of sparkling water. He was dressed the way he usually did, old jeans, faded shirt with a frayed collar (at least he'd washed it), and the same worn-out tweed jacket. Quite a contrast to the high gloss of the guests at tonight's festivities.

"Yeah. Feef, short for Fifi. Which my boss prefers instead of just calling me Fay. That's Tristram's thing. I indulge him. He's harmless." Fay was feeling good. It had been her brainstorm to have the Athenaeum host an evening that combined her Joey's music (she said "her" only to herself, she didn't want to spook him) with some selections from her psychographically dictated manuscript. Head librarian Nancy Clayton had OK'd the idea and then persuaded the managing director in turn. So if Tristram tonight wanted to call her Fifi or Feef or Fee-Fi-Fo-Fum that was fine with her.

To mark the occasion she was wearing the silver stud earrings that had first prompted the whole adventure. "Bob Howard the iguana would be pleased," murmured Bonaventure. Fay was surprised and happy he noticed.

"Joey B! My man. Senior Statesman of Rock! Lemme shake your hand." Treff Boudreau, insisting on selfies with Bonaventure. After which Treff asked if he'd mind posing for more selfies with Treff's band crew—"my Raptors"—and maybe providing an autograph or two.

Bonaventure said he wouldn't mind and sighed so softly no one save Fay was likely to have heard. He showed signs of exhaustion—*No wonder,* she thought, *after everything he's been through*—and restlessly he rubbed between forefinger and thumb a two-inch-long glass flask.

Treff Boudreau sat heavily beside him a moment. "Thanks, bro. Thought we'd open with your all-time fave. 'Queen of Diamonds.' You'll see I added horns. Trevor here plays a cool alto sax. Plus I decided to play it in E. That okay by you?"

The ex-musician shrugged. "Man, it's your gig tonight. Play it any way you want. I'm just taking up space in a chair."

Treff clapped him on the shoulder. "Listen. We're not done setting up. Still a shitload to do. Gotta talk to my lead guitarist. He can't tune his ax worth shit. Zero hour minus ten!" He hurried in a swirl of dreadlocks to the front of the room, where crew members were adjusting microphone stands and reverb amps.

"You sure you're gonna be all right tonight?" Fay knew she'd already put this question to Bonaventure a half-dozen times in the past hour, but she couldn't help worrying. So many people coming up to him, hailing him, exclaiming "Welcome back, Joey B!", saying "Awesome what a thrill to meet you in person." While all the time he kept his head down as much as he could, contemplating the dried beetle husk in the glass flask.

"Yeah. Sure. I'll be fine. I mean, for ninety-nine per cent of the night all I gotta do is sit and watch someone else do all the work. I just have to get up for two minutes and croak out this new number called 'Providence Blue.' With the help of the other member of my duo."

"You mean trio." Augustus Valerian Tessario sat on the other side of Joseph Bonaventure, cradling the Chihuahua who lay curled up within his hoodie. "Cheddar's gonna be up there with us. She'll make all the difference."

For the first time that night Bonaventure smiled. "You're right. She *will* make all the difference."

Sitting on the other side of Gus was Janey Evans. She interrupted their conversation to pat Cheddar's head and hug and fuss over her nephew, something she did at intervals of every five to ten minutes. She'd developed this habit ever since Gusto's safe emergence from the hospital.

While Gus talked with his aunt, Bonaventure turned to Fay MacConnell. "Sorry I'm not at my best. Just feels strange to be at a gig where they're gonna play my old numbers. Haven't listened to this stuff since, well, since the Pacific Bacchanale."

She wondered aloud for the umpteenth time whether organizing this event had been such a good idea.

He said it was all right really. "I mean it's a great fundraiser for the Athenaeum, isn't it? Plus maybe it's a way to take account of my own past and put it all away. Anyhow, ever since I jumped through that fire last week out by the College Street Bridge, nothing will ever seem so bad again." In a low voice he whispered—*not that he need worry about being overheard*, thought Fay, *not with the chatter of so many people in the room*—"I mean, Gus came back from the dead, and so did his doggie. That's what's most important. But I have to say I'll be glad when tonight's all done. Guess I'm not much for socializing anymore." He raised the glass vial to eye level, contemplated the beetle husk. "Melville here's got it easier. He gets to relax."

"If you consider it easier," riposted Fay, "to be stiff on your back for a hundred fifty years with your six legs curled up." At that they both had to smile.

Melville the husk made them think of the same thing at the same time, and both turned their gaze to the Egyptian Cabinet at the far end of the room. To mark the special occasion it had been brought out for display, complete with its sculpted columns, pharaonic sun-boat, and painted goddesses and gods.

"That's how it all started," remembered Fay. "You talked me into checking the cabinet's drawers. Otherwise we'd never have found Novalyne Price's journal."

"Not to mention finding Melville here. The guy who gave up in discouragement at the halfway point of his trek through that cabinet drawer."

As they reminisced—*amazing*, she realized, *how much has happened these past few weeks*—she surveyed the room to make sure all was in order. It was imperative that everything go perfectly. Her boss Tristram Schaefer was the conservative sort, had been reluctant at first—to put it mildly—to have the Ath host a combined raunch-rock-nostalgia gig twinned with a Poe poetry slam. He'd expressed doubt that anyone would attend, that a Joey B tribute band could possibly bring in any of the library's subscription members.

But Nancy Clayton, bless her, had sided with Fay, had said this would be a lovely fundraiser plus an opportunity to attract a fresh population of Athenaeum members. So Tristram had been won over, albeit with the caveat that if the event drew "the wrong kind of attendee" and anything was stolen he'd consider two employees culpable—Nancy Clayton, and "you especially, Fifi MacConnell, for coming up with the idea to begin with."

Well, so far, so good. They'd chosen the library's downstairs chamber as the venue—it was the largest meeting space in the Ath—and had decorated the room with Poe-themed memorabilia to provide ambience for the second half of the program. Rare volumes of the famous writer's work in display cases. A stuffed raven mounted on a wooden stand in a corner near the entrance, beside a flickering light display that flashed the one word "Nevermore" (which also did service as the Ath's nickname for the bird). Wall-sized daguerreotype portraits of the poet. (*As always*, reflected Fay, *poor Eddie looks defiant, despondent, dyspeptic.*) And—"just for general Poe-esque atmospherics," as Fay had said to Nancy—swags of funereal ebony cloth draped everywhere. Similar swags adorned the refreshment tables that beckoned with food and drink.

The two librarians had wondered what kind of response to the décor they'd get from attendees who showed up for the first part of the program. "Not very rock and roll," Nancy had fretted. But Treff Boudreau had set their minds at ease the moment he strode through the door. "Dig the black," had been the first words from his mouth. "Some kinda punk Goth flair. Cool." So on that score all was well.

And no one could complain about the turnout. Full house, every seat taken. Even Tristram was pleased. Subscription members, of course, who'd shown up thrilled at the prospect of learning about newly discovered poems of Poe. In their role as hosts, Fay and Nancy greeted attendees as they came through the door. Plenty of Riverglow volunteers: Barb and Captain Linda and Father Cypriano (who'd brought as his guest Reverend Gladys from First Baptist). Plus Stubby Rattanak, trailed by his day-shift workers from Guild Metal—assistant foreman Jorge Ramirez, along with Dree Duarte and Crazy-Chester Metcalf and the rest of the loading-dock crew. (They shouted "Hey how are ya?" at Gus Tessario, who let them feed popcorn to his Chihuahua. "Wasn't so long ago," said Stubby, "this little dog spent her time hiding under food trucks.") Gina and Tommy Deluca from the downtown diner were there. ("Miss a night of Joey B's music? No way!") And shortly before the show started, in walked Dieter Konrad in a freshly laundered flannel shirt, bearing—impressively—no trace of Haven Brothers ketchup. With him as his guest he brought fellow Peerless resident and rooftop watcher Zahra Beheshti.

Yes, a full house. In fact, however, twenty seats remained empty by the time Treff's Raptors were tuned up and primed to start. These seats were in a roped-off quadrant marked "Reserved for Premium-Access Sponsors." "Mega-buck donors," said Fay. "Strange they haven't shown up yet after paying so much to reserve twenty tickets."

Even stranger, she said, was that these premium-access sponsors had reserved seats at the very rear of the room farthest from the performers, in the corner where the stuffed raven stooped in brooding solitude by the flashing "Nevermore" display.

"Well, it's their money," shrugged Nancy. "They're still supporting the event whether they turn up or not."

She turned to Fay. "Ten minutes past the hour. Those premium people are probably going to be no-shows. Let's get started."

Fay waved at Treff to give him the go-ahead and sat beside Bonaventure. Stratocaster slung over one shoulder, Treff Boudreau bounded to the mike at center stage and bellowed, "We are apex predators, spin you on your head-ators: ladies and gentlemen, Rhode Island's finest tribute band, Treff and his fricking Rap-ta-tors." His guitar crashed out the opening chords of the song made famous by the Fox Point Punks, and the other Raptors joined in:

> Been hanging on this corner all afternoon
> Ain't slept so long look just like a junk
> I freeze every time I see a police car
> Cuz the cops got me listed as a wanted punk.
>
> Woman I need a home for tonight
> Nothing to my name but a hot Cadillac
> If midnight find me out on the street
> I'll catch a dum-dum bullet right through my back.

Half the crowd (the younger set) seemed to know the words. They sang each verse along with the lines bellowed out by Treff. Tommy Deluca, ecstatic, raised his arms and swayed them back and forth. His inked-in go-go girl waved her checkered flag.

> Girlie you look like the Queen of Diamonds
> Burning your cigarettes right down to the bone
> Don't know damn it if you even notice me
> Don't want to stay out here all alone.

Drums, bass, horns, sax. Lead guitar, rhythm; Treff Boudreau on vocals. Atop them the voices of a roomful of happy fans. They held up their phones and snapped photos of the band. Friends took snaps of each other and then turned again and again in their seats to see Bonaventure where he sat in the back and they yelled "Hey Joey B!" as they took snaps of him as well. He tried to smile each time—*senior statesman of rock*, with an offhand salute of acknowledgment—but Fay could see it was costing him.

Maybe if you take me I won't be so scared
My blood's still drying on my jacket sleeve
If you leave me here to fend for myself
Machine-gun wizards kill me right on the street.

Noise level: deafening. Nancy Clayton on Fay MacConnell's right frowned and made a face. Fay shouted in her ear "Dance club music. No choice but to play it loud."

To her left Joseph Bonaventure hunched smaller and smaller in his seat. He pulled and tugged at the sleeves of his tweed coat, pulled and tugged where the tattooed verses writhed up his arms. "Girlie you look like the Queen of Diamonds." Fay recalled the nickname she'd silently bestowed when she'd first spotted him on the Riverglow skiff: *Mister Twitch*. Well Mister Twitch was certainly at it now: *pull and tug, pull and tug*, as if doing so would hide the tattoos better.

The band sang the final stanza:

You wouldn't believe how bad I need a friend
Darling girl I don't see why it can't be you
You know one jaunty joker when the joker is wild
Could pair with a queen if she'd just deal him a try.

Mister Twitch persisted in twitching at his sleeves. *Pull and tug. Pull and tug.* She laid a hand on his arm, leaned in to him. "Hey." Louder. "Hey. It's all right."

End of number. The twitching eased.

Claps and roars from the enraptured crowd. Treff Boudreau—in what Fay always remembered later as a very handsome gesture—pointed with his guitar toward the back to direct the applause to Bonaventure, and the audience yelled "Joey B."

Bonaventure waved back weakly in thanks, turned to Fay and said, "Dopey stupid goofy lyrics. From a long time ago."

"The fans don't seem to mind."

"No, they never did." A melancholy smile. "Never did."

"Cool. That was cool," enthused Gusto to Joey's left. "But that last stanza's new, ain't it? 'You wouldn't believe how bad I need a friend': cool. But I never heard it before."

"I added it just last night," confessed the one-time star. "Kinda made it up on the spot and asked Treff to include it."

"Hey jaunty joker." Fay tapped her chest. "Here's one well-worn and somewhat crumpled queen that's more than willing to deal you a try."

Bonaventure looked back at her, blinked, swallowed with effort as if catching his breath. "That sounds good to me. Sounds good. Guess that makes us two of a kind." They sat and held hands as the Chihuahua scrabbled out from Gusto's hoodie to lick both their faces.

The Raptors played a few more Fox Point Punk oldies. Bonaventure had only one more comment for Fay—"Last time I heard all this was on the West Coast, the last night I ever played"—and she nodded to show she understood. By the time the final number ended, his face shone with sweat as if he'd been on stage himself all that time, but a no-longer-agitated Mister Twitch seemed more or less at peace.

"And now, for you discerning connoisseurs of rock and roll," warbled Treff Boudreau into the mike, "here's a dynamic duo who're gonna offer us a hot item entitled 'Providence Blue.' "

"You mean Terrific Trio!" Augustus Valerian Tessario stood up and held his Cheddar high. He turned to where Bonaventure still sat hesitant. "Come on, Joey." With one hand Gus cradled the Chihuahua, with the other he coaxed the rock-star senior statesman from his seat.

Claps and applause urged the trio to the front. Once there, they turned to Treff and his musicians. Treff Boudreau spoke into the mike. "Folks, we're just jamming up here, it's all improv, so I need to check with our guest vocalists to ask them what tune goes with their 'Providence Blue.' "

Bonaventure said he'd consulted with his partner, asked Treff if the Raptors knew the melody accompanying the refrain to something from the sixties by Eric Burdon and the Animals called "It's My Life."

"Shit yeah. Course we do."

Turned out the crowd did too. With snuffled accompaniment from the Chihuahua, Gusto and Bonaventure sang the two stanzas of the song:

Hey I'm a pest
And I'm out of control
I'm big and I'm blue
And I'm just on a roll.

Hey I'm a bug
And I'm feeling just fine
Cuz I'm spreading my wings,
And I'm learning to fly.

After the first round, Treff shouted "Now everybody," and then the pair led the audience in singing the stanzas, over and over and over.

And when they were done and took their bows amid the applause, Janey Evans shouted "That's my Gussy" and hugged Fay MacConnell and cried till her makeup ran. All of which gave Fay the feeling the evening's effort was worthwhile.

An intermission break—the rock and roll gear stashed away, a podium established up front—and then the second part of the night's entertainment was underway. Nancy Clayton stood to introduce the speaker.

Fay MacConnell sat in the front row during Nancy's introduction, breathed deep to calm herself. *Nerves a bit jangly but hey girlfriend that's understandable*, she told herself. Tristram and other boss-folks in the audience, all sitting in judgment. Uncertainty in her mind about how the Ath's subscriber-members would respond to the poems she was about to reveal. Even more uncertainty about the hard-core scholars who had shown up, a half-dozen specialists in Poe. From Yale, Harvard, Cornell. Brown too of course. Tristram had introduced them to her. Sterling Professor of this. Endowed Chair of that. Tailored suits, surprising amounts of jewelry, lots of unsmiling self-assurance. *Huh, so you guys are Edgar Allan Ravenologists*, she'd said by way of attempted feeble jest. She'd regretted it as soon as the words left her mouth. The look they gave her made her wilt as badly as Joey's beetle husk in that flask.

Hey at least I took the time to dress up a bit. Tonight she wore black linen trousers and a black linen jacket, paired with a white oxford shirt and a silk scarf colored black and violet. It made for a good contrast, she decided, with her cropped blonde mane. Earlier that evening as she'd dressed before the mirror in her Arcade micro-apartment she sang out to Dupin the cat (who'd been watching from the couch): "I seldom look this good so get an eyeful." That's when she realized *Hey I'm feeling all right. Keyed up, but all right.* Partly because of Poe of course, but also partly because of one Joey Bonaventure.

She sat now in the front row. Nancy was almost done with her introduction, was saying something about the exciting manuscript find and how the whole story had begun right here in the Athenaeum. Fay had sternly instructed herself to keep her eyes straight ahead and not to wriggle about to see how the people behind her were responding. (*Especially all those scholars.*) At the last second she gave in to temptation and turned in her seat just to check on how her Joey was doing. *Still in Mister Twitch mode or now more or less functional?* Head no longer bent, he actually looked right at her and smiled and gave a thumbs-up of encouragement. *Functional: yay!* She smiled back at him and touched the silver stud in her ear by way of private signal (what she silently identified as her "iguana wavelength") and then rose as Nancy invited onlookers to join her in welcoming the Ath's own Fay MacConnell to the podium.

In retrospect, Fay would say later, the first fifteen minutes of her talk proceeded perfectly before everything just went *smash.* Prior to her presentation she'd already decided to minimize the sensationalist truth of how she acquired these new verses, so she said nothing of having taken psychographic dictation from a transmogrified Robert E. Howard. *(Besides, they'd just think I'm nuts—something I'm half-convinced of already, or would be if I hadn't experienced all this alongside Mister Twitch.)* Instead she made quick cryptic references to the Ath's own Egyptian Cabinet, a suddenly discovered manuscript of verses, and the nineteenth century's vogue for psychometry.

"Suffice it to say," she added, "that the verses I'm about to recite constitute hitherto overlooked and unpublished poems of our own Edgar Allan Poe. And I think we're entitled to say 'our' because after all Poe came here frequently to this very Athenaeum when he was courting his celebrated fellow poet Sarah Helen Whitman."

Tristram Schaefer was beaming. The Ath's board members were all smiles. This was familiar stuff, after all, and none too weird. Romance, tragedy, high drama in the library where everyone now was sitting. The public loved it. The scholars were still unsmiling but at least they didn't seem offended. *So far, so good.*

She took a deep breath. *Here comes the strange shit.* "The poems I'm about to recite have reached us via psychometric transmission, whereby a great-hearted sensitive soul from the past conveyed sublime literary treasures to a like-hearted sensitive soul in the present."

The audience began to stir and murmur. *Psychometric transmission? Like-hearted sensitive soul? Who's this woman talking about anyway?*

No choice but to plunge on. She knew she was going to get in trouble with these poetic discoveries, but what was the alternative after all? Withhold them from the world? No, that wouldn't be right.

"These psychometrically transmitted verses I'm about to recite for you may seem a bit out of character for Poe, but he himself seems to have thought of them as pioneering a new vulgarian mode."

New vulgarian mode? The murmuring grew louder. She faltered, hesitated. Tristram Schaefer, ever alert to what might please his audience, darted glances right and left.

What would her dad have said? "Girl, in this world you gotta have moxie." Well, he was certainly right. With no further hesitation, she recited loud and proud the poems Bob Howard had transmitted via iguana wavelength to the silver stud in her ear. (She omitted the detail that Poe had improvised these verses while serving with fellow-Vespertine Bob in the third cohort of Rome's Valerian Legion.)

The Worm impels us 'cross the sandy wastes.
It doth choose our fate, it chews our face.
Condemned are we to die—some foreign place;
Condemned to drop and croak without a trace.

When Conqueror Worm next bars my way in deepest gloom
I'll ask it: Bear a message with this tune
Salute her when you're next within her tomb
My evanescent love, my Dom'na Thume!

The murmur swelled to tumult. The scholars had gone from unsmiling to indignant. She distinctly heard the word "forgery," delivered with a sneer. Oh how she longed to shout "This stuff's no forgery, I'm a Poe fangirl and I'd never fake it with him, besides Mister Twitch was there and he can testify."

But she never voiced such a defense because of the intrusion that scrambled the dynamic in the room. Down the staircase to the ground-floor meeting space came a gray-clad group, each member wearing collar pins that read "GGCG" and "HPL was right." With quiet confidence they filled the seats in the roped-off quadrant marked "Reserved for Premium-Access Sponsors." This was in the back corner of the room, near the table with the stuffed raven and the light display that flashed its mournful "Nevermore." Most of the newcomers she didn't know but there was one Fay knew for sure: Alicia Wheatley.

The surprise made Fay lose her train of thought a moment. But she wasn't the only one to show dismay. All the Riverglow volunteers were glaring at Alicia's gang, undoubtedly thinking the same thing that raced through Fay MacConnell's mind: *This Yog-Sothoth baroness has got her nerve, showing up here all nice and calm after trying to ram the* Icarus.

But the rest of the Athenaeum audience had no notion who she was, probably figured she was just one more wealthy donor. And the scholars were still quarreling over Poe, so she told herself to go ahead and recite another poem; this might be her only chance:

> Nasty cockroaches are we,
> with nasty cockroach teeth;
> We eat and we excrete
> Then die off on the street.

From murmuring to tumult to eruption: Fay was given no opportunity to recite further. "Nasty cockroaches are we," roared some scholar in scorn. "I'll stake my career Poe never penned such a verse in his life!"

"Granted," one woman replied (was this the Yalie? Fay had trouble telling them apart), "the poetic meter is ragged, and I'll warrant 'We eat and we excrete' never appeared in the canon, but another verse we heard a moment ago may have more claim to authenticity. 'My evanescent love, my Dom'na Thume': words like that might convincingly comprise a lost fragment from a work like his masterpiece 'Ulalume.' "

The scholar from Harvard, or maybe it was Cornell, said he found the argument unsound. Fay tried to resume but found herself wordless at the podium and forced to wait as the critics hashed things out.

Which gave her time to notice a development at the back. No one else seemed aware: the audience was watching Harvard versus Yale versus Brown. But the GGCG group was paying attention to someone else. (And she remarked that Alex Finster wasn't among them, *which makes sense,* she thought, *since Tagger was left in the river treading water when that speedboat made its escape.*) The entourage silently watched Alicia Wheatley, who was sitting with a book open on her lap—a small volume, antique, leather-bound, with pages that might well be of vellum.

But Alicia wasn't simply reading. Her lips moved in what seemed a recitation. She held her hands before her face and interlaced first her thumbs, then her fingers, after which she suddenly extended her arms to full length and directed both hands palm out so they pointed straight at Fay.

Whatever it was definitely hit Fay hard enough to make her stagger. She gripped the podium for balance, held on for dear life. Rapid blinking; short of breath. She could still see the action at the back, knew it was disturbing, knew she should cry out, but somehow lacked the strength to sound a warning. *And meanwhile everyone's just watching the scholars quarrel about "We eat and we excrete." The spell must be blanketing the room, for folks to be so oblivious.*

While the audience sat enraptured, Alicia got up and tiptoed to the table with the light display. She approached the raven that stood stuffed and upright on its wooden stand.

Fay tried again to shout. Her throat grew tight. She tried to move but swayed and lost her balance. Again she had to grip the podium, had to hold on hard. No one in the Ath audience seemed to notice.

Meanwhile one of the critics was saying something about how "The phrase 'Conqueror Worm' from tonight's recitation does in fact appear in an authentic verse by Poe embedded in his well-known tale 'Ligeia.' "

Now Alicia had picked up the stuffed bird, tucked it under her arm. A nod from her, and her GGCG entourage all rose and followed her as she headed toward the stairs.

Can't shout, can't speak. But there is one thing I can do. She closed her eyes and put all her strength into one thought: *Joey.*

She never knew if it was the iguana wavelength ear-stud that both of them had handled, but whatever the reason, Joseph Bonaventure suddenly exchanged glances with her, then turned around to the back at her wordless urging. He saw what was happening, gave a shout. "Hey that's our Nevermore—you ain't stealing that!"

Which was enough to break the spell. The room snapped alert. Riverglow volunteers rushed to the retrieval. The Baroness formed her entourage into a defensive formation to cover her own retreat. Stubby Rattanak led Jorge and the whole factory loading-dock crew in a charge that overran the phalanx: Guild Metal versus Gnostic Guardians. Crazy-Chester Metcalf and Dree Duarte grabbed folding chairs and swatted their foes aside.

Fay rushed around the melee and caught the retreating Baroness halfway up the stairs. She grabbed the woman's arm from behind and only then realized that the thief was carrying not one object but two: the stuffed Nevermore and the small leather-bound volume from which she'd been reciting. Fay glimpsed on the spine a one-word title. *Necronomicon.*

The librarian pulled on her opponent's arm, yelled for her to stop. Alicia yelled back, something to the effect of "I've got to find the cosmic gate and no one's going to stop me I've got to seal Yog-Sothoth against the incoming alien hordes." Even as she howled this, Alicia tucked both bird and book under one arm and with her free hand gripped Fay MacConnell by the throat.

Not much bigger or heavier than me, thought Fay, *but boy she's scary strong.* Alicia tightened her constrictor grip. Fay feared she might black out.

Just at that moment, a dash up the stairs by someone else, and a second person rushed at the Baroness. Through her choke-out blur Fay saw a slim young woman with a wild dark mop of hair head-butt the Gnostic Guardian in the belly.

The collision unbalanced all three and tumbled them in a tangle down the steps. At the foot of the stairs lay the long-lost *Necronomicon.* Nearby: the stuffed Nevermore, which had landed upright on its feet. Alicia Wheatley lay motionless and stunned.

The young woman who'd done the head-butt disentangled herself first. "Zahra Beheshti," she introduced herself as she helped Fay to her feet. "From Lahore. Now at RISD."

"Hey. Pleased to meet you." Fay complimented her on the tackle.

The two would have said more, and Fay would certainly have scooped up the book of black magic, but something unexpected intervened.

From the floor where the stuffed raven stood sounded a sudden *graaack*. "A cough," said Fay later on, "the kind of gasp anyone might make if they've got something stuck way down their throat."

Graaack again, from where the stuffed bird stood. Cautiously Fay stooped and picked it up, expected it to flap its wings, hop or fly about.

But no. In her arms Nevermore lay rigid, motionless, not at all alive. A product of some taxidermist. A stuffed bird, nothing more.

She turned it upward and bent close so they were nose to beak. Which was when she noticed the thing clenched within its mouth. Clenched fast, whatever it was. Unyielding, fixed in place.

Zahra helped her and the two of them eased the thing from the bird's closed beak.

Curled and rolled up tight, the thing. Sheets of paper. Faded ink. Handwriting that by now Fay recognized.

"A manuscript," thrilled Zahra.

Fay turned and called to Joey to show him the treasure they'd just rescued from Alicia Wheatley.

Speaking of whom. Fay realized they'd best secure their prisoner and pick up the volume of black magic stolen from the Ath by H. P. Lovecraft so many years before.

But when Fay and Zahra turned they realized two items had slipped away.

The Baroness.

The *Necronomicon*.

Fay and Zahra looked at each other, said the same thing at the same time.

"Uh-oh."

42

The night out at the Athenaeum was exactly what Zahra Beheshti needed.

She'd had another dreadful phone call earlier in the day with her mother. The usual: "How could you do this to us? The dishonor you've brought on our family, the shame. And all because you had to have your way and write your dissertation on that horrid heretic and *kafir* from five hundred years ago, what's his name."

"Prince Dara Shikoh, Mommy-ji. And he wasn't a horrid heretic. He was a freethinker and a pluralist, the kind of person our nation needs today."

Which had only made her mother angrier. "Our nation: Who are you to talk? You've made our family's name into a nationwide disgrace!"

"Nationwide" wasn't too far off: just today she'd received denunciatory emails from at least a half-dozen different locales within Pakistan. All showed fury with her for honoring a man who'd tried to reconcile the Muslim and Hindu populations of the Moghul Empire.

The worst of today's electronic fulminators had been some big-bearded mullah from Islamabad. He'd been harrying her with condemnatory *fatwas* for months. The fact that she was now living in American exile as a "refugee of conscience" didn't slow the man a bit. His email from this afternoon had striven to prove to three decimal places that "since as is universally known all Sufis everywhere are unbelievers and the unspeakable Dara Shikoh belonged to not one but two Sufi brotherhoods and since this diabolical prince monstrously claimed that spiritual worth could be found in the Upanishads and other non-Muslim scriptures of India, then it is manifestly clear that this idolater richly deserved the sentence of death to which he was subjected—a sentence to be applied to you too, O accursed of God, should you ever dare return to Lahore." She'd seen the blustering face of this fanatic once on a YouTube screen as he thundered a Friday sermon, and she could imagine with what satisfaction the mullah had typed up today's excoriation and complacently clicked on "send."

After this digital hot-acid assault she'd snapped shut her laptop in revulsion and taken the elevator up to the Peerless building's rooftop retreat. The downtown sky-high view calmed her, cleared her mind a bit. Quiet up here, no one about except for a pair of falcons (maybe the same ones pointed out to her by her neighbor the other day). Flapping and fussing they were, many stories above, as they dived at one of the upper windows in the nearby Industrial Trust Building.

The sight of those birds reminded her of a favorite excursion back in her girlhood days in Lahore. She loved to stand on the bridge over the Ravi River, would dawdle there for hours. Hot Punjabi sun and an offshore breeze that blew away the city's stink and haze. Below, black water-buffaloes, submerged to their eyes, cooling off in midstream. Above, pariah kites wheeled and rode midday thermal air-spouts in a slow helix in the sky. Neighbors derided these birds as scavengers of corpse meat (also scolded them for swooping down crowded alleys to snatch up a chapatti from a baker's bread display or a treat from a tiffin tin). But young Zahra exulted in their flight, studied them as they flew south-southwest along the river and disappeared from view. At home she consulted an old atlas, with her fingers tracing the Ravi's course to learn where the kites might have flown. The Ravi debouches into the Chenab, and the Chenab in turn merges with the great Indus River. Which in turn opens wide into the Arabian Sea. The child didn't know if her pariah kites ever flew that far. *Someday*, she dreamed as she stood upon the bridge, *I just might join them*. Little could the dreaming girl have known that one day the Indus and the Ravi would flow with her right into the Providence River.

In the midst of such memories both bittersweet and sad, Dieter Konrad had startled her by appearing at her elbow with a sudden last-minute invitation. "Rock and roll plus a Poe poetry slam, tribute to a Fox Point Punk local legend name of Joey B." She'd never heard of any Joey B but it all sounded so improbable, so American, she'd instantly said yes. *Much better than moping with my memories on the roof.* A last glance at the falcons still scolding at that upper window of the Superman Building, and she was off with Dieter Konrad resplendent in his gaudiest flannel shirt.

Watching the speaker Fay MacConnell up at the podium that evening, Zahra knew at once this woman was having a case of nerves but was nonetheless proceeding pluckily. Yes, very plucky this young Fay. And when the critics in the audience began carping, calling out "improbable" and "forgery," they reminded her of a row of jowly mullahs crying "heretic" and "*kafir.*" Zahra saw the speaker falter in dismay, felt indignation on her behalf. She longed to help this Fay, to be her friend.

So when someone yelped "Hey that's our Nevermore—you ain't stealing that," Zahra had no idea who or what Nevermore was but she did see Fay the speaker rush up the stairs to chase the thief. Which was more than enough to impel the impulsive Lahori to dash up the stairs after her and crash headlong into the miscreant. Only at the instant of collision did Zahra realize she knew this fugitive: Alicia Wheatley, who'd been so charming in chatting her up at RISD's museum. Who'd shown so much interest in the museum's two surviving canopic jars—the same jars that had mysteriously been stolen only a few days after their chat. As Zahra's head smacked into the Gnostic Guardian's midsection there came the thought: *This is what the locals call payback.*

And a moment later she was helping Fay to her feet and being introduced to Joey B and Janey Something and a host of other brand-new friends.

Amid this excitement Dieter Konrad approached from the refreshment table, his mouth engaged with an oversized pastry puff. Sugar dust and cream adorned his shirt. "Nifty job you did on the bird-snatcher," he complimented her as he extended a paper plate atop which three more pastry puffs lay piled. "You having a good time?"

Her eyes shone as she replied with a favorite Americanism. "You bet your ass!" Exuberantly she bit into her puff.

By now the raven-thief's gray-clad followers had long since scampered up the stairs and out the door, joining their baroness in her retreat. Two minutes after that, the police arrived, followed by news reporters and a TV broadcast crew.

Zahra saw Fay MacConnell look distressed. "Are you not feeling well?"

"Afraid my boss is gonna fire me. Before the gig he warned me I'd be the one to blame if this event attracted the wrong crowd. And now just look at the place. Broken chairs, fistfight on the stairs, plus the police and a hundred-per-cent guarantee the whole freaking mess will be on the eleven o'clock news tonight. Yeah, I guess you could say I'm not feeling well."

Before Zahra could decide what to say to offer comfort, Fay's boss strode up, followed by the head librarian. The Lahori saw her new friend stiffen, brace herself. Fay raised her hands in surrender. "I know, I know. All this was my idea. And now it's turned into a mess."

But Tristram Schaefer surprised both Fay and Zahra by enfolding Fay in an enthusiastic hug. "It's a mess, but a good kind of mess. No one got hurt. A few chairs broken, but who cares. The important thing is all the great publicity we're getting. Nancy tells me we're already trending on Twitter." Behind him the head librarian offered Fay and Zahra a big wink. "Look, look." He tapped at his phone. "See? 'Only at the Ath: Kick-ass mosh pit meets manuscript hidden in big-mouthed crow.' Actually a raven, but so what. Headlines like that, Nancy says, are just what we need to attract the younger generation. Six hundred likes in twenty minutes. Membership is going to go up, up, up. And it's all thanks to you!" He said Fay was definitely in line for a promotion and a raise.

An hour later, after the police and the public and the press had gone away, after the food had been eaten and the quarreling critics all dispersed, a quiet conclave of friends assembled in the Athenaeum's downstairs vault. Zahra Beheshti and Dieter Konrad. Tristram Schaefer and Nancy Clayton. Father Jim and Reverend Gladys. Atith Stubby Rattanak and Janey Evans, who both sat close beside Gusto and his Cheddar. All of them gathered around Fay and Joey B, who carefully unfolded the creased papers that had been stashed within Nevermore's beak.

"It's dated July 1936," announced Fay, "and it's in the handwriting of someone Joey and I have encountered before: Novalyne Price, a one-time Athenaeum employee and the close companion of pulp-writer Robert E. Howard. I suspect"—she grew silent a moment as she glanced through the sheets—"yes, I suspect the things written here are the last journal entries she ever wrote before her metamorphosis, before turning into ... but I guess all of you should just listen to the whole thing here. It might make more sense that way." She and Joey took turns reading aloud from the faded ink on the sheets:

43

Journal of Novalyne Price

Benefit Street, Prov., RI
July 12, 1936

Am I already too late to help my poor Bob?

I put in my first day's employment yesterday afternoon as a part-time cleaning lady at 66 College Street. Of course even as I mopped and swept I searched for clues. The study with its big work table interested me most. I felt driven by the dreams I've had—or visions, or hauntings, or what you will—of Bob appearing to me in insect-form and struggling to speak. I felt sure if I could just get close to the vivarium atop the table I might find answers.

The two caterpillars who struggled with that Mercury dime on my last visit, who did everything they could to tap it against the glass: surely it was a signal they were sending. And who else could they have been signaling but me? And the one caterpillar who stared at me so beseechingly with its bright red eyes: that, I know now, had to have been none other than Robert E. Howard, formerly of Cross Plains, now somehow ensorcelled like a captive prince in the Arabian Nights.

My plan was simple. I had things all worked out in my mind as I walked from Mrs. Torrance's boardinghouse on Benefit up to H.P. Lovecraft's lodgings. Greet the gentleman pleasantly as if I had not a suspicion in the world, set about my work, remove the burlap from the vivarium, announce the glass surfaces need cleaning. That would give me ample time to study the tiny inhabitants kept confined within.

But I found myself baffled. The table stood bare. Burlap sacking gone. Vivarium vanished. No sign of the caterpillars.

Lovecraft raised a dismissive eyebrow and said the insect realm had been only a passing fancy and he's moved on to other amusements. "So I've tossed away those worthless trifles." But even as he said this his eyes fixed me with a shining glitter as if to mock me, as if to say "I know very well why you've taken this job, I know very well what you're after." Yet he said nothing further.

I turned, feeling another pair of eyes on me. In the corner on its coatrack perched the crow Kavva. I expected a gaze fully as mocking and cold as Lovecraft's but instead I saw something else. Sympathy, I think. Concern. And—I know as I write this that it sounds strange—even a desire to warn me.

The bird flapped its wings and I stepped nearer. But its master frowned and Kavva settled back motionless on its perch. I had no choice but to busy myself with chores.

Swept, mopped, dusted, all while asking myself, What can I do now? Is there any way I can help Bob? I was as silent as Kavva, awaiting any chance that might guide me to learn more.

Lovecraft settled himself at his work desk by the west-facing window. From a stack of volumes he selected a certain book, old and thick and bound in black leather. Stamped on its spine was a title: *Necronomicon*. Reverently he turned its pages, making notes on a sheet of writing paper as he read.

At first he perused his text quietly enough. But the more he read the more impassioned he became, the more hastily he jotted. He seemed increasingly unaware of my presence, ever more absorbed in his *Necronomicon*. I watched him with hooded gaze even as I labored.

Faster he scratched his notes, even as he turned the pages of the book in frenzied jubilation. He muttered as he wrote. "At last," he cried to himself, "at long last."

So abstracted had he become that I took the risk of edging close behind his desk. He'd filled a sheet with densely written script. I could all but see what he had scrawled.

At which moment he stood abruptly and pushed back his chair.

Had he seen me? Was he about to berate me for attempted spying?

Not at all. Agitated, boastful, he bent and flung open the window and shouted to the street: "I tell you this is big!" All unheeded, the sheet with its scrawled notes fluttered to the floor.

Unmindful of me, my employer leaned forward and shouted again out the window: "The quest is done!"

I snatched the sheet from the floor and quickly scanned the jotted lines:

> Abdul Hazred writes of having encountered in his travels a merchant named "Abdallah Yaqut", who set up a trading emporium in Madinat al-Roum (Constantinople). There Yaqut had met a warrior of the Byzantine Varangian Guard who hailed from Norway, by name Thorvaldr Herjolfsson. This Norseman claimed to have sailed with Leif Eriksson when the latter voyaged westward from Greenland to Vinland in what is now North America. "Our captain decided to winter in Vinland," Thorvaldr reportedly told the Arab, "but restless grew I and a group of Vikings, so in company with our thralls we took two dragon-ships south along the coast until we reached a bay and a river inlet. Up this river we ventured till we found a rock-crevice from which surged forth a storm of winged frost-demons—a sight at which we wondered greatly."
>
> The detailed description recorded by my *Necronomicon* author convinces me that the Norseman Thorvaldr must have brought his longships to the very site of what would later become Providence. There he apparently glimpsed Yog-Sothoth itself, the cosmic gate through which Cthulhu's cosmic minions have streamed unimpeded to invade this Earth of ours. Frost-demons indeed: well might the sight of them freeze a man's heart.
>
> I dare not entrust further details to the written page but will merely note here for my own satisfaction the Arabic phrase my dear Abdul Hazred employed to name this portal between the worlds as described to him by Thorvaldr: *Majma' al-Bahrayn.* I leave the phrase untranslated as a safeguard against unworthy eyes. But for those of us who have been properly initiated and instructed: what secrets will this name disclose!

Once more Lovecraft shouted, as if demanding long-withheld recognition from the world at large: "I tell you this is big!"

Then he gulped, scolded himself for indiscretion, hastily closed the window. Still exhilarated, still aroused, he murmured the same phrases over and over, clearly treasuring the words. "Yog-Sothoth, Majma' al-Bahrayn. Finally, finally." He all but pranced before his desk. "With long-gone Abdul Hazred's help I've located the cosmic gate. Majma‘ al-Bahrayn: for those who know the meaning, a well-chosen designation for Providence's own vulnerable entry point through which alien hordes may stream from the howling wastes of starry space. Yes, the name is suited perfectly, perfectly."

Lovecraft's words puzzled me but I'll note them here in case my journal is ever found by a reader to whom the words convey more meaning.

"But soft, I must take counsel." Still careless of his cleaning woman, my employer strode right past me to the coatrack, raised a hand in a commanding gesture, addressed the crow. "What think you? Now that we know where the gate is, we must stuff it full with fresh apotropaia to repel Cthulhu and his hordes of aliens."

Kavva reacted not at all. No cawing, no flap of its wings. It stared straight ahead, unresponsive.

"So." Lovecraft crossed his arms in irritation, said this wasn't the first time the crow had shown itself recalcitrant.

Suddenly he turned to me as if realizing he'd been indiscreet. For a long moment he stood calculating. I knew he was reviewing everything he'd just said to check whether he'd trumpeted something I shouldn't have heard. I bent to my dusting as if cosmic-gate ravings were all in a day's work for a housemaid.

And after that I finished up and cleared out as fast as I could.

July 15

Crows talk. They speak. They speak English.

Or at least one does. I found out as follows.

When I returned to Lovecraft's apartment today I found a note on his door: "Miss Hopkins—Am away all day on business. Please be sure to dust the books in my study. HPL."

As good a chance to snoop further as I'd likely ever have. Sure enough, Lovecraft was absent. Kavva was present but sat perched where I'd last seen him, motionless on the coatrack. No wing-flutter, no sense of life.

Quickly I donned an apron and did the dusting as ordered, remarking book titles while I tidied. The *Necronomicon* nowhere to be seen; I'm convinced my employer stole his copy from the Athenaeum. But I found something else, left on his writing desk in plain view—an open notebook with a freshly penned entry on which the ink seemed barely dry: "Transformation spell as recorded by Abdul Hazred al-Majnun, sufficient for rendering humans into insects or reptiles or sundry other forms."

I thrilled as I saw the jotting. Could this be a way to reunite with my Bob? I read through the contents quickly, both the incantation and its list of attendant paraphernalia (all of it quite everyday), candle, thread, fluttering moth at twilight. (Fluttering moth? I told myself no time to think; ponder all this later.) Hurriedly I searched for paper and pen and copied out the jotting for myself, shaking my head at my own actions as I did so. Look at yourself, girl. A bare six weeks ago you'd have scoffed at such things, would have rated yourself four-square, tough-minded, hard-headed. But that was before Bob Howard's death and the vivarium caterpillar wielding a Mercury dime and the dream in which the same caterpillar communicated with its beseeching eyes. Now you're in a horror-master's house in Providence, not in Cross Plains anymore.

A voice speaking behind me shot me bolt upright with fright. "It's a trap."

I spun about. Lovecraft? No. Not a soul in sight.

I was wrong. The voice spoke again. "It's a trap."

In the corner. The coatrack. The crow. As in a dream I spoke back. "You mean this spell doesn't work?"

"Oh, it works all right. All too well it works." Kavva fluttered from the corner, landed on the desk. For a moment he stared out the west window, then turned his gaze on me. "The Magus knows your name's not Hattie Hopkins. He knows you're Novalyne Price, the special friend of that suicide Howard."

At the word "suicide" I bit my lip.

The crow continued. "The Magus wrote out that transformation spell and left it for you to find, hoping that you'd use it."

I asked why would Lovecraft do that.

He said because the Magus sees me as a nosy, prying female asking too many questions. "But he also sees you as a busybody who can be easily disposed of. If you perform the spell and become a Vespertine, you risk forgetting your purpose, your inner self. Then you'll be added to his roster of servants, like Howard, like Poe, like all his Elementals. Like me." The crow paused as if caught up in sad reflection.

Risk forgetting your purpose, your inner self. I tucked the jotting in a pocket, said I'd take that chance. "But why are you telling me this?"

"To warn you. And maybe to remind myself I too once had a purpose."

The beak came up sharply. "He's returning. He'll be here in five minutes. Go now. He must not know we spoke. His punishments are dreadful." Kavva flapped back to the coatrack.

I removed the apron, put on my coat. "Punishments?"

"No time for talk. Study the spell but do not attempt it until we speak again. I can advise you further, perhaps tomorrow. Now go! He must not see us speaking." He folded his wings, settled in his perch. A few seconds his onyx gaze regarded me, with compassion, I think, with kindness. Then the eyes shut as he feigned stillness.

"Until tomorrow, then," and in gratitude as I left I lightly touched the beak. A soft *grriick* in reply, and the crow settled once more upon its rack.

I hurried down the stairs and out the door. As I turned from College onto Benefit I looked once over my shoulder and saw Kavva's Magus descending the hill toward his apartment. I turned my head away and walked faster. I don't think he saw me.

Eight o'clock, evening coming on, and I couldn't sit still in my room any longer. Too keyed up from the day. I went down the hall, knocked on Maggs Johnson's door. "Gosh Novalyne, where you been keeping yourself? Looked for you this afternoon." She yawned. "Sorry. Just took a nap. This heat and all."

I suggested a nighttime stroll to Brown's campus. "It'll be cooler outdoors."

We sat on the grass. "See," I said. "I told you it'd be cooler." The spot I'd picked was by a lamppost not far from Manning Hall.

From my bag I produced some fruit and cloth napkins and two bottles of soda pop. "Your choice." I held out the bottles. "Nehi root beer, or RC Cola?"

"Royal Crown Cola. Like the radio says, 'Best by taste-test.'" She saluted me with her bottle. "Well, here's to ya."

Insects circled the lamplight. I cut up an apple and pear, offered Maggs a slice, laid the rest on a napkin. She drank her RC Cola and watched idly as I took out my notes from earlier in the day and pulled from my pocket a candle and a length of thread. I glanced at the notes, wrapped the thread around my right index finger and pulled the thread tight.

"Well get a loada that," marveled Maggs. "Whatcha doing anyway?"

I said I guessed I was rehearsing.

"Oh yeah? Rehearsing what?"

I said I was just talking silly. Full twilight now. The lamp stood circled by many winged flitterlings. I asked her to tell me something. "How much would you risk to help a fella you were dating?"

Maggs gulped more RC Cola and eyed me shrewdly. "We talking hypothetical or down-to-earth brass-tacks serious?"

"Hypothetical." One glance at her twisted grin, and I laughed at myself. "Okay, serious, yeah. Brass-tacks serious."

She said "well okay then," she liked having all the cards out on the table so to speak. "Take my boyfriend for example. Now he's a swell guy. But I don't think I'd risk too much for him. He's always forgetting to show up for our dates. Nah. Not sure how far I'd stick my neck out."

She asked how about me. Several moths left the lamplight, settled on my fruit plate. Most stayed only a few seconds. Abundance of caution I guess. But one showed confidence. Big, five-inch wingspan. Reddish gold, with brown eyespots.

"Pretty," said Maggs as she drank her soda pop.

Cautiously I squeezed a pear slice, formed a pool of nectar on the plate. The moth advanced and dipped its proboscis in the liquid.

"How about you?" Maggs asked me again. "How far would you go to help a fella?"

"Guess it's all depending."

She asked depending on what.

For a long minute the moth imbibed the sweetness. Its head faced me as it drank. Fearless, confident. If you feel any gratitude, I prayed as I gazed back, would you be willing tomorrow night to guide me through the dark? Same time, same place?

"Depending on what?" said Maggs again.

"Depending on if I trust a crow."

"Hey. Have you gone loco?"

I apologized even as I watched the moth drink up the last of its nectar. "Sorry, kid. How much I'd do for the fella I have in mind, it really comes down to the question"—I tapped my chest for emphasis—"does this gal have sand. Does this gal have the grit to see a thing through?"

"Well girl for what it's worth"—she drank the last of her soda pop, wiped her mouth—"I think you got the grit."

I told her thanks. The moth faced me a moment longer, then fluttered up from the plate and off across the campus lawn into the summer night.

Maggs stood up, said we'd best get back to the boardinghouse. "Rest up and all. We'll probably have a lot of work tomorrow."

I agreed that was probably all too true.

July 16

This morning at work Mrs. Dexter told me a gift had been left at the Athenaeum's door from that nice gentleman Mister Lovecraft.

First she showed me the note that accompanied the gift. "Perhaps to be of use when you next stage a reading from the verse of the illustrious Edgar A. Poe. In which case it may be apropos to name the enclosed: Nevermore."

Then she showed me the gift. "See, Miss Price?" she said brightly. "We can use it as a display prop." The prop, as she called it, was someone I'd begun to think of as a sympathetic presence, even as a friend. A bird, stuffed and mounted on a wooden stand. Wings forever motionless, onyx orbs that lacked all light. A stab of grief. Kavva, what did he do to you?

"Miss Price." Mrs. Dexter wanted my attention. "There's a personal note here enclosed for you as well."

Lovecraft's missive read:

> The thing was becoming a nuisance and hence was of no more use to me. When its immaterial spirit returns from Egypt it will find itself in durance vile. This bird will stay immobilized for as long as I see fit. The question now facing you, O Hattie Hopkins, is: Do you have the requisite courage to help your Two-Gun Bob? If you do, and if you become a Vespertine, I may also arrange to make the spell currently binding Kavva the Elemental somewhat less than eternal.

But even before reading the note I'd already made up my mind. Even if I have to attempt this without Kavva's counsel, tonight will be the night.

Six o'clock

Library chores done for the day. Sitting now in the quiet of the downstairs reading room, reviewing the notes I jotted from the *Necronomicon* spell on Lovecraft's desk. "Thread to be wrapped around right index finger while outdoors at twilight. Light the candle, recite the incantation. Attract a winged creature, taking care it not get scorched in the flame."

Here I'm careful to read over the notes most meticulously: "And if the moth to which you attach yourself is agreeable, it will guide your ectoplasmic self to any destination you may desire. But upon emergence at your destination the body you'll be assigned will be nonhuman."

Nonhuman. Ay, there's the rub. But I've made up my mind. And with luck my moth-guide this evening will be the same creature I met last night: reddish gold with a five-inch wingspan, hopefully retaining a sense of gratitude from last night's refreshment. Must remember to bring more pear nectar to strengthen it for our journey.

Seven-thirty

Nothing further to prepare. Made sure to give Maggs a big hug when she left for the day. Told her to take care. She looked at me strange. "Gosh, Novalyne. You take care too." She knows something's up.

Not quite time yet. Feeling a bit keyed up. For distraction I leaf through today's *Providence Journal*. First the fashion ads. "Kandy Stripe Sport Frocks, $7.85. Our seven-eighty-five dresses are the talk of the town." Sorry, no interest in shopping.

The entertainment page: more promising. "RKO Albee double feature, 100% new technicolor. Exciting adventure across the China Seas!: *Roaming Lady*, with Fay Wray and Ralph Bellamy. Followed by *The Girl from Mandalay*: Outcast woman ... living dangerously ... loving recklessly! Drama flames at white heat!" Yeah, that's me all right: loving recklessly, living dangerously.

Am I scared? You bet.

Let's have a look again at that entertainment page. What might Bob like to go see with me? Here's one. "Sylvia Sidney and Spencer Tracy in *Fury*: Remember the terrific kick you got out of *The Big House* and *Fugitive from a Chain Gang*? That was nothing compared to the powerful, spell-binding thrill of this great new M-G-M entertainment!" Yes, Bob might take me to go see that.

Must remember to bring his letters tonight. Will make it easier for the moth to follow his psychometric trail, wherever it might lead.

Seven forty-five

Almost time. Page through the news. Here's an item. "Dogs, Stranded Nine Days on Ledge above River, Saved by Rope Climber":

> Two nondescript mongrel dogs were rescued today from the perch they had occupied for nine days on a precarious ledge 200 feet above the swirling waters of the Fraser River in British Columbia. The dogs had swum to the ledge nine days ago when an old rowboat in which they had gone adrift capsized in Cisco Canyon. Two hikers performed the rescue. While his companion, Bob Pinto, stood watch above atop the cliff face at the anchor end, Ray Washgrove slid 400 feet down a ¾-inch rope to the spot where the dogs were marooned. He coaxed them into a haversack and climbed up the thin rope with them to safety.

Now that's something I'd like to do. Rescue helpless creatures from swirling waters.

But what am I thinking? That's precisely what I'm about to attempt. Lower myself down a rope to the darkest depths of death, with no one but a moth to stand watch at the anchor end. Though I think Bob Howard at five foot eleven and two hundred pounds might be a bit big to coax into a haversack!

I know the task will be hard and take me through the grimmest nighttime realms. But with God's help my love will be strong enough, will maybe make up for my absence back then, when Bob despaired and pulled the trigger on himself, when he threw his life away. But I've got the grit and I've got the sand to see this through, yes to descend and extend my hand and retrieve his soul from the fiery floor of hell itself.

I will not leave him to wander endlessly. I will seek him out and search for him in his afterlife. I'm ready for any transformation, any suffering to help give Bob a second chance. That's all any spirit wants. A second chance.

Time now. I'll fold this up and hide it with Kavva-Nevermore. He'll keep it safe until he sees someone to whom he can entrust these secrets.

And now to find that moth.

44

"Dear Lord." Pastor Gladys Trevor shook her head. "That woman sure had guts. Can you imagine? To subject herself to who knows what kind of magic spell, with no idea what she was going to be changed into." What echoed strongest in her mind was one of the very last lines in Novalyne Price's journal: "Extend my hand and retrieve his soul from the fiery floor of hell itself." She nodded, reflecting on her own vocation: "That's ministry work, all right, extending a hand, when we feel the strength, with heaven's help, to those we find in hell wherever we happen to spot them, in the gutter, on the street, in our daily life."

"Gutsy all right," agreed Fay MacConnell. "And I think Novalyne's journal also gives us a fresh clue about this 'cosmic gate' Lovecraft was so obsessed with. She says he was so excited he'd figured out its location that he started shouting the news from the window all over College Hill. I can't picture that somehow, doesn't sound like him, he was such a control freak."

Joseph Bonaventure said she was right. "'Control freak' sums up the man's style. But by July 1936, the date of Novalyne's last entry, Lovecraft was pretty ill. He knew he was dying of intestinal cancer and had only a few more months to live. He was absolutely set on finding Yog-Sothoth before he died so he could fill that cosmic gate of his with every magical protective device he could steal, buy, or borrow. And he was willing to raid the RISD museum, the antique shops on Fox Point, and any other place he could think of, to get hold of apotropaia to fortify Yog-Sothoth and keep out the alien hordes. So once he figured out its location here in Providence, he must've been plenty excited. No wonder he started babbling and yelling out the window."

"Whoa, man, slow down." Dieter Konrad looked both intrigued and confused. "This all strikes me as plenty apocalyptic, right down my investigative alley. Could someone please explain what's going on?"

Even as Bonaventure began an explanation, Fay interrupted. "Hey, we've gotta focus on our newest data point. This name we've never heard before for Lovecraft's cosmic gate. Majma' al-Bahrayn. This is promising, except I've got no idea what it means."

"Sounds like Arabic," ventured James Cypriano.

"It is!" exclaimed Zahra Beheshti. "It means 'the place where the two oceans merge' or 'the convergence point of the two waters.'" Her face shone with delight at the chance to expound what she knew. "Originally comes from the Qur'an, but it's also the title of a mystical treatise by my hero Dara Shikoh. He wrote the book to show how Sufi Islam and Vedantic Hinduism flow harmoniously together in their wisdom. Of course he made many of his fellow believers angry at him for that book." She frowned in thought, twining strands of hair around her fingers as she pondered. "But I don't know Providence's topography well enough to figure out which location is symbolized by Majma' al-Bahrayn."

Pastor Gladys snapped her fingers, said she thought she knew. "Citizens Plaza, also known as Confluence Point, right here downtown, you know? That *V*-shaped spit of land in the middle of the Providence River, where the two streams of the Woonasquatucket and the Moshassuck come together right at its tip. 'The convergence point of the two waters': it fits!"

"Then what're we waiting for?" cried Janey Evans. "Let's get out there and find that gate before the competition gets to it first."

Tristram Schaefer counseled caution. "Shouldn't we wait to notify the authorities before attempting anything on our own?"

Nancy Clayton gently remonstrated. "May I remind you that *we* are the authorities. We've got representatives from the two institutions most nearly concerned with this potential find, the Ath and the RISD museum. We've got experts here on all things Cthulhu and paranormal. Plus people knowledgeable on matters spiritual and archaeological. So I think we're as entitled as anyone else to check this business out. Besides, Tristram"—and here she gave her dubious boss an impish grin—"how often do we librarians get a chance to hunt for what could turn out to be a cache of buried treasure?" She grinned again.

"But I do have a question." Nancy looked about the room. "If we're going to investigate a convergence point of two waters, we'll need a boat. And where are we going to find one at this hour, considering it's getting on towards midnight?"

Atith Rattanak said no problem. "I've got the *Persephone* tied up right now at the Dyer Street dock. All clean and swept out."

"What an opportunity," said Gladys Trevor. "I've never been out on a Riverglow ship before."

"Time to address that woeful gap in your experience," smiled Jim Cypriano. "Let's do it."

Atith was the first to hurry out the door, saying he needed to load some gear from Riverglow's storage locker onto his boat. "I've a hunch we just might need it."

It was only when they were all aboard and the mooring lines had been cast off and the skiff was out on the nighttime river that the Jesuit suddenly groaned in dismay and disappointment. "I've just remembered something that could scramble our calculations."

Gladys, Tristram, and Nancy chorused what was that.

He reminded them that in the 1980s and early '90s—"long after Lovecraft's death"—the city had undertaken an urban renewal program called the Providence River Relocation Project. "Which involved a lot of dredging and rerouting so that the confluence point of those two smaller rivers today isn't exactly where it was in Lovecraft's era."

Atith cut the motor. The boat drifted in the dark. "Then which way do we head?"

"And how do we find those treasures," lamented Tristram, "that Lovecraft stole from RISD's museum and all those other places?"

At that moment Cheddar the Chihuahua voiced an opinion. From her cocoon within Gusto's hoodie she had been staring at the water. Suddenly she growled and yipped, then yipped again.

Gus Tessario pointed to where the dog stared. Floating beneath the surface just beyond the skiff's prow lay two long and narrow forms, one grayish green, one orange gold. Atith clicked his flashlight, shone it on the water. The forms flickered in shimmering undulations. Light rippled as the creatures twitched their tails. Then with a sudden *S*-curve the pair reversed direction and swam away upriver.

"Goldfish and iguana," said Fay.

"With another mission to fulfill," added Bonaventure.

"Which means we follow them," concluded Atith Rattanak. Cheddar yipped full-throated encouragement, and everyone concurred in following the dog's advice.

North the swimmers led them, under the Crawford Street Bridge, then beneath College Street and the Washington Street Bridge as well. Cold, damp exhalations breathed down on them from the arches overhead. The *Persephone* motored on through the river's concrete underworld.

Now ahead of them midriver loomed the jutting *V* of a high stone promontory. "Confluence Point," announced Atith. "Ahead off to starboard, the Moshassuck. Portside, the Woonasquatucket. But I've lost sight of our swimmers and I'm not sure which river branch to follow from here."

The black skiff idled on black water. Crew and passengers murmured indecisively.

"Starboard," decided Gladys. "Let's follow the Moshassuck." She explained why. Lovecraft had been a keen historian of colonial Rhode Island, and he would have known that Roger Williams had first established his settlement only two hundred yards upstream, on the east bank of the Moshassuck, "where North Main Street is now. They called it Towne Street back then."

She reminded her companions that Lovecraft blamed Williams for bringing into Providence a host of ethereal presences that the horror-Magus considered pestiferous.

"The alien hordes of Cthulhu," suggested Dieter Konrad.

"That's right," said Gladys. "Even though Roger Williams interpreted those presences in a radically different way." But it would have made sense, she continued, for Lovecraft to have wanted his apotropaic deterrents somewhere in this vicinity. "Because this was ground zero of the infestation, as far as he was concerned. He apparently believed the cosmic entry point was located right in the city's historic center, and he was desperate to plug it and block it so nothing could ever get in. So let's head up the Moshassuck, but take it nice and slow, Stubby, and everyone look sharp."

Atith responded with an "Aye aye Ma'am," and the *Persephone* chugged past the starboard face of the promontory.

Only to cut speed abruptly as Cheddar barked and Gusto shouted "Look!" There in the water close by the promontory, patiently waiting, lay the two swimmers. Stubby's flashlight played over the surface. One of the swimmers raised its head clear: golden mandible and fins, great round luminous eyes. It studied them and nodded.

"Novalyne," called Fay MacConnell and waved in salutation.

The goldfish flapped a fin in silent reply and then turned its head as if to guide everyone's attention. "There," called Atith, and his flashlight shone on the promontory's pitted stone. Straight up the granite surface climbed the iguana, its claws fighting for purchase on the slippery wet rock. Some fifteen feet up it climbed. A pause. And then—with a mouthful of pointed teeth that gleamed white and needle-sharp in Atith's beam—it abruptly chewed at the lichen that grew around a jutting stone.

Dieter Konrad made a nervous joke. "Random impulse-snack?"

Joey said he didn't think so. "I think Bob Howard's trying to signal us something."

And so it proved to be. More gnawing, and then the iguana twisted free and plunged with a splash back into the water. "X marks the spot," shouted Dieter in excitement. "Looks like that critter's notched the place we need to check."

Cautiously Atith brought the boat closer so that the *Persephone*'s gunwale gently bumped the wall of stone. "There's a ladder stowed in the stern," he said. He asked for someone to fetch it forward.

Gladys and Jim steadied the ladder upright against the rock face of the promontory. "Now," said Cypriano, "we just need someone to climb up and investigate what these water-folk are trying to show us. Joey, you're the Lovecraft scholar. Would you like to do the honors?"

"Would I? You bet!" Eagerly Bonaventure clambered up the ladder as Fay MacConnell joined the others in steadying the rig and urging him to be careful.

"See anything?" Fay voiced the question everyone in the skiff was thinking.

"Not yet." Balanced on the topmost rung of the wobbly ladder, the grad student ran his fingers along the portions of the granite surface where the lizard had gnawed away the lichen. "No, not a thing. Nothing but ... wait a sec. Stubby, could you shine that flashlight up here, where my hands are?"

In the dark, Atith's beam lit the pitted rock face, then Bonaventure's tweed coat and the spot where his hands rested. "Thanks,

Stubby. Yeah, I was right. There's a crevice here." The watchers in the skiff stared upward and strained to see as Bonaventure traced the narrow aperture. "Yup, the opening makes a right-angle turn. Think it might be a door of some kind. Do we have anything in the boat I could use to pry this thing open?"

"Just you wait one second." Atith hurried to the stern and came back with a crowbar. "Here you go."

"Definitely an access point or something," grunted Bonaventure as he applied the bar to the crevice. "But a bit stuck. Definitely hasn't been opened in a wh—Wait. Here we go. Got it." A small metal portal swung open.

Gasps from the boat below. "Whoa," muttered Dieter Konrad. "This is way cool."

Atith shone his light up on the door. Its outer surface had been covered in granite to make it blend in with the rest of the promontory. "Clever camouflage," commented Tristram.

Bonaventure handed the crowbar down to Fay, asked Atith if he could borrow the flashlight. "Looks like some kind of recessed compartment. Gonna poke my head inside, check this out."

Fay told him to be careful. An excited Dieter said, "Screw careful" and shouted up the ladder "Can you see anything?" He grinned to the boat at large. "This is like opening King Tut's tomb."

"You guys are not gonna believe this." Bonaventure's words were muffled. From below his companions could see his head and shoulders were squeezed inside the chamber's mouth. They heard a sound of scraping, as if he might be pulling something from deep within the compartment.

"It's a container of some kind. A chest. Made of metal. Sealed up tight. Waterproof, I think, with some kind of padlock. And ... yup, stamped on the lid is the name of our delightful H. P. Lovecraft." He dragged it to the entrance. "Heavy. Thing weighs a ton. Here, I'm gonna pass it down to you guys." Eager hands received the chest as he eased it down the ladder.

Dieter Konrad was all for opening the box on the spot but Nancy and Tristram said it could wait till everyone was safely back on dry land. "Joey," called Fay from below. "Anything else up there?"

"Yeah. Yeah, there sure is. Way at the back. Not sure what I'm looking at. But whatever it is"—the listeners below heard him hesitate as if awestruck—"I think this is more in your line of work, Pastor Gladys. You too, Father Jim. Both of you ought to come up and have a look."

Gladys Trevor felt a tremor go through her at these words. *The same thrill I felt when I found the lost manuscript in that desk in the Arcade building. Except even stronger, because something tells me this is going to be much more important.* She turned to James Cypriano. "How about it? Sounds like this is a task for the two of us to tackle in tandem."

Atith hurried from the stern. "Here. Luckily I brought a second ladder."

Bonaventure descended and handed Gladys the flashlight. "Not sure what to make of it," he puzzled. "Definitely alive, to judge from the movement. But not like anything I've ever seen. Best approach with caution."

Jim Cypriano rubbed his hands in anticipation of the task, tapped her on the shoulder. "Shall we?" Priest and pastor ascended their ladders side by side.

At the top they pushed the portal wide and together they peered into the chamber.

At first what they saw seemed simply a radiance, a brightness, a warmth. But Gladys could see why Bonaventure had said it was alive. Whatever this being might be, it throbbed and pulsed: tentative, inquisitive, uncertain.

Correction, thought Gladys. *Beings, not being. More than one of whatever it is.* The brightness resolved itself into a retinue of lights at the rear of the hewn stone chamber, diminutive globes that bobbed and touched one another, as if to converse each unto its neighbor.

They stayed bunched at the very back of the space, crowded against the far wall. She suddenly realized *They're afraid, afraid to come forward.*

Jim Cypriano seemed to realize this too. "They've been blocked in here, inside this cosmic gate," he said indignantly, "for who knows how long. Made to feel unwanted and unwished-for, and, I suspect, all on account of the devilments in the box that was placed in here by Lovecraft. They're scared to come out." He rubbed his chin, said he wasn't sure how to proceed. "Well, maybe let's just be straightforward."

Gladys saw him direct a smile at the radiant retinue and speak a simple sentence. "We bid you welcome."

In return within their narrow space the retinue bobbed and dipped as if in salutation.

Gladys Trevor was to know Jim Cypriano for many years to come, but she knew now she'd always remember this night as one of his finest moments. For in response to the retinue, as best he could while perched high on a rock face on an unsteady ladder, the Jesuit courteously bowed and bobbed his head in return.

Which made them bob and bow all the more. And Gladys, being after all a historian of seventeenth-century Rhode Island, had the presence of mind to recall three historic words suitable to the occasion. She too nodded and hailed the huddled aliens, saying in a loud voice, "What cheer, Netop?"

At this the huddled lights danced in what she knew had to be pure joy. *It's as if some of them remember*, she thought, *having heard this greeting once before.* Then as she and Cypriano retreated and descended the ladder, the lights streamed from the cold chamber out into the warm summer night.

The crew members of the *Persephone* afterward each recalled in their individual ways for the rest of their lives the starburst display that followed as they looked up into the sky. Zahra Beheshti wished her prince Dara Shikoh could have been there to see it: *Truly a vision in which believer and nonbeliever can both rejoice; here the oceans in truth converge.* Nancy Clayton told neighbors it was the high point of a long, eventful career at the Ath. Tristram Schaefer bemoaned having been so overwhelmed that he forgot to pull out his phone and make a video. Dieter Konrad said things like "Revelation and apocalypse-conspiracy: I mean wow."

But Gladys Trevor remembered it in the words used by Roger Williams himself to describe his own first experience of these celestial refugees:

> For I awoke one dawn by the shore of the river called Seekonk to behold a Sight wondrous: Sublimities of radiance, descending from the Heavens. Most like unto six-winged Angels, wherefore I named them Seraphim ... Then turned they to me and did dip and bow with Curtsies most gracious and formal, so that by their kindness of Presence I knew them to be Envoys of our own Father of Mercies and His Son our Lord Jesus Christ. And thus reassured I did return

their Salute. For every Exile in a strange land doth long to hear the word Friend.

Which reminded her of the title of the book once penned by Williams so many years ago: *A Key into the Language of America.* In her life Gladys had sometimes wondered: *What is in fact America's true idiom? Is it Lovecraft's lingo of xenophobia and fear directed against all foreigners whether earthling or galactic?* But tonight she felt the seraphs showed a different answer: *America speaks a language of hospitality and welcome.*

Her heart full, she sighed as she watched the angels cavort in gratitude above the *Persephone.* "Reverend Roger," she breathed, "you sure pegged it right: everyone, every exile—and that includes all of us—doth long to hear the word 'Friend.' "

A long moment of radiance, and then—as if eager to make good for the lengthy expanse of lost time—the seraphs scattered to illumine Providence with their grace.

Gazing after them from the water: an iguana and a fish. With the angels liberated, they turned once more to the skiff and then dived and disappeared from sight.

"Okay," said Gladys Trevor. "Let's head back to shore."

45

Late at night it was by the time everyone returned to the Athenaeum, with a half-dozen volunteers lugging the big metal chest through the library's portico past the dark Doric columns.

They laid the box on a long wooden table. Gladys read aloud the inscription on the lid:

On the occasion of
Rhode Island's Tercentenary AD 1936
This Time Capsule has been deposited
As a remembrance of past history
Through the philanthropy of
Howard Phillips Lovecraft of Providence.
Not to be opened until
Another Tercentenary has passed
In the year AD 2236.

She said this had been a clever move on Lovecraft's part. "Somehow he managed to have this thing hidden in the promontory at Confluence Point. But he must have anticipated that someday the river could be dredged and the promontory might be shifted and reconstructed." Labeling his apotropaic bulwark a "time capsule," she continued, would have discouraged anybody who found it from breaking the thing open to see what was within.

"Yeah," said Janey Evans, "and stamping it with the instructions 'Do not open till 2236' would have kept this stuff locked up tight for a good three hundred years."

Cheddar the Chihuahua snuffled at the box. "I doubt there are any Slim Jims in there for you, baby," said Gus Tessario, "but I hope we're not gonna wait no three hundred years to get a peek inside."

"Not at all," said Pastor Gladys. "Stubby, would you pass me that crowbar?"

Ten minutes' work. Padlock broken, seals forced apart, lid pried up and open.

Nestled within the box lay many rarities. Fay cried softly in excitement. "Do you recognize this, Joey?" She lifted up a severed bronze head: sightless glass eyes, frowning metal lips.

"Wow." Bonaventure marveled as she passed it to him to handle. "From that statue of the emperor Augustus. It's gotta be what our buddies in the Roman cohort were sent down to that Kushite temple to retrieve."

"Yup," she agreed. "This is what Bob Howard and good old Eddie Poe brought back from Egypt."

Packed densely within the capacious box were many more artifacts. Juju fetishes. Ghost daggers. Statuettes of plague demons and gods of war. Tiger masks for summoning and holding the spirits of beasts of prey.

"With all these things," mused the Jesuit as he helped sort through the contents, "poor Lovecraft thought he was keeping Providence safe from Cthulhu and its ilk. And instead all he did was exclude a host of penitent angels who wanted nothing more than to help us down here on earth in this our exile."

"And look!" exulted Zahra Beheshti. One after another, she pulled from the box a pair of alabaster vessels, one human-headed, the other in the likeness of a hawk. "The two canopic jars that've been missing from RISD's museum since that lizard heist in 1936. Boy, my boss Heather is going to be so happy to get these treasures back."

Atith said he'd heard there were two other jars still missing from the museum.

"That's right," said Zahra. "Stolen from us just recently by Alicia Wheatley's Gnostic Guardian gang." With grim determination she added, "And I aim to get them back."

"Don't worry," Tristram Schaefer assured her. "I've provided the Providence police department a full description of Alicia Wheatley and her group. Warrants have already been issued for their arrest."

Dieter asked what were the charges.

"Unlawful possession of the Athenaeum's copy of the *Necronomicon*, for starters," was Tristram's prompt reply. "Plus trying to steal our stuffed Nevermore raven as well as those missing canopic jars. Not to mention casting a hostile spell on our staff member Fifi Mac

Connell. Don't worry. Wheatley and her Guardians won't be free for long."

A sudden slam of the library's outer door. A rush of retreating footsteps down the outside stairs. Dieter and Bonaventure sprang to their feet, sprinted to the door.

Only to return a moment later. "We were all so excited when we got here we left the outer door unlocked," said the grad student. "I think someone snuck in after us to listen in on what we found. But he's gone now."

Dieter Konrad said they got a glimpse of the intruder as he ran off and descended College Street, headed for downtown.

Fay asked if they could tell who it was.

"Yeah," said Bonaventure. "Someone we know. Alex Finster. Also known as Tagger."

"Tagger," said Atith sympathetically. "I wonder what'll happen to him now."

"He'll probably get picked up by the cops tonight," said Fay, "unless the Baroness of Yog-Sothoth comes up with a spell to save him fast."

"Or unless," offered Father Jim, "he has a change of heart that gets to him first."

"How likely is that?" snorted Dieter skeptically.

"Don't forget," said Gladys Trevor, "we've just released a stream of penitent angels out over the Providence River. Let's give them a chance and see what they can do to help."

"Amen, Reverend," said the Jesuit, and at that they all shared a smile.

46

"I'm telling you the cops are probably on their way this fricking minute," Alexander Finster all but bellowed into his phone. "You'd better haul ass outta there. That's what I'm aiming to do. I don't have time to run more errands for the Guardians."

"Of course you do," came the smooth reply, "as long as you don't panic." Alicia Wheatley's voice retained its normal tone, detached, superior, superbly in control—*the same tone she had*, came the memory to Finster, *that first night when I was wandering by the river and she and her groupies first approached me and roped me in with their offer.*

Which is just what she's doing now, he thought. "You still want to be Baron of Yog-Sothoth, don't you?" Yes, he knew that tone, its mix of imperious and flirty.

Except now a lot of the charm was gone. Now as she spoke, his thoughts went back to the last time he'd followed her commands: *faithfully obeying her orders trying to net that spike-headed swimmer-thing, falling headfirst into the water, and then flailing helplessly while her speedboat sped away and left me on my own.* It was only his fast footwork scrambling ashore that had kept him from getting arrested on the spot.

Now here she is, big-league Baroness of Yog-Sothoth, giving me more orders, figuring I'll just faithfully obey.

She was saying something about dirigible craft and being holed up on the top floor of the Industrial Trust Building. "I know very well the police are likely to come charging up to my penthouse lair here on the top floor. Ideally I'd like to escape by zeppelin and laugh at them all while I sail away in my airship. But unfortunately the *Necronomicon* doesn't seem to have any sorcery addressing the making of such vessels. Or maybe it's just that I'm new to the Magus' text and still a bit of a novice when it comes to casting spells. No matter. I've mapped out a plan B. I can escape from this tower by way of bug."

"Leave the bug out of it," he pleaded. "Don't ask me to do it. I told you already. I've been having bad dreams about that thing. It can't sleep at night. And I can scarcely sleep either. I don't wanna mess with it no more. Don't wanna put it through any coercion."

Purring reassurance. "I thought you wanted to be Baron of Yog-Sothoth."

"I did. Now I dunno."

"You know, you show more potential than any of these loser locals. Maybe that's because you're an artist, a graffiti master with a real creative flair." A voice silky, insinuating. "You could share a throne alongside me. You'd like that, wouldn't you?"

He had to admit he would.

"Well then. I just need you to return to that building. What's it called? Yes, New England Pest Control. Climb up to the roof just as you've done before but this time recite a certain spell from the *Necronomicon* that I'll dictate to you now."

Tagger said that would be risky. "I've been up there twice. No way I can pull this off a third time. Cops'll be watching for me."

She wasn't listening. "The spell is something Abdul Hazred learned many centuries ago on the island of Java from the court necromancer of the sultan of Yogyakarta, an incantation entitled 'How to animate automata made of metal.' I've contemplated this and feel certain it'll work. And what a splendid exit I'll make! Laughing at my foes, flying off on a fifty-eight-foot termite, something I've brought to life that's under my total control."

He protested maybe it didn't want to be under her total control. "I told you it's been having trouble sleeping. It doesn't like all those restraints that've been holding it down."

"Alex. You and me. Baron and Baroness. We'll share a throne. You're better than these luckless losers."

Share a throne. You and me. No question she could still cast spells. He sighed and said "Okay."

"Wise choice. Stand by and I'll dictate to you the animation incantation."

He heard the turning of parchment as she leafed through her *Necronomicon.* In the background, high-pitched shrieks—those falcons, no doubt, still diving at the window of her lofty gondola perch.

Ten minutes later he was in a taxi, her spell recorded on his phone. The driver looked to be from West Africa, smiled a lot and showed a pair of gold front teeth. "Where to, my man?"

Tagger asked if he knew the address in Providence of New England Pest Control.

"Home of the Big Blue Bug? Of course I do." A flash of gold teeth again as he smiled into the rearview mirror. "Tourists come to this state, they want a tour, they ask for the Bug, they love it. Me, I'm Yoruba, I'm from Nigeria, but now I'm a Rhode Islander and I like to show visitors points of pride. We all love it. So of course I know the Bug and its address."

Big Blue Bug. Point of pride. We all love it. Alex Finster writhed in his seat. *What am I about to do?* He stared out moodily as the cab raced through the nighttime streets. They descended the hill, crossed the College Street bridge, turned left at Memorial Boulevard and drove by the river.

Baron and Baroness. You and me. An enchantress.

And then, out on the water: a hovering, a glimmering of wings, a sighing susurration. And a breathed-in thought, an inspiration: *You don't have to do this. There are alternatives. Think.*

Alternatives. Alternatives to coercion, to servitude. Again the susurration, a flickering of light behind the clouds, winged inspiration. *Alternatives. Think.*

Alex leaned forward and tapped the driver. "Hey. You know where the nearest Newport Creamery is?"

"Sure do. I like that place. Go there for my breaks." He said his passenger was in luck. "Open 24/7 nowadays. Special summer hours."

The clerk at the Creamery looked at Alex Finster funny when he put in his take-out order. "You sure you want that much?"

He said he was sure. "Don't worry. It won't get wasted. I got a pal with a humongous thirst."

After the Newport Creamery he had the driver stop again for one more take-out order. Then they headed straight toward the industrial wharf area and Eddy Street and New England Pest Control.

"You want me to give you a hand with all that?" The cabbie offered to help him carry his take-out stuff. Alex thanked him and said no he'd be fine.

It took three trips from the street to the roof because of what he'd bought en route but he'd been here before and knew his way. Three trips up the ladder and topside, wrestling his purchases, trying not to spill them. Thankfully no one in sight, street empty at three A.M.

He stood in front of the termite, its wings bucking in the night wind, its thorax tugging against the restraints, the cables and guy wires thrumming with the tension. Restless, this metal bug, just like in the dream. Jumpy was how it felt. Which was the way that he felt too.

He walked around to the bug's head, careful to keep from the roof's edge and the steep pavement-drop below. A gust of breeze, and the bug bucked and dipped again. *It knows I'm the jerk that tagged it. It doesn't trust me. And I don't blame it.*

"Whoa," he said aloud. "Easy now." And he reached up to pat its snout.

His phone pinged loud. He knew who that'd be. He ignored it.

Carefully he placed before the bug's head the three take-out orders. "A ten-gallon serving of Del's Lemonade. Plus ten gallons' worth of Awful Awful flavored ice milk. And an equal-sized coffee cabinet: milk shake extra thick. And I even remembered to bring super-long straws for your convenience, which proves I ain't as dumb as I might look."

Nothing. He waited. *It knows I'm the jerk that tagged it.*

His phone pinged again. A text from Alicia Wheatley: "Bring me my bug!" Imperious as always.

Still no action from the termite. Patiently he waited. *It doesn't trust me. And I don't blame it.*

More whisperings in the air, more inspiration.

Good idea, he thought, *wherever that came from.* He picked up the waxed-cardboard container with its ten gallons of coffee milk shake. *Whew, feels like it weighs a hundred pounds.* He lifted up the container until the elongated straw just touched the maw of the blue bug.

He held the waxed container up high, felt his muscles tremble from the weight. *Come on, bug, you gotta trust me.*

More pings from his pocket. Another message, for sure the same: "Bring me my bug!"

His forearms, biceps, neck all trembled. *Can't hold it up much longer.* The termite towered overhead. *Come on, you gotta trust me.*

And then from overhead a sound. The slightest sip. Tentative, unsure.

Then another sip.

Followed by a prolonged slurping and suction and smacking that denoted an end to prolonged suffering and thirst.

The carton in his arms grew lighter as the liquid flowed up into the maw.

Empty. Quickly he tossed aside the container, picked up the Awful Awful. *Try this one.*

No hesitation. The flavored ice milk was sucked up fast.

To be followed by the lemonade. The creature had picked up confidence. The ten gallons drained off pronto.

Alex Finster stood back and watched. All along its fifty-eight-foot metal length the termite trembled. The night wind rose. The wings rocked back and forth.

Shuddering: head, thorax, abdomen. Upward tug and strain as the nutrients did their work.

And then a *snap* and *whip* and the human had to throw himself flat on the tarpapered roof as bolts and stanchions burst. Guy wires whirred, cables gave way. All restraints came loose.

He looked up just in time. The Big Blue Bug was in the sky and flying high. It circled the rooftop once and flapped its wings and disappeared out over the bay.

More pinging from his pocket. He took out his phone. Same message. "Bring me my bug!"

He texted a reply. "Sorry. Out of service."

He stood up, stretched his arms wide. Roof empty now, nothing further for him here. He crossed to the ladder and rapidly descended. *Have no notion where I'm headed. But I'm out from under, and that's a start.*

He reached the street, ran off toward the wharf and its freighters in the harbor. *Feeling strangely lightweight, strangely free.*

47

A ping on her cellphone. "At last," she fumed. "An answer." She wondered what'd been taking him so long.

"Sorry. Out of service."

She knew what that meant. No escaping in grand style. No rooftop departure via bug.

But this wasn't Alicia Wheatley's only problem. She'd also just gotten a text from the Guardians' Governing Council. "Yog-Sothoth has been breached," it read. "This was your responsibility. We require an accounting."

A serious matter indeed, to incur the Council's displeasure. She sat brooding on her throne in the penthouse Gondola Room of the Industrial Trust Building. Flanking the throne were the two canopic jars she'd so laboriously stolen from the museum. How recently it was that she'd sat here caressing their alabaster heads, luxuriating in the memory of how skillfully she'd contrived the theft. And now they stood as a mute reproach: she'd failed to find the cosmic gate before her rivals, failed to install these jars as additional apotropaia to repel the alien hordes of Cthulhu. *Yog-Sothoth has been breached.* Yes, an accounting would be swift to come. *I'll have to get out of here fast.*

Fast indeed. A glance at her camera monitor screens showed chaos at ground level. Swarms of police squadrons were overrunning the lobby. Beneath the entranceway's chandeliers and painted Zodiac gods, her gray-shirt minions briefly fought to hold back the police.

As if to accent the crisis, those falcons outside were at it again, shrieking and diving at the window, still striving to drive her away. "Be patient just a bit longer," she addressed them as they shrieked. "I'll be departing soon enough."

As a girl when rejected and excluded she'd always taken comfort in her Milton. And even now, when she should have been scrabbling to find an exit and safe haven, she pulled from the reading stand beside her throne the volume she loved most.

She opened the book and read at random verses from the poet's *Samson Agonistes*. The captive Samson, eyes gouged out by his Philistine foes, is now an object of mockery for the grinning mob that holds him prisoner and thinks him helpless. Nonetheless he contrives to topple the giant pillars of the hall within which he's being held for mass amusement while his enemies feast and jeer:

> But he, though blind of sight,
> Despised, and thought extinguished quite,
> With inward eyes illuminated,
> His fiery virtue roused
> From under ashes into sudden flame ...
> Straining all his nerves, he bowed;
> As with the force of winds and waters pent
> When mountains tremble, those two massy pillars
> With horrible convulsion to and fro
> He tugged, he shook, till down they came, and drew
> The whole roof after them with burst of thunder
> Upon the heads of all who sat beneath,
> Lords, ladies, captains, counsellors, or priests,
> Their choice nobility and flower, not only
> Of this, but each Philistian city round
> Met from all parts to solemnize this feast.
> Samson, with these immixed, inevitably
> Pulled down the same destruction on himself ...
> O dearly bought revenge, yet glorious!

A thud and rattle at the glass. Again the falcons dived and shrieked. Another glance at the camera monitors showed her that her minions were now scattering like ants. The police had reached the lobby elevators.

Arrest, humiliation, now riding up the shaft.

She, submit to handcuffs? Baroness of Yog-Sothoth, an object of mockery for the grinning mob?

No!

But what to do?

Here she had her Samson to show her. "O dearly bought revenge, yet glorious!"

She put aside her Milton, plucked up the *Necronomicon*. Quickly she leafed through the chapters till she found the section she needed. Yes, this was it: "Conjuration for toppling a dwelling."

Another glance at the monitors. Two elevator cars ascending, each crammed with enemies coming to make her captive. *Not much time.*

She began the invocation. Still an amateur at all this, she had no idea how effective this untried spell might be. But with luck it would bring down all twenty-eight floors of Superman's vaunted Industrial Trust, topple stone and concrete into rubble that would bury police and unworthy acolytes alike. In her fey and reckless mood she gave no heed to what this meant for her own fate.

Linking forefingers and thumbs, she turned her hands palm outwards and extended her arms full-length toward the elevator doors. She felt the sorcerous strength well up from within. *Yes, it's working!*

But even as she chanted, even as the charm rippled up along her spine and shot out through her mouth, she sensed a sudden blockage.

Not from within, but from without. Something serving as a shield, protecting the whole building.

She summoned a second spell, then hurled a third.

And now, glimmering before her, near the elevator doors, she could see what this shield was. Curtains of flickering light, arrayed in sets of six wings. In the shimmer of these winged entities she caught glimpses of faces: faces of radiant beings, first a guardian lion, then a lamb with a banner that read "Agnus Dei." The wings caught her conjurations and made them ricochet round the room. And each time one of her spells recoiled, a voice resounded like a bell: "Sanctus Sanctus Sanctus."

Now Alicia Wheatley experienced something close to panic. *This must be what's managed to come through the cosmic gate.* These winged things didn't project the kind of force she'd always anticipated. They seemed serene, even mild, rather than Cthulhu-style demonic.

But she didn't stop to analyze all this. She knew only that these things were baffling her own power. Hers!

From behind her a keening shriek. Those falcons again.

Not much time. The glimmering guardian wings before her stood ready to defend the building from conjuration-collapse. The police would be pouring out of those elevator doors in a minute to put the cuffs on her.

The scratch of raptor claws on glass. *Those birds really want me out.*

Which gave her an idea for one last desperate gambit.

Once more she snatched up the *Necronomicon*, turned to its well-thumbed section on transformation spells. From penciled notes in the margins she could tell that Howard Phillips Lovecraft had also once consulted these pages. *He must have*, she thought feverishly, *in order to turn humans into caterpillars and lizards. Yet the difference here is that the Magus never tried it on himself. But if Samson could bring a temple down on his own head, I can try directing a spell to turn inwards on myself.*

A last glimpse of the elevator monitor. The doors were about to open.

Here goes, she breathed as she recited the spell. *Just you and me, Samson.*

And when the doors parted, the rapid-response team found no one on whom to clap their cuffs. By the throne, a discarded gray polo shirt with lapel pins: "GGCG" and "HPL was right." A few torn feathers on the floor. An open window in the twenty-eighth-floor Gondola Room. And far away in the predawn sky a flight of falcons, shrieking and chasing off a bird of some kind.

"Difficult to tell for sure, given the distance," was what the subsequent police investigation reported, "but it seemed the bird clasped in its talons a black volume bound in leather."

48

"Sorry I'm late." Fay MacConnell was all apologies as she joined Joseph Bonaventure at the Dyer Street dock. "I stopped by the Ath. Can't seem to find that stuffed Nevermore raven. Don't know what happened. Nancy says it went missing right after we discovered that manuscript crammed in its beak."

Bonaventure said not to worry, that the bird was bound to turn up. "I mean it can't have just walked off, right?"

"Well, never mind that for now. Did you bring that other thing like I asked you to, the one you always carry around with you?"

"Got it right here." He reached into his tweed coat pocket and pulled out a small glass flask. "My buddy Melville, six-legged husk and all." Affectionately he studied the beetle with its dried carapace. "But why'd you insist on my bringing it here out to the riverbank, and why do we have to do this ritual of yours—and that's what you called it in your text message, right, a ritual?—why do we have to do this so early in the day?" He rubbed his chin's unshaven stubble. "I mean, it's not even five-thirty."

"It's on account of this." She tapped the silver ear-studs she wore. *The studs that started this whole deal*, she thought, *the time I wore them to my first Riverglow outing*. "Remember how I told you I didn't think there was any more psychometric juice left in 'em? Turns out I was wrong. Because when I woke up a little while ago, I realized I'd fallen asleep still wearing my earrings, and there was my cat pawing at me for attention, and when I opened my eyes the first thing I saw was this scrap of paper Dupin was batting all over the couch. I picked up the paper and turns out it had a few sentences scribbled on it. Sentences containing very specific instructions, as you'll see in a second. In my handwriting, too, even though I have zero memory of having written anything like that before I fell asleep."

"So let me guess. More psychographic dictation from ol' Spike-Head."

"You got it." She showed him the scrap with its scribbling:

"Bring the vial with the insectoid remains of Herman Melville to the Providence River. Steer for midstream. Set the insect free and afloat at first light. Then wait."

To the east and south, massed clouds above College Hill and Fox Point glowed pink and rose red in the cool air of dawn. Beside them at the dock the *Persephone* rocked gently as a breeze slapped waves against the boat. "Too bad neither of us is licensed as a skipper," said Bonaventure. "We could just borrow Stubby's tub here for the job."

"Speaking of whom," replied Fay, "I sent him a text, too. And here he comes. Looks like he brought company."

An old sky-blue Impala pulled up at the curb. Out stepped Atith Rattanak and opened the passenger-side door for Janey Evans. From the rear seat came Augustus Tessario cradling his Cheddar, who dozed comfortably in her human's zipped-up hoodie. Both teen and Chihuahua yawned.

They all joined Fay and Bonaventure in climbing aboard. The *Persephone* motored south and downstream for several minutes. Atith guided the vessel until it reached midriver, then turned to Fay. "How far?"

"This should do it."

Quiet on the water as Atith cut the engine. Cries of gulls; distant traffic on Memorial Boulevard and 95. But up close there was simply the sound of rippled splashes tapping the skiff. That, plus snuffles as Cheddar poked her head out from the hoodie.

Fay nodded, and Bonaventure crouched low over the *Persephone*'s prow. Uncorking the flask, he gently tapped the insect out onto the water.

"Now what?" asked Gusto.

"Now we wait," said Fay.

As they waited Gus announced he had good news. "Stubby says I can have my old job back at Guild Metal. The pay's not bad and he says he'll pick me up every morning so I don't oversleep plus I can bring Cheddar to work. That's a pretty sweet deal, ain't it, Joey?"

Bonaventure agreed it was.

"Plus Aunt Janey says me and my dog can stay with her as long as we want. Get us back on our feet and all." Janey Evans and Atith Rattanak both beamed like proud parents.

Still cradling his Chihuahua, Gus peered over the gunwale. "That beetle of yours. Not doing much. Curled on its back, legs up in the air."

Fay said give it time.

The teen extracted from the hoodie a beef Slim Jim, unwrapped the plastic, tore off a piece for Cheddar, then a bite for himself. "Been thinking about all the trouble I caused, the way I let you guys down, disappointed everyone." Janey tried to interrupt, told him not to fuss about such things, but he persisted. He said he'd been thinking about ways he could try to make amends. "Truthfully, make it up to the world, do something worthwhile." He said since he loved animals, he'd decided to use his spare time to volunteer for the Humane Society or someplace like that. "You know, rescue dogs. Rescue as many as I can. Give 'em attention. Stuff like that."

He studied the water. "Hey. The beetle. It's moving. Not bad."

He was correct. The insect had righted itself, was paddling in slow, labored circles.

"Step one in recovery," said Bonaventure.

"Recovery. Beetle recovery. I like that." Gus Tessario laughed, then sobered again. "Joey, I been meaning to ask you. I know you've had bad dreams and all, that nightclub fire and everything, but do the dreams ever go away? Cuz ever since that night you dove in after me over by the bridge I'm still having these bad nightmares. Not every night, but two, maybe three times a week." He said the dreams involved opioids, fentanyl. "China white, temptations from the pills. Then my doggie in the water, and me drowning along with her, and all of it my fault."

Bonaventure came and stood beside him, patted Cheddar's nose as she asked for more Slim Jims. "I don't know if the dreams ever go away," he said, "at least not a hundred per cent. I know I still have my share. But the important thing is you wake up and you remember you're not facing this alone."

Atith Rattanak spoke up then, said he'd had his own share of nightmares since his boyhood in Cambodia. "What happened to my family. Being captured by the Khmer Rouge. And this." He held up both hands, showed his stumpy finger-stubs. "But I wake up and remember I have friends to pull me through. Maybe that's the message of the seraphs." He smiled at Janey Evans.

Who smiled back and then said to her nephew, "You just look after all those dogs you want to rescue. And we'll all look after you. Deal?"

"Deal." The teen grinned with relief, studied the insect again. "Hey. It's not paddling any more. It just climbed up on a piece of trash on the water, looks like a . . . yeah, a Reese's peanut butter cup wrapper. Yeah. Looks like the beetle's taking a breather."

So it seemed. The beetle crouched motionless on the plastic wrapper.

Bonaventure turned again to Fay MacConnell. "We keep waiting?"

Fay had been asking herself the same question. She'd done what she'd been ordered via psychographic scribble, had rousted her buddies to help her deposit the withered husk of Herman Melville upon the river. And now here he sat in his beetle-self on a Reese's wrapper. Melville was looking livelier, seemed even to be taking an interest in the chocolate peanut butter remnants on the plastic. Maybe their job was finished.

She was just about to say so, about to say "Let's head for shore," when a loud *graaack* came from overhead. She looked up startled. Beside them on the gunwale alighted a big crow.

Fay didn't have to ask to know who it just had to be. "Kavva-Nevermore?"

For reply the crow peered at her meaningly. It croaked again, a croak she took to signal "Wait."

So she did. So did they all.

But not for long.

A pair of elongated subsurface forms swam up from the stern alongside the *Persephone*, one to port, the other to starboard, and converged at the skiff's prow. One swimmer, with spiky crests, glimmered a dull gray green. The other gleamed orange gold.

The Chihuahua yipped a greeting. "Goldfish and iguana," cried Gusto.

In gentle undulations the pair nosed up to the candy wrapper where the beetle crouched. Without hesitation the insect climbed up on the iguana's snout and found a perch atop the tallest of the spikes that crowned the lizard's head. Their passenger secured, fish and reptile swam side by side out toward the open bay.

Kavva stirred, and Fay recognized it too was about to depart. She asked if it could do her a favor, take a message. "Tell Eddie Poe hi from me when next you see him." The crow *graaacked* once in reply and then flew up. Eyeing the two swimmers, the bird cawed in a bright clear cry that Fay thought at first was directed only to Bob Howard. But on second thought she realized the words were directed to them all, to the pulp-writer lizard, to Novalyne Price the goldfish, to all the creatures in the skiff.

The crow cried, "Still your friend."

Then it soared up, only to be met by another flier, although this one was much larger. Big and blue and fifty-eight feet long, it flexed its wings slowly as if it was still learning to fly.

"Hey," exclaimed Gusto, "that's our metal Bug!"

Side by side at a majestic measured pace, the crow and termite led the swimmers on a course into Narragansett Bay and beyond.

Janey said, "Where do you think they're headed?"

"South Seas," speculated Joey. "Probably Nuku Hiva. That's what Mister Moby-Dick always wanted."

Gus sighed as he fed more Slim Jims to his Cheddar. "I wonder if they'll ever come back."

"First they have to help Melville get his beetle-self back to Polynesia," said Joey. "But as soon as they get done with that, and they sense how much we miss them, they'll turn around and be here before you know it. They want to continue to be part of this city's story. That metal termite will guide them. It'll figure out the way."

"You think so?"

"Oh yeah, I have faith. You see, like Roger Williams, our Blue Bug trusts in Providence." He smiled. "I know I sure do."

END

AUTHOR'S AFTERWORD

The first question you might well ask after finishing *Providence Blue* is: Wait—did H.P. Lovecraft really contrive to push Bob Howard into suicide?

The short answer to that is no, he didn't. Nor, for that matter, were Robert E. Howard, Novalyne Price, Edgar Allan Poe, and Herman Melville ever transformed (as far as I know, at least) into (respectively) a lizard, fish, caterpillar, or beetle. What you've just read, after all, is a work of speculative fiction, a meditation on life-and-death issues: Is there hope for the dead after suicide? Is there a way to transcend despair?

For the historical record I'll note here that Novalyne Price actually outlived both Howard and Lovecraft by many years. She eventually got married and had a child and enjoyed a distinguished career as an educator before her death in 1999. The memoir she wrote of her friendship with Bob Howard (entitled *One Who Walked Alone*) provided ideas for some of the dialogue in *Providence Blue*.

In fact even the most phantasmagoric of my Vespertine explorations were prompted in part by bits of biographical data that the novel tries to represent faithfully. Howard began his correspondence with Lovecraft as an admirer of the older man's work. But estrangement and increasing tension manifested themselves in their letters, in part because of their very different views on barbarism versus civilization, and partly because of Lovecraft's championing of Benito Mussolini and his enthusing over the Fascist's "civilizing" invasion of Abyssinia (a view that considerably angered Howard). Lovecraft admired both Mussolini and Adolf Hitler.

The pro-Nazi sentiments he expressed are closely linked, I think, to his own personal xenophobia and racial obsessiveness. What most horrified this horror writer was the idea of foreign immigrants in a New England he fantasized as Aryan and Yankee. Two types of aliens spooked him: boatloads of foreigners washing up in

Providence and New York from overseas, and tentacled Cthulhu-grotesques emerging from distant galaxies through cosmic gates. Lovecraft fused the two fears in tales such as "The Horror at Red Hook." He saw the universe as lacking any animating spirit of compassion. In a world as cold as this he had little regard to spare for people he deemed different from himself.

As a Rhode Islander who was born and worked in Providence, I discovered Lovecraft's writings at a very early age. As a boy I was too young to figure out what it is about the Magus that entices. Like other horror stories, his tales implicitly hold out the promise of revelation: they tease us with the hope that by narration's end we'll get a glimpse of the way life really is. In the case of "The Rats in the Walls" the glimpse amounts to a flash of fangs separated from us by the thinnest curtain hangings, and hostile gnawing forces for as far down as we can see. What I've tried to do in *Providence Blue* is talk back to this bleak worldview and draw on the city's history to offer a radically different vision, one inspired in part by Rhode Island's one-word motto: *Hope.*

The legionary desert expedition joined by Poe and Bob Howard has some basis in history. What inspired me was an account by the ancient Greek chronicler Strabo in his *Geographica* (17.1.54), where he describes a raid by Kushite warriors against the Roman outpost city of Syene (today Aswan) on the Egyptian-Nubian frontier. The Kushites carried off statues and images of Caesar Augustus as trophies of war. A retaliatory raid by a Roman legion detachment succeeded in recapturing some of these statues—but not all. For in 1910 British archaeologists excavating the Kushite capital Meroë (in what is today the Sudan) made a curious discovery. Beneath the buried staircase of a temple to the god Ammon, they found the severed bronze head from a statue of the Roman emperor Augustus—carefully positioned for purposes of ritual humiliation. The severed head can now be seen in London in the British Museum.

A word now concerning "penitent angels." As a Catholic Christian I'll use this opportunity to acknowledge the speculative liberties I took with aspects of Church doctrine. Articles 391–393 of the *Catechism of the Catholic Church* specify how "radically and irrevocably" the rebellious angels allied themselves with Satan in rejecting God and the divine order in the "war in heaven" alluded to in

Revelation 12:7–9. Consequently, decrees the Church, "It is the *irrevocable* character of their choice, and not a defect in the infinite divine mercy, that makes the angels' sin unforgivable."

This pronouncement is part of the reason why I subtitled my novel "A Fantasy Quest": that is, a counterfactual reverie. I'm not the first to speculate on these fallen beings. Dante in Canto 3 of his *Inferno* refers to uncommitted angels: "Neither mutinous nor loyal, they kept themselves separate and apart" in the rebellion against God. As a result, muses Dante, such lukewarm spirits are welcomed by neither hell nor heaven.

Providence Blue poses the question: What might happen if some such threshold angels sought to avail themselves through penitence of the "infinite divine mercy" described by the *Catechism*? My story concerns a quest in which a number of characters strive for spiritual healing and redemption. It's a quest in which various beings, human and angelic, corporeal and incorporeal, and under the yoke of metamorphosis, do their best to help each other even as they open themselves to receive God's grace. What they want is what so many of us long for, whether in this life or the next: a second chance.

ACKNOWLEDGMENTS

Part of what made writing this novel so much fun was visiting my hometown and exploring old haunts. Staff at the Providence Public Library on Empire Street downtown (a destination for bicycle expeditions in my high school days) helped me with microfilms of the *Providence Journal* from 1936. Personnel at the Peerless Building and the Arcade showed me rental apartments and answered strings of "what-if?" scenario questions. Ms. Stephanie Ovoian, reference and special collections librarian at the Providence Athenaeum, graciously allowed me to examine the Egyptian Cabinet up close and was kind enough to open the long-closed cabinet's drawers—which is how we happened upon the bird illustrations that had been excised from a copy of the *Description de l'Égypte* (an incident that made its way into the novel). While going through these drawers we also found a dried insect husk that spurred its own subplot in *Providence Blue*.

Speaking of insects. Employees at New England Pest Control (now known as Big Blue Bug Solutions) generously allowed me to climb up onto the roof of their headquarters for a one-on-one encounter with the fifty-eight-foot termite. The rooftop bug's-eye vista I enjoyed on that visit—especially the skyline view of Superman's Industrial Trust Building—inspired several scenes in the story.

Sharp-eyed College Hill residents will have noticed that the boardinghouse where Novalyne stayed (144 Benefit Street) is in fact the address of The Old Court Bed and Breakfast—by far the best lodgings you can find anywhere in the state of Rhode Island. Innkeeper Max Gallagher and his staff are outstanding in the hospitality and welcome they provide for their guests.

Volunteering with the Waterfire festival was an extraordinary way of experiencing the Providence River. On several summer evenings in recent years I helped tend the fire braziers by both canoe and woodboat-skiff. The volunteer crews I met in this work came from Stateside and abroad but were united in their love for Providence.

The skippers showed me how to feed the flames without singeing my face or plopping overboard before a riverbank audience of thousands.

To all of these individuals and institutions throughout the city I express my thanks.

The final draft of *Providence Blue* benefited enormously from the close reading undertaken by members of the editorial staff at Ignatius Press. In particular I thank Mark Brumley, Vivian Dudro, and Thomas Jacobi for their encouragement and insightful comments. Special thanks too to copy editor Abigail Tardiff for her perceptive criticisms and meticulous work on the manuscript.

In creating works like this I undergo spasmic flesh-torn moments of being besieged (to borrow a Lovecraftian image) by rodents of gnawing doubt: *Is what I'm trying to write too crazed, too strange to make sense to anyone but me?* But here's where I'm lucky. Friend and spouse Dr. Jody Rubin Pinault carefully critiqued each chapter as it was written. She helped me see the hope and promise in the salutation "What cheer, Netop?" She kept the rodents at arm's length. And that made all the difference.

Also by David Pinault

FICTION

Museum of Seraphs in Torment: An Egyptological Fantasy Thriller

NONFICTION

The Crucifix on Mecca's Front Porch: A Christian's Companion for the Study of Islam

Notes from the Fortune-Telling Parrot: Islam and the Struggle for Religious Pluralism in Pakistan

Horse of Karbala: Muslim Devotional Life in India

The Shiites: Ritual and Popular Piety in a Muslim Community

Story-Telling Techniques in the Arabian Nights